Secrets Best

Kept

by

Clara Rodriguez-Marts

ISBN-13: 978-1-7371897-6-3

For the Boriquen keepers of heritage, language, and resistance,

And my mother

Aurea Morales Casilla

Content Note:

This story is inspired by actual historical events that include the murder, rape, enslavement, and torture of Indigenous peoples. While these topics are acknowledged within the narrative, they are not graphically described.

Reader discretion is advised, particularly for those who may be sensitive to these themes.

Chapter 1

"Bella, I need the case report on the Smith case on my desk today by 5:00 pm."

Bella looked up from her laptop screen and saw her supervisor, Laura, standing in front of her desk and staring at her.

"Did you hear me?" Laura, noticing Bella's distressed look, saw how tired she was. "Hey, is everything alright? You seem tired and distracted today. What can I do to help?"

Bella felt embarrassed that she once again drifted into her daydreams. "Yes, everything is fine. I am sorry about that. The truth is that I have had some weird dreams lately, and I feel awkward and out of sorts."

When was the last time you took a break?

"Huh? Time off, I'm not sure. But I have so much to do that I can't take time off right now," Bella said as she tried her best to put a smile on her face to avoid worrying her supervisor.

Uh, uh, that's not good enough, Bella. You need to take care of yourself, or you'll end up getting sick. What if...:

Bella's phone rang. She saw her mother's name on the screen and asked Laura if she could take the call. Laura smiled, "Of course. Let me know if you need anything."

"Yes, this is Bella. Mami, ¿cómo estás? ¿Todo bien?"

Bella's mom replied urgently, "No, no, mija, something has happened, and you need to come home."

Bella stood up, reacting to the news that something had happened. "Mami, que paso? Tell me."

Bella's mom lowered her voice and, with a tragic tone, she told Bella that her father had died and that she needed to return to Puerto Rico for the funeral. Bella immediately felt anger at the idea of going back home for a man she barely knew.

As she recalled how suddenly he had left them, crying out to him as he drove away, her tone grew exasperated as she told her mother, "Hay, Hay, no mami. I'm sorry. But that man left us, left me, and never reached out. Every decision I made while growing up was influenced by his abandonment. If it weren't for your sacrifices, I don't know how I would have fared. You know, I was rebellious and angry because he rejected me, he rejected us. I refuse to attend his funeral and be surrounded by family members who forgave him. I will never forgive him."

Hay mija, this is your chance to tell him how you feel and say goodbye," her mother stated.

"Look, think about it. The funeral is on Friday, and your brothers and sisters will also be coming. You all should be together to close this part of your lives. If you don't want to forgive him, that is up to you, but help your brothers and sisters through this passing. Bella, ben por favor."

Bella didn't want to argue with her mother. She knew her mother had been both father and mother to them; she provided for them and did her best to help them succeed in life.

Her mother just didn't understand that Bella regretted not reaching out to her father. She regretted not telling him how she felt and making him feel guilty for what he did to them. And now, she won't get that chance.

Yes, she was angry. She was furious at her father, upset that life had to be so hard growing up, angry at herself for the mistakes she made as a teenager, and upset that she had made her mother cry during those tough years. In a melancholic tone, she tells her mom, "Mami, dejame pensarlo. I have to think about it, and I will let you know."

"Está bien, Bella. Let me know if you are coming, y cuidate."

Her mom understood that Bella had more trauma than her brothers and sisters because she was the youngest when her father left them. For years, sibling rivalry was intense, and Bella struggled to control her strong emotions. She often fought with her siblings and accused them of having more time with their father than she did. Bella often blamed them for how his leaving and abandoning them affected her, making her feel rejected.

Now, the moment to tell him everything she had kept bottled up was gone. All those things she was going to blame him for, all the pain and hardship she had endured growing up. As she looked at her cell phone, a teardrop landed on it.

"Damn him!" exclaimed Bella.

Bella looked up to see Laura still standing in front of her, a worried look on her face. Bella quickly wiped away her tears and cleared her throat. "I am sorry, Laura; I didn't realize you were still here. Actually, I forgot I was at work. That was my mom. She called to tell me that my father passed away, and she wants me to come to the funeral back home."

Laura quickly offered her condolences to Bella.

Bella was irritated by the display of sympathy for her father's death. She had pretended for years that her father was dead, which helped her disconnect her emotions and move on.

Bella looked up at Laura, "I am OK, Laura. I don't need condolences because my father died when I was six years old, when he abandoned us. I don't feel any kind of loss over that man."

In Bella's determined eyes and the unshed tears Laura saw that she was only convincing herself that her father had died years ago, as a way to control the emotional pain of being abandoned by a parent.

Bella looked out the window of her office. It overlooked the staff garden. It was her favorite place to go when she got stressed. The company supported holistic wellness for its staff and developed a garden for their use. Now, she was looking at the quiet, serene space that was often her place for Zen. But she felt nothing. She wiped tears from her face again, tears for the good memories she shared of her father. She remembered him swinging her around.

Then the painful memories flooded over her, and she felt overwhelmed.

She remembered the pain she felt watching him come out of her parents' bedroom with a suitcase in his hand. She remembered her mother trying to hold him back while pleading for an explanation. She asked him again and again what she had done wrong, why he was leaving them.

Bella's parents were married for fourteen years. They had four kids: two girls and two boys. Bella was the youngest. She was six years old when he left. She recalled her brothers and sister crying and begging him not to go. Antonio the oldest, was 13 years old at the time. He stood in front of the front door with his hands out, barring his father from leaving. Bella heard him plead, tears on his face, "No, papi, don't go. I will be good now, I promise." She saw her brother Carlos and her sister Amelia try to pull their father away from the front door.

Bella felt a hand on her shoulder and looked up to see Laura staring at her with compassion and understanding. Bella had been open with Laura all these years because she felt supported by her. Although they came from two different cultures, Laura had also experienced childhood trauma. Her mother, though had taken her to counselors and specialists when her father died in a horrific car crash. Bella never had that support. She felt that Laura's loss was different from hers because, unlike her experience of pretending her father had died when he left, Laura's loss was authentic, a tragic accident and loss, not abandonment.

"Was your mom asking you to go to the funeral?" Laura asked, her voice soft.

"Yes, she wants me to go back home to Puerto Rico to attend that man's funeral. Hah! As if I would cry a single tear for him. I don't want to see him or the rest of his family."

"Go, Bella. You will live to regret it. I didn't get a chance to say goodbye to my father, and I had to find a way to deal with those emotions. I was angry at the world. For years, I hated God for taking him away. I was angry at my mother because he went to the store that night to pick up something she wanted." Laura gasped and her eyes widened, "Hey, do you think this was the reason why you've had strange dreams these past few days? Maybe you are meant to go to the funeral, or those dreams will keep haunting you."

Bella did not want to be convinced. She refused to discuss her father, and rejected Laura's suggestion to attend the funeral. She brushed off the issue.

"Nah, I'm ok, Laura. Really. I don't plan to pretend to mourn an asshole who abandoned his family twenty years ago. I don't want to talk about it. I just want to get back to work and hand you those reports at the end of the day." Bella opened the file on her screen labeled "2024 Case Reports" and went back to working on the administration expenses.

Laura had known Bella for six years. She did her internship at this law firm. She was impressed by how her investigative mind worked, she caught things none of the other lawyers noticed. After she graduated from college with her law degree, the firm hired her.

Practicing law became a challenge for Bella. She learned that she was not a public speaker, so Laura offered her the opportunity to work in investigations, researching cases. Laura was always impressed by the way Bella was able to discern whether a client was lying or hiding something. Now, years later, the law firm viewed Bella as a vital part of the practice. Laura knew Bella well enough to know that she was done talking.

"Ok, Bella, I hear you, but if you need anything, you just let me know, alright."

Bella looked up and, smiled, "If I need anything, I will ask you. I promise."

As Laura turned away to walk off, Bella stopped her, "Laura, I want to thank you for your support. Listen, I don't know what dreams I'm having because I can't remember them, but I'm pretty sure they're not about a man who left me twenty years ago. I don't have any feelings for him. I'm OK, really, I am OK."

Laura smiled, "Yeah, ok, remember though that you have plenty of sick time and bereavement time if you decide to go."

Bella frowned at the thought of going to the funeral.

As she saw Bella's face she said, "Alright, alright, I will leave you to your report."

For the rest of the day, Bella focused on numbers and item lists. She was absorbed in her work and didn't notice the office staff starti to leave for the day.

As she worked through the numbers, Bella received a text from her sister, Amelia.

Hey sis, mom told me that she talked to you, and you know about dad's passing. Can we talk about it?

Bella sighed.

She didn't want to talk about it. She told herself that the man didn't mean anything to her, so his death didn't matter either. Bella ignored the text and went back to the last few expenses she needed to include in the report. Her phone beeped again.

I know you don't want to go home for the funeral. You don't have to. But could you please call me? Hermana, I need to talk to you. I've had weird dreams these last two days.

Bella paused. She picked up her phone and responded.

Dreams??? What kind of dreams?

Bella reflected on the times she and her sister shared feelings or dreams that later came true. It made their father uncomfortable when the girls started to find things he had lost or guessed correctly when someone called their father or approached their house. After Luis left, Bella and Amelia's shared dreams and premonitions grew stronger.

As they grew older, their mother warned them not to tell anyone about their gift. She called it a gift, but to them, it felt more like a curse.

The girls had many sleepless nights filled with frightening dreams that made them feel disaster was imminent. They spent many anxious days waiting waited for something terrible to happen.

Now, Amelia had just told her she had been having bad dreams over the past few days. Her phone chimed again.

Bella, they're weird dreams, and I can't remember them clearly. But I wonder if they were about Dad. Tell me, have you had strange dreams too?

Bella froze. She hadn't thought that the dreams were a sign of upcoming death. Unlike the dreams she had over the past few days, those dreams from her past were informative and easy to understand.

Bella didn't want to answer. She wanted this whole thing to disappear. Bella reassured herself that she had decided not to go to the funeral. Bella didn't want to talk about it, not even with her beloved big sister.

Bella's phone chimed.

Please, hermanita, can we meet and talk about it like we used to do? Please.

Bella felt the weight of her sister's sorrow. She felt conflicted but stayed committed to helping her sister. Growing up, they were inseparable for most of their early years. Bella knew that it was Amelia who protected her from her own fractures.

Their mother had to work two jobs to pay the bills, buy food for them, and cover school expenses, including school fees, field trips, and club fees, keeping her very busy outside the home. As she grew, Bella's behavior became erratic and defiant. At school, she struggled to earn good grades and make friends, and she soon found herself skipping school and hanging out with the wrong crowd.

It was Amelia who went to look for her in the neighborhood whenever Bella escaped the house after arguing with Carmen. Amelia would threaten to call the police whenever she found Bella with an older man. Amelia also mediated the arguments between Bella and her mother. They argued whenever her mother received notices from the school about Bella's behavior. Bella knew that her mother had neighbors keeping an eye on the house and Bella's whereabouts. They would call her to tell her that Bella had skipped school, that Bella was walking around the neighborhood, or that the police had brought Bella home again. Amelia often defended Bella and kept her mother from beating her.

Now, Amelia was feeling scared about the dreams they both were having. She worried it may have something to do with their father's death. Bella felt like she had to agree to meet up with Amelia.

She typed into her phone.

Look, we can meet tonight at my place, but don't try to convince me to go to the funeral. I told Mami that I wasn't going. I've thought about it, but I am too angry at that man to go. Is it a deal? I am almost done with a report I am writing. How about my place at 6:00, and we'll cook something to eat? I don't want to go out. I just don't feel like it right now.

Amelia quickly responded.

Yes, yes, I agree. I don't feel like being sociable with people right now, 6:00 is perfect. I'm getting out of work soon and will meet you outside your apartment. Thank you, Bella.

No problem, sis. I will see you around 6:00.

Bella looked up to see a few co-workers still at their desks, typing away. Once again, she gazed at the Zen Garden outside her office window. Her peace was once more disturbed by her sister's conversation. Bella wanted to make sense of it all, but she couldn't. She tried to relax and breathe to clear her mind and refocus on the quarterly report.

Bella heard one of her co-workers tell her goodnight and waved back. "See you tomorrow, John. Have a good night." Bella realized that most of the office was dark because the desk lamps had been turned off. She looked at her smartwatch, which read 4:45 p.m., and realized that she had to finish the report.

Chapter 2

Bella approached her parking spot. She was thinking about what had happened earlier and how much she wished it all would just disappear. She sat in the car, letting her thoughts drift to her mother, her siblings, and returning home to Puerto Rico. A rush of excitement surged through her at the thought of going back to Puerto Rico.

Geez, Bella, she said to herself, *how long has it been since you went back home to the island?* Bella smiled as she answered her own question, *Too damn long, that's for sure.* Bella recalled the food, the music, the beaches, and how spending time with her family was hectic but wonderful at the same time.

Initially, after Bella's father left them, their mother refused to return to the island. She never told the children why she wouldn't go to Puerto Rico. Instead, her mom would take them to other great places on vacation. Being as young as they were, they never considered the reasons why their mother chose different vacation spots whenever they asked to return to the island. It was years later that Bella's mother told them that their father had moved back to the island after leaving them, and he had been living in Puerto Rico for many years. The children were angry that she had known where he was living and hadn't told them before. They demanded that she explain why she had kept that a secret, exclaiming that if they had gone to him, they could have convinced him to return.

Amelia accused her mother of keeping their father away from them. Carlos demanded to know why she hadn't told them. Carmen told them that she didn't understand why Luis left, and emotionally, she wasn't willing to face him. She instructed them to forget about their father, reminding them that if he had wanted to come back, he could have at any time. Carmen also reminded them that she still loved him deep down, that she had never remarried, and that they should not direct their anger at her.

After that day, their father was never mentioned again. They shifted their focus to their futures. Antonio got married and had two children. Carlos became a social worker. He hated his career because he felt useless in helping fatherless households and struggled with intimate relationships. Carlos met his current wife, Linda, when his boyfriend at the time introduced her during a company holiday party. Linda was a perfect partner for Carlos because they both didn't want to have children. Linda was a few years older than Carlos and set in her ways. Carlos told himself he would become a bad father if he had children. The two often traveled, had close friends, and were sociable in their community. Amelia became a nurse, married her long-time girlfriend, Torry, and they have a daughter named Angelica; everyone called her Angie. All four remained close, and family get-togethers were hectic and fun. Bella made her work her main focus and had reservations about committed relationships and starting a family. Bella dated people for a few months, but then the relationships would somehow fall apart. She told her family and some coworkers that she had "bad luck in romance,"

Carmen applied for a job in North Carolina and was hired. Her children were teenagers at the time, and she knew they would be upset about leaving their schools and friends. However, everything was much harder in Florida without Luis. The neighbors in the development where they lived hardly talked to any of the surrounding neighbors. People were more introverted, mistrustful, and independent. It almost felt as if hatred was a tangible thing that filled the air. In both Florida and North Carolina, there is a strong sense of a "someone is out to get you" mentality, making it difficult for them to build a strong community. In North Carolina, Bella and some of her siblings found it tiring to constantly explain to neighbors and coworkers that they weren't Mexicans or that they hadn't crossed the border into the United States. Bella felt hated by some of her neighbors and coworkers simply because she was a woman of color, and she spoke Spanish. It never made sense to her why some people hated others just because of their skin color or because they spoke a different language. After all, Europeans naturally spoke many languages, and research had shown that the more languages a person spoke, the higher their IQ. Luckily, Carmen realized that living in North Carolina was just as tough, and she decided to move the family back to Rio Piedra. They moved into Abuela's house and stayed there for several years. Although her boys were almost seventeen and eighteen and had plenty of reasons not to move, Antonio and Carlos agreed to go back to Puerto Rico. Bella was overjoyed to return home. Amelia had told Bella that Antonio and Carlos didn't argue with their mother because they'd always known how unhappy Carmen was, feeling so alone with the rest of the family back on the island. Bella admired her brothers because they had friends and played sports. They had adapted well to North Carolina, and Amelia always explained that Antonio and Carlos were 'passing.' At the time, Bella didn't understand what that meant.

Bella's car turned off by itself, snapping her out of her thoughts. She grabbed her bag and headed to the exit when she saw an older man standing by her gardenia bushes in front of her apartment. The sight filled her with dread, thinking a stranger was watching. She bent down to grab her pepper spray, ready to confront the trespasser, but when she looked again, the old man was gone. Bella felt unnerved, worried that someone might be watching her. She hesitated about getting out of her car. As she tried to peer into the darkness around her, she saw headlights and a car parking beside her. Bella let out a sigh of relief. She recognized Amelia's car. Bella had always felt protected by Amelia. There was an energy about her that could make anyone smile and feel safe. Those warm feelings returned now as Amelia looked at her and smiled.

"Hermana! Como estas? It's so good to see you!" yelled Amelia from inside her car. "Did you just get here? I was running late from work, so I was worried that I was keeping you waiting."

"Oh no, don't worry about it. I just got here myself," Bella said, feeling that telling Amelia about a phantom man in the bushes might sound crazy. "Let's go inside. I prepared chicken soup in my crockpot, and there's plenty for both of us."

"Hay que rico! I love your chicken soup! It's just like mami's."

Both sisters loved spending time together. But COVID came and created distance between families and friends. During those years, many people who believed the rhetoric from the President at the start of the virus suffered for their strong beliefs. People in power convinced some that the virus would disappear quickly. Others convinced people that the virus wasn't real and that there was nothing to worry about. Scientists, doctors, and nurses knew otherwise. They suspected the virus had been around since early 2019. But the administration pushed ignorance. To some, it seemed as if science was everyone's enemy.

Bella often thought that the idea of science being considered fake and an enemy was frightening. It was confusing that some truly believed science was harmful. Yet, these same people would flip a light switch when entering or leaving a room. They got into their cars, buses, trains, or planes to reach their destinations. They used cell phones to communicate with family and friends, watch censored news, and listened to podcasts about issues they could relate to. Science was all around us and part of us. We have invented tools to make work easier, technology that helps people and children with special needs, and devices that ensure a comfortable life, like air conditioning and heating, yet people still railed against science as if was an evil religion.

Amelia, a nurse, was an essential worker. She still fought PTSD from her time working in the ER at Charlotte First Hospital. Amelia would call Bella to cry over the senseless deaths. She contracted COVID, and everyone in the family feared losing her. Many times, Amelia told Bella she was going to quit and give up the profession because of the toll it took on her. The senseless deaths of so many men, women and children had become hard for her to bear. Patients were dying in ICU rooms alone, hooked up to machines that helped them breathe, cleaned their blood, and pumped them full of medicines to relieve their symptoms. Amelia called Bella and the family to remind them to wear masks and stay away from people who refused to do so. She constantly supplied them with hand sanitizer, masks, Lysol, and goggles. Bella appreciated that her sister was looking after everyone. Still, she was worried that Amelia's anxiety was overwhelming her and that she might get sick or burn out from the profession she had loved since she was a little girl.

Bella remembered that Amelia always asked her to play nurses and doctors, with their mother pretending to be the patient. Amelia loved helping people and was passionate about her career. However, as the COVID pandemic and the spread of misleading rhetoric continued, Amelia reported that the hospital's management would guilt them into staying. Bella would cry with Amelia on the phone because they shared emotions and the nightmares that had become a regular part of this period.

Amelia and Bella supported each other. Bella discovered that back in Puerto Rico, she had lost her grandmother, an aunt, two uncles, and four cousins. She also learned about the deaths of several school friends.

That time felt unreal to her. She began to feel oppressive thoughts, and she restarted Cognitive Behavior Therapy when her niece and nephew contracted the virus when schools reopened. Her nephew Jr.'s lungs were scarred by the virus, and he now needes medication and nebulizers to breathe.

Poor administrative decisions and a President more focused on his popularity, his desire to bully others, his wealth, and the power that comes with the presidency cost the lives of over a million Americans. Sadly, Bella realized that COVID would never truly disappear. Worse people had been motivated to hate those who din't look like them, worship like them, or share their beliefs. Politicians and the media exploited those divisions, leading to loss of life and trauma. The sad part was that most people didn't realize they had been deceived.

Amelia and Bella often felt sadness and fear when hearing about attacks on people fighting for equity and equality. On January 6th, 2021, the president's followers, who believed him and those around him when they falsely claimed that the 2020 election had been stolen, stormed the U.S. Capitol. That event further tarnished American history.

The U.S. has a long, ugly past of taking what colonists—and now politicians and corporations—wanted, enslaving people, dehumanizing those enslaved, and reducing them to property. The American story was filled with pain, blood, treason, rebellion, wars, lies, torture, and corruption, built by so-called great men. Along the way, many stood up for liberty, equality, equity, gender expression, education, and freedom.

Those who benefited from the old systems convinced people who felt forgotten and nostalgic for the days when a white man was on top, that America was a better place.

Bella and Amelia would talk about these issues for hours on the phone. And ask each other, "Great for whom?"

Sometimes Bella considered moving back to Puerto Rico, but the pandemic was spreading there, too. Puerto Rico had never had real representation in Congress. American politicians and corporations exploited the land and the people. Medicine and supplies to protect from the infection were scarce, and many Puerto Ricans died needlessly.

During the last year of the pandemic, Amelia and Bella kept their conversations going. Bella found time during her busy work schedule to join a nonprofit affiliated with the American Civil Liberties Union to defend innocent victims mistreated by law enforcement, wrongly accused of crimes, or denied jobs based on race or ethnicity.

She would tell Amelia about the horrible cruelty inflicted on many of their clients.

Amelia shared stories of the thousands of uninsured patients her hospital cared for during COVID.

She remembered individual patients and families begging for help. Bella hadn't realized how costly it was to treat someone with COVID without insurance. Amelia often discussed how these patients and their families were frequently referred to the local Department of Human Services, only to find out they didn't qualify for assistance with medical bills.

Hearing about these injustices, their brother Carlos also joined a group to volunteer his resources. As a social worker, Carlos had seen terrible abuse inflicted on parents and children. He understood the monster called poverty and despised politicians and corporations for creating it. Now, these same politicians and corporations prioritized profit over caring for the people who elected them. The get-togethers between Amelia and Bella became a trio. Carlos brought the wine, Bella cooked, and Amelia cleaned up.

But life had gotten busier. Although they still met up, it was less frequently.

Seeing Amelia again made her feel safe. Together, they entered her apartment.

"Oh man, that smells good," Amelia said to Bella. "Do you think there is enough for me to take some home? You know I hate to cook."

Sure. I think there's enough. Bella went straight to the kitchen and gathered bowls, bread, and glasses of wine. "Toma, Mel, come eat. Buen Provecho, as mom would say."

As the sisters ate their meal, they discussed the changes happening at Amelia's workplace, and Bella talked about the workload at her job.

Bella felt comforted to have her sister with her. She wasn't sure what she was thinking after hearing about their father's death. She felt disconnected and didn't want to forgive him for leaving them behind. It seemed strange to her that a daughter wouldn't be sad when her father died.

Bella asked about her niece, Lulu, and her sister-in-law, Torry.

"They are doing well. Torry just got a raise, and we're finally considering buying a house. The problem is that houses have become so expensive. For now, we're saving for the down payment. Lulu is a sweet kid; she reminds me of you when you were little. She has two best friends, as she calls them. She's learning to read and is about to start kindergarten. Her favorite place to go is the library. Can you imagine a child wanting to go to the library?" The sisters laughed as they remembered the countless hours they spent at the library during the summers.

"Well, I guess she's like her brilliant mom," Bella joked.

"Sure, but which one?" Amelia shot back.

They laughed and continued discussing family. After dinner, Amelia went straight to the kitchen to clean up.

"Hay, Mel, deja eso. You wanted to talk about your dreams, didn't you? You don't need to clean up. Come, let's sit on the sofa with our wine and tell me about your dreams.

Amelia agreed and walked into the living room. On her way, she refilled her glass of wine and prepared herself to talk about what was frightening her. She gulped her wine and started her story.

"Ok, so last Tuesday night around 2 am, I started screaming in my sleep, and I woke covered in sweat. Torry had to shake me awake. I could see the worry on her face. Sweetheart, she said when she brought me a glass of water. You were crying out. All the years we've been together and out of all the dreams you've had, this one was your worst and you scared the hell out of me!."

My head was swimming, my head was pounding, my heart was racing, and for a moment, I forgot where I was. I could still hear someone crying and a voice saying, 'Don't go.' Torry watched me as if I might start crying again at any moment. I could see how worried she was for me."

Amelia gulped down the rest of her wine, then continued her story, "Torry told me that I started crying out, words like 'why,' 'why didn't you tell me,' and 'Bella run!' The strange thing was that I couldn't remember the dream."

Bella sat stunned. "Do you remember anything at all?"

"I woke with the worst headache I've ever had. Torry handed me a writing pad and a pen and insisted that I write down anything I could recall."

"Why didn't you call me?" Bella asked.

"I don't know. Maybe because the look of concern on Torry's face worried me, and I didn't want you to worry about me too. For the rest of that day, my eyes played tricks on me."

A flicker of trepidation passed through Bella; earlier, she too had believed she was going crazy, seeing things that weren't there.

"What do you mean your eyes played tricks on you?"

"Well, I thought that I kept seeing things that weren't there."

Like what?" Bella asked, both intrigued and worried at the same time.

"Crazy things like images of people suffering, racked by disease, being assaulted by old-time soldiers. It would only last for a second or two, and by the time I blinked or wiped my eyes, the image was gone. Oh, and as I was leaving the bathroom at work, I thought I saw an old man in the mirror. "

Bella's blood ran cold.

"Can you tell me anything about the old man?"

"No, it happened so quickly that I can't give you details. I just told myself that I was tired from lack of sleep."

Amelia poured herself another glass of wine and kept telling her story.

"Bella, the next night, Torry woke me up by shaking me again. She hugged me and said that this time I got out of bed and ran around the room crying out, 'Help them, they are being slaughtered.'" Amelia explained as she gulped wine. "She said that even though my eyes were open, I wasn't responding or seeing her. Torry said I was screaming, 'Why didn't they tell us?' Hermana, I don't remember any of this."

Bella was frozen in place. Her dreams flooded her mind with vivid images of a dilapidated building and chaos, people crying out for help, men, women, and children chained on a dirt floor. She couldn't imagine what any of the dreams had been about; nothing in them looked familiar. A chill ran down her spine. Carefully, Bella got up, put on a sweater, and handed Amelia a throw. Amelia wrapped the throw around her shoulders and continued her story.

"Last night I woke up screaming. Poor Torry. She jumped out of bed, ready to act. I felt so guilty. My dreams were affecting her too, but she didn't complain; she just hugged me until my breathing slowed, and I regained my senses. This time, though, she demanded that I call you to see if you're having the same dreams."

"She knows we shared dreams as children," Bella said.

"She knows most of it. We talked about it when Lulu had a spell of nightmares a while back."

Bella was concerned for a moment; she felt a slight surge of resentment for Amelia sharing something so personal between them without talking to her about it. She wondered whether she would tell her husband if she ever got married, then realized it was a foolish question. Of course, she would if she truly loved the person; she would share everything. Amelia's voice snapped her back to herself.

"I remembered something new about this dream. I remembered Dad asking for forgiveness. Bella, I couldn't understand him very well, but I saw sadness in his eyes as he pointed to the chaos of people running and crying. I think Conquistadores were chasing them."

Bella gazed at the wall as if seeing the space where similar visions from her own dreams haunted her. The image of people fleeing and running to escape some disaster overwhelmed her with sadness, and tears streamed down her face.

"Bella, I am scared. And now, Mom called this morning to tell us our father died. What does it mean?" Amelia held her sister's hands and leaned closer. "Please, Bella, tell me, have you had bad dreams too?"

Bella was now more concerned than ever. A heavy sense of doom began to weigh on her. Bella looked out the window; she hadn't realized how late it had gotten. The little light in the room came from the lamp post outside her living room window, which cast long shadows into her apartment. Since childhood, she had been afraid of the dark. She kept the darkness at bay with many floor lamps. Her family would often come over and joke about how Lowe's ran out of floor lamps because Bella bought them all. The day had turned into night, and shadows filled her apartment. Bella quickly moved around the room and turned on all the lights. The lamps gave her a sense of safety. Her therapist had advised her to start turning some lights off to confront her fear of the dark. Bella tried one night, but she couldn't sleep until she turned on some lamps and the nightlight in her bedroom. She decided not to try that again and found another therapist.

Chapter 3

Bella saw the look of desperation and fear on Amelia's face. After all, their shared gift had never been of forlornness and trepidation. This was the first time Bella could remember sharing nightmares of this magnitude with Amelia. When they were kids, they both dreamed that their grandmother would come to them to say goodbye. She told them to forgive everyone, including themselves, because the past is the past. As she faded away, she told them that she loved them and would always look out for them. When Bella woke from that dream, she went crying to her mother. Carmen was making the bed when Bella stormed into her room. Amelia followed shortly after.

"Chicas, que pasa?" cried out their mother.

Both Amelia and Bella ran to their mother's arms. Carmen knew that the girls had the family gift. It skipped Carmen, but it was obvious that both girls had the ability to dream when they were toddlers. Carmen knew that Luis didn't want to talk about it and was glad that Carmen didn't have the gift. When they were babies, he often reassured himself that the girls were "clean of any of that witchcraft stuff." As each of the girls developed, Carmen came up with excuses whenever the girls had bad dreams or blurted out things at the dinner table about a family member they shouldn't have known. Carmen would quickly interject and say something like, "Oh, yeah, my mom called today just to talk about family gossip. The girls must have overheard me on the phone." Those types of replies would relieve Luis, and he would dispel any thoughts of his little girls being witches.

Carmen disliked the feeling of isolation she experienced from not sharing this with Luis. After all, these two girls are his flesh and blood, and he loves them. But somehow, Carmen knew that his love for the girls would be tested if he discovered their gift.

As the sisters grew older, Carmen would turn their dreams into games and tell them that these were their special games, and they couldn't tell anyone. She instructed them that whenever they both had a dream or a nightmare, they were only to tell her and no one else. Amelia discovered that the reason their father left them was because he had found out about the girls' gift. A few years later, Amelia told Bella about that day and the argument their parents had. Amelia explained that she had overheard their parents arguing about something the girls had done. She quietly listened through the door and learned that their father had heard Carmen talking to her mother on the phone about the girls' gift getting stronger as they aged. He also heard Carmen say that Luis didn't know, and it was becoming harder to hide the girls' abilities. Luis slammed the partly open bedroom door and stood in the doorway, yelling at their mother. Amelia couldn't hear much beyond her mother saying she wanted to tell him, but was scared that his disgust for people with gifts might change how he treated their daughters. She couldn't catch her father's exact words, but she heard terms like "witches" and "they are an abomination to God." She was shocked when her parents' bedroom door suddenly swung open, and she saw her father holding a suitcase.

"Papi, where are you going?"

Luis didn't look at Amelia. He pushed her aside and kept walking. Amelia could feel hot tears welling up in her eyes. She was confused.

She cried out, "Papi, what did I do? I am sorry if I did something wrong."

Luis paused in the living room when he saw the rest of his children. They had worried looks on their faces because they didn't know what was happening. Luis told his sons to take care of their mother and the house. Antonio stood between the front door of their house and his father. He asked his father if he was going on a trip and when he was coming back. Luis didn't answer. He reached for the doorknob and told his son to move out of the way. Antonio had always been stubborn and confrontational. With his chin held high, he told his father, "No, papi. What is going on? Where are you going?"

Luis looked at his son, tears welling in his eyes. "You are too young to understand these things. I have worked hard to provide for you and keep our family happy, but that is no longer possible."

Amelia hugged her father around his waist to show how much she loved him. Through tears, she begged her father not to go. "Papi, please don't leave. I promise I will be good. Dad, I love you, and I am sorry for what I did. Don't go, daddy, please don't go."

Luis emotionlessly pulled her arms away from around his waist and handed her hands to Antonio. With that last act, Luis walked through his front door and never came back.

Bella and Amelia always hoped their father would return through the front door one day. They waited with bated breath during Christmas, Father's Day, and their birthdays. Yet, they were always left waiting for him to come back. On those nights, Bella and Amelia would cry themselves to sleep. Bella knew Amelia was coping better with their loss because she was older. She understood that, being a teenager, Amelia's interests would include boys.

Carmen, realizing her children were hurting after Luis left their lives, took down all of his photos. She focused on being both mother and father to her kids. She would remind herself that she was doing just fine without him. Carmen also followed the counselor's advice to keep the children busy with extracurricular activities. Antonio played soccer, Carlos joined the school band, Amelia signed up for the girls' soccer team at her high school, and volunteered at the local library. Bella, being the youngest, couldn't join any sports teams, but she showed interest in gymnastics. Bella did gymnastics until her junior year of high school, when she joined the school's math club. Carmen knew her kids were resilient and were moving forward with their lives.

Carmen, on the other hand, was angry. She was furious at how narrow-minded Luis had been. She felt betrayed by the man who had taken a vow and by the man she had shared her life with. Life had become difficult. Carmen reached out to Luis's mother to pass messages to him. She told her mother-in-law that the children needed clothing, school supplies, and money for the clubs they participated in. Their grandmother would say she was sorry and that Luis was alone, living in the old homestead. She updated Carmen on the condition of the house and how he had tried to repair it over the years. But the house should be condemned, and Luis should return to his family. Carmen had to make his mother believe he wasn't welcome back in their lives. But he could still help his children.

The conversations never led anywhere. A few days after each attempt to get help from Luis, Carmen would receive $75-$100 in the mail from Luis's mother. Carmen knew that Luis's family came from a wealthy background. They had known each other since childhood, and everyone in the village was aware of their wealth. Their house sat on a hill, covered by trees and shrubs in front. From there, you could see the beach a few miles away and the mountains beyond. Carmen's anger grew each time she received the 'charity' from Luis's mother. Carmen stopped calling her and focused on working to support her children. "Desgraciado, I hope you burn in hell!"

As each of her children grew into adulthood, started their careers, and began their own families, Carmen was very proud of them. And now, they were taking care of her.

And now, both of them were facing uncertainty in their dreams. Bella noticed how tired Amelia looked. As she moved through the living room, turning on lights, she looked in the mirror and saw that she appeared exhausted. They had endured heartache, relationship problems, and a pandemic. And now, they were facing horrific dreams of people being slaughtered and burned. Bella thought they should call their mother tonight and talk to her about their dreams.

Chapter 4

Bella refilled her cup with wine and sat on the couch facing Amelia. She was prepared to share her dreams with Amelia.

"So, Amelia, I have had some weird dreams these last few days."

"You have!" cried out Amelia, "Why didn't you tell me?"

Because they didn't make sense to me. I didn't know what to make of them. Were they about things to happen or things in the past?

Right! I don't think that we ever dreamt of the past," said Amelia as she forced herself to remember the dreams from their childhood.

"No, I'm pretty sure we hadn't, unless when we were little, Mom didn't tell us," Bella said aloud. "How about if we call her now?" Bella reached out for her sister's hands. "What do you think? You know, after Dad left, life became hard for Mom, and she worked two jobs to pay all the bills and give us what we needed. Maybe she doesn't remember, but we should ask."

Amelia believed this made sense. Her memories returned to her childhood and how busy their mother had been. But she always found time to take them to their meetings and was their biggest supporter.

Maybe that's why they all wanted to care for her and make sure she lacked nothing.

Yeah, that is a good idea. She told me that she was going to Puerto Rico before the funeral so she could spend time with her family before returning to the States. I bet she is there, and there is an hour difference at this time of year. Amelia looks at the time on her cell phone. "Ok, I don't think that she is in bed yet."

Amelia dialed the number and put the call on speaker so they could both talk to her.

"Hola, Amelia."

Listening to their mother's happy and loving voice always made Amelia feel good.

"Hola mami, esta es Bella. How are you? Is it too late to call you?"

"No, girls, you can call me anytime. What is happening? Wait, have you two had a dream you are worried about?"

Carmen always understood how the girls felt and what they thought. She could banish the monsters in the corners of the room, make them feel better after losing a game or a match, and empower them to believe they could endure and try again.

So, Bella and I have been having strange dreams. Torry has had to wake me up from nightmares where I am screaming.

Bella interrupted, "And mom, we are both hallucinating about an old man and people being killed and burned. Mami, their screams have haunted me over the past few days, both at work and at home. The old man tells me not to go. Go where? I am confused. I haven't had a good night's sleep in a few days. My supervisor, Laura, told me today that she was worried about me. What does this mean, Mami? Did something like this happen to us before?"

Amelia asked, "Yeah, Mom, did we suffer from nightmares when we were kids?"

There was a long silence on the phone.

"Mom, are you still there?"

"Yes, I am still here."

Carmen's voice lost its optimism and became wary of what she was about to tell them.

It started with you, Amelia. When you were nearly three years old, you experienced night terrors. Oh, baby, those were tough nights. Your screams would wake me. I would run to your bed, and you were either swinging your arms or patting your pajamas. On other nights, you would burst into my room and beg me to help you. I could tell that you weren't focusing on me, and you weren't really in our world because you kept looking around, and your voice sounded desperate. 'Help me, they are trying to catch me!' The only way you would calm down and fall back asleep was if I told you I would hide you from the bad people. I made you stay in bed with me on the nights your father was out on business, and you would fall asleep again. Whenever your father was in town, I told him that you had vaccines that day and that you had a fever. Those nights I helped hide you and stayed with you in bed.

Amelia was in disbelief. As hard as she tried, she couldn't remember that time. Bella noticed that Amelia's eyes widened, and her mind wandered through childhood memories. Bella also noticed how scared Amelia was.

Amelia begged her mother to explain. "Pero mami, I don't remember any of this. How long did the night terrors continue?"

Until your father left. The therapist told me that the intense feeling of abandonment was overpowering other emotions and might affect long-term memory. The therapist explained that you blamed yourself for your father leaving, and in counseling, you would say that you were a bad girl because you made your father leave. Oh, I would tell you that the only person who made your father leave was your father. I tried to reassure you that you were a wonderful child with a big heart, and someday you would help other people. After a few years, you entered middle school, and other things mattered more than your father. I was relieved.

Bella moved to the sofa and sat close to Amelia so she could talk to her mother. "Mom, this is Bella. What about me? Did I have night terrors, too?"

Well, yours were different. For one thing, I noticed that whenever Amelia had her night terrors, you would start crying at the same time. I would pick you up, but the crying continued. While holding you in my arms, we would help hide Amelia from the bad people. As your vocabulary grew, you would tell me about the people burning. I took you to a counselor. She showed me pictures you had drawn, and they were of people being burned at the stake. Other drawings were of men who scared you. The counselor talked to me about not watching adult movies. She told me she was required to report any abuse or lack of supervision. I felt like I was going to lose you if she didn't believe I wasn't letting you watch inappropriate things. I made an excuse that your older brothers must be watching adult movies and shows, and that I would talk to them. That seemed to satisfy her.

Are you telling me that the counselor was planning to report you to child protective services? Amelia, did you know that?

"Of course, I didn't know that! I was only two years older than you, and I don't even remember having these night terrors."

Bella, you were so scared of everything. You were afraid of the sound of thunder and lightning, being alone, and your closet. So, I removed the doors. You also feared being under your bed because you thought bad people hid there. I placed boxes under your bed. And since you were afraid of the dark, I put nightlights in your room, the hallway, and the bathroom. Luis would complain that I was feeding your fears. I lied to him and told him that you found a rat that ran into your room from the hallway, and now you were scared it might come back. I reassured him that you would get over that fear soon.

Bella was curious, "Mami, did he not know about our dreams? I mean, how could he not see that Amelia and I were sharing dreams, and we know things that we shouldn't have known?"

"Well, I hid it from him. Listen, when you two come to Puerto Rico for the funeral, I promise I will explain everything. Tell me more about this dream."

Bella described her dreams and hallucinations. "Well, like I said, I keep dreaming of people running, screaming, being attacked, and burning. The dreams aren't clear. They are more like segments, similar to a movie trailer that only shows you parts of the movie. But, Mom, the screams stay with me even when I'm awake, at work, and anywhere. Their screams, Mami, scare me. They sound far away, but I can close my eyes and see the faces that are screaming."

Amelia told her mom about hers, "Yeah, and I see images of men chasing people; some have what I think are muskets, and others are hurting people. The men's faces scare the shit out of me! They look like crazed men out to kill. And now I think I am hallucinating because I can catch glimpses of a woman and an old man out of the corner of my eye, but when I turn, they aren't there."

"Yeah, I see them too. I mostly see the old man. In my dream, I can hear him telling me not to go, but he never tells me where I am not supposed to go. I have caught a glimpse of him outside my office window, in the bathroom mirror, and here in my apartment. I am starting to think that there is something wrong with me."

Carmen tried to reassure her daughters that there was nothing wrong with them. "No, listen, girls, there is nothing wrong with you two. You have a gift, and this gift has sometimes turned into a curse. And now it's back. We will face what's about to happen together."

Bella thought that her mother saying 'what's about to happen' sounded cryptic and like a sign of bad things to come. Bella had to find out what was going on. She was determined not to cry over a man she didn't know or show affection toward his family. But she was now convinced that she had to go back home if she wanted the nightmares to stop.

"OK, mami, I'll take time off work and catch the next flight home. I'll call you when I land. Good night, Mom. I hope we didn't cause you any worry." Amelia agreed, "Yeah, Mom, sorry if we worried you."

Don't even think like that. I'm glad you called me. These sound like terrible visions that you shouldn't face alone. Your rooms are ready here. I made sure to add an extra bed in your and Torry's room, Amelia, for your daughter.

Amelia smiled and thanked Carmen for always thinking ahead.

Amelia thought maybe it wasn't too late for Bella to catch a flight with the same airline, and they would arrive home together.

"Look, Bella, when Torry and I bought our tickets, there were seats available."

Bella thought that it was a good idea to travel together. "Ok, Mom, then we will see you tomorrow."

"Great, call me when you land, and I will go pick you up. See you tomorrow, girls."

Bella turned to Amelia and asked, "Did you notice the strange way Mom said what's about to happen? What do you think that was all about?"

Amelia was still staring at her phone and thinking about the childhood she didn't remember.

"Yeah, I don't know what that was about. Mom had never sounded like that before. Plus, sis, I want to know why she never told us about our night terrors."

That was strange to discover something about yourself that you have no memory of. It felt like she had a big, dark secret to reveal to us. And why do you think she kept everything from Dad?

Amelia thought about it, and something started to make sense. "I don't know that, but do you think that was the reason why Dad left us?"

Bella was quick to reply, "I have no idea why that man left us. But I know it wasn't because of anything you or I did. He was selfish, and there's a special place in hell for him!"

Amelia knew that Bella harbored a lot of anger towards their father, but she now realized that the anger had turned into hate. Amelia understood that she was justified in feeling that way. Bella was the only one who had genuinely forgotten about their father and adapted to the situation better than the others. Maybe because they spent the most time with their father, and Bella was so young at the time.

"Well, I am glad that you are going with me. We had always done things together, and it would be strange for us not to be together at this time."

Bella opened the airline app and bought her ticket. She was curious about the mystery that awaited them.

"Hey Amelia, you had like three glasses of wine. Go ahead and call Torry and let her know that you are staying here tonight. Our flight doesn't leave till 11:30 in the morning, so you will have plenty of time to pack."

Oh, I am already packed. I was determined to go, if only to comfort Mom. You know they spent many years together. And I know you can't remember, but they were so good together. She used to smile from ear to ear whenever he came home from a long business trip. I figured I would be there for her. I'm glad you decided to come with me. I will call Torry and ask her to swing by here in the morning, and then we can head to the airport.

Chapter 5

For the first time in nearly a week, Bella slept deeply and felt rested. She opened her eyes when the sun peeked through her bedroom window, gazing through the lace curtain. Outside, she marveled once again at the beauty of nature. Since childhood, Bella loved being outdoors—climbing trees, walking trails, swimming in the river, and playing outside. Even as an adult, she enjoyed having lunch outside in the Zen Garden, spending time in her garden, and on weekends, exploring new destinations. Nature brought her joy and a calming sense of peace. Her backyard was small, but she had covered it with honeysuckles, roses, and jasmine that grew along the fence.

As she lay in bed, gazing out the window, she recalled what had happened up until last night. Her peace was broken by memories of the nightmares she and Amelia had been experiencing. Fear now took hold because she understood the dread of going to Puerto Rico. What was she going to find out? What did her mom mean when she suggested she had things to tell them? And was she ready to attend her father's funeral with his family around him?

Bella remembered how close-knit her family was when they lived in Puerto Rico. They say that Puerto Ricans celebrate anything. After being colonized, slaughtered, and enslaved for hundreds of years,

Puerto Ricans developed a strong sense of resiliency that helped them survive through the centuries. Most Puerto Ricans carry the idea that 'It will be alright' and 'What can I do to help?' The belief is that if you are lucky enough to endure hardship, surrounded by family and friends, and celebrate life, you can survive anything. Bella often missed that kind of fellowship — the large family gatherings, holiday celebrations, and community block parties.

Although Luis moved the family from Puerto Rico to Florida when Bella was nearly six years old, they made frequent trips back to Puerto Rico to celebrate holidays, attend weddings, and visit for funerals. Bella grew up believing everyone had the same experiences. However, she quickly realized, while living in Florida, that people who lived on the mainland often had sheltered lives, many distancing themselves from their extended families, fostering a culture of "I" and "Mine" rather than "Us" and "We." Bella couldn't understand why anyone would prefer to be separated from family rather than be part of a community of family and friends.

Bella's childhood felt full and supported by her extended family until her father abandoned them. She remembered the turmoil that followed that day, and quickly she did what she always had; she blocked intrusive thoughts and pushed aside the emotions of those painful years. Bella believed that if she didn't look back at those days and years, she would be fine.

Bella's strength was gradually growing as the sun rose. She loved watching the rays of the sun cast soft shadows on the lace curtains. From her vantage point, she could see clearly across the room. The sunlight lit up the corners. Bella sat in bed and took three deep breaths. With each inhale, she welcomed peace; with each exhale, she released fear. She heard noises from the kitchen—voices, in particular. A smile spread across her face as she recalled that Amelia had stayed the night.

She recognized the smell of coffee and bacon. It felt good to have her sister there.

Bella walked into the kitchen and saw her sister-in-law, Torry, serving her niece, Lulu, bacon. Torry and Lulu looked up and smiled at Bella.

"Titi. Good morning."

Bella picked up Lulu and gave her a big hug.

"Lulu, you are getting so big!"

"Yeah! I am all grown up. Mommie told me that I am going to the big kid school soon."

Bella looked up to see Torry wrapping her arm around Amelia's neck to comfort her. Bella knew that Amelia was struggling with the idea that Lulu was growing up and would soon be in kindergarten.

Bella greeted her sister-in-law, "Hey Torry, how are you? It means the world to me that you are coming with us."

Don't forget about me, Titi. I'm going to see Mima too," Lulu said as she went back to the table to finish her breakfast.

"What do you want to eat? Amelia made an omelet with bacon. And of course, we have coffee."

"Thank you, Amelia, for cooking. It reminded me of Saturday mornings when we were kids. No matter what, mom made egg omelets, bacon, bread with butter, and coffee." Bella served herself and sat down to eat. Torry handed her a cup of coffee and went to the kitchen to start washing dishes.

The conversation in the kitchen shifted from talking about the places they planned to visit in Puerto Rico to making plans for taking Lulu to the beach. The sisters didn't mention what their mother had told them the night before. With Lulu present and listening closely, Bella thought it wasn't a good idea to discuss their concerns in front of Lulu. So, they talked about their travel plans and last-minute arrangements.

They had agreed to ride in Amelia's car. She owned a crossover with enough space for everyone and their luggage. Amelia parked her car at the overnight parking lot at the airport. Lulu couldn't contain her excitement. She was 3 years old the last time Lulu traveled to Puerto Rico and didn't remember her visit there. They went through the ticket counter and the TSA checkpoint. Bella could hear Lulu telling the airport staff that she was going to Puerto Rico on a big airplane. Some of the staff smiled and wished her a safe flight. Others looked at her without responding. Amelia grabbed Lulu's hand and led her to their gate.

"OK, our plane is on time, and we have an hour to wait. Lulu, sweetheart, do you need anything?"

"Yes, mommy. I need to go potty."

Amelia turned to Bella. "Can you watch our things while I take her to the bathroom?"

"Sure thing."

"I will go and find us something to eat," Torry told Bella. "Is there anything in particular you want, sweetheart?"

"Yes, mommy, I want chicken nuggets."

You, Bella? Is there anything that I can get you?"

"Yeah, a large coffee, please," Bella said to Torry as she dialed her mom on her cell. "You got it." Torry walked over to one of the nearby restaurants at the Gate.

"Hola mami, how is everything?" Bella greeted her mother.

"Hay Bella, would you believe that the family is already arguing about what your father left to his remaining brother and sister? It's terrible to see them fighting over money and property they already have. Honestly, querida, if your father had anything to leave anyone, it should be you kids because you were his children, and your aunt and uncle are wealthy and own several houses, cars, and boats," said Carmen to her daughter.

"Well, you know how it is, Mom, the rich always want to get richer even if they don't need the money. From what I remember of my childhood, we never heard from his family, never received a single birthday card, and they never helped us when we needed something."

"You are right, baby. They never reached out to us. When your father's older brothers died, they left behind a lot of money and property. None of you was mentioned in the will. You all had to work hard and borrow money for college, which your aunt and uncles never had to do."

Torry arrived with the food and drinks. "I know how you like your coffee, Bella, large coffee with four creams and six sugars." Torry handed the coffee to Bella.

Torry looked up and realized that Amelia and Lulu had not yet returned from the restroom.

"Hey Bella, have they returned at all? What bathroom did they go to?"

"They haven't returned, and I don't know which of the bathrooms at this gate they went to, but knowing Lulu, she probably dragged Amelia to one of the gift shops with toys," proposed Bella, and she blew on her coffee and took a sip.

"This coffee is good! Thank you, sis."

"Good, I am glad you like it."

Torry noticed the phone in Bella's hands and felt that she had interrupted Bella.

"Oh, hey, I'm sorry. I hadn't realized that you were on a phone call."

"No worries, it's Mom."

Torry smiled and wanted to greet her mother-in-law. "Hey Carmen, this is Torry. How are you?"

"Oh, Torry, it's so good to hear your voice. Listen, don't get me started as to how I am feeling."

Torry glanced at Bella, signing as to what was going on.

Bella whispered, "I'll tell you later."

Torry nodded and smiled. She returned to her conversation with Carmen. "Well, I am curious, Carmen. I can't wait to hear the gossip. You can tell us all about it tonight. Our plane lands in San Juan airport at 3:30 pm."

"Yeah, I will pick you all up around that time. I'm eager to see my grandbaby again. I saw the photos you sent, and she's growing too fast. I have a special surprise for her."

"Carmen, you are always spoiling her."

"Well, what are grandmothers for?"

Torry responded, "To spoil grandchildren, I guess. So, listen, I need to find Amelia. I think Lulu dragged her into one of these gift shops, and you know how expensive airport gift shops can be. I'd better rescue Amelia before she ends up buying too many toys for Lulu. I gotta go. Love ya, and I can't wait to see you."

"I am excited to see all of you. Adios mija.

Torry handed the phone back to Bella and went to look for Amelia and Lulu.

Bella returned to her conversation with her mom, "So, Mom, what is my uncle and aunt arguing about?"

"The usual, who will get his share of the family house, the stuff in the house he had been living in, and the money he has in the bank. You know that your father's family came from wealth."

"I knew they had money, but honestly, Mom, I don't know what they did to earn it."

"Ah, well, they have inherited wealth from generation to generation. Your father's ancestors were aristocrats in Spain as far back as the 1300s."

Bella couldn't believe what she just heard. Her paternal family were aristocrats. "Wait, what?? His family were aristocrats. Where did they come from?" Bella was astonished and continued to ask questions. "I don't understand, Mom, why didn't we know that? Do they still have family in Spain that we are related to? How did they keep the money going for centuries?"

"Yes, there is still family in Spain. The titles have changed over the generations, and I will have to tell you all the history when you are home. Either way, your father's family has managed to increase their wealth with every generation."

Bella couldn't believe what she was hearing. She remembered all the struggles they had gone through after her father abandoned them. It made her angry to think that her mom had to work two jobs to pay the bills, while her father, who had money, could have given her mom money for child support. When he left, it was for good, and he never contacted them again. Bella's blood was boiling. She had known that they had money, but she hadn't realized they were actually wealthy.

"Mom, but how come we had to struggle so much growing up. You worked so hard to pay the bills, buy us clothes, and put food on the table. And all that time, my father was wealthy? How can that be? I am confused and angry."

"I know, baby. Back then, I never showed it to you, but I reached out to your father, asking him to help us, and my letters would be returned. Several times I reached out to your bitch of a grandmother, and she would tell me that she hadn't heard from him, but I knew that had been lies. Look, there is a lot for me to say to you, but I want you all together to hear your father's history and the arguing that is going on now that he has passed away. "

"Ok, Mom. We have about 30 minutes before they start boarding the passengers. We will see you tonight. Have you heard from my brothers? When do they arrive in Puerto Rico?" Bella looks up to see Torry, Amelia, and Lulu returning. Lulu was holding a new stuffed animal that was almost as big as she was. Torry was right, Amelia caved in.

"Your brothers are landing soon. Your cousin Juan Carlos is on his way to the airport now. Abuela is roasting a pork shoulder with onions and rice. We will talk tonight."

"Ok, Mom. We will see you tonight."

Amelia approached Bella, curious to know who she was talking to. "Hey, was that Mom? Torry told me that you were talking to her."

"Yeah, I called her to let her know that everything was good and remind her to pick us up at the airport." Bella was curious about what her mother had just told her, and she couldn't wait until later tonight.

"Hey Amelia, you are older than me."

"Not by much, tho."

"But you remember more of our childhood than I do."

Amelia became curious as to what Bella was getting at. "Yeah, I guess. What's up?"

Bella leaned in to get closer to Torry and Amelia and whispered, "Did you know that dad was wealthy and that his family's fortune goes back to the 1300s in Spain?"

Amelia jumped back and said, "What? What the hell are you talking about?" Amelia was stunned. "I mean, I knew they had money and that they were self-centered and greedy bastards, but WEALTHY?? Is that what you and Mom were talking about? Wealthy, like real, real money?"

Bella was able to tell from Amelia's response that she hadn't known anything about her father's family coming from wealth. "Yeah, mom told me that our aunt and uncle are arguing about what dad may have left them in his will. They are staking claim to things Dad owned, including large amounts of money."

Amelia's head was spinning as she recalled long-buried memories of the poverty they had grown up in. "That son of a bitch never sent Mom any money to take care of us, and you're telling me he was wealthy?"

Bella nodded her head and continued her story, "Yeah. Like the top percent wealthy."

Amelia sat down in shock. Torry sat next to her and held her hand. Amelia began to cry quiet tears as she recalled the struggles of their childhood and the selfishness of her father and his family. Amelia balled her hands into fists. Torry whispered to her that everything would be okay and she should worry about Lulu. Amelia realized that Lulu was staring at her with a worried look on her face.

"Yes, you're right, Torry."

Amelia smiled at Lulu and reassured her daughter that she was ok. "I am sorry, Lulu. I got mad, but I am ok now."

Lulu got off her chair and hugged her mom. Lulu returned to her chair to eat her nuggets.

"Ok, Bella, what's this all about?

"Well, Mom said that the family was squabbling about inheritance crap. She told me that our father's family were aristocrats in Spain back in the 1300s and have managed to keep their fortune growing and expanding all these centuries."

"What? Aristocrats? How did they make their money?"

Well, she didn't tell me that, but she said she will explain everything tonight after dinner. She wanted to make sure we were all together before she went into this history. So, I guess we'll have to wait." Bella gave Amelia a few minutes to process what she just told her, then asked, "So, you weren't aware of any family wealth?"

"Family wealth? No! Of course not!" If I had known about our father's wealth, I would have found him years ago and demanded that he help Mom raise us. I mean, you know, I wouldn't forgive him for abandoning us, but for God's sake, I would have helped Mom take his sorry ass to court for child support! God! Is this for real? And Mom drops this bomb on you and expects us to wait until tonight so she can tell us the story. That's incredible!"

"To say the least," exclaimed Torry as she approached Amelia and hugged her. After almost 8 years together, Torry knew that Amelia's anger would explode if she didn't get answers tonight. Torry thought that a distraction might be a good idea until they boarded the plane. "Hey Mel, how about you and I go to that bar and get us a glass of wine?"

Amelia's head was swimming with memories and countless questions she wanted to answer. But Torry was right; if Amelia stayed angry, Lulu would worry.

"Yeah, a glass of wine sounds good right now. You know what, forget the wine, I need a bourbon."

Torry smiled, "ok, bourbon it is." Torry turns to Bella, "Hey Bella, can you watch Lulu while we are gone?"

Bella understood Torry's distractions. She was the only one who could help Amelia break out of her angry moments and process her feelings. "Sure. You two go ahead. Hey, on your way back, can you bring me a Coke?"

"You got it." Torry smiled at Bella, "Thank you!"

"No problem, sis, Lulu can tell me all about her new furry friend here."

Lulu smiled.

Chapter 6

Bella had offered to let Lulu sit next to her during the flight so Amelia and Torry could have some alone time. Once they join the family, there will be no more alone time for anyone. Bella smiled as she thought of her crazy Puerto Rican family.

"Why are you smiling, Aunt Bella? Did you see something funny out the window?"

Bella was pulled out of her memories as Lulu started to climb onto her lap to look out the window. Bella put Lulu back in the child seat and buckled her in.

"Remember, Lulu, for your safety, you have to stay buckled in your chair." Bella adjusted Lulu so that the seat belt wasn't too tight. "There, how does that feel? Not too tight?"

Lulu smiled at Bella and nodded. Bella saw Lulu's new furry friend on the floor between the seats and reached for it. Lulu quickly grabbed her plush animal, hugged it, and thanked Bella. Like most children, Lulu was curious about why Bella was smiling. "So, what was funny?"

Bella leaned closer to Lulu as if she had a secret to tell her.

"Well, I was remembering how everyone in our family behaves around each other."

"What do you mean?"

Well, Lulu, you haven't been back to Puerto Rico since you were a toddler, so you don't remember how loud our family can be. We're a very close family, and we love spending time together. But because we've all been so busy these past few years, we haven't been able to be together in a while.

"Why?"

Bella thought about how to explain the changes that life brings when you're an adult; there are bills to pay and family responsibilities that get in the way of everyone getting together more often. Bella realized that the last time she visited her family in Puerto Rico was when she, Amelia, Torry, and Lulu went to see their grandparents. Once word got out that they were visiting from North Carolina, the family gathered at their grandmother's house. Bella recalled that week fondly.

"Well, little one, when we grow up, get jobs, and become mommies and daddies, making time out to go back home becomes hard to do."

"Why?"

Bella heard Amelia and Torry giggle in the seats in front of her. Amelia turned around to face them and said to Bella, "Yeah, Bella, why?"

Bella sighed at Amelia. Then she turned to Lulu and tried again to explain.

"Ok, so whenever you talk to Mima and your great-grandmother, you can use your tablet, right?"

Lulu nodded.

"Well, it is easier to talk to our family on Facebook because we can do it anytime. However, going back home or visiting your uncles or Mima in Florida means that we have to arrange the trip, and sometimes that is hard to do. You know that we had to pay for this flight, right?"

Lulu nodded and put her hands to her ears as she complained, "Yes, but this plane is loud."

Amelia laughed and agreed with Lulu, "Yup, you are right, baby girl, this plane is loud. Don't forget to ask Aunt Bella for your headset if you need it."

Lulu nodded, "ok, Mommie."

Bella continued, "And Lulu, your mommies, and I have jobs that we had to check to see if we could take time away from our work to go to Puerto Rico. And don't forget your new clothes and everything your mommies needed to get for the trip. All of that costs money. So, going on trips takes a lot of planning. But you will see how big our family is. Abuela and the others haven't seen you in over two years. When they see how big you are, they will want to hug you and talk to you. Hey, and don't forget your cousins will be there too, so you can play with them."

"What can I play with in Puerto Rico?

Bella's smile grew wider as she remembered the fun she had as a child whenever her mother took them to Puerto Rico to visit Abuela. Carmen worked so hard to provide for the family after Luis left them. One thing she made sure of was to save money so that every two years, they could return to the island and reconnect with family. Memories of going to the beach, climbing mango trees, fishing, and having big get-togethers—often with the family, where the food and music never stopped—were among the best moments of Bella's life.

Bella had never felt more at home than when she was back on the island. Growing up, she was fascinated by the stories she would hear about her family. As an adult, Bella took a DNA test to learn more about her heritage. She discovered she was related to people from Africa, the Tainos, Spain, and Portugal. She was determined to create a family tree showing all the generations. Now, she felt she needed to inspire Lulu to keep her family heritage alive and appreciated.

"What to do, huh?"

Lulu nodded.

"Well, we will go to the beach for starters."

Lulu became excited. "I love going to the beach and playing on the sand!"

"Yes, I know. North Carolina beaches are nice. But wait until you see the beaches in Puerto Rico. Puerto Rico's beaches are green and beautiful. You can play in the water with me and your mommies. And, Puerto Rico has many trees with fruit."

"WHAT KIND OF FRUIT?"

"Lots of fruit. You love fruit, right?"

Lulu nodded with excitement.

"In Abuela's house, there were mangoes, oranges, bananas, and lots more fruit trees. And this is the time of the year when all the trees have sweet fruit for us to pick." Bella spoke to Lulu in a storytelling way that made Lulu yawn. "And, Abuela's house has a garden with berry bushes and rose bushes inside the house."

"Wow! Like mommy, she has plants inside the house." Lulu yawns again.

"Kind of, but this garden is open without a roof, and the rooms surround the garden. Abuela's house sits on the edge of a forest that we were little, your mommy, and I would go exploring to look for fairies."

Bella noticed that Lulu's eyes were now closed. She covered Lulu with a blanket.

Amelia looked behind her when she didn't hear her daughter talking anymore and noticed that Lulu had fallen asleep.

"You have a talent, sis. You can make our childhood into a wonderful story, and she loves it. Thanks!"

"Yeah, I guess it was somewhat, and I miss it. I should tell you, Amelia, that I have been thinking about moving back to Puerto Rico and moving into Abuela's house."

Amelia had suspected how unhappy her sister had been. She hadn't had time to think about what she wanted after Lulu was born. She thought about the ideas that came to mind while Bella told Lulu their story. Amelia couldn't help but smile as she remembered the large groups of family members, the music, and the food.

She looked at Bella with concern and asked her, "How long have you felt like this? I mean, I kinda knew that you weren't happy, but I had no idea that you wanted to return to the island."

Torry turned around on her chair and joined in the conversation. She had questions to ask because of her concerns. "Bella, I wish you had confided in us. Do you feel lonely? Are you having trouble at work?"

Bella appreciated Torry's directness and smiled as she tried to explain, "No, I don't feel lonely, and work is fine. I have a great supervisor. It's not about that." Bella thought about some of the social problems she had experienced and witnessed living in the continental US. "Look, we have discussed this before. We've noticed how more and more people have become isolated."

Torry herself had brought up the same topic to others.

"People hate people. Sometimes it feels like everyone is out for themselves. Racism and discrimination are expanding all around us. Ignorance about cultures and ethnicities has spread throughout this country, and it's now acceptable to be close-minded and hateful. It's become a stressful situation to speak to Abuela over the phone in public because she only speaks Spanish, and people around us might overhear me speaking Spanish."

"Yeah, I get that. I have had looks by people around me when I speak in Spanish over the phone." Amelia recalled a situation where she had a problem that ended in an argument with a total stranger who yelled at her for speaking Spanish in America."

Torry immediately responded to Amelia's statement, "What? You hadn't said anything to me about that." Torry was concerned. "Baby, you know these crazy fuckers are usually carrying a gun and they are trigger-happy morons that will shoot first and then claim, 'stand your ground' bullshit."

"I know Torry. But I felt attacked. These 'morons' don't even know that Puerto Ricans are American citizens. I wanted to educate her, but I quickly realized that nothing I could say would change her mind. So, I walked away."

Torry noticed two people sitting behind Bella and Lulu were staring at them. When Torry made eye contact, they quickly looked away. Torry saw that the man was wearing a Trump hat. She quietly laughed because racist people who vote for leaders like Trump still go to Mexican restaurants and vacation in Spanish-speaking countries, all while voting for strict immigration laws aimed at removing anyone not white from the United States.

"Yeah, I get it. I have noticed the increase in racism and bigotry. I mean, it's always been there, but now they have been given the 'green light' to be hateful and dangerous. Amelia and I have had our share of looks from Trumpers and Libertarians. We are not only offensive because we are a lesbian couple, but I married a Hispanic, brown-skinned woman, and my daughter is brown-skinned. Amelia and I have discussed leaving North Carolina, but our finances are tight, and Lulu was in an excellent daycare."

"I understand you two are choosing what's best for Lulu, but I don't have a boyfriend or children, so this might be the best time for me to move back to the island."

"Ladies and gentlemen, we are approaching San Juan International Airport. Please buckle your seatbelts. Flight attendants prepare to land."

"Hey, Belle, can we exit the plane last? With a plane full of people, I don't want to shuffle with Lulu through 200 other passengers."

"Sure, Mel, no problem."

Bella could see how excited Lulu was. Lulu grabbed her plush toy tightly with one arm and Torry's hand with the other.

"Mommy, it's hot in here. Is the air conditioner broken?"

"No, sweetheart. Puerto Rico is an island that is usually hot," Torry responded to her inquisitive daughter. Torry couldn't help but smile with pride at their daughter because she was curious and wanted answers for everything she saw."

"Why is it hot?"

"Well, it is in the Caribbean Ocean south of where we live. The sun is bright here, and the sky is a deep blue. To stay cool, we wear light-colored clothes, drink plenty of water, enjoy snowballs, and sip iced coconut water. But it's not so bad. The sun keeps the ocean water warm. Our beaches back home are usually cold all year, right?"

Lulu nodded. "Yeah, the water is cold."

"Right, but in Puerto Rico, the water is warm and shallow. When we get closer to the beach, it will look like an emerald under the pretty blue sky."

Amelia and Belle grabbed their luggage and joined Torry and Lulu.

"What are you guys talking about?" asked Amelia as she took Lulu's cardigan so she could adjust to the temperature change.

"Mommy was telling me that it is hot here because the sun is brighter here."

Amelia smiled at her daughter and nodded in agreement.

"Mommy also told me that the beaches here are green and warm."

"Oh yeah, baby! And most beaches have white sand. Some beaches have sea glass along their shores, and others have black sand from volcanic rock a long time ago." Amelia was excited because this time, Lulu was older and could do so much more while they were in Puerto Rico. Amelia also thought about how wonderful it would be when Abuela meets her great-grandchild; she looks just like her.

The group exited the airport. When the doors opened, the bright Caribbean sun made them all squint. Amelia squatted in front of Lulu to put a pair of child-sized sunglasses on her.

"Ok, Lulu, do you remember what you are going to tell Mima and Abuela when you see them?"

Lulu excitedly nodded, "Uh-huh, when I see Mima and Abuela, I will give them a big hug and say hola Mima, como estás."

"You are so smart," Amelia said, hugging her little girl. "Your Spanish is really good. Your grandmothers will be so proud of you!" Amelia stands up and looks for her mother. "Mima should be here any moment to pick us up.

Outside the airport, vendors were selling flavored shaved ice called 'piraguas.' Bella quickly went over to the vendor and ordered four small snowballs in tamarind flavor.

The group just arrived in Puerto Rico, and they were hot, so piraguas are the best way to cool down. Bella handed everyone one. They sat on their luggage and enjoyed their piraguas. Torry used a moist wipe to clean Lulu's face and hands. "Well, what do you think about your piragua?"

"It's so good, Mommy. Can I have another one?"

"Not right now, sweetheart. Mima should be here any minute, but don't worry, you will have piraguas again." Torry heard a car blow their horn. "Carmen! Hello!"

Carmen drove up and stopped in front of her daughters. She jumped out of the car and ran to her family. She headed straight to Lulu, swung her around, and brought her in a tight hug. "Oh, Lulu, it's so good to see you." Carmen kissed her granddaughter on the cheek before hugging her daughters.

Lulu wanted to greet Mima in Spanish because she had practiced, but Lulu was curious as to why Mima was crying. "Mima, if you are so happy, why are you crying?"

Carmen laughed as she turned away from Bella, Torry, and Amelia. "I am crying tears of joy because I am happy to see you." Carmen grabs Lulu's suitcase and helps Lulu into the car seat she borrowed. "I know that I get to see when we talk on WhatsApp. But it's not the same as seeing you in person." Carmen adjusted the restraining belt around Lulu and pulled on it to ensure it was locked in tight. "You are so big and smart. I can't wait until Abuela sees you. You look just like her." Carmen kissed her granddaughter on her forehead and slid into the driver's seat.

"Thank you for picking us up. It's so good to see you!" Bella leans over and hugs her mom again. "I've missed you."

Amelia joined Bella in hugging her mom from behind. Torry followed. "We had planned to visit you in Florida, but Florida has become a state that would not welcome people like me and Torry. I am sorry, Mom."

"Mija, don't worry about it. I agree with you, Florida has changed ever since that idiot became governor, and he cares more about getting re-elected than doing right by his citizens. He is willing to sacrifice our children's education for so-called moral laws. He smiles and tries to convince everyone that Florida is stronger and more secure now than ever before. Still, on the other hand, he enjoyed America's immigration laws when his family immigrated to the United States." Carmen pulls away from the airport and gets on the main road heading to her mother's house in Rio Piedra. "He is a hypocrite, and people blindly follow him. However, we have time to discuss that and other things later. Right now, Abuela has made lunch, and a couple of your cousins are coming over."

All three ladies became excited, thinking they would get to eat Abuela's food. They are hungry. Bella pictured Abuela's Spanish-style house sitting on the hill. Fruit trees surrounded her house. On sunny days, she could see the ocean from the back veranda.

Chapter 7

During the ride to Abuela's house, they talked about their jobs, asked how long Carmen had been in Puerto Rico, and Carmen asked questions about Lulu. Lulu was excited to tell her mima that she would be starting kindergarten soon.

Bella was happy to be back in Puerto Rico. She and her siblings were born in Rio Piedra, but their father took a job in Florida, which caused them to leave the island. Bella was three years old when they moved to Miami. At first, she and her siblings adapted to the change. Her family seemed happy, at least until their father abandoned them. However, in the years that followed, Carmen supported the family, encouraged her children in their sports and activities, and saved money to take the family back to Puerto Rico every few years. With each trip back to the island, Bella's anxiety about returning to the mainland grew.

Carmen's car drove through Rio Piedra's market. "Mom, I want to take a time out to go to the market for souvenirs."

"Sure, baby. We are going to take our little princess around the island so she can see where her family came from." Carmen made her way uphill along a winding road, getting closer to Abuela's house.

They passed the elementary school that her siblings attended when they lived in Puerto Rico.

Amelia had fond memories of her siblings walking home from school, and she and Carmen waiting for them on top of the hill. Her brothers would race to see who could reach the top the fastest. Her mom would declare the winner and hug both of them. Back then, the neighborhood was full of activities. Family and friends lived up and down the hill, creating a close-knit community. Mothers would greet Amelia and her siblings. Her mom would have conversations about the blocks, gossip, or telenovelas. Amelia knew that her mother was the happiest when they lived in the small house on top of the hill. Abuela's house was a few houses further up the hill. Her brothers would run into the house to change their uniforms and meet up with neighborhood kids to play, get into trouble, and climb trees to pick fruit. Amelia's mom had strict rules. The boys were expected to change out of their uniforms, finish their homework, and make their beds before going outside to play. Carmen would grab her sandal and wave it, asking the boys, "Where do you think that you are going?"

The sandal, also known as 'la chancla', was a feared tool used by parents to discipline their children for many generations, often without actually ever having to use it to spank them. The boys would rush back into the house and focus on their homework. They also understood that their homework and chores needed to be finished before their father arrived home from work.

Bella rolls her window down. She was able to smell the scent of food and the sound of music in the air. Women ran to their gates and their porches to welcome Amelia and Bella back home.

"Hola ninas!! Amelia!!! Como estan?"

"Llegaron! Carmen te veo mas tarde en la casa de tu mama!"

Amelia and Bella stuck their heads out of the car windows, waving and saying hello to old neighbors and friends. A friend of Amelia's ran over to their car to say hi.

Amelia was excited to see her old friend.

"Hey Angelica! How are you?" Amelia noticed that Angelica was pregnant. "Angelica, you're pregnant again? What is this one, your third?"

"Yes, my third and my last. Tony and I discussed stopping after this one. But listen, I will visit you later, ok?"

"You better!"

They arrived at their grandmother's house and saw their cousins and Abuela walking toward their car.

"You're here!"

"Hey, Uncle Juan Carlos!" Bella gets out of the car to greet her uncle. "It's so good to see you again!"

"Hay mi linda, it's good to see you." Juan Carlos hugged his niece. "You know you are looking more and more like your mother." Juan Carlos turns to Amelia and Torry to greet them as well. "Girls! You are more beautiful every time I see you!" Carlos looks toward the house to see Carmen handing Lulu over to Abuela. "Is that Lulu?? Wow, she's grown so tall. And you know what, she looks just like Abuela. Wow!"

Juan Carlos's son, Angel, came over after they put their luggage in their rooms.

"Hola, prima!" Angel hugged his cousins. "Hey, cousin Torry." Angel hugged Torry. "Don't forget, Torry, if you ever feel like you've had enough of my cousin, I am still available," Angel grinned and winked at Torry and Amelia. Bella giggled and thought to herself, 'Same old Angel,' as she walked to her great-grandmother. Seeing her grandmother standing by her mom filled Bella with strong emotions of being back home. Others had always told her mom that she looked too young to have grown children. And now Bella took a good look at her grandmother and noticed that she had barely aged in the last two years since they had visited the island. Abuela stood tall and graceful, her hair shining in the sunlight, and she barely had any wrinkles on her face. Bella thought to herself how wonderful it would be if she aged as well as her mother and grandmother.

Bella stepped closer to her grandmother, standing in front of her Spanish-style house with orange clay roof tiles. Under the warm sunlight, the flowers shimmered and sparkled. It was clear to Bella that it had rained overnight, judging by the water droplets on the shrubs and trees. She saw Lulu run to the plants in front of the large windows of the house to smell the flowers and pick blackberries from the vines growing along the wall. In her garden, Abuela had local tropical plants like hibiscus, as well as gardenias and roses. The scent of flowers was strong in the air, and the breeze carried it throughout the yard. Abuela's garden was also full of butterflies, hummingbirds, and local birds zipping back and forth. Abuela loved her garden, spending a lot of time outside tending to her plants and animals. Next to the large wooden doors, she placed a bench and a light post. It was a picture-perfect scene.

Bella approached her grandmother and embraced her. Bella inhaled the smell of roses from Abuela's body spray.

"Hola Abuelita." Bella kissed her grandmother on the cheek. "Todo bien?"

"Si mija, todo bien," replied Abuela with tears in her eyes. Abuela was overwhelmed with emotion upon seeing her granddaughters and great-granddaughter. Who could have guessed that they would grow up to be kind and loving people after the trauma they went through because of their father? Abuela looked at her granddaughter with fondness. "Bella, you are a beautiful young woman. When are you going to get married?"

Bella knew this question would eventually come. Abuela wasn't the only family member who would ask why she was single. Bella understood that her aunts and uncles would ask too. She mulled over her response, aware that culture heavily influenced gender expectations.

"Well, I am not looking for a boyfriend right now, Grandma. I received a promotion at work, and I am still trying to figure out the ropes."

"Sure, sure, but you get home from work to an empty house. Aren't you lonely, baby?"

"No, not really. Amelia, Torry, and Carlos often come over. But look, Grandma, I'm working long hours, and no man is going to put up with that. That will lead to problems and heartache in the relationship. So, for now, I am enjoying being myself, I enjoy my work, and I work long hours. I am okay without a partner."

Carmen approaches them to join the conversation, "Listen to your Abuelita, Bella."

"Look, I expect that this question will come up often over the next few days. But I grew up with a strong mother who raised us without a partner." Bella turned to face her mother. "And mom, although I have been angry at my father for abandoning us, I never felt like I needed a father." Bella hugged her mom and added, "I never felt like I needed a father because you gave us love, discipline, and you provided for us. I hope to be as strong as you." Bella then turned to her grandmother and expressed her admiration with love, saying, "And you, Grandma, you lost your husband twenty years ago, and you've never hooked up with anyone else. You raised the last four younger children, and you've maintained this beautiful property. You even started a career so you could provide for your kids." Bella hugged her grandmother. "I want to be like you two." Both Carmen and Abuela had tears in their eyes and felt proud of Bella.

Carmen was all too familiar with this argument and understood that Bella was free to make her own choices in life. "OK, Bella, I know. I'm glad you're figuring out who you are before committing to someone else. We Puerto Rican women tend to be very outspoken and passionate."

Torry and Amelia approached them. Torry joined the conversation, "Yup. That would describe Amelia."

Amelia quickly responded to Torry's comment, "Hey! Is that supposed to be a subtle way of saying that I am stubborn?"

Lulu runs to the group with blackberry stains on her face, hands, and clothes.

"Lulu, did you enjoy those blackberries?" Amelia bent over to take a photo of Lulu, covered in blackberries. "Come on, let's get you cleaned up.

Antonio stepped out of the house with his usual bright smile. "Ok, ladies, your bags are in your old rooms." He kisses each of them on the cheek. I have to go, but Abuelita, count on me to come over for dinner tonight."

"Of course, Antonio. I am making your favorite foods tonight."

Bella stood in front of her grandmother's house, gazing down the hill at the place she missed so much. The green trees of the forest still held the heights, but the edges had been pushed back and replaced with concrete, tin, and tile houses. The neighborhood stretched up the distant slope in a patchwork of weathered tin, faded pastels, and concrete. It was more crowded than she remembered. Some homes had fresh coats of bright turquoise and sky blue, but most sagged under rust and time. The outlines of familiar streets were still there, but the rhythm felt different, more open sky, less shade, fewer trees. It was strange and stirring. Life buzzed differently than she remembered. Music still played in the distance, but rather than the lively, joyful sound she knew, it seemed muted and strange, as if the air itself was afraid of what the future held. Bella felt like she was caught between two worlds: the steady hum of the forest behind her and the buzzing pulse of a town that desperately waited for her to return.

Together, they all walk into the house.

Chapter 8

Bella loved this house. Isabela's house was a Spanish-style, two-story colonial with large windows and high arches around some of the doorways. The inner courtyard featured Spanish tiles on the floors and up the stairs, depicting images of the family history on each tile. Every generation added more painted tiles to share their story with future generations. Bella would spend hours looking at the tiles and felt a sense of pride knowing that her family line went back to pre-colonial times. Unfortunately, tiles with pre-colonial history were few, so she knew very little about that part of her history. In the courtyard, roses, gardenias, and hibiscus bushes were planted along the boundary wall. As a child visiting her grandmother, she would sit on the wrought-iron bench between the roses to read or sketch. Abuela's house always smelled like flowers. Breezes traveled through the house, keeping it cool. This house had been in the family for over 150 years. Abuela would tell stories of how the house was built on the land of a northern tribe of Taino people, from whom we are descended. Abuela had a collection of Puerto Rican art, Spanish antiques, family art, and a couple of Picassos. My family has embraced all parts that make up Puerto Ricans, including Taino, Spanish, Canary Island, Portuguese, Italian, and African lineage. Bella took a deep breath as she stood in front of an old family photo with her father in the center of the group.

She remembered seeing a sketch of a Taino woman in a frame at the end of the hall. The sketch looked very old, and the artist's name was barely visible. Her grandmother noticed that Bella often stared at the sketch. Once, her grandmother asked her why she liked staring at it. Bella was five years old at the time. At first, she shrugged. Her grandmother already suspected that Bella had the gift because Carmen often called to discuss Bella and Amelia's gifts. That day, Isabella managed to get Bella to answer her question. With warmth in her eyes, Isabella told Bella it was okay if she wanted to tell her why she liked the sketch. In a whisper, Bella leaned in and said, 'Because I see the lady sometimes and she plays with me, but mommy told me not to tell anyone.' Isabella realized there was no doubt about Bella and her gift. She told Bella her secret was safe and she wouldn't tell anyone. As Bella explored the house, she remembered her father playing with her at Abuela's house. But then he left the family, and she couldn't forgive him. Once again, like many years before, Bella found herself staring at the sketch of that lady. She felt a connection to her, even though she didn't know who she was.

Bella walked through the familiar hallways, remembering the times she spent in this house. She recalled all the places she would hide while playing hide and seek. She thought about all the walks Abuela took her on in the woods. Her stories about their ancestors described a strong people who were almost wiped out by the colonists who arrived on their shores and claimed the island. The woods were a magical place for Bella—nearly 32 acres of lush, tall trees, fruit trees, coconut palms, berry bushes, taro plants, a beautiful creek feeding a small pond, cliffs, and ancient rock formations. Abuela and Carmen would take Bella and her siblings on hikes into those woods to teach them about their indigenous and African heritage. Within this 'Garden of Eden,' some Taino and African ruins still survived, mostly hidden by vines and hard to find unless you knew where to look. Bella always felt a sense of peace and belonging in the woods. It was also the perfect place to play hide and seek with her siblings because she knew every part of this small forest. Adjusting to city and suburban life, with more houses and asphalt than trees, was difficult for Bella. Going from her personal yard to concrete backyards always felt alien. One of the hardest things to get used to was not having fruit on trees, as store-bought fruit often tasted bland and tasteless. She also felt a loss of connection to her community and struggled to adapt to the American individualistic way of life. Puerto Ricans have a culture that values living for today and a deep love for the island because all Puerto Ricans are connected to each other and the land.

Bella knew that Abuela had nine children. Some moved to the mainland for career opportunities, while others stayed on the island and remained close to their families. Abuela gave parcels of her land to her children so they could build their own homes and stay near family. Bella remembered how often she walked to her cousins' houses by cutting through the woods. After a certain age, Bella and Amelia would walk to the homes of family and neighbors around the neighborhood to babysit or do odd jobs. In this village, everyone knew each other, and a strong sense of community thrived.

Bella remembered the day they left the island as one of the saddest days of her life, even sadder than the day her father abandoned them. Bella's mom met her husband at work. They both worked for the same company in different departments. When their company opened an office in Miami, Luis thought it would be a great new start to move the family to Florida. At first, Bella didn't like Florida and kept asking her parents when they would go back to Puerto Rico. But eventually, Bella adjusted to living in Florida, helped her mom around the house, and played with her siblings. Even at a young age, Bella noticed the difference between living in Florida and living in Rio Piedra. For one thing, her mom and dad didn't have time to play games with them. They had to work one or two jobs to pay the bills, and they seemed tired all the time. Bella was overjoyed when Carmen told them she had made arrangements with Abuela to go back to Rio Piedra and move into her house. Carmen asked the children if they would be willing to do that. At first, Amelia seemed upset because she had good friends there, but she eventually agreed to the move because, thanks to Carmen, who had taken the children back to the island on vacation, Amelia made friends in Rio Piedra. And Carmen didn't know that Amelia had been talking to a boy she met on their last trip to Puerto Rico. Bella saw her giggling and talking to a boy on her laptop, and she quickly closed the computer when Bella walked into the room. Amelia tried to reassure Bella that he was just a friend and not to tell Carmen. Bella kept Amelia's secret and used it to get her to do chores she didn't want to do.

Returning to Puerto Rico as a teenager, Bella found the village, the house, and the woods more enchanting. She felt a profound connection to the land. Bella remembered her favorite spot by the pond that she loved to visit. The waterfall from the creek poured into a pond—an awe-inspiring sight. Bella enjoyed sitting in a small cave behind the waterfall to draw. On cloudy days, she would sit on a large boulder that extended into the pond, watching frogs, some turtles, and small fish. At that spot, the canopy of trees opened up to reveal the sky, sometimes full of clouds, other times bright blue and sunny. Bella would spend hours on the rock, sketching, painting, or simply relaxing and listening to the forest's sounds. These sounds transported Bella to a different time, when these woods and many others across the island were home to thriving indigenous peoples. Bella remembered how strange it felt that she never felt alone in the woods. In fact, she felt a strong pull toward the trees, as if she was one with nature.

The hallways were inside the house. Large paned windows, when opened, let the breeze flow in and out. Over the big, sculpted doors, stained-glass windows sat. These windows showed Catholic scenes with Jesus blessing the family and home with open arms. When they returned to the island as teenagers, Bella wondered why Abuela hadn't taken those windows down and replaced them with glass artwork showing Puerto Rican scenes. Abuela told Bella that their family line was not only Taino and African but also Spanish and Portuguese. She explained that the colonists who came to take the island were Catholic and decorated their homes with religious artifacts and decorations. Abuela said that embracing part of their legacy is good, as long as Bella doesn't ignore the other parts, because by accepting all that you come from, those cultures and ethnicities will shape who you become. And still, Bella would struggle with her sense of identity for years to come.

The stairwell leading upstairs was made of cast iron. The tiles that decorated the hallways and garden also covered each of the steps leading up to the upper level. They told a story of stages in the family's history, almost like a quilt made of tiles. Every generation added more tiles that represented what was happening in Puerto Rico as well as in their family. Some tiles bore the names of family members, and over time, images of the family and the house were added to the tiles. Abuela taught her children and grandchildren about the importance of protecting the land from corporate exploitation. The land wasn't worth much, but it was the ancestral home of Puerto Rico's original people. Over time, colonists and the slaves they brought transformed the land. Slaves who escaped from sugar plantations found refuge here and formed a symbiotic relationship with the Taino. Enslaved Africans and people from the Canary Islands arrived when Spain claimed the islands as Spanish territory. These people, forcibly taken from their land, homes, and families, possessed skills they shared with the Taino. The Taino, in turn, shared their own skills with the newcomers. They thrived for many years until a massive hurricane struck the island, destroying the trees and plants that served as food sources. That hurricane forced the inhabitants to move closer to the cities the colonists were building. The towns made of brick and stone survived the hurricane better than the clay and palm leaf structures where the indigenous people lived. With the trees, plants, and some animals gone, they had to relocate to the towns and cities, where colonists enslaved, raped, and wiped out most of the indigenous population. Once slaves to the wealthy, it became almost impossible to leave a few years later, once the land healed from the hurricane that had caused so much destruction.

Abuela would tell the children stories about the bravery and creativity of their ancestors, who had to adapt to their new fate as slaves after being free and having autonomy before the hurricane. She retold stories passed down through generations, recounting how these ancestors found their way back to their ancestral land and remained hidden from the colonists. Even today, some pockets of Taino stay secluded and evade capture by the enslavers. Abuela also educated the children on how their people came back to this land, the very same land they live in now. She explained that, by the time some of their ancestors escaped their captors, the invaders had raped and sired children with them. Many Taino slaves died from bacteria and illnesses that Europeans brought with them to the island. Those who survived worked as slaves until they found a way to escape. Occasionally, a man, woman, or child would escape and return to their birthplace, only to find Europeans had taken control of their land, cut down the trees, and built small towns where lush forests once thrived. Abuela would tell the children and anyone listening how fortunate it was that their property consisted of hills, large trees, and cliffs—features that kept the land out of the colonists' reach, preventing them from taking it for themselves and building on it. When their ancestors returned, they could replant, build homes, and repopulate the area.

Bella made her way up the stairs to her old room. Abuela hadn't changed much in the room except for replacing Bella's old twin bed with a full-size bed better suited for adults. Bella chose this room years ago because it faced the backyard garden, some medium-sized fruit trees, and the woods. On rainy days, she would sit on the bay window to sketch while enjoying the view of her woods. Now, she stood at that very window and stared at the trees that always called to her.

Lulu jumped on Bella's bed. "Hey, Aunt Bella, did you see my room? It's great! I have toys in my room, and I can see the ocean from my window."

Bella was happy to see Lulu enjoying her visit to Puerto Rico. "Yes, I know. The ocean is far away, though. But because this house sits on top of a hill, we can see just a little bit of the ocean on clear days." As Bella began to turn around to face Lulu, she thought she saw a woman standing just inside the tree line. She thought to herself that maybe one of her cousins was coming to greet them." Bella grabbed Lulu's hand and asked her to show her the room.

On the way to Lulu's room, Lulu asked Bella many questions, such as who the people in the paintings and photos in the hallway were, why the roof was open, what happened when rain came in through the open roof, and why Abuelita's house seemed old. Lulu also asked Bella what the Wi-Fi signal was so she could use her tablet, and where the TV was.

Bella laughed because it was obvious that Amelia and Torry hadn't told their daughter that Abuela's house didn't have a TV or computer. Abuela's phone was a basic model that she bought just to access Wi-Fi for FaceTime with the family.

"Well, Chiquita, there aren't any televisions or computers in Abuela's house."

Lulu reacted immediately, "What? How can I see my videos or play on my tablet? Who doesn't have a computer? I am going to be so bored."

"No, you won't," Bella explained that Abuela believed children should be outside playing and exploring. "When I lived here, I never missed not having a television or computer because there's always something to do here and lots of family to do things with."

Lulu looked up at Bella with a look of surprise, "Really? So, what did you do when you were bored?"

"Lots of things like playing hide and seek. Have you noticed how big this house is? And all the cabinets you can hide in, not to mention the outdoors. Abuela's house had three gardens, one in front, one inside, and one out back in the yard." Bella walked into Lulu's room, sat her on the bed, and kept talking about the different ways she entertained herself as a child, with a fondness for the home and land it sat on. "And don't forget the woods."

Lulu made a scary face and informed Bella, "I am scared of the woods. What if a monster lives in the woods, and at night, it comes out to get me?"

Bella laughed and comforted Lulu's feelings of fear, "Lulu, there aren't any monsters inside those woods."

"Are you sure?" Lulu asked with trepidation, looking outside the window at the trees.

"I am positive. I wouldn't lie to you, sweetie. Look at what you'll find in those woods: fruit trees, berry bushes, a waterfall that flows into a pond, and many birds and animals." Bella stepped out of bed to stand in front of the window and look at the trees. "Oh, and best of all, the pond is a beautiful emerald green that shines when the sunlight hits it."

Lulu became curious, "shines how?"

Bella looked at Lulu and thought about how she would explain that, since it was something she often wondered about and asked Abuela about. "Well, Abuelita told me once that the woods are special, and magic makes the pond glow on certain days."

"Magic! Wow! Can I see the pond one day?"

"Absolutely, but I will take you, or another adult will take you." Bella bent down to look at Lulu eye-to-eye. "Lulu, you have to promise me that you will not go inside the woods alone."

Lulu became disappointed. She wanted to see real magic. "But, why? I am a big girl now, and I won't do anything bad."

Bella found it heartwarming that her niece was just as brave in character as she was when it came to exploring new things. "Because of the pond. Although it's not very deep, it is still a pond. I know that you can swim, sweetheart, but in a pool. A natural pond is not like a pool. Because the waterfall feeds the pond, and then the water continues down the hill, a current is created as the water moves. So, promise me that when you want to go into the woods, you will ask me or another adult. OK?"

Lulu looked out the window again, still fascinated by the woods, but she agreed to her aunt's request and promised not to wander alone, "OK, Aunt Bella. I promise. When can you take me?"

"Well, let me talk to your mommies about that, ok?"

Lulu, smiling, kissed her aunt on the cheek and agreed, "Ok, then when you talk to them, will you take me to the woods?"

"If they say yes."

Lulu hugged her aunt.

Torry walked into the bedroom. "Hey, are you giving away free hugs?"

Lulu ran towards Torry and hugged her. "Aunt Bella was telling about the magic in the woods."

Torry looked at Bella and smiled, "Was she? Yeah, your aunt has always loved the woods, and maybe someday you and she can go exploring."

Lulu became excited, "Really, Mommy?"

Bella looked at Torry for confirmation of consent. After all, Bella would love to teach the next generation about the wonder of their ancestry so they can also protect this land.

Torry told Bella and Lulu that she needed to ask Amelia how she felt about that first. "Anyway, I came to let you both know that lunch is ready, and some of our cousins are outside. We are eating in the backyard garden.

Chapter 9

Bella asked Abuela if she could help take the dishes outside. Abuela replied that her cousins, aunt, and uncle were setting the outdoor table. Amelia was carrying the bowls of food outside. Abuela asked Bella to wash her hands and join the celebration. Bella felt at home! Gathering at Abuela's house was always a special kind of celebration. Conversations around the table were filled with laughter, small arguments, and loud voices. The joke was that if anyone asked why they were talking so loudly, the answer was 'because I am Puerto Rican.' Like many islands in the Caribbean, the people of Puerto Rico had a unique way of celebrating life. Puerto Ricans were no exception. They love family, the land, food, and rum. The common belief was that life and food should be thoroughly enjoyed. Abuela always said she didn't want to live anywhere else. She visited her children who lived inland, but she was always happy to return home. Abuela would ask herself why life outside the island was so complicated, busy, and anxious.

Family members approached Bella to hug and kiss her. They expressed how great it was to see her again. Aunt Julia asked if Bella was dating yet. Cousin Clarissa asked if Bella wanted to start a family.

Bella responded with her usual answers: "No, I am too busy at work to make time out to date anyone."

Clarissa responded with a concerned look on her face, "Bella, why do you want to work so much? Do you have friends to hang out with? Do you take time off from work?"

Bella had been pondering those same questions for years. Why was she still living in North Carolina? Why fill her days with work? Was she unhappy and hiding her true feelings?

Bella smiled at her cousin and tried to explain, "Look, I don't know how it happens, but living in North Carolina has become so expensive that I have to work long hours to earn overtime and impress management, hoping for bonuses and raises just to pay for rent, my car, and food. I have a small garden in my backyard where I grow vegetables. But with food prices rising, I can no longer afford to splurge anymore. It's all a trap!"

Sitting beside Bella was her brother, Antonio, and next to him sat Torry.

"Bella is right," Antonio said. "Check this out: Makayla and I both have to work because of too many bills. Look, if you work, you need a car; if you have young children, you must pay for daycare. Get the picture? A third of my paycheck goes to my car and insurance so we can get the kids to school, appointments, and our jobs. Lulu is still in preschool, which costs money. Our Maria is in second grade and needs clothes, school supplies, and money for field trips. Housing prices have tripled, and the banks won't give us that kind of credit, so we just can't buy a house. We're forced to pay rent, and our greedy landlord raised the rent by 50% last year. It's like Bella said, the whole American life feels like a trap. In fact, Makayla and I dip into our savings most months just to get by." Antonio looked at Carlos for support. "Carlos, didn't you tell me your rent has also gone up?"

"Yeah. My greedy bastard landlord also raised my rent by nearly 40%. I transferred to Child Protective Services to earn more money, but now I work almost 10-hour days, sometimes 7 days a week. I have friends, but I don't have much time to hang out with them because I work on weekends too. So, don't ask me about having kids. I can't afford any more expenses."

Everyone shook their heads and expressed concern that they were all working too hard. Clarissa was confused, "But, if it's that bad, why don't you come back home?"

Amelia jumped into the conversation, "because our credit cards are maxed out. Every time we put gas in the car, repair something in our house, do car maintenance, buy groceries, or pay taxes, it chains us to our jobs just a little bit more. Bella's right, it's a trap."

Julia responded to the latter, "Wait, we all pay taxes."

"Yes, but you pay sales taxes and federal taxes. We pay sales tax, federal tax, Social Security tax, property tax, services tax, and income tax, whether we earn the money working or we win the money. We are taxed to death. We are drowning in taxes." Amelia turned to Torry, "Am I missing any other taxes? Ironically, the US went to war with Britain when the crown continued to impose taxes on the colonists."

Torry sighed, "Not sure, babes. Taxes are out of control. And what's worse is that every year the government cuts back on education, health care, and social programs, so where is that money really going?"

Amelia continued to vent, "The trick is not to get into debt, right? Simple, right? But it's not that simple. Credit cards are also a necessary trap. When all your bills are practically doubled, you have no choice but to use credit cards to get by." Amelia took a drink and took a deep breath. Amelia had known that Bella hadn't been happy living in North Carolina, and she longed to return home. Amelia understood that sense of longing. "That's one of the reasons why Torry and I are excited about Lulu starting school in the fall. We will be saving over $800 per month once we don't have to pay the daycare."

All eyes at the table turned to Amelia. Maria's eyes widened.

"$800?? Every month??" Amelia and Torry nodded.

"Oh, and the daycare makes us pay for extra accident insurance for Lulu, and we have to pay for field trips. It actually adds up to another $500 extra every year."

Abuela couldn't believe how much daycare cost for children. "Pero Amelia, that's so much money. I think I understand what 'the trap of America' is." She turned to Carmen with more questions, "Was it the same way for you, Carmen? Were you trapped in America?"

Carmen talked about how often she had to work two jobs to pay the bills. She always felt guilty about not being at home with her kids. "Yeah, you all know that Luis left me with nothing but the house and the debt for the house. I had to hire a lawyer because I couldn't afford to divorce Luis and sue him for the house. But the house wasn't fully paid off, and I sometimes had to work two jobs to pay the mortgage. When I found a job in North Carolina and looked into the cost of living, I felt I had no choice but to rent out my house and move to North Carolina. But I dealt with too much racism, hatred, and discrimination in North Carolina to stay. Once the kids were grown, in college, or living on their own, I moved back to my house in Florida. I had paid it off, so moving back saved me money. I felt bad leaving my children in North Carolina and returning to Florida, but Carlos started his career, Antonio had his first baby, and Amelia and Torry moved in together." Carmen turned to Bella and asked, "But Bella, I always wondered why you didn't want to move to Florida with me."

During that time, Bella knew that she wasn't happy in North Carolina, and she wouldn't be happy in Florida. She was still trying to figure out who she was and where she belonged.

"I was sad that you were moving away, but I didn't want to leave my siblings. I had just started my job at the law firm."

Abuela said, "Well, I am glad that you ALL were able to come home together this time!" Abuela got up from the table and went back to the kitchen. "Wuala! Anyone ready for coffee and dessert?"

The group simultaneously said, "Yes!"

Bella helped Abuela serve the coffee and her famous dessert, tembleque.

Lulu was curious about the desert. "Ooh, mommy, what is that? Is it a white Jell-O?" Lulu accepted the piece that Bella handed to her.

Torry answered, "No, Lulu. It is called tembleque. It's like a pudding made of coconut. Your grandmother makes the best tembleque on the island. It's sweet and creamy with a little bit of cinnamon on top."

Lulu took a bite of her piece, and her eyes lit up. "Wow! Abuela, this is so good!"

Abuela felt a great sense of pride at seeing her grandchildren enjoy her dessert. "Thank you, Lulu. I am glad you all like it. It makes me happy to see that you are enjoying a dessert made from an old family recipe. My great-grandmother taught generations of Rodríguezes this very same recipe. I pick the coconuts from my own trees, and I grind them to get all the coconut milk out of them. Anyone for seconds?"

All the children raised their hands. The family spent their lunch reminiscing about lost memories, asking questions about their lives in North Carolina, and discussing what they wanted to see while in Puerto Rico. No one wanted to talk about Luis's funeral. No one wanted to ruin the splendor of the gathering by reopening old wounds. There will be time to talk about the funeral and the arrangements. Bella didn't really care. She was there to support her mother and her siblings.

The children finished their plates and were excused so they could play. The adults cleared the table of leftover lunch and put the dirty dishes in the sink. Abuela always interjected when she saw everyone clearing the table because she insisted that she could do it herself. Everyone laughed and expressed gratitude for Abuela's hard work in feeding them, insisting on helping around the house.

As Bella stacked a group of plates to take to the kitchen, she asked the group, "Hey, who was that woman with the long black hair? I thought she might be a family member because she looked familiar. I expected her to join us for lunch."

Bella didn't notice that everyone, except her siblings, had fallen silent. She looked up to see some of her family's faces staring at her with wide eyes, as others avoided her gaze. Bella, Amelia, and Torry seemed confused about the reaction.

"What is it?" Bella asked the group.

Everyone seemed hesitant to answer her. Carmen spoke in a hushed voice, showing concern for Bella, "Baby, where did you see this woman?"

Bella became worried about who this woman was that her family seemed to be afraid of. Bella pointed to the woods, "There, standing between the trees and bushes at the edge of the woods. Why? Who is she?"

Carmen approached Bella to speak to her and Amelia. "Look, girls, that's why I asked you to come home. There's a lot we need to tell you, but I was hoping we could talk about it when your Aunt Maria arrives later today. But it figures that you saw her today. You've been gone for several years, and I thought we wouldn't have to talk to you both about the violence in our family's history."

Bella grew worried. Amelia stood up and asked what violence was. Torry looked at Amelia's face and became concerned. They all wondered what this family secret was really about. Abuela glanced at the children and noticed how Lulu and Crystal, who were preschoolers, needed to take their naps. She then looked at Amelia and Carlos and reminded them that it was 1:00 pm.

"Amelia and Makayla, do your kids still take naps? Look at them, they are running around, but I think Crystal is getting tired."

Carlos and Torry turned to look at the children. The older children seemed to be having a great time playing, but Lulu and Crystal, exhausted from their playfulness, clearly needed their naps.

"You are right, Abuela. It's definitely time for Lulu to nap." Torry knew Amelia was dealing with her emotions right now, so she got up from the table to get Lulu. Makayla followed. Makayla knew that if Crystal didn't take her daily nap, she would struggle tonight.

Abuela asked Bella and Amelia to be a little bit more patient. She was waiting for her sister, Maria, to arrive before telling their story.

The family cleaned up after lunch and bid everyone goodbye. The plan was for them to return later today for dinner and bring a dish to share with everyone. Parents checked on the older children, talked to them about the heat in Puerto Rico, and ensured they knew what drinks were in the refrigerator. Abuela reminded them that she did not have any sodas. She would often tell them how bad sodas were for children, and fresh juices from fresh fruit were better for them.

Carmen hooked her arms around Amelia and Bella's arms, and they walked back inside the house.

Chapter 10

The afternoon sun was at its highest, making it uncomfortable to be outdoors. Abuela had a recreation room on the second floor of the house, where the older kids would play, talk, and hang out. Abuela placed her pork on the spit to start roasting. Abuela used to say that the pig had to roast slowly and steadily after being seasoned with herbs, spices, and mojo. Abuela had a wood grill in the kitchen with a flue that drew the smoke outside. Abuela had a bowl of cut-up fresh fruit and berries that she placed on the coffee table for all to enjoy.

Bella seized her chance to escape the house. She needed a moment of solitude. Her curiosity and worries had become too much. She found herself walking into the woods. Instantly, she began to relax, and her mood shifted. It was always such a familiar feeling. She smelled the earth beneath her feet, the trees, and the flowers. In the air, she heard the songs of hundreds of birds nesting high up in the trees and flying around, feeding on bugs. Even the sound of the leaves rustling felt like a song sung just for her. There was so much life and energy in this small forest. She wasn't exaggerating when she described this place as magical to Lulu. As a child, she had played with the idea that magical creatures lived in these woods. Bella would spend hours searching for fairies and elementals. Bella thought the mist rising from the pond at dusk was one of the most beautiful sights in the forest. As a teen, Bella believed that will-o'-the-wisps lived in the forest and came out at night to lure her to the pond. Her brothers would tease her whenever she told them that she 'almost found where the fairies live.'

Along the path, Bella snacked on blackberries, which she plucked from the bushy vines while walking. She noticed that the cherry bushes were also heavy with fruit. She took off her hat and filled it with cherries. At this time of year, the fruit is very tart and firm. Puerto Ricans turned these berries into a delicious, tart, and sweet candy called 'Cerezas'. Carmen and Abuela taught Bella how to make cerezas. Bella then found herself in front of the pond. The pond was more like a freshwater lagoon. It had a sand embankment that led up to a boulder. Bella stood in front of the pond, admiring its water's color. It was magical to see rays of the sun land on the water's surface, making the pond glow a beautiful light teal. A waterfall from a creek fed the pond. On a short climb up the embankment walls, one could see rocks and fallen trees in the creek. The water rushed down the embankment into the pond. Bella sat on a rock in the creek, feeling the cool, fresh water rush past her. The sound of the water traveling down the creek was relaxing to Bella.

As Bella admired the beauty of this place, she felt eyes on her. Bella turned her head in the direction from which the sensation came. At first, all she saw was trees and bushes covered in shadow. As her eyes adjusted to the darkness of the forest, she thought she saw that woman again—a woman of average height with long black hair. The shadow hid most of her features, but Bella recognized her as the woman she saw outside her bedroom window. Bella called out to her, but the woman disappeared. Bella ran through the bushes to reach her. When she stood where the stranger had been, she looked for any signs of where the woman had gone. Bella noticed the area was muddy from last night's rain, but there weren't any footprints in the mud. She thought that the stress of everything happening was making her crazy, and she was hallucinating.

Bella returned to the boulder to look for fish and frogs in the pond. She lost track of time, caught up in her magical world.

Amelia approaches Bella and smiles, "I knew that I would find you here."

Bella sat up, happy to see her sister. "Hey sis, I am sorry that you had to come looking for me."

Amelia climbed up the boulder to join her sister. "Nah, don't worry about it. Everyone knew where I would find you. You had always had a strong connection to this forest. Hey, I was curious about that woman you saw today."

Bella wasn't surprised that her sister believed her. Amelia had always been the one person she could talk to about anything, be it dreams, boys, or anything else. "Mel, look, I am not crazy. That woman was standing at the tree line. She was looking straight at me. She seemed familiar, but I didn't know where I knew her from. I wish I could have seen her better so I could remember how I knew her. She has long black hair. I think she has brown skin, but she's always in the shadows, so I can't get a clear look at her."

"Always in the shadows? Bella, how often had you seen this woman?"

"Well, I saw her earlier today, and just now I thought I saw her standing by those trees across the pond. But she looks like a woman in my dreams. In my dreams, she is calling out to me, but I can't make out what she is saying. But, it doesn't make sense that the woman in my dreams is the same woman I saw today."

"Where did you see her just now?"

"Do you see those two trees that are kind of wrapped around each other?"

Amelia nodded. "Yeah, I know those trees. We used to say that the trees were kissing. Didn't you sketch the trees?"

"Yeah, I called it *The Kiss*. She was standing between the two trees behind the bushes. Unfortunately, that area was hidden in the shadows, so I wasn't able to see any details. I went over there and looked around and did not see her."

Amelia stared in the direction Bella pointed, long and hard, as if somehow she could see the woman. "Maybe she took off when you spotted her."

"Yeah, I thought that too, but Abuela told us that it rained last night."

"Yeah, so what?"

"Well, that area is very muddy. If she had been standing there, she would have left footprints, but there weren't any in the mud. Very weird!"

Amelia looked at Bella and softly grabbed her by her shoulders. "Listen, Bella, that was not the first time you saw that woman."

Bella's eyes widened while her mind rose through her memories to remember who the woman was."

Listen, when we were little, Mom and Dad brought us to Puerto Rico several times. We stayed at a hotel so that family members' feelings wouldn't be hurt because we didn't stay with them. We have a large family. Anyway, one day, visiting Abuelita, we played hide and seek. We couldn't find you, though. Carlos and Antonio searched for you in the house and the woods. I have to tell you, it was terrifying to walk into those woods alone, but I was more terrified of you jumping into that pond. I ran to get to the pond in case you were drowning or hurt when I saw you talking to someone. Belle it was a woman with black hair. Now, many Puerto Rican women have black hair, and we have families living in the surrounding area, so I just thought you were with one of our aunts. I heard you talking, but I couldn't make out any words. I called out to you and saw that the woman was gone. I became more worried that a stranger was living in this forest and that you were in danger. I ran up to you and asked you who you were speaking to.

Bella was frozen in place. She didn't have any recollection of this, but now that Amelia was talking about it, Bella thought that it did sound familiar.

"Bella, you told me that you were talking to the woman, and you pointed to her. Then you giggled and asked the woman that I couldn't see, 'Why can't she see you?' Bella, my hair stood up, my heart was pounding, and I knew that either you were sick, the woman was a ghost, or you were crazy. You were as old as Lulu is now."

"I was talking to someone you couldn't see?? How is that possible? Was it a ghost?"

"I don't know Bella, but you told me that she was as real as you. I asked you to tell me what you and the woman were talking about, and you said that she told you to take care of our people and the land. I thought that was an odd thing for a preschooler to say, so I figured that you were talking to an adult. I couldn't figure out how the woman ran away so quickly when I called out to you."

"What did you do back then?"

"Nothing. I believed that you had spoken to a lady in the woods, but I was worried that if I told Mom and Dad, they would take you to a bunch of doctors because they wouldn't believe you."

They both climbed off the rock and began to walk back to the house. Bella thought about it carefully, "Yeah, I think that mom would have believed me, but your father, on the other hand, would have yelled at me for making things up."

Amelia noticed how Bella had disassociated herself from their father. Amelia knew that Bella always felt abandoned, and she had missed out on the years the rest of them had with their father. She respected Bella's feelings and never tried to change her mind.

"So, you saw your little sister talking to a ghost and you kept your mouth shut," Bella smirked as she wrapped her arm around Amelia's arm.

"Of course. We were on vacation, Mom was happy to be back home, and I didn't want to cause anyone to treat you differently because you claimed to see a ghost."

"You said that I didn't say that the lady was a ghost."

Amelia laughed.

"No, you said that she was real. But I didn't know if anyone would seem concerned about you. So, every time we visited Abuelita, I kept you close. I knew you loved this forest, so I came in with you. Shortly after our last family visit, we couldn't come to Puerto Rico for several years. The bills got bigger, and Mom didn't want Antonio and Carlos to take on part-time jobs. So, we didn't return to Puerto Rico for several years. You never mentioned the woman again, that is, until today."

"But why can't I remember all of this?" Bella became confused.

Amelia embraced her sister and held her hands. Bella knew that look well. Amelia had a way of easing Bella's anxiety about the unknown. And now she had just learned that Amelia had been watching over her her entire life.

"You know, Bella, I think that tonight we are going to learn a lot about our family."

Bella nodded. "Yeah, you're right. I can't help but feel a little bit annoyed that family secrets had been kept from us all the while, for years, you and I have had terrible dreams."

"Well, let's get back to the house. Aunt Maria just got here, and the party is about to get going. Let's have fun with our family tonight." Amelia led Bella out of the forest.

The sisters talked about how great it was to be back home. Amelia seized this opportunity to discuss her discontent and her desire to return to the island with Bella.

"Listen, Bella, can we talk about what you said about moving back to Puerto Rico?"

Bella agreed to explain her feelings, "You know, Mel, I don't want to move away from you. You and I are like tide at the hip. As far as I can remember, you have always been there for me, wiping away my tears and taking away my bad dreams. You even helped me when I was not making good choices, and things could have ended badly for me. Plus, I don't want to miss watching Lulu grow up. But I feel disconnected from my life. I guess that doesn't make sense. I suppose I'm talking nonsense. Forget what I said." Amelia and Bella strolled so they had time to talk. Amelia thought of how much she would miss Bella if she moved out and what her absence would do to Lulu.

Amelia turned to face Bella. "Bella, I am going to be honest with you. Right now, I am feeling selfish because I don't want you to move away. I don't think you and I have ever been this far apart, and your moving back here will mean that I won't be with you. And Sis, Lulu is at an age where she will feel your absence in her life. I want my child to grow up with family around her."

Bella couldn't help feeling hot tears welling up in her eyes.

"Bella, I just wanted to share my feelings with you. And at the same time, I understand yours. That sense of belonging to something like this family and the land that surrounds us. There have been times, even when we were growing up, when I felt we needed to come back to our family." Amelia could see through the trees their aunts, uncles, cousins, and children setting up for the feast. Amelia turned to face Bella. Bella saw tears on Amelia's face. At that moment, Bella felt terrible for making her sister sad. This was the reason why she had kept her feelings about leaving North Carolina to herself. "Bella, don't worry about it. Of course, it hurt to hear you say you wanted to move away, but if I'm honest, I was more worried about how sad you've been, and I hadn't realized. I'm sorry. And if I'm honest, I envy you a little bit."

Bella snapped her head up and gave Amelia a confused look.

"Of course, Torry and I owe so much on our house that we can't just get up and leave. With this trip, our credit cards are maxed out, and paying for Lulu's daycare costs a small fortune. There have been times when Torry and I casually wished we could drop everything and leave this crazy trap we fell into. 'The American Dream' my ass!" Amelia looked around and spread her arms wide. "Look at this place, Bella. I can feel magic in the air. The energy pulses and reminds us that we are sons and daughters of our mother island. The American culture teaches people that they are on their own, they have to work hard, and end up in debt or with health problems." Amelia turned to look at her family laughing and hugging. She saw Lulu running around with her cousins, and Torry enjoying himself with our cousins. Amelia could hear the laughter and feel the energy from the scene. Amelia faced Bella with a gentle smile. "You're right about this place having a life force that every Puerto Rican feels deep inside. It calls us all home, and it's been calling you to return for a long time."

Bella hugged her sister. "Thank you, Amelia. We can talk about it another day. I needed to hear that you would understand."

Chapter 11

When both sisters entered the clearing, Torry saw them from across the glade and walked over. Angel waved and called out to ask if they wanted him to make them a drink.

Amelia hugged Torry and waved to Angel.

"Yeah, do you still make the island's best pina colada?"

With a big grin on his face, he spread his arms.

"Cousin! Are you doubting that I still make the best pina colada on the island?" Angel chuckled. "I got you couz!"

The afternoon was exhausting for Amelia, Torry, and Bella. They found a quiet moment to take a breath while they watched Lulu play. Amelia stretched her arms and yawned. "I forgot how much island people love to party, and our family is no exception."

Torry leaned on her wife as someone spoke behind them.

"Are you saying that you are too old to party cause your mom still can out-party all of us!"

They all turned. Coming down the stairs was a familiar face.

"Tia Isabella," they all yelled together as they moved to embrace her.

"Hola, niñas! You are all so beautiful." Isabella hugged her grandnieces.

Torry helped Isabella as she walked toward the outdoor patio. "Abuela Isabella! How old are you now? You haven't aged a bit since we last saw each other!"

Isabella laughed and said, "Are you kidding, Torry! Listen, we Moraleses age well, but our joints remind us every day that we ARE old." Isabella stopped walking, her face turning serious as she addressed Amelia and Bella. "Your mom told me about your recent dreams. And you are right to be concerned. So, I want to take some time tonight after the children are in bed so we can talk."

Bella quickly responded, "Talk about what, Tia?" Bella was eager for answers. "Does this have anything to do with Luis's death?"

Isabella noticed how Bella referred to her late father by his first name. Bella can hold grudges, and being abandoned by her father was one of those 'you never forget' situations that she will probably never forgive. Isabella felt sad for Bella, but at the same time, she felt pride because Bella was not only named after her, but Bella was also a lot like her. "I promise, girls, we will talk tonight, and it may lead to more questions. But you just got here. Let's celebrate your homecoming." Bella, Amelia, and Torry looked at each other and agreed to just have a good time with their family.

Amelia quickly called Lulu over to introduce her to her great-aunt. Lulu, sweaty and red-cheeked, ran to her mother. "Lulu, have you been drinking water?"

"Uh-huh. Mima gave me coconut water. It was so good."

Amelia picked up Lulu so that Lulu was at eye-to-eye level with Isabella. "Good, coconut water is good for you. Baby, this is your great-aunt Isabella."

Isabella beamed with love and joy as she stared at her great-niece. "Well, Lulu. You are so big. I thought you were a baby, but you are grown."

"Yeah, I'm all growed up. And auntie, guess what? I am going to kindergarten soon."

"Wow! That sounds like fun."

Sofia was Carmen's niece. Her father, Miguel, was Carmen's brother. Carmen and Miguel were only a year apart, so they behaved more like twins. They shared a strong connection. For years, they were as close as Amelia and Bella. Carmen was maid of honor at his wedding to Elena. Miguel and Elena were married for twenty years and had three children. The family was devastated when Miguel contracted COVID at work. He fought the symptoms for eight days, but Miguel succumbed to COVID-19. His death deeply affected everyone in the family. Carmen grieves for her brother. While Carmen lived in Puerto Rico, she babysat Miguel's kids often and became more like an older sister to Sofia. Sofia had a bigger-than-life personality that reminded Carmen of her brother. Sofia walked inside the house to tell everyone that the food was ready, and they all gathered at the table.

"Aunt Isabella! You look great!"

"Thank you, Sofia. I noticed that you didn't come with your husband tonight."

Sofia placed her hands on her hips and scowled at her aunt. "Now you know that I am not married, Titi. Will you ever stop trying to force me to get a husband? You know I was just accepted to the University of Puerto Rico, and I start in August."

Sofia wrapped her arm around her aunt. "Look, Titi, today women have more options. I want a career in archaeology, and that means I will be out in the field, and most men don't do well when the wife is independent, has her own income, and is not home to cook for him." Sofia looks at Bella to indirectly ask Bella for help.

"Titi, I hope that Sofia and I won't be asked when we are getting married again and again while we are here."

Isabella faced both Bella and Sofia, "Look, girls, my husband died a few years ago. You have no idea how lonely it is growing old without your companion. I know that you are young and have plans for your life, but don't dismiss marriage. Finding your soul mate can be special."

Sofia was quick to respond, "Or finding your manchild can lead to a happy divorce."

Isabella made a sour face and waved Sofia's comment away as if she were swatting a fly, "No, Sofia. I can see that you are convinced marriage can be a lot of work for the wife. And of course, you are right. It usually is. However, there are some positive aspects as well. You know, you are right, you are young. The truth is, if I had the choice to go to college or get married, I would have chosen college first."

All three of them burst out laughing.

Stepping outside, Bella looked up at a sky filled with orange, blue, and yellow hues. As the sun set, the colors in the sky grew more vivid. The clouds were sparse, and the sky was beginning to glow with bright pink shades. Bella stood there in awe of the view. Antonio approached her holding a pina colada.

"What, did you forget our Puerto Rican sunsets? Nothing else compares." He looks at Bella. Antonio had been sensing Bella's discontent. "You know, Bella, you belong here." He pointed to the ground. "This land is in your blood. Our ancestors lived in harmony with nature, helping this island flourish. It has been taken away from us for too long." Antonio moved behind her to grab her shoulders from behind and point to the tree line. "You sense it, don't you. The forest calls you. It has been since we were children. And now it's calling you home."

Bella was startled.

"Did Amelia tell you how I have been fighting myself to return home?"

"No, wait. Seriously, you have been thinking of moving back home?"

Bella nodded while her eyes remained fixed on the tree line. There in the shadows, the lady stood, staring at Bella. This time, she had a gentle smile on her face. Bella knew that Antonio couldn't see her. "Yes. I love living near my sister, and I like my job, but I feel as if another part of me is here waiting for me to return home."

"Listen, you know that Abuela will let you stay here. She has a big house, and even though we visit often and help her with the maintenance, I bet she could use your company. You should think about it."

Antonio and Bella walked over to the table. That's when Bella saw Amelia holding Lulu in her arms. Lulu looked upset, and Amelia was staring right at Bella. Bella hurried over to Amelia and Lulu, "What's wrong? Did Lulu get hurt?"

Amelia looked at Bella and whispered, "No, it's not like that." Amelia then turned to Lulu and said, "Lulu, tell Aunt Bella what you were doing."

Lulu's eyes were downcast, and in a hushed voice, Lulu responded, "I was in the woods."

"What! Lulu, sweetie, remember that I told you that you cannot go into the woods by yourself?" Bella faced Amelia, worried that Amelia would be mad at her, "Mel, I swear I told her not to go into the forest by herself."

"I know you did. Lulu mentioned it to me earlier today. I am not mad at anyone. Just listen to her story. Lulu, finish your story."

"Ok, mommy. I am sorry, Aunt Bella. I know you told me that I can't go into the woods by myself. But I wasn't by myself."

Bella looked up at Amelia. Amelia had a 'wait for it' look on her face.

"Who did you go into the woods with? One of your cousins?"

"No, it was your friend, the lady."

Bella's blood ran cold. "What did the lady say?"

"I couldn't understand what she was saying. She pointed into the woods, and I followed her. I climbed the waterfall."

Bella gasped.

"It's ok, Auntie. The lady showed me that I had to dig. But then, mommy found me."

"Yeah, Bella, she was on top of the waterfall picking up rocks. You can imagine how I felt."

Bella's mind was spinning.

Amelia was able to see that Bella was trying to figure things out. She noticed that everyone was gathering at the table.

"Look, Bella, how about you and I talk about this later? Lulu, I don't care who wanted you to go into the woods. You, young lady, are not allowed in that forest without me, Mommy Torry, and Auntie Bella. Got it?"

"Yes, mommy."

"Come on, Bella. Everyone is gathering for dinner, and I am hungry." Amelia turned to Lulu, "Are you hungry, sweetheart?"

Isabella nodded and smiled, realizing that her mom wasn't mad.

"Yes, I am so hungry."

"Good, let's join the others."

Chapter 12

The celebration was a grand affair of traditional Puerto Rican foods, delicious desserts, and Antonio as a master bartender. Some family members danced salsa and merengue. Neighbors came to welcome everyone home. The neighbors brought food and desserts. Bella thought that the food would never end tonight. She took in the scene of her family celebrating and remembered childhood memories from Puerto Rico that were similar to what was happening now. She missed this, her family, the house, the forest, and being Puerto Rican.

Bella was lost in thought when her cousin Lucas sat down beside her.

"Hola Bella. It is so good to see you and your family here." Lucas gazes at the family dancing and laughing. How is North Carolina?"

"Beautiful, but expensive. Many people have settled in North Carolina. Houses and apartments are springing up everywhere. Thousands of acres of lush greenery are being destroyed. I see the slaughter of trees and wildlife. For what reason, so some goddamn millionaire can buy the land, build cheaply made houses and apartments, then sell them for absurd prices."

"Yes, cousin. That is happening here. Corporations are buying land and even whole ghost towns. They are knocking down historical homes, and they are even building on protected land. Bella, those fuckers are buying politicians, buying our heritage so that rich people can buy these million-dollar homes on our mountains and beaches."

"Are you kidding me? So, it's happening here too. The rich are taking whatever they want. I wouldn't be surprised if corporations haven't looked at this town yet."

Lucas turned to face Bella. "Bella, they have. They've offered some of our neighbors' money to buy their homes. Bella, these are working people who have struggled their whole lives. These people are offering them $100,000 for their simple houses."

"How many have sold their homes?"

"So far, none. They are seriously thinking about it, though. The only thing keeping them from selling is that they know that they won't be able to afford to buy anything else. They can't buy half the house they have now with what is being offered. The prices have gone sky high, and some people are being evicted from their homes because the government says they have no ownership papers."

"So the corporations are taking Puerto Rico apart?"

"Corporations and politicians. But the truth is that Puerto Ricans have been trapped in debt, made homeless, denied rights, and our land has been auctioned to the highest bidder, and yet we love our island. Being Puerto Rican is like being part of something grand, and it's in all of us; no matter if you leave the island, Puerto Rico is in your veins. And sooner or later, the island of enchantment calls you back home."

Bella understood that feeling of being summoned back to the island. Bella saw people saying goodnight and mothers gathering their kids. Bella and Lucas joined the group to say their goodbyes. Amelia and Torry said their goodbyes and took Lulu upstairs to put her to bed.

Carmen came to Bella, hugged her daughter, and together they walked inside the house. After cleaning up, the house was quiet, and the light from the lamps and chandeliers gave the home a warm glow. Amelia and Torry came downstairs, conversing. Bella figured that they were talking about Lulu and the lady. Amelia and Torry looked up and spanned the room. Torry noticed Isabella, Carmen, and Maria talking. She saw the worried looks on their faces. Amelia tapped Torry and pointed to Bella, "There's Bella."

"Hey, is Lulu asleep?"

"Oh yeah. She played so much today that the minute her head hit the pillow, she started to yawn. Torry started to read a story, and in a couple of minutes, Lulu was fast asleep."

"No kidding, Bella, fast asleep. Torry, do you ever remember a time when Lulu fell asleep so early?"

"Nah, bedtime is difficult at our house. Did you notice that Lulu never asked for our phone or her tablet today?"

Bella had noticed that Lulu spent a lot of time with her cousins today, rather than on her tablet. "Well, I noticed. She had no problems getting to know her cousins and playing today. It was terrific to see her having that much fun."

Carmen approached them, "Hey, sweethearts, your grandmother and Isabella are ready to discuss with you some things about our family." We are gathering in the family room.

Carmen, Bella, Amelia, Torry, Maria, and Isabella sat down, all facing each other. Maria drew in a deep breath and whispered a sort of prayer that Bella couldn't make out. "Bueno, girls, let me first say that it wasn't anyone's intention to keep secrets from you or anyone else. These situations don't happen often because the family curse had skipped a couple of generations. Carmen had always suspected that you two carried the gift. But it wasn't until you all visited us several years ago that you both said specific things like dreams you had, and a woman with long black hair. We prayed that it was just a coincidence because we knew from our family history that life becomes difficult for the gifted ones. Carmen informed us of your nightmares growing up, especially your nightmares, Bella. Carmen and Luis had moved to Florida, and a year later, you came home to visit us. Your mom, let me know about some of the dreams you and Amelia were having. Your mom confided in me that she was afraid that the gift was in both of you, and she wasn't sure how she was going to keep it from your father."

This confused Bella, "But, why did she have to hide this so-called 'gift?'"

Isabella responded, "To explain that we have to go back to the beginning. You both are familiar with Puerto Rico's colonial history. But not much is known about the history of our indigenous people and what happened to them. Long before the Spanish and Portuguese arrived on our beaches, the Arawak people had been present for at least a thousand years, well before European colonists claimed our island. The Arawak on the island eventually became the Tainos. They had a strong sense of stewardship over this land and spread throughout the continent and other Caribbean islands. They were polytheistic and worshiped nature's gods, utilizing plants, roots, and herbs for both healing and nourishment. "We," Isabella points to everyone in the room, "we are all part of that bloodline. I mean, sure, there have been centuries of blending bloodlines with the Europeans, slaves, and other nationalities. But we hold more indigenous heritage."

The mood in the room was tense. Carmen silently cried. She knew their history. She knew of the horrors that the Europeans did to her ancestors for the glory of land and money. Of course, they renamed our home from Bonrinque to Puerto Rico, meaning the port of riches. The riches that they stole from our people to make their king richer. A few of them lined their pockets with gold and silver as well. Carmen knew the history all too well. She hoped that her children wouldn't show the family mark of foresight through dreams. Carmen looked at Bella and thought that she had always known Bella would inherit their ancestors' abilities. She hoped that she was wrong, but she wasn't.

Isabella joined the conversation. She explained the importance of the land to the people of this town. "Antonio, Carlos, Amelia, and Bella, you haven't been told all of this that you are about to hear because we were hoping that the family curse would not pass down to you. In our family, the curse passes down through the women, but every once in a generation, it skips the females." Maria stood up and walked to the large paned window. She continued her story, "This is a small village. For a millennium, this land has provided for us, and we have taken care of it. That is how it's always been. When the Spanish landed on our shores, they decimated the land, kidnapped the young to work their fields, and burned entire forests to build their houses. There are still original colonial houses and streets made of stone and brick throughout the island. They raped and killed women and children. In our small town, the Europeans and their minions removed as many of us as they could to enslave us on their sugar plantations. Some of our families were able to hide deeper in the forest and caves. This house sits on cliffs and volcanic rock that Tainos and then African slaves immigrated to. The forest was dense and hard to maneuver through. But those miserable bastards tried to smoke out the rest of the Tainos from where they were hiding."

Maria gazed at the darkening forest and the few lights from homes around them. She had heard these stories growing up, and she shared them with her children to pass on their history, so no one would forget where they came from or how hard their ancestors worked to endure the violence and brutality of the colonists, which changed their way of life forever. She often told this story because the Tainos did not leave written records. After years of hearing and recounting her people's stories of conquest and murder, talking about their ancestors' stories makes her sad, even centuries later. From the window, Maria listened to the coqui frogs and the night birds. She also heard the sound of the wind and, in the distance, music coming from homes up and down the hill.

Noticing Maria was getting upset, Isabella took up the tale.

"Shortly after Europeans arrived, they seized the native lands belonging to the Tainos, who had lived on the island for over a thousand years. They were also starved after their lands were taken. Young girls and women were kidnapped to be used as sex slaves for the labor force. Others were forcefully impregnated to provide the elite with personal slaves for their estates."

A tear drop ran down Bella's face. Torry stood up and paced in anger. Amelia was becoming angry that their mother hadn't told them all of this.

Isabella continued, "Somehow our ancestors managed to escape and return to settle this land. Some had to leave their loved ones enslaved. They found the forests surrounding these hills and hid to ensure their people's survival. There are caves located behind waterfalls and along the cliffsides of this property. Those ancestors who endured slavery were bred with Europeans, which is why many Puerto Ricans have European ties. For example, your father was a Puerto Rican with European roots. His lineage deliberately continued the European bloodline. When Carmen met him, she didn't know he was a Castillo. Castillos have direct ties to the Spanish, who took this island for themselves. But we will get to the Castillos later."

Maria brought out a bottle of dark rum and several glasses. Torry quickly grabbed a glass, and Maria poured her some rum. Others followed Torry's example. This get-together had turned out to be more than they expected. Bella's thoughts were scattered. She wondered if that was the reason her father left.

Isabella took a sip of the rum and took a deep breath before continuing with the story, "Our direct ancestors were able to evade the Europeans for many decades. They flourished in this land. Their population grew. They healed the land. They were self-sufficient, and they reformed their hierarchy with tribal leaders. Our ancestors lived off the land, and they thanked the nature gods that provided them with sanctuary, food, and hid them from the Europeans. Over time, the hidden homes in caves evolved into structured mud and stone houses, then wooden houses, and finally cement homes with clay roof tiles, which are famous and often owned by the elite. In the late 1600s, one of our ancestors began to write their history. We have her journals in our safe. The University asked to borrow the journals for their research on Caribbean Indigenous history. But we decided not to let anyone borrow them because we didn't want her to be dissected by research students and then written up in some journal for many to read. Her name was Nayeli. Nayeli was the village healer. Today, she would likely be described as an alchemist and a Wiccan. She used roots and herbs to heal her townspeople. She protected the land and her people. Even after she was 'joined' with her husband, she continued to heal people and the land. Nayeli had two children before she experienced problems with a third pregnancy, and she died for just a minute. She lost the baby and the ability to have more children. In her diary, she mentioned that while she lay dying, she experienced what she called a miracle by the one great God. She wrote that she saw her body lying on the mat, and everyone around her was crying and placing their hands on her. Outside of her house, there was a bright light. Nayeli described the light as warm and comfortable. From the light, there came a flash and thunderous sound, and she came back to life.",

Carmen's children were captivated by Nayeli's life, especially that of a woman in the 1700s who was able to be a prominent member of her society and write. Carlos poured himself another glass of rum. Torry nudged him on the shoulder and handed him her glass to refill.

"After a few days of healing from the miscarriage and the moment when she died, Nayeli began to write about having strange dreams."

Carmen looked at her daughters with apologetic eyes. Everyone else in the room cast their eyes at Amelia and Bella. Bella felt awkward.

The villagers regarded her as an enlightened figure because she could predict natural disasters that might destroy the village or foresee an upcoming injury. But all good things come to an end. Word spread that Nayeli was a witch who had sold her soul to the Devil. The Catholic Church exploited fears of the unknown and hell, using its wealth to bribe those in power and the elite. Some people believed the propaganda so deeply that husbands betrayed their wives, neighbors accused neighbors of witchcraft, and children reported their parents as witches. Hundreds were arrested, tortured, and some were burned at the stake. Others were imprisoned and forgotten.

Amelia interrupted her grandmother, "Wait, abuela, this happened here in Puerto Rico? For how long?"

Maria turned away from the window to face the group. With tear-filled eyes, she answered Amelia's question. "Amelia, the Catholic church had a lot of power. And they dealt with what they saw as threats to their rule and control over people. They heard about Nayeli and immediately recognized the dangers of ignoring her. They arrested her and declared her a witch and the Devil's daughter. Back then, only the elite, royalty, and members of the church were educated. They believed their role on Earth was to save souls. The harsh truth was that they enjoyed feeling powerful and in control. The elite and noble families often forced a son or daughter who lacked influence to join the church, ensuring they had a vested interest. Since most people were uneducated, they depended on their priest or monk for guidance.

Maria poured herself a glass of rum and sat down to continue the story. "So, people basically feared the unknown, and they relied on their religious leaders to tell them what to do and what God wanted from them. Nayeli stayed tucked away, forgotten. Her jailers believed that killing her would make her a martyr. Nayeli was the daughter of a chief and not someone who could be easily killed. So, they stopped feeding her and erased her name from the records as if she had never existed. But not everyone forgot about her. Her husband and her father were determined to bring her home. Karma is a bitch for sure because the woman who reported Nayeli to the authorities ended up being accused of witchcraft by her husband a year later.

"Nayeli's husband, Yaniel, was able to find his way inside the fort where they kept prisoners. He worked inside the fort as a general laborer. Her father worked outside the fort as a butcher. They kept this facade for a month until they found her. Now they had to wait for the darkest night of the year. That night, they hid inside the meat cooler. At night, the soldiers change shifts, and for a brief moment, there is confusion, laughter, chatter, and they aren't paying attention to who would be breaking into the fort. Yaniel had checked all the cells in the front corridors of the fort over the last couple of weeks. This time, they were going to check the area at the back that only the soldiers went to. That area is not visible to most people because the rocks and the ocean obscure it. There is no escape once you are there."

Carmen got up and went to the kitchen. She set down a tray with coffee for everyone.

"Well, they found her, but she was weak and emaciated. Her large eyes recognized her husband and her father, but she lacked the strength to wrap her arms around them. They gave her water. Her husband cried with anger at finding her in that condition. Yaniel let them know they had to leave the fort before sunrise. He explained that if they crawled through a sewer tunnel that drains sewage to the sea, they could escape by going through the volcanic rocks on the cliffside. Days later, she would write in her journal that they were all willing to risk their lives for her freedom. Together, they crawled through the tunnels until they reached the rocky terrain. They climbed over sharp rocks and driftwood. Yaniel wrote that it took them a while to get far enough from the fort, but they succeeded by staying in the shadows. Once back in their village, her family hid her in the old caves."

Antonio asked what happened to Nayeli.

"Well, Toni, they made it back to the village, but Nayeli was weak and suffering from a high fever. Nayeli dreamed of her death and the coming battle for this land. Nayeli asked for paper to start writing her memoirs. She described her health fading. Nayeli wrote about the family history spanning the past thousand years, including stories passed down from generation to generation, and then shared her own story. Nayeli wrote about a dream she had regarding the upcoming battle. She talked about the light that visited her. The voice whispered that she had to prepare her descendants for this battle for this land. The voice explained to her that her daughters will carry the gift the gods gave her to prepare the future generations to come."

Bella was astounded by what she had heard tonight. Was she a descendant of Nayeli and her people? Is this the reason why she had dreamt of a woman and seen her in her childhood, and lately?

Isabella continued the story, "Nayeli knew that her goddess was granting her the blessing of dreams, and now she understood that her children would become the next generation of warriors for this land. She wrote that she wasn't afraid of her death because she would transcend to another spiritual plane. She recorded that the goddess had healed her and allowed her to have more children who would defend their land, and she was granted foresight of her death. Nayeli made the most of the time she had left. She wrote about teaching her children the gift of healing and how to understand the land to protect it. She spent time with her family and prepared them for her death. She provided detailed instructions on how to prepare her body for the spirit world. She explained what the goddess had told her: how she was to be buried in a sacred place, unseen by anyone except the gifted one, at a time when the land was in danger. Her husband wrote in her journal after she passed away. He documented that he followed her instructions. He hid her burial site in the forest, and only the gifted one will be able to find it. He also took this opportunity to send a message to the family, emphasizing the importance of the village for future generations.

Maria produced the journal from the family safe. Everyone gasped. Bella noticed how fragile the book was. It was made of vellum. The book should be protected from the climate and being handled. Maria put the book on the coffee table and opened it to Yaniel's passage. It was written in old Spanish, and Bella was barely able to make out what it said. Isabella knew the passage by heart, so she recited it from memory. He explained that at her deathbed, Nayeli had him write a message from her to their future generations:

'My children, the greed of the white man and their church is vast. As Puerto Ricans, you have a responsibility to teach each generation about the importance of the land, trees, rivers, oceans, and the forests. Over the past centuries, land was taken from us. Our people were murdered, women raped, tortured, separated from their families, and sold or traded into slavery by those who call us savages. I was given a great gift, and now I wait in the spirit world to guide the gifted ones to their destination.

Please don't lose your love for this island, continue the bonds, teach your children their responsibilities for one another, and may the goddess give you the strength you will need to endure.'

Chapter 13

After Maria finished reading the journal, she removed the gloves she had used to handle it and placed the journal back in the safe. Everyone had tears in their eyes. Suddenly, everything made sense to Bella. She realized that she was Nayeli's descendant, and she understood that it had been Nayeli she had been seeing.

"So, are Amelia and I the gifted ones Nayeli wrote about?"

Isabella was careful as she answered, "Well, yes and no."

Amelia raised her eyebrow, looking confused.

"Let me explain that we have known both of you have the gift of dreams, but only one of you has had contact with Nayeli. I think that you, Bella, are the gifted one that Nayeli wrote about."

The room fell silent. Antonio spoke first, "Well, Bella, I always knew that you and Amelia were cursed with these dreams, but you, Bella, I felt that you had been touched with the abilities of a medium. You were a creepy kid."

Carlos described his experience, "Yeah, Bella, one time you fell asleep on the sofa watching TV, when out of nowhere you sat up and tracked something moving from the kitchen to mom's room, and you said, 'I will.' Girl, you have me the hibbie jibbies.''

Bella couldn't believe what they were saying. There was so much about her childhood that she just didn't remember. "Wait, Amelia also has dreams, too. Maybe Amelia is the one Nayeli spoke about?''

Amelia gently held Bella's hands and said, "Bella, you're right, I have dreams. Since we were babies, you and I have shared the same dreams, but you have extra abilities. Antonio and Carlos were right. When you were little, you were creepy. You saw people who weren't there. You were also the only one to interact with the lady in the forest. You have even seen her in your dreams. We now know that the lady you've seen over the years is Nayeli, and she has been trying to tell you something. So now you have to figure out what she wants to tell you.''

Bella didn't even know what she wanted, let alone what a ghost wanted. She had been feeling torn for a long time, but her insecurities and traumas made her hesitant about change. Now she had just been told that the ghost she'd been seeing wanted her to lead some kind of revolution. *What the hell!*

"So, children, there's more that we have to tell you." Both Maria and Isabella looked at each other as if saying, 'It's okay, go on.'' Isabella pulled out old documents; some looked older than others. "The women in our family have had this ability throughout hundreds of years, skipping a generation or two. With each generation, we learn more about our story. It's important for you to know the history of both sides of the family." Isabella turned on some lamps so everyone could see the documents better. Some of the documents were faded. No one had noticed that it had become dark, and the limited light cast shadows in the corner of the room.

Bella's eyes widened when she saw the documents. They looked like antiques that should be preserved.

Isabella continued with the story. "When your mother met your father, she didn't know his background. They seemed like a great match, and they were happy. I want you to know that. Your father was good to your mom. He was a proud father when each of you was born. But, your father had a family history as well, and you all need to know it so you can understand, if nothing else, why he abandoned you all."

Maria unrolled an old map of Rio Piedra and continued with the story. "Most children are taught that Christopher Columbus discovered Puerto Rico and the Americas. But they are not taught about the indigenous people who lived on the island for more than a thousand years before Christopher Columbus landed on our shores. The Europeans' greed for gold was like a contagious disease. The gold stolen from the Americas and the Caribbean Islands filled the pockets of the monarchy and the nobility, at the cost of human lives. In the Americas, children learn about the heroes of the Revolutionary and Civil Wars, but they aren't taught about the cultures and how they lived. Their names aren't in school textbooks. American Indigenous 'heroes' who fought against the theft and destruction of land they had occupied for thousands of years were destroyed in the name of conquest and gold. Mining gold is extremely dangerous, and life expectancy is short. That's why slaves were used, because they are seen as disposable. Along with conquest came the spread of religion. At that time, the dominant religion was Catholicism. Powerful men made the rules about who was God's favorite and who was meant to work for the European man. Their belief was that the whiter your skin, the closer you were to God and his protection. Everyone else was meant to serve God's people." Maria took another drink.

Isabella continued, "Most of you here know some of this information. Puerto Rican schools still teach about the hero

Christopher Columbus and others. In these last decades, we have seen that schools are integrating Taino and African history as well." Isabella unfolds a document with an image of a 1500s conquistador. "Schools in Puerto Rico teach about the island's first governor, Ponce De Leon, but they don't teach the details of the policies he put in place. Christopher Columbus renamed the island from 'Boriken' to San Juan Bautista after the Catholic saint. In 1508, Ponce de Leon established the first colony in Puerto Rico and named it Caparra. It's an archaeological site now. Eventually, he relocated the colony to what is now known as San Juan. De Leon saw an opportunity to strip the island of all its gold and silver until the mines ran dry of metal. In only a year, Ponce de León had subjugated a majority of the native population and had control over most of the island. He even had a name for it, encomienda. The right of colonists to demand tribute and forced labor from the islanders. Encomienda was simply a form of feudal genocide."

Maria stood up and paced the room. "Encomienda forced the indigenous population into a forced labor class that was subject to the Conquistadores. The Tainos worked from sunup until sundown. They also died from the many bacteria and diseases the colonists brought with them to the island. To extract gold and silver, the Tainos and African slaves were exposed to dangerous chemicals, inhumane conditions, and malnourishment. Can you imagine a population of people who never knew hunger, only to now be starving to death? They lived off the land and sea, and everyone in their tribe ate and supported one another. All of a sudden, they were being separated from their families, communities, watching their loved ones be killed, and forced to work until they dropped or go hungry. The Tainos did not have the antibodies to fight these silent killers, such as smallpox, measles, influenza, and others. It was believed that De Leon enjoyed the power he had and was willing to inflict cruel punishments whenever the enslaved fought back." Maria's voice lowered in sadness as she told the story.

Eventually, Ponce de Leon was sent by the crown to explore Florida in search of the 'Fountain of Youth.' However, regardless of which governor was in charge, the enslaved people suffered at their hands. There was a symbiotic relationship between the ruling class and the Catholic Church. Some would argue that the church had more power than the governor because they worked behind the scenes to influence new laws and enforce what they considered moral justice. For example, the Tainos and African slaves were seen as less than human because they worshiped false gods and because of the color of their skin. The church leaders were brutal in carrying out sentences, and the rationale was that they were doing God's work to save a heathen's soul. Monks worked locally to teach the enslaved their role in life according to God. They also took their teachings into the dungeons to enlighten the damned.

"By the time he left the island, Ponce de Leon was responsible for the loss of thousands of Taino, to the point where it was believed they had become extinct." Maria sat up tall and proudly said, "But, no, we didn't go extinct. We are still here."

Maria took out a paper with many names on it for them to see. One by one, everyone leaned in to look at the document. No one wanted to touch the form, as it was delicate and could be damaged. There was a sense of respect and sadness as they looked at the thousands of names written down. Maria pointed to a name halfway down the list. The writing was faint, written in Spanish, and the document was weathered, but Bella was able to make out the letters spelling Nayeli, wife of Yaniel, and the youngest daughter of Chief Agüeybaná. Both Amelia and Bella gasped when they saw their ancestors' names on the list of prisoners, and that she was descendants of a chieftain.

Bella was the first to ask a question, "Why was Nayeli imprisoned? What did she do?"

"She was imprisoned for witchcraft."

Isabella was also shocked when her parents showed her the list. She took out smaller documents from an old, weathered leather pouch. Isabella gently placed them on the coffee table as she explained what they were, "So, you are not able to understand everything written on these documents. They are Nayeli's journals."

Everyone was confused.

"Let me explain. When she was imprisoned, Friar Gabriel Sebastian, a monk responsible for her reform, was in charge. Nayeli wrote about her imprisonment and the terrible conditions she had to endure. Her captors often withheld food, pushing her toward dehydration and starvation. Rats and roaches were her companions, and at night, she feared the rats might harm her. She wrote about a religious man who visited her daily. At first, he seemed patient as he taught Nayeli Spanish. The governor declared that the enslaved were not allowed to speak their native languages. They were forced to learn and speak only Spanish. The monk noticed how quickly Nayeli picked up Spanish, so he started teaching her how to write.

Torry leaned over the back of Amelia's chair and asked, "Abuela, how long was she in those dungeons?"

"Well, Nayeli was keeping track of the time because she had a small window where she was able to see a portion of the moon. She wrote that she had been imprisoned for four months. Nayeli wrote that she was afraid that she was not going to survive the imprisonment, so she began to document her life and her imprisonment. She wrote about the slaughter that she witnessed when they hanged enslaved people in the courtyard. She saw proud people trying not to show fear. They stood erect, defiance etched on their faces. On the day they were to take her to De Leon, she saw an execution being carried out. One of the detainees, about to be executed, looked at her. She says in her writing that for a moment she was able to see his hard stare, his head held high, and for a moment she saw him nod at her. At that moment, Nayeli remembered that she was the 12th child of a chief, and her life partner was a minor son of a chief, Agüeybaná, who originated from Guaynia. Neyeli straightened her back, held her head high, and nodded to the man in gratitude. Moments later, he was hanging from a rope along with the others. Nayeli wrote that in that brief encounter, she found her strength to fight whenever the situation called for it, and she found the ability to endure. In front of the governor, Nayeli stood tall and unapologetic before Ponce de Leon. He noticed that, unlike the other detainees, Nayeli was unafraid, and her stare was challenging to his authority."

Maria rolls out a scroll with an image of his honorable Governor Ponce de Leon. She pointed to the image of De Leon. He was dressed in splendor in what looked like metal armor.

De Leon saw Nayeli's attitude as a threat to his rule, and she could cause problems if other Tainos defied the establishment. And he couldn't allow that. After all, he was the King's representative in San Juan Bautista. He looked at Nayeli and ordered her to lower her eyes. She did not. De Leon did not take that well. He called her a savage not fit to be in his presence. She still did not lower her eyes. Instead, she lifted her chin slightly in defiance. Nodding to one of the soldiers, Nayeli was whipped. And yet, her eyes never lowered, and she stood tall. She was beaten again. The other prisoners kneeled in front of the governor in fear that they would be whipped. Nayeli wrote that the white men in the room whispered to each other that 'the governor was being gracious, and he should have her executed'. Their whispering became murmurs of 'who does she think she is?' 'Heathen.' 'The governor should cut her down while she stands there.'

The governor realized she was challenging his authority in front of his subjects and other slaves; those facing him and those serving him. He knew that her defiance could ignite a revolt, and the social order he maintained could end the feudal system that had been in place in Europe for over a thousand years. She overheard these vile men talking about her in such a way that she reacted by freeing herself from the soldier's grasp. Nayeli was emaciated and dehydrated, but she was the daughter of a chief. She had been taught to fight and how to survive. She kicked her leg out to strike the soldier near her in the gut. The governor quickly backed away to get out of her reach and shouted orders to restrain her.

The governor observed the frightened faces of his council and clergy. He also noticed the expressions of the slaves in the room. Their eyes shone with pride as they saw her fight back and resist her captors. Their gaze stayed fixed on her, and De Leon did not like that. He sensed a threat to his rule and authority. De Leon understood that he needed to stop her, but he also had to make an example of Nayeli to crush any hope among the enslaved.

De Leon pointed to two soldiers standing guard at the door of the hall. 'You two, restrain her!' he ordered. The guards grabbed the chains on the wall and reacted quickly. By the time they reached her, one soldier was already on the ground, and Nayeli drop-kicked the other soldier. The two guards wrapped chains around Nayeli from behind, quickly immobilizing her and holding her down. Once De Leon felt the situation was under control, he knew he had to show strength and remind her who her superiors were.

"De Leon yelled out orders to stand her up. 'Quickly, stand her up! This slave is going to pay for trying to fight back!' He turned around to face all the enslaved people in the room. De Leon knew that he had to crush any spark of rebellion or risk losing his absolute power as governor of Boriken."

'You are a savage! It looks like I must teach you to respect your betters!' Don Leon slapped Nayeli across the face hard enough to split her lip. But Nayeli's hard and proud stare did not waver. She locked eyes with De Leon, displaying authority. De Leon knew that he had to demonstrate his superiority over everyone in the colony. 'Take her to the yard and tie her up to the pole.' He turned to face everyone. He was angry. His voice echoed in the hall. 'No one is allowed to help her! Guards take her, and she is not to receive any water or food. And, if anyone goes to her aid, they will be joining her at the yard strung up for the buzzards to pick at your skin and eyes.' Everyone cowered as he threatened to punish them just as equally as these heathens."

"Nayeli wrote about the days she was tied to that pole. She stood tall and straight. She remembered the chief she saw waiting for his execution, her mind recalling his look of strength, pride, and determination not to let these monsters strip him of his dignity. Nayeli noted that, as a minor child of a chief with limited status, she was still a symbol of hope for other prisoners in the fort. So, she kept her emotions in check, didn't ask for water, or plead for her life. Even when her strength waned, she refused to lower her head, keeping her eyes fixed on the upper window of the central tower where the hall was. When no one was watching, De Leon would look out that window, hoping to see her slumped, crying. Instead, he always found her eyes staring back at him, proud and defiant. Her unwavering resolve infuriated him, fueling a blinding rage. De Leon was perplexed by her contempt—who did she think she was? Just a savage who believes she's better than him. Each day, he ordered Nayeli to be whipped, convinced that he wouldn't win this battle of attrition unless she died."

"Don de Leon, why are you showing pity on this heathen. Why don't you execute her? She has to be an example that no one stands up to the establishment.'

" Because if she is executed, she will be a martyr to her people.' De Leon turned to face the man he was talking to. Nayeli could see that the situation was grave. She wrote that she was going to die. Nayeli, having the gift of foresight, closed her eyes, stood tall, and took deep breaths. She could hear the ocean, feel the breeze on her face, feel the sun on her skin, and hear the sound of the trees and animals all around her. She found herself relaxing and ascending. In her mind's eye, she saw thousands of faces all around her. She recognized the faces of her people. Her ancestors were the Arawak. Nayeli realized that they were telling her not to give in. They gave her strength and the energy to foresee the future. She saw herself running and hiding; she saw her sons and daughters. The vision showed Tainos running, screaming, women being violated, children, and people being hanged and burned. Nayeli saw the flow of time, and she understood. As she comprehended her obligations, she saw the souls of her people look at her; they held their heads up, nodded at her, showing approval, and Nayeli said that they smiled. Everything faded away. Her spirit returned to her body, and the bodily pains returned. Nayeli wrote that the pain was unbearable, but she knew she could not show a sign of weakness. Nayeli knew what she had to do."

Chapter 14

The room was quiet. Everyone was listening to the story. With his head lowered, Antonio said, "I didn't know all of this history." He ran his hand through his hair and walked toward the wall full of old family photos. Antonio looked at pictures of parents, grandparents, aunts, uncles, and cousins. They stretched across the centuries. On the opposite wall, Antonio examined the artifacts on the shelves. Some of these objects also spanned centuries, including religious trinkets, clay pottery, and woven baskets. On the walls, there were sketches and paintings of ancestors, some of whom were Spanish men and women, as well as Taino sketches from the 1600s. Antonio turned to face the group. His eyes welled with tears and regret.

"I didn't know that our family was enslaved. I guess most of us don't consider that slavery was a global form of power and control. I believe this is another pitfall that modern civilization often falls into. We are so worried about our bills, acquiring wealth, buying the latest cell phone, we care more about losing access to our technology than worrying about the problems of the world, past and present. It's like they keep us distracted so that we don't think about the horrors of the past, the manipulation of the people by the elite, and we vote for selfish idiots that have sold their souls to whoever can line their pockets."

Antonio punched the table between the sofas. Everyone else understood what he was saying. They all felt trapped, but Bella felt angry that she fell into the trap herself. Somehow, she felt that time was slipping away, and she had something to do.

Carmen was saddened to see her children's anguish. She hugged her son and then turned to face the others. "In America, human slavery is a stain that it is desperately trying to erase from history. We know why evil politicians are changing history textbooks so they can teach the next generation the history they want them to know and remove the vile acts their ancestors did to other humans for the sake of wealth. Here, Puerto Rican politicians have done the same. For generations, powerful men have enslaved and murdered our people. When the number of Taino decreased to near extinction, they brought African men and women to replenish their slave numbers. Using the slaves, they took all the silver and gold. When those mines were emptied, they used the slaves to work on farms. They found that the second source of wealth came from human labor. They made their wealth by selling the crops that the enslaved died tending the fields. Large plantation houses were built for the elite. From their plantations, they ruled with cruelty for centuries. That's what the politicians don't want you to know, and they have been actively shaping people's thoughts, desires, religion, and history."

Isabella continued Nayeli's story.

"De Leon walked up to Nayeli. As he got closer to her, he saw renewed strength in her eyes. He was mystified about where that kind of strength came from. He had to remind her that she was an inferior creature who had to be taught to respect. 'Who do you think you are, challenging my authority?' He spat in her face. Nayeli did not react.

She stood still, her eyes meeting his as equals. De Leon hated this situation because he knew that he couldn't execute her without risking a rebellion. To humiliate her with his hands, he tore the front of her tunic, exposing her breast. 'Now you will stand here for everyone to look at you. You will be for the pleasure of my soldiers.' He turned around and saw prisoners being brought in; he saw soldiers completely enthralled by what they were seeing, and from the windows high up on the fort, he saw the clergy, wealthy merchants, and his council focus on the scene below in the courtyard. De Leon faced the soldiers and gave instructions, "I want the gallows built here where she can see her people executed.' He raised his voice, spread his arms, and addressed everyone, 'Feast your eyes on this savage animal! Many would consider her beautiful if it weren't for the devil's blood that runs through her! She has proven that these people are unintelligent and need to be controlled by the supreme class, us! God ordained it! I give permission for the soldiers to enjoy themselves.' He faced her and found her staring straight at him with her head held high. 'Why do you defy me? You will stay tied to this post until I decide to have you executed.' Nayeli finally spoke to De Leon, 'You cannot kill me without risking a revolt.' She smiled at De Leon as if he were an idiot, 'I am a daughter of a chief. We are a proud people, and our women are trained in combat just as the men. You cannot make me beg for my life. If you kill me, I will be the force for change of your evil system. You cannot kill me! I curse you and your children and your children's children for all time. My bloodline will continue and will be the force of ruin for your descendants. Your children and their children will learn of the monstrosities you brought to my people, and they will learn of your cowardice.' De Leon slapped her hard enough to loosen a tooth. He leaned in and, through clenched teeth, he growled at her that he would make her disappear and no one would remember who she was."

"De Leon was furious. He knew she was right. He could not kill her. But maybe a few more days on the pole would weaken her, and she would have to give in. However, the opposite happened. Nayeli described the looks on the faces of those condemned as they saw her tied to a pole with her breast exposed. Nayeli was heartbroken to see that strong people had become emaciated and their spirits broken. Every few days, people were lined up to face death. But when they looked up at her, their backs straightened, and their heads were held high. Many smiled at her and bowed their heads slightly to pay their respects. She believed that this made their passing easier, and without fear, they would go to their ancestors carrying the pride of their tribes."

Nayeli wrote about how the men abused her body. They taunted her as they treated her less than human. She also described the pains she had to endure and how close she came to giving up. But the memory of her vision of her ancestors and the future to come gave her the strength to keep living.

De Leon noticed the change happening around him. His henchmen reported that word was spreading about her defiance, and she was becoming a symbol of rebellion. De Leon had heard the same reports from the plantation owners. The wealthy merchants and elites complained that they had started to see a difference in their slaves. Some were making eye contact with their handlers, while others were losing their subservient mannerisms. The elites were afraid she was influencing people toward rebellion, and their wealth was at risk."

"De Leon decided that instead of executing her and making her a martyr, which would threaten his feudal system, he would take a different approach. He yelled for his guards and instructed them to take her to a cell on the bottom floor of the dungeon. 'She will receive one meal a day and one glass of water, just enough to keep her alive, but at the point of death, she will pray for death.' De Leon walked to the courtyard with his men. Before they pulled her down from the pole, he wanted her to know what was going to happen to her and that he had won the challenge."

"Nayeli described the proud expression on De Leon's face. De Leon saw bite marks on her neck and chest. He also noticed bruises on her breasts and neck. The men took her to the new cell. Nayeli said that it was a dark hole at the end of the row. To reach it, they walked two levels and passed through moldy doors. They opened the iron door into the cage that was her new home. They threw her into the darkness and slammed the door behind them. Within seconds, they disappeared into the dark hallway. As her eyes adjusted to the darkness, she noticed a skeleton chained to the wall. She saw rats and roaches, and the cell smelled like death. Once again, Nayeli noticed a small window high above her head. She would use the bucket to reach the window. The window was a connection to the outside world. Some of her moments of peace came when she could look out at the ocean, listen to the waves, and breathe in the sea air.

"Throughout the days she spent in that hole, she heard the trap door of the gallows daily. She thought of her people. The Arawak were a proud people with a rich history spanning thousands of years. They landed on these beaches and flourished. Now, her people were being slaughtered because the colonists wanted the gold and silver that Mother Earth provided. Nayeli described them as a plague that wouldn't stop until everything was gone, and her people would disappear. Nayeli also wrote about the other women imprisoned. She wrote that she heard the women screaming and then the jail door slam shut. She assumed that the soldiers were helping themselves to the women locked up in the dungeon."

"Angered by everything that had happened to her and her people, Nayeli climbed up to the window and prayed to her gods to punish these people. She repeated the same prayer every night to strengthen the curse she had placed on De Leon. Her hatred for De Leon and his people was the driving force that made that curse linger on De Leon's bloodline throughout time."

"Nayeli tracked her days in that cell. She proposed that she had been locked up in that cell for over four months, until one night when a familiar face approached her bars. Nayeli's health was not good. Her sight had adjusted to the darkness. Without the sun, her skin looked pale. Nayeli also wrote about sores in her mouth and two loose teeth. Being at the end of the cell block, hidden in a dark hole, she only had interaction with the guards when they brought her food and water every three days. One day, she heard a noise that woke her from sleep. She pressed her face against the bars. It didn't sound like the guards, and they are due to feed her for two more days. The noise got closer. She recognized a voice. She became excited because the voice she was hearing was her husband's voice. Nayeli called out to them. On the other side of the bars, her father and her husband tried to hug her through the bars. She was able to tell that they were overwhelmed by the smell that radiated from her and the cell. They brought tools to break her out. They explained to her that she had been imprisoned for more than six months. They brought her a pouch of water, dried fruits, and nuts. The food energized her, but having contact with her family was even more healing."

"We must go. The next change of guards will be soon, and then there's a short window when the guards are distracted. Nayeli knew she wouldn't be fed for two more days. That meant the guards wouldn't notice her absence during that time. If they moved through the jungle and hid in the caves, Mother would provide for her children, and they could escape. At the sound of the church bells, they knew it was time to act. Nayeli's eyes had grown accustomed to the darkness of the hole, allowing her to navigate the dark hallways and crevices within the depths of the dungeon. The group worked together to find how the two men used to break in. They understood how serious the danger was, so no one spoke. They relied on a deep understanding of nonverbal cues, like hand gestures, to communicate. Nayeli didn't let her weakened state show. She was determined to escape De Leon. She wrote that she knew her escape would retaliate against Don Leon's regime, that her escape could inspire her people to fight back against their enslavement and murder, and she was determined not to die in this hellhole far from her homeland and her people, so she kept pushing toward liberty."

Chapter 15

Carmen turned on the last lamps in the room. She appeared with coffee and coconut pudding. She knew that all this history was a lot to take in in one night, and she regretted not telling her daughter sooner about their lineage and their connection to Nayeli.

Isabella continued with the story.

"So, Nayeli discovered that Tainos throughout the area had heard of her rebellion against Don Leon. Many now saw her as a queen in her own right, fighting the enemy for her people's freedom. Word had spread among the enslaved and the still-hidden villages. The group did not want to bring the wrath of De Leon's men down on innocent people, so they carefully planned their route to a hidden path that led into the deep caves in the mountains. Legend tells the story of how the island was formed. The Mother goddess Atabei rose from the earth out of the depths of the ocean and the volcano's fire to create the island the Taino called Boriken. Atabei spread her hands and formed the mountains that collected the rain, providing food and fresh water for her children. As the Arawak spread across the Caribbean, they were guided by Atabei to these islands, which we now call the Caribbean. To protect her children from hurricanes and the intense summer heat, Atabei wove through certain mountains, hidden tunnels, and caves where her people could find shelter. The group decided to head toward those cliffs. From the cliffs and hillsides, they planned to gather as many of the enslaved as possible. They understood this was a fight against genocide, and they were willing to die fighting—rather than be locked up in a cage in darkness away from the sun, the moon, the wind, and their people."

"For weeks, they trekked unpaved trails that led them deeper into the mountains. To avoid the white man's dogs searching for them, they often waited until nighttime to drift down rivers and climb waterfalls. Along the way, they encountered other hidden Tainos who were more than willing to feed and resupply them. These people were often escapees themselves. They updated the group on what happened after the soldiers realized that Nayeli had escaped. De Leon reacted exactly as Nayeli predicted. He went crazy. He demanded that they find Nayeli. De Leon punished the soldiers from that night shift by placing them in hanging cages to die. It served as a warning to the other soldiers that De Leon wasn't a lenient man, and he would not tolerate failure."

"Unfortunately, De Leon was crazed, and he punished a few thousand Tainos for aiding the fugitive. Nayeli was brokenhearted that her escape cost so many of their lives. Her father-in-law reminded her that Atabei chose Nayeli to save her people by creating a direct connection to Atabei herself. His father-in-law, Loquison, informed her that once she was safe, he would leave to join his father, Loquillo, in his fight against the Spanish. During their journey into the mountains, he learned that his father, Loquillo, was leading a rebellion to push out the Spanish. Yaniel wanted to go with his father to help his people fight. Loquison asked his son to come with him on the way back home to bring women, children, and youth to the hills. He trusted his son to help ensure his people's survival by taking them to safety. Loquison also entrusted him with the responsibilities of a chief. He told his son that the gods revealed his role was to fight against the

Spanish, and Yaniel's role was to join Nayeli in rebuilding their community. Nayeli already knew Loquison planned to return to their village to rescue as many villagers as possible. Atabei spoke to her in her dreams, showing her the massacres still to come. Nayeli felt as if she were flying with Atabei. She saw visions of the land being stripped of its natural resources. She heard screams and fighting. She was among the enslaved brought in chains to Boricua to replace the Taino slaves who had died. Atabei also explained that when the gold and silver run out, the Spanish will turn to the land itself for wealth. They will clear large areas of natural land, fill in marshes and small bodies of water to plant more crops. Atabei showed Nayeli how the Tainos used the mountains to hide and survive. She also revealed Nayeli's fate. Nayeli wrote that Atabei showed her what she needed to do in the coming years. She explained that six months in prison had affected her health. Over time, she will lose her energy, and her diseased body will die and join her ancestors."

With sadness, Isabella explained that Nayeli had contracted some of the diseases the Spanish brought with them.

"Atabei showed her how her connection to the goddess had given her the ability to fight diseases, but only for so long. Nayeli was told that she would eventually wither away and die slowly. In the meantime, she was to teach her daughters how to use the gift that Atabei had passed down to her. This gift will continue to be passed down through many generations. It will help them make choices based on their dreams and premonitions. While this gift exists in all of Atabei's daughters, not all of them will have Nayeli's direct genes.

"With the expansion of Europeans into the Caribbean, the Tainos merged with African slaves and Europeans. Atabei's gift will skip a few generations, depending on what happens in the lands she created, when destruction returns because of greed in men. Throughout these islands, women have taken the mantle to bring about change using Atabei's gift."

Amelia is confused, "But abuela, what is happening in Puerto Rico that Bella will have to change?"

Bella whipped her head to face Amelia.

"Me!!! I am not Atabei's representative! What the hell are you talking about?" Bella looked around the room and realized they had already discovered that Nayeli was one of her direct ancestors. "What are you all looking at? Show me some proof that I'm supposed to be a Nayeli soldier who'll save people when I don't even know how to save myself!" Bella stood up and started to pace. "I don't even know what I want to do with my life."

She turned to face Isabella and Carmen. "How do you know?"

Carmen grabbed her hands and embraced her daughter.

"Because, baby, your whole life you have been seeing and talking to Nayeli."

"Wait, Amelia has dreams, too. So maybe it's her."

It was Amelia's turn to respond. She figured it out, and now she had to help her sister with whatever mission Nayeli had given her. "Bella, what is your birthday?"

"What!! My birthday!! What does that have to do with anything?"

"What is it?"

"November 19th, 1993, why?"

Maria explained, "Christopher Columbus arrived back in the Caribbean on November 19th, 1493, and they anchored on this island to explore the islands. Talk of gold piqued De Leon's greed for money and power. In 1508, De Leon was appointed governor. Hija, you were born on the anniversary of Columbus's landing on our shores."

Bella sat down, feeling confused and scared. Still, memories of countless dreams over the years flooded back, reminding her of how often Nayeli had tried to speak to her in those dreams. She didn't want to believe she was a hero.

"Throughout the centuries," Isabella continued, "Nayeli's bloodline has endured. Direct descendants have left the island, and others have stayed. Our bloodline is one of Nayeli's descendants. Her gift has skipped a few generations. And those who sensed they had the gift chose to ignore it, but others responded. For hundreds of years of colonization, the gifted have led rebellions, fought poverty, and demanded civil liberties."

Everyone turned to face Isabella.

"Do any of you remember your father's name?"

Antonio responded, "Juan D.L. Castillo."

"Do you know what the D.L. stands for?"

Antonio replied with a scowl, "I don't know, and I don't care. That is how his name is written on my birth certificate."

"The D.L. stands for De Leon."

There was a collective response, "What!!!"

Amelia turned to Carmen with tears in her eyes, "Mami, did you know?"

Carmen wanted to comfort her children. After all, it's not every day that someone finds out they are related to a monster that nearly caused the extinction of the Taino people and made slavery of humans a widespread and profitable business. "No, your father and I were young, and we loved spending time together. I suspected he came from a wealthy background because of some of the clothes he wore, and he didn't want me to meet his family. We initially eloped, but my mom insisted on a small church wedding. His family didn't show up to the wedding when they found out we were married.

"We were young and full of dreams. He never liked talking about his family, instead focusing on our little family. It wasn't until a year into our new life that we filed our taxes, when he had to spell out his full name. I remembered a family legend involving the Europeans and their colonization of this land. But it was a couple of years later when Abuela sat me down and told me the Nayeli story."

"Once Amelia's gift began to grow, and then you, Bella, came along and showed signs of the gift, I reminded your mother that she had to keep your talents a secret," Isabella said.

"Why?" Amelia was demanding answers.

Maria stepped in to continue, "Because of Nayeli's curse. When she cursed De Leon, she cursed his bloodline. When the gifted become active, they unintentionally affect the health and wealth of any of De Leon's descendants. The De Leon wealth survived for many generations, and they actively took steps to preserve their wealth and lands. Some have become community leaders, religious figures, and politicians. Those whom the gifted interact with often end up poor, arrested, or powerless. Ponce De Leon himself died from a poisoned arrow during one of his Florida expeditions. His greed and ambition were never satisfied. These colonists, along with many more that came after De Leon, take what they want, and they will remove anything or anyone that gets in their way. It was said that as death approached him, he was hallucinating; or so they thought, because he seemed to talk to a woman who was not in the room. His aide wrote that 'my poor lord is not of his mind. He is talking to a woman. He laughed at her. He told her to go to hell. And just as he slipped into moments of unconsciousness, he would yell to this phantom to stop laughing at him.' We can only speculate about what happened to him at his deathbed."

"Your father's family had always conducted background checks on outsiders marrying into the family. By keeping his relationship with Carmen a secret, his family was unable to find out that Taino blood runs in our veins. His mother was furious when she found out about the marriage. She tried everything to persuade your father to get a divorce, but he refused. She even threatened to remove him from the will, but he still wouldn't agree. His mother reminded him that if he had daughters and they had the 'gift,' their wealth would be at risk."

Carmen sat down in front of her kids to continue the story.

"Your father told me that his mother threatened to remove him from the will. He said he would work to provide for his family no matter what his mother did. He didn't tell me about the curse—that he kept to himself. When I noticed Amelia having dreams and sometimes answering 'yes' or 'no' before she was asked a question, I asked your grandmother to help me figure things out. That's when I learned everything, and I decided not to let Luis know that Amelia was showing the gift. Then, you, Bella, came two years later, and it was obvious that you and Amelia shared the gift. But yours, Bella, was a little different. I walked into your room one day and found you talking to someone who wasn't there. I asked you to tell me who you were talking to. I remember you gave me an 'are you blind' look and told me you were talking to the lady. Well, you saw the lady in dreams and in the real world."

"Why can't I remember her if I had years of interactions with this lady?"

Chapter 16

Carmen was determined to tell her kids everything about their heritage. "Because I would remind you that there wasn't a lady and I didn't want you to say anything in front of your father, so I told you that the lady wasn't there. Then school came, and your teacher contacted me about you arguing with fellow students about playing with a lady who wasn't there. I know I messed up, sweetheart, because my telling you that the lady wasn't real and asking you to keep it a secret from your father and the school was wrong. You must have been so confused. And then your father left us. Well, the years that followed were difficult for you, and you preferred to run away and hang out with your friends. At one point, I took you to see a counselor, but that didn't help because you refused to talk to the counselor. I think those years were so painful for you that you blocked them out."

Antonio was quick to respond, "You mean to tell me that our father left us because of some 'gift'? He abandoned his four kids over money! That doesn't make any sense! He never even sent money for you to buy us clothes. He forgot about us because of his inheritance!"

Carmen was filled with sadness. She knew it was hard to hear that their father cared more about money and his status in the family than about his children. Carmen worked so hard to provide a life where they lacked nothing, but the pain of being abandoned never left her. She couldn't comfort them. They had to accept the reality of what their father had done, and she knew it would take time.

Amelia was confused. "Mom, why did you ask us to come to his funeral? I had never forgiven him for abandoning us." Amelia was heartbroken and couldn't sit still, so she paced the room. "I made myself believe that he had a mistress, and he ran away with her. That was bad, you know, but finding out that he abandoned us for money is so much worse!"

Carmen wrapped her arms around Amelia, trying to ease her pain. "No, Amelia, your father never remarried, had a partner, or other children. When I visited his mother, she was confused about why Luiz had left us and moved into their old family farm. I went to see him once, and he stood at the doorway yelling at me to go away." Carmen sat down with her shoulders slumped forward. "I demanded answers. At that time, I hadn't heard Nayeli's story, so I didn't know anything about an inheritance or anything like that. I kept yelling that I was his wife and that he had children who needed him. He yelled at me for not telling him sooner that you girls had that gift. He didn't make any sense, but he kept yelling, 'It's a curse, I am cursed, I am ruined just like the curse said!' The farmhouse was a two-story Spanish Colonial house made of cement blocks, stucco, and clay roof tiles. It looked ancient and was falling apart. Your father looked unrecognizable. He had a long beard, haunted eyes, and smelled of alcohol. He refused to speak to me and slammed the door shut. I was left standing there, confused and shocked at who this man was. I didn't recognize the man I married. When I returned to your grandmother's house, I found you three playing outside and was told Bella was in the woods again. Your grandmother sat me down and told me Nayeli's story." Carmen reached out and squeezed her mother's hand tightly.

Isabela comforted her grandchildren, saying, "I know that this is a big shock for you to learn this history. But you had to be told. When your mother returned that day, she was distraught and couldn't stop crying. She didn't understand anything about a curse, so she didn't understand what Luiz was talking about. I asked Maria to come over so we could share the story with her. I watched you three kids playing outside and went into the woods to find Bella. As always, Bella was sitting on that large rock in the pond. I noticed that Bella was staring at the waterfall and smiled. Of course, I didn't see anything or anyone, but Bella did. It reminded me of the time when she was five years old, and I would find her staring at Nayeli's portrait."

Bella snapped her gaze away from Carmen and to Isabelle, "That is Nayeli? All this time, I had been staring at her image. Maybe I made up Nayeli because I saw that picture?" Bella was hoping that all of this was a mistake.

Isabella replied, "No, Bella. That sketch was done by your great-great-great-grandmother Teresa almost two hundred years ago. In her journal, she wrote about her love for the woods and a lady she would meet there every day. She also noted that as she grew older, the lady became clearer and clearer, and was able to communicate with her in her dreams. She wrote about what Nayeli told her in her dreams so that Teresa could prepare herself and protect the land."

Amelia was curious, "Protect the land from what?"

"From the greed of powerful men who took lands that weren't theirs in the name of their crown and God. They saw themselves the same way Christopher Columbus and Ponce de Leon claimed to be explorers expanding Spain's reach and saving savages from a heathen life. Spain colonized Puerto Rico for four hundred years. The colonization led to wealth and power for the Spanish men who came here in search of land. For those four hundred years, they became rich while Puerto Ricans experienced poverty, cruelty, enslavement, genocide, repression, and taxation. The poor stayed miserably poor. Many villagers lost their homes to the expansion of sugar and tobacco plantations. These people found themselves in low-wage labor. At the time, this town was being considered for a housing development for slaves and indentured servants to live in while they worked on the plantations. Teresa formed a campaign to expose the plans of these plantation owners. She helped empower the residents to unite and rebel against the plantation owners. From what I was taught, word even got to Spain of the misery Puerto Ricans were living in, and the plans to expand plantation lands and build squalid houses for the people who worked for the plantation owners. Although the monarchy and the elite didn't care about the plight of poor people, many common Spaniards did. There was controversy with their views on Christianity and the atrocities being done to these people. The King was informed of protests throughout his kingdom and vandalism. That forced King Philip V to change those plans. He took his plans to another island, also conquered by Spain. Unfortunately, here in Rio Piedra, Teresa was taken from her home in the middle of the night and arrested. Governor Brigadier General Enrique Grimarest declared Teresa an enemy of the state. Teresa was given a quick and corrupt trial and imprisoned for ten years for inciting the public. She wrote in her journal that she would endure any punishment because her town was safe, and she had a home to go to when her sentence was over. After ten years, like Nayeli, Teresa was malnourished and sick. She was glad to be home, but she never regained her strength, and after a few short years, she died. She wrote that she didn't regret her choices because she had saved her home and taken away another conquest by greedy, wealthy men. The last thing she wrote in her journal was a sentence,

'Resa que siempre puedan contar nuestra historia a cada generacion para que nunca olviden lo cerca que estuvimos de perder nuestro hogar. Levántate pueblo mío y lucha por lo que te corresponde. Nunca más serás esclavizado.'"

Carlos looked at the last page of Teresa's journal. She stared at the words written in cursive and cursed the asshole who thought teaching cursive writing to kids in public schools was unimportant. He, Bella, and Amelia were not able to read it. "Grandma, I can't read that. What does it say?"

"It says,

I pray that they will always be able to tell our history to every generation so that they never forget how close we were to losing their home. Rise, my people, fight for what is rightfully yours, and never be enslaved again."

A thousand things raced through Bella's mind. She wondered why Nayeli had chosen her. Bella didn't see herself as a hero, activist, or warrior. She lived in a quiet, isolated bubble, only allowing a select few into it. She preferred staying in the background. She wondered why Amelia couldn't be the so-called 'chosen.' Bella looked up to Amelia because she was friendly, optimistic, supportive, and strong. *Amelia could take on a challenge, not me.*

Tonight, Bella discovered why her father abandoned her. She also realized that money was the reason he broke up the family. Bella learned about Nayeli and the struggles of the Tainos and African slaves. She found out she was the chosen one carrying Nayeli's bloodline and was supposed to be a hero. She also learned about Teresa and the sacrifice she made for listening to Nayeli and getting involved in starting a revolution.

Bella's head was pounding, and she felt nauseous. Suddenly, a deep-seated fear about the unknown took hold of her. She wished she could turn back to the day before her mother called to tell her that her father had died—when her life was safe and predictable. Bella didn't feel well. She quickly stood up and ran to the bathroom to vomit.

Everyone else stared as she rushed out of the room. Amelia felt pain for her sister's suffering. She was angry at her ancestors and how life had worsened for Puerto Ricans. She was angry at her father and the trauma he caused when he left. Amelia knew Bella's past behaviors came from feeling abandoned. Now, she had just been told that she was chosen by one of our ancestors and had a mission to fulfill so that Nayeli could rest. Amelia followed Bella to the bathroom to check on her.

Isabella knew how Bella felt because of what she had been told about the family history. The difference was that Isabella wasn't the 'chosen' one. Her job was to keep the family history alive by passing it down to the descendants so it would never be forgotten. Bella and Amelia returned to the room. Everyone saw that Bella was pale. As Bella stepped into the room, she blacked out. Amelia reacted by supporting her sister upright. Antonio ran to Bella's side and picked her up.

"Abuela and Mom, thank you for sharing Nayeli's story. I've learned that I come from a people who lived and died for what they believed in. It's also hard to accept that my dad chose money instead of us, but at least I know he didn't leave because of anything we did wrong. He left because he was selfish and, like his ancestors, greedy. I'm going to take my sister to her room and then get some rest."

Carmen kissed her son on his cheek. Thank you, Antonio."

The rest of the group agreed with Antonio and chose to rest and process all this information tomorrow. They hugged each other and walked out of the room, leaving Isabella, Carmen, and Maria still in the living room.

"Bueno, we did it. Your kids finally know the truth," said Maria.

Carmen was sad seeing her children in pain. She was mainly concerned with Bella. This was a lot to accept. "Yes, that is good. They can finally relieve themselves of any guilt they felt over Luiz's abandonment. But I don't know if Bella will be ok."

Isabella reached out for her daughter's hand. "I know that you are worried about her. We both are, too. But Bella is strong. She had endured a lot over the years."

"And she is not alone. Now that they know the history, they can help Bella figure things out and support her. I, for one, am extremely excited that Nayeli's descendant is among us because this island desperately needs help. Puerto Ricans are struggling, protected land is being secretly sold to corporations, and many Puerto Ricans are poor and feel a sense of hopelessness. We have to support Bella and give her time for her to figure out what she is supposed to do."

"You are right. We are with her." Although Carmen was worried for her daughter, she was going to support Bella in whatever she faced.

Chapter 17

Bella was walking in the woods. She was surrounded by mist. As she walked further into the woods, she saw people cooking and children helping adults harvest vegetables. At one point, Bella noticed that the people all around her stopped what they were doing to watch her walk by. She realized that they were smiling at her, and she smiled back. Bella heard the sound of a waterfall and realized that she was at her favorite place in the forest, the pond. She saw a woman beckoning her to come closer. With every step, Bella felt as if someone was moving her, and she didn't have any control. Bella stood in front of Nayeli. This time, the apparition appeared to be a living person.

"Why did you choose me?" Bella was angry. "Why me? My whole life, I thought that I was a freak because you had been coming to me since I was a child. And this entire time, you were real. Imagine how I feel. Bella cried tears for all the years of pain. Her words came through as a whisper in between her tears, "I am no warrior."

Nayeli looked at Bella with soft, warm eyes. "You are stronger than you think. Bella, you have an attachment to this island. Every tree, flower, forest, and river is part of you."

Bella noticed that the people she had seen along the trail were now all standing behind her. They all looked concerned. She was able to see that they were a proud people. These were some of her ancestors supporting her. Seeing their faces brought a smile to her face. Since moving to the US, she had felt unplugged from her life force. She thought that it was because her family was broken. But now she realized that she had been taken away from her people and her land.

"I don't know what it is that you want me to do. Please tell me what it is that I am supposed to do."

Nayeli waved her hands, and the scenery changed. The people opened a passage for her to see the vision Nayeli wanted her to see. They were running and screaming. Bella saw huts burning, smoke everywhere, and she saw Tainos being tied up, chained, and dragged off by men in armor, riding horses. Bella heard screams and women crying. She saw Taino men fighting the white men who came to kidnap them. Bella cried as she gazed at the horrors in front of her.

"The people of this island and the African slaves who were enslaved and killed fought for their independence. For centuries, Boriken's people have been denied freedom when governments and companies have taken their lands to build factories, encampments, and large houses for their leaders."

The scene changes. It reflected the decades and centuries that have passed and how colonization affected the Puerto Rican people. She saw villagers enslaved to cane plantations. Nayeli showed her people living in squalor and going hungry. Bella wasn't sure how much more she could take. The image turned into more recent times, and she saw millions of Puerto Ricans leaving for the continent because of the loss of work. Trade agreements and business deals born of corruption have weakened the island. It's people fleeing to the US, where they were forced to work day and night, sacrifice their families to work, and earn so much debt that they…"

"Trapped!" Bella knew all about this trap.

"Yes, they become trapped in a work culture that sacrifices the family."

"Nayeli, I am sorry for what you have been put through. You are a strong woman. I don't know what to do."

"You will when the time is right. For now, open your eyes and pay attention to the joy and struggles of your brothers and sisters of this land. You are all connected to each other and to this land. The island will provide you with what you need to sustain yourself and bring joy to your life. Too many Puerto Ricans have fallen for the illusion of opportunities that are not real. Some Puerto Ricans and their children have awakened from their dreams of opportunities outside of this island just to become trapped in it with no way to get ahead."

"So, what do you want me to do? Can you give me details? Will you help me?"

"I will always be here when you need me. I want you to pay attention. I want you to find me."

With that last statement, Nayeli was gone. Bella sat up in bed. She realized that it was a dream. The visions were still in her mind. "That's it, it was just a dream." Bella uncovered herself and found mud on her feet. "What the hell! Did I sleepwalk?" Bella decided not to try to figure everything out. She was going to do what Nayeli told her. She was going to pay attention. But what did she mean by 'find me?'"

Bella awoke abruptly when she heard her mother knock on her door.

"Bella, are you awake?"

Bella was groggy, yet still able to see the images of her ancestors in her mind. Her mother's voice broke the haziness of her grogginess. She responded, "Yeah, I'm awake. Come in."

Carmen wasn't shocked to see Bella pale. The story of the ancestors is something difficult to hear, and to hear that you are a chosen person who is supposed to help your people must be overwhelming. Carmen walked up to her bed and handed Bella a cup of coffee before she opened the drapes and French doors that led to the balcony in Bella's room. Bella heard the birds and the rustling of the trees. Bella felt the cool morning breeze enter the bedroom and took a deep breath. There was something wonderful in the morning scents. Bella walked up to the window facing her bed and stood beside her mom, admiring the greenery of the land all around them. Bella and Carmen walked out to the balcony and sat in the bistro chairs to talk.

"Bella, I just want to say that I am sorry I didn't tell you when you were growing up."

"Yeah, Mom, that was messed up. Why didn't you tell me?"

"Well, at first I was afraid of your father's retaliation. It was his ancestor who helped to wipe out a large population of the Taino people, and I knew that his family was a group of people so proud of their European roots. No one in your father's family had ever married someone brown-skinned, and they didn't like that your father did. They offered your father a lot of money not to marry me. Once we were married, your grandmother would ask him what color each of you was when you were born. So, when he found out about yours and Amelia's abilities, he was afraid that his family would find out and demand that he separate himself from us or cut him out of the will."

Bella was shocked that racism was still a factor in hatred. She stood up to lean against the railing. "I don't get it. If my grandmother knew about me and Amelia's abilities, why did she invite all of us to the funeral?"

"Because she didn't know, I found out the day I went to face him that he never told his family about you two. He told me that he didn't want them to hate you enough to place a curse on your kids. He said that it was the least he could do for his children. I asked him if he planned to return home. Luis told me that he couldn't because if his mother found out that you and Amelia carry Nayeli's curse, he would be removed from the will. I was shocked that he would choose an inheritance over his kids. I decided that I was done crying for him. I vowed to be both mother and father to you kids. That day, I turned around and left him standing there without saying another word." Carmen leaned against the railing. "Did I do wrong? Should I have begged him to come home? The truth is, I was so angry at him that I was disgusted with him."

Bella faced her mom. "No, Mom, you did what any of us would have done. Maybe he was afraid of losing his inheritance, and maybe he was afraid of what it meant for him to have daughters that would bring shame to his family's name. Who knows and who cares? He made his choice, and now there are no apologies to be said, and it's not like he can repent." Bella hugged her mom. "You gave us what we needed, love and your time whenever you could."

Bella took a deep breath and finished her coffee. She stared at the woods surrounding her grandmother's house. She knew that some kind of mystery was hidden inside. How would she fulfill her destiny? How will she know where to find what she is supposed to do? The images of her indigenous ancestors smiling at her filled her with warmth and motivated her to face her new responsibility head-on. She said to herself, 'I don't want them to haunt me for the rest of my life if I don't take on this challenge.' Bella knew she was not alone. Her family was with her. Nayeli was with her. And the community was with her.

Whenever she returned home to Puerto Rico, she felt that sense of community that she had not experienced in the United States. On the continent, people have been manipulated into being distracted from the issues that truly matter. Advertisements, social media, corporations, and politicians rely on Americans adopting an individualistic mindset. They are being told what to eat, what to wear, and who to believe in, working to pay for things they do not need but want to have, to keep up, and buying the next trendy product. Many Americans focus their time and energy on themselves, their individual families, and their careers. They live to work and find themselves in the "trap" of debt. Many are too focused on what other people are doing, who they are with, what gender they are showing, and how popular or famous they can become. These distractions keep them from recognizing their responsibilities to their communities, to other people, and to the land that has supported their families for generations. Americans who live on the continent are stressed to the breaking point.

At this moment, Bella took in the landscape and felt a sense of connection with the land, the community, and her family. As she appreciated the wonder and beauty of this place, listening to the sounds of birds all around her and smelling the scent of flowers in the air, she was reminded that she was not alone and that she belonged here. Bella was reminded that she was part of something greater and that others were counting on her. She once again turned to face Carmen and exclaimed that she would never have chosen this 'gift,' but the ancestors of their people had visited her, and she knew this was a very important challenge, and the time to act is now.

Carmen reached out to Bella's hands and squeezed them tightly. "Bella, I am scared for you, but please know that we are all here to help. Tell us what we need to do."

Bella looked at her mom and sensed how much she loved her daughter. Bella knew her mom would always be there to support her. "Thank you, Mom. I promise that when I figure things out, I will reach out to everyone for help."

"Oh, hey," Carmen said, "I forgot to tell you that your cousin Olga came by to see you earlier this morning. She asked me to tell you that she will be home today and would like to spend some time with you to catch up on things. Come downstairs and grab some breakfast. You know that your grandmother prepared a huge breakfast. Your brothers went to buy some things they needed, and Amelia and Torry went to the butcher to order a pig for roasting before you all headed back. So, let's go downstairs so you can eat, and maybe you'll want to go see Olga."

Chapter 18

After enjoying Isabella's breakfast, Bella went to Olga's house. Olga lived with her parents to help care for her mother. After her father died, her brothers and sisters moved out to find jobs in the city and the U.S. Being the youngest, she stayed to finish school and figure out her future. But Olga's mom suffered from severe depression, so Olga had to stay home to care for her. A few years later, she met her husband, Orlando. Orlando was a contractor, and he handled the house's repairs. They dated for two years before he proposed. Olga was thrilled, but she knew she couldn't leave her mom. Her older siblings couldn't help her physically because they had jobs, families, and debts. Orlando agreed to move into Olga's house. They had two kids, Pepito and Carla. Bella was excited to catch up with Olga again.

Olga was outside in her flower bed when she saw Bella heading to her house. Olga could not contain her excitement. She ran to Bella and gave her a warm hug.

Cousin, it's been too long! Why haven't you come back home sooner?

Bella loved Olga's energy. She knew that Olga also had her share of pain and loss, but somehow she always smiled. Olga was nothing like Bella. Sometimes, Bella struggled to find joy in things, but Olga always found a way to cheer her up and help her get through depressive moments. "Olga, you look great!" Bella noticed that Olga was pregnant. "Girl, are you pregnant?"

Olga was excited to tell her cousin that she was six months pregnant. "Yeah, this will be the last. It's hard to have a big family these days. We already know that the baby is a girl. We decided to call her Esperanza because she represents hope for a better life. Listen, come on in and see the kids. You're not going to believe how tall Pepito has gotten, and Carlita looks just like my mom."

They entered the house. Bella saw familiar family photos on the walls and shelves. She recalled all the times she had stayed at Olga's house when they were younger. Bella noticed a framed picture of Olga's father on the wall. "Your dad was a great man, Olga. I know that you and your mom must miss him a lot."

"Yeah, we do. Mom will stare at his photos a couple of times a day. I hear her crying sometimes at night. I told her that we will ask her psychiatrist for new medication to treat the depression."

Bella was shocked that her aunt was still struggling with severe depression. "Olga, I am so sorry. I know you must be worried about her."

Olga wiped a tear from her eyes, "Yeah, I really am worried about her. You know my mom was always happy and energetic. People have come to get her to take her out. They tell me that when she's out of the house, she's her old self again. So, I have scheduled a few times a week to go to the beach with the kids, meet up with her siblings, and sometimes we go shopping together. I started to look for a counselor who specializes in grief."

"That's great. I can also visit her while I am here."

Olga served Bella guava juice. Bella thought about telling Olga her plans to stay in Puerto Rico with her. "So, listen, Olga, you and I have shared a lot of secrets growing up. Can I share a secret with you now?"

Olga was intrigued. She and Bella shared secrets as they grew up. She noticed that Bella was becoming rebellious and angry as a teenager. "Of course. You know that we keep each other's secrets to the grave. Girl, spill it."

Bella took a deep breath and said, "OK, I think I am not going to return to the United States. My heart tells me to stay here and help my grandmother. I mean, she is not feeble for her age, but the house and other things need tending. I am a paralegal, so I think I could find work here too."

Olga hugged her cousin. "Bella, are you serious? It would be so wonderful for you to stay. I know that your grandmother would love it. What did your mom say?"

"Ah, well, that's the secret. I haven't told anyone but you. The truth is, I will miss my family a lot. Antonio and Amelia have children to consider, and Carlos has his partner, who has a great career as a digital designer; no one would want to move out of North Carolina right now. I guess I needed to talk to someone and get their feedback on how realistic my ideas are. You're supposed to talk me out of it." Bella walked to the window. She looked around the neighborhood and realized how run-down everything looked. It saddened her to see the devastation caused by Hurricane Maria in her old hometown. Before her were abandoned houses with graffiti and boarded-up windows. She couldn't understand why people left their homes, their land.

"Olga, why is the town so run-down? Where did everyone go?"

Olga walked into the kitchen to pour Bella more juice. She handed her the drink.

"Well, Bella, whatever the news said about Hurricane Maria, it was a hundred times worse. This town sits on two hills. Maria stripped trees bare, blew roofs and walls from the homes, and we were flooded for over a week with no way to get clean water. The people living at the bottom of the hills were hit the hardest because their houses were flooded with up to four feet of water. Without America's help, many of us couldn't make repairs."

Olga showed Bella photos on the wall. "I took these photos after Maria hit the island. Look, here is where your uncle Emilio's house used to be. Now nature has taken back the ruins of the house.".

"Oh yeah, I heard him talking to my mom a few weeks after Maria. She did mention that he moved to Texas."

"That's what a lot of people from town did. It wasn't just that we didn't have water and electricity for weeks; we didn't have jobs. Federal funds for recovery were cut, and small towns like Rio Piedra were last in receiving any help from FEMA."

Olga opened a drawer in the side table and handed a stack of photos to Bella, then sat down. Bella was horrified by the images as she looked through them. There were places she recognized from her childhood, ravaged and destroyed. As she sifted through the stack, Olga continued her explanation.

"So you had the hurricane, loss of employment due to big box retailers from the States forcing local businesses to close without ever reinvesting in the community. Then the US cut the budget, and hundreds of government workers here were out of jobs. I don't understand it. They make hundreds of billions from goods that come from this island and its people, but they refuse to support us like they do the States."

She raised her hands in a sad, 'what can you do about it' gesture, then continued.

"Eventually, young people began to leave the island for work on the mainland. We were thinking of moving to the States as well, but Bella, we love this land. I love being Puerto Rican and feel the connection that all Puerto Ricans share with their island. My mom absolutely refused to move to the States because she and my dad had lived in New York for a few years. They did not like living in the States."

Bella put the pictures down and turned to face Olga.

"How did you survive?"

"Our grandmother's house sits on one of the hills, and her house didn't flood. So, she had some of the neighbors whose houses were destroyed move into the house. Grandma was amazing. She provided people with food and clothes. Here, I took these photos to show how well everyone worked together." Olga took more photos out of the drawer.

Bella saw Isabella cooking and serving food surrounded by dozens of people. She saw family members processing wood from the fallen trees to repair neighbors' homes. There were photos of people she recognized cooking and children helping with laundry. Most importantly, the images showed how united they were in their common purpose to survive. Bella was moved by her family and friends' resilience and wished that she had been here to help. With tears in her eyes, she looked at her cousin.

"I am so sorry that I wasn't here to help."

Olga hugged her cousin.

"Bella, you were dealing with a lot back then. We had to survive because it became clear that FEMA wasn't going to help us in time to save some of our family and friends. Thousands of people died because of Hurricane Maria. We were determined not to lose any more people in this town. Some moved to the States to send money to their family. Today, refugees have moved into some of the abandoned homes. Other abandoned buildings have become headquarters for criminal gangs. Have you seen any police presence since you arrived here in Rio Piedras?"

Bella realized that she saw police officers and cruisers leaving the airport, throughout San Juan, and in the better neighborhoods. She hadn't even noticed that as they drove further into the low-income communities, the police presence became increasingly less noticeable. "Actually, no. You are right, I haven't seen any cops in this town."

"Nope, and you won't. The gangs control some of these neighborhoods. Our young boys join the gangs to survive. I think that those of us who live on this hill have kept the gang activity out of it, but it takes all of us to look out for each other. Listen, Bella, you might as well stay living in the States because soon this neighborhood won't exist."

Bella looked up at Olga in shock. "What are you talking about?"

Olga grabbed an envelope from the bookshelf. She handed it to Bella to read. As Bella read her letter, her face grew more stressed. "Are you planning to sell your parents' house?"

Olga sat down. Bella saw Olga look defeated. "I am not selling anything. You are a lawyer. Does that letter say anything about money?"

"No, it doesn't."

"That's right. The Morning Glory Corporation has offered the county an undisclosed amount of money to buy all of this district of the county. We all have thirty days to provide the Department of Housing and the Legal Department a copy of everyone's house deed."

Bella understood clearly what the Morning Glory Corporation was doing. "Please tell me that you have the deed to your parents' house."

With tears in her eyes, Olga explained their situation, "No, cousin, my mom does not have a deed to the house. My mom explained that when her great-grandmother and great-grandfather bought the house, they purchased it from one of their uncles. They paid their uncle cash, and they moved in. My parents' family has lived in this house for over seventy-five years. They never thought they needed a deed because it was just understood that this was their house."

As a lawyer in North Carolina, Bella knew that without a deed, they would lose their home. "Olga, I am so sorry! Did you go register the house under your mom's name?"

"I tried, but they told me that because the land had already been purchased, they wouldn't be able to help me register the house under my mom's name. So, we will have to move. My mom is distraught that she is losing the home she has known her entire life." Olga tried to put a smile on her face. "Hey, maybe we will move to North Carolina, close to you. Listen, Bella, this isn't just happening to us. You should talk to some of the neighbors. Many face the same problem as we do. They just never knew that they would have to present a deed to show ownership."

Bella asked Olga if she could hold onto the letter for a day or two. "Olga, I am going to read this document to make sure that it's legal."

"I appreciate it, Bella. Thank you so much!"

Bella wanted to speak with the neighbors who had received this letter. "Does Tia Tita still live up on the hill?"

"Oh yes. She is now living alone. All but one of her kids moved to the States. Her daughter, Cecilia, moved to San Juan. She works as a nurse at a doctor's office there. Cecilia visits her on weekends and helps her get to appointments. But Tia's other four kids barely contact her. She makes excuses by telling everyone they are so busy. But the truth is, they are struggling with hardships. One of her sons has been married twice. I bet she would love a visit from you. I know she gets lonely sometimes." Bella and Olga hugged. Olga made Bella promise to return for a visit.

Chapter 19

The afternoon was filled with family visiting Abuela's house. Bella noticed there was always something on the stove for everyone to eat. It made her genuinely happy to see her mom and grandmother happily socializing with everyone. At one point, Bella felt she was wanted. She looked around the yard and saw the spirit of Nayeli just inside the tree line, a few feet away. Bella wondered if it was a trick of the light, especially since the day was hot and bright. She thought she saw the lady in the woods beckon her to enter, and she was drawn to follow. It felt strange, like being in a dream. Was she sleepwalking? That must be it—she was dreaming, sleepwalking. Bella saw people from different eras smiling at her from between the trees. They called out, but she couldn't understand everything they said. She felt a strong connection to everyone around her. Ahead, she saw the lady floating over the pond, and her beauty captivated Bella.

Bella cried out, "What do you want me to do? I don't feel like I am the one you need."

In her mind, she heard what she could only assume was Nayeli's voice, "Find me."

Feeling anguish at the task ahead, Bella started to cry. She was frustrated because she didn't want to be the one to save anyone. "How, Nayeli? How do I find you, and once I do, what should I do? I don't understand."

Suddenly, the spirits spread out in the forest, encircled her, and placed their transparent hands on her. Nayeli felt their pain, which made her cry out. She looked at the faces around her and realized that although they shared their pain with her when they reached out, they were all smiling, almost as if they believed in her. It was clear that they believed more in Bella's abilities than Bella did in herself.

Bella beseeched them in a soft voice, "Please tell me what to do. I need your guidance."

Immediately, Bella saw the image of Nayeli's journal in her mind and heard voices telling her to read the journal. Just outside the circle, Bella saw images of Spanish ancestors. Some were dressed in colonial attire, and others wore multi-generational clothing. One slowly approached Bella and spoke to her in Spanish. He was dressed in what looked to her like Renaissance clothing. Bella was able to assess that the material and style were made of expensive materials. She was also able to see the gold rings on his fingers and the gold threading on his hat and vest. He spoke a dialect of Renaissance Spanish, but she was able to understand it in her mind.

"Daughter of our daughters, know that what was done to the people of this land was evil. During those times, the greed in men brought death, disease, and genocide to the Taino and African people. It looks like men are weak when it comes to the desire for gold. Today, men still make decisions based on how much gold they can get, regardless of the evil deeds they do to obtain that gold. You must save your people to protect the land that you love so much. Go back and read Nayeli's story and find the answers you need. In my time, I was the chosen one,

but I chose land and riches over the gift. You are strong and intelligent. You will have to figure out what you need to do or lose all that you love."

Bella dropped to her knees as she watched the specter speak. She was transfixed. She wondered if he was one of her ancestors or a perpetrator of the violence done to the people of this island. Perhaps he was both and repented for not taking on the cause laid upon him in his time.

He looked at her and gently smiled.

"Yes, my daughter. I am one of your ancestors. I committed many evils against people I thought were beneath my station in life. I had riches, slaves, and several sons who continued my legacy. When Nayeli came to me, I was but a child, and my parents forced me to believe that Nayeli was a demon trying to take me away. Later, as an adult, she spoke to me. I cowered at her message. My family grew wealthy from the backs of men and women, and they didn't matter to us. Nayeli wanted me to give that up, to fight alongside those who were fighting for their freedom. I chose to focus on the riches, not the lives of others. My torment in death is great!"

Bella heard screams and gunfire all around her. She realized that the specter was putting images in her mind from his time, images of what had happened to the Tainos and Africans who were enslaved by elites like him. "I carry these screams with me for all eternity. Don't make the same mistake I did." With his final words, all the spirits surrounding her disappeared—except for Nayeli. Nayeli floated just in front of the waterfall, her face showing tranquility. Bella found strength in Nayeli's compassionate look.

"Ok, I will try."

Amelia found Bella drinking coffee in the garden. From her body language, Amelia saw that Bella was lost in thought.

"Everything ok, Bella?"

Bella was brought out of her thoughts. She looked at Amelia with an intense gaze."

"Whoa, what is going on? I know that look."

"I visited some family today. First, I went to see Olga. It was great seeing her again. She keeps excellent records of Hurricane Maria and what this neighborhood went through to survive. I then visited Tia Tita; she looks well, but I can tell she's lonely with so many families and friends no longer living here. After that, I came back to talk to Grandma about what I discovered."

Amelia was concerned. She knew that Bella wouldn't seem this upset if it weren't serious. "What did you discover?"

"Bella took the envelope out of her shoulder bag and handed it to Amelia."

Amelia read it calmly until she reached the end of the first page. "What the hell?! Is this saying what I think it's saying? Did some Texan company buy the town?"

Bella's eyes were fixed on the woods behind her grandmother's house, searching for Nayeli's spirit to show her the way. "Yup, the county officials sold the land to a company based out of Texas. I've read the entire document. It claims that they held a community forum to discuss the sale. The problem was that the politicians and the Texas company failed to post information about the meeting, so the people of the town weren't present. And, what's worse is that the county politicians sold the land because they knew that not everyone had a deed for their homes."

"What does that mean?"

"It means that some of our friends and family are being evicted because no one thought about registering their properties to obtain a deed of ownership."

Amelia instantly reacted to this information. "Does grandma have a deed to her house?"

"Yes, she does. I spoke with her. She let me know that when grandpa died, she created a will for her belongings. That was when she registered the house under her name."

"So, grandma won't be evicted from her house?"

"It's not that easy. She has proof of ownership, so her letter is different. She told me that the people who have a deed were offered half the market rate. The letter also outlined the plans for this community, making it difficult for those with deeds to remain. Grandma said that everyone is devastated over this because their homes are full of history, and many do not have the money to move somewhere else."

"This is terrible! Can anyone do anything about this?"

"I don't know. I sent a copy of the forms to Laura to review for me. We are looking for any loopholes."

"Abuela must be so scared."

Bella chuckled and rose to stand up. "You would think that, but you know Grandma is a strong person. She isn't giving up that easily. She is gathering the neighbors to take their case to the city council in next month's meeting. For now, she is helping others find the deeds to their homes."

"Yup, that sounds like grandma." Amelia smiled and grabbed Bella by the shoulder. "Come on, let's get lunch going for everyone."

Bella was still troubled. "Nayeli showed herself to me today."

Amelia stopped walking. She was determined to help Bella with her quest.

"What did she say?"

"The same thing she tells me in my dreams. To find her. The thing is that I don't know where to look, and I don't understand why I have to find her. And our ancestors also came to me today and touched me. Mel, although they smile with pride at me, they are in pain. I felt it when they touched me." Bella's eyes became watery. "It was the centuries of pain they had endured at the hands of colonists. I don't even understand how they can be smiling at me when they suffered so much."

Amelia felt bad for her little sister. She hugged Bella and tried to comfort her.

"Bella, maybe they are smiling because they know that the future of our community is in good hands."

Bella chuckled, "My hands? No, I don't think so."

"Come on, tell me what else happened."

Bella recounted her experience in the woods. She described the Spaniard and what he said. Amelia was in shock. Bella explained the torment that he has had for eternity. Amelia wondered if the Spaniard was a direct ancestor of their father.

"Wait, did you say that you were able to see an image of Nayeli's journal?"

"Yeah, why?"

"Maybe that is where you're supposed to start. Look, I know that Nayeli spoke and wrote in a different language, but Abuela had a college professor translate it. So, we don't need to touch the original in Abuela's safe. She has the translated copy, and I am sure that to help you in this quest, she will lend it to you. Let's ask her for it."

Bella knew that Amelia would come up with a plan. Growing up, she could always count on Amelia to look at things from a different perspective and offer new ideas. Bella was relieved that Amelia wanted to help her.

"Yeah, that sounds like a good start."

"Come on, let's go find grandma."

Chapter 20

Amelia and Bella found their grandmother going through old boxes filled with essential documents.

"Hey abuela, what are you doing?"

Their grandmother looked up at them and smiled.

"Hijas! Can I make you anything?"

It was typical of Grandma to make someone feel good by cooking for them.

"No thank you abuela. Amelia and I are going to prepare lunch, but you look busy looking through those boxes. So, can we help you? What are you looking for?"

"Ah, that's nice of you two, but no. I am looking for old family documents that show family lineage and property exchange."

Amelia realized that she was helping the family members who did not have a deed to their homes. "Oh, I see. You are looking for any official documents that mention family members who were given their homes and lands to register their properties under their names now."

"Kind of, but not quite. You see, the town's registry office is no longer accepting applications for ownership deeds. Did Bella explain to you what is going on?"

Amelia nodded. "Yes, and I think that it's horrible what they are doing! The fact that people voted into position lined their pockets with money from this Texan company and sold the land from under their feet. It's despicable!! It's as if some Puerto Ricans will never be free from the greed of certain men."

Abuela was proud of her granddaughter's world views. Carmen taught them to be strong women and to go forward in life to accomplish their dreams.

"Well, you know women have also had a part in the colonization and enslavement, too."

"I know abuela. It's just really messed up that forever, the driving force for people of privilege has been to grow their wealth at the cost of lives. Even today, corporations and government agents would sell their souls to the devil to gain MORE. More of what they already have. I mean, seriously, can Jeff Bezos spend all of his money in one lifetime? NO! His kids will not be able to spend all that money in their lifetime. So, when is enough, enough? When do they stop raping the earth and its people for their wealth? All I am saying is that it's not fair. Some of us will work our entire lives and never have enough money for homeownership, having families, or enjoying life."

"You are right, Amelia. I am enraged at what is happening here. I think helping our neighbors figure out what they can do to save their homes is the most important challenge facing us right now."

Amelia knew that Bella and her grandmother were right. She just felt this rage at how, no matter the era, rich men ruled over everyone's lives, particularly women. She and Torry have had to fight for their right to live life together and have a family. But right now, doing something to help her friends and family is what she has to focus on.

"Oh yeah, I almost forgot. Grandma, can we read the translated copy of Nayeli's journal?"

Isabella stepped away from the boxes of papers she was looking through. She was intrigued that Bella and Amelia wanted to know more about Nayeli.

"Of course, what's going on?" Isabella headed to the study to retrieve the copy of the journal she had locked inside her bottom desk drawer.

Bella and Amelia followed her and realized that she had three boxes of family history out on the table.

Amelia was curious about how far back her records went. "Abuela, are all these boxes filled with family history information?" Amelia opened one of the boxes and saw weathered documents and yellow letters. Amelia noticed letters dating back to the 1950s, as well as some that dated further back to the 1920s.

Isabella took out the keys to open the drawer when she was distracted by Amelia's question.

"Oh yes, dear. Those records date back to the 1800s. Before that, most of our family was not educated, so they weren't able to write things down, but they did gather letters and documents for the future generations." Isabella pulled out some of the older documents wrapped in sheet protectors to protect them from deteriorating. She handed some documents to Amelia.

Amelia was amazed to hold letters from 1838 in her hands. "Abuela, this is from 1838! These should be digitized and shared."

Isabella had never thought about that. "Hija, that is a wonderful idea, but I don't do a lot of technology here. As you can see for yourself, here in Rio Piedra, we don't always have reliable internet access."

"Can I do this for you while we are here? I can visit the library to scan the documents and create a digital file. You can share it with anyone who may need information on our family history while keeping the originals safe and secure."

Isabella was proud to see that her granddaughters were eager to learn more about their family history, as well as using their knowledge and abilities to pass this information on to future generations.

"Of course, mija. How would you do it?"

"First, I need to go through the boxes and create a catalog. For those in a fragile condition, I will use my camera to take quality photos of them. I may be able to do that with all of them."

"Sounds wonderful, Amelia. Oh, can I ask you to wear gloves when working with them? I want to protect them from any bacteria."

Amelia realized she hadn't thought about the bacteria and oils on her hands when she picked up the form. She also just realized that Isabella had been wearing gloves the whole time they were talking to her. Isabella grabbed an antiseptic wipe and carefully wiped the outside of the sheet protector.

"It's ok, Amelia. I got it. I do appreciate that you offered to help. I guess I am passing the title of family archivist down to you."

Bella was waiting by the desk, smiling at her grandmother's happiness. Isabella looked up and saw that Bella was still waiting for her to give her the journal.

"Oh, Bella, I am sorry. Here, let me get you that journal."

Isabella handed Bella a copy of the journal. On the cover was a description of its content:

This is a digital copy of The Journal of Nayelis, daughter of Caguax.

Cagua, Puerto Rico 1522, translated 2019 by Professor Francisco Casilla Montera.

University of Puerto Rico Anthropology Department

Some of the translations summarize interpretations of the Taino language based on existing records. Finding exact translations into our current Western language was challenging. Please note that this university used its resources to provide the most accurate translation possible.

Bella was intrigued by the document she was holding. Nayeli's thoughts and life experiences seemed right there at her fingertips. She reflected on what the ancestors told her earlier that day and how frustrated she was that they had instructed her to find Nayeli, but perhaps the journal would offer her a clue.

Isabella noticed that her granddaughters were deeply engrossed in the documents they were reviewing. She didn't want to disturb them, so she excused herself to the kitchen to make lunch. Hearing the noise of pots from the kitchen caused Amelia to snap out of her concentration. Torry and Lulu were expected to return home shortly, and she remembered that she had to prepare lunch for Lulu so they could let her lie down for a nap.

"Grandma, I was going to make lunch for us."

"Don't worry, mija, I will make lunch. I picked some fresh fruits from the trees in the backyard, so I planned to make a fruit salad. I bet my grandbaby is going to love it. I will make lunch; you go back to what you are doing."

"If you are sure?"

"Of course, claro que si."

Amelia noticed Bella sitting by the window that faced the backyard. She seemed engrossed in what she was reading.

"Boy, it must be good reading."

Bella looked up with tears in her eyes.

Amelia was startled to see Bella become emotional because of the journal.

"Bella, what's going on? What does it say?"

Bella handed her some pages. "Here, I have only read the first four pages, but you take a look. I think I'm moved because the woman who has been haunting me is now a character from my past. Look at how she started the journal:"

'I, Nayeli, eighth daughter of Chief Caguax, leave this written history of my life to teach all the ones to come the importance of fighting for what you believe, standing up to tyranny, and always being true to who you are. The journey is often long, exhausting, dangerous, and heartbreaking, but it's your life's journey, and it will challenge you. You must be ready for the fight to survive.

At my current age of what the Spaniards call forty-eight, my health is failing due to the imprisonment I endured under Ponce de Leon's command. They took me away from my home and my people. He jailed me because I refused to humble myself to their authority. I defied them when they tried to enslave me. They controlled my fate by imprisoning me. Ponce de Leon had me stripped, tied to a pole, ordered his men to abuse me, and locked me in a dark hole in their deepest dungeon; never to see the light of day, smell the ocean, be with my people, or walk through our vast forests. But he was wrong. He only made me more determined to survive. And he made me a role model for our people to follow.

My children, as you read the story of my life, remember that Boriken's future rests in your hands. Our struggle is not finished. The greed of men will persist, and their power to destroy and conquer will fall to you as time goes on. We embraced the newcomers, the Spaniards, with open arms, but all they did was take, claim what was not theirs, and kill those in their way.

Your land, wherever it may be, is precious. I hope my words in this journal will give you strength. My descendants will carry on my work and teach the next generation. Remember to be free, live your life, and never forget what came before you, so it can guide you through what is to come.

"Damn! She was an incredible woman. We need more people with Nayeli's strength and unflinching determination." Amelia handed the journal back to Bella.

"Here, you need to read this more than I do to find clues on how to find her. I will get my camera and start this digital archive. Let me know if I can help."

Bella took the book back and flipped the pages. "Yeah, I sure will."

Bella was distracted by the sound of Amelia's camera. She decided that her favorite spot was the best place to read this journal. She grabbed the book and headed into the woods.

Chapter 21

As Bella entered the woods, she felt she wasn't alone. Throughout her life, the woods always connected her to the land and its people. It also had a sort of sad feeling to it that she was able to relate to. Bella thought that maybe this sadness was part of why she felt more at home in this forest. This time, the forest felt lighter, and for the first time, Bella's senses were heightened like never before. Her sense of smell was stronger, and she could pick up the scents of flowers, dirt, leaves, and even the water from the pond. Everything smelled sweeter. The heaviness in her heart also lifted. As she walked toward the pond, she was sure she saw the faces of people from the distant past in the shadows between the trees. It gave her strength as she moved forward.

She walked far enough to hear the sound of the waterfall. Her excitement increased as she quickened her pace. Through the shrubs and trees, Bella saw sunlight streaming through the canopy and shining on the pond's surface. It was a magical scene. In the area where the sun's rays touched the water, it shimmered as if reflecting pixie dust into the air. The sun also illuminated the large boulder Bella liked to sit on. She thought how perfect it was that the sun was lighting the rock for her, making it easier for her to read.

Bella made herself comfortable on the boulder. At first, she looked all around her. This time, things appeared brighter. She looked into the water and saw fish below the surface. Bella closed her eyes, felt the breeze on her, heard the sound of water, and saw parrots flying above the trees. Bella struggled with the thought of leaving this place again. She had to push those thoughts aside for now and start reading.

Bella was deep in Nayeli's story when Amelia approached her.

"There you are. With a big old Spanish house with many rooms to read in, you choose this boulder." Amelia giggled. "How far have you gotten?"

"Hey, Amelia. Sorry, I was completely captivated by her early years. Wait till I tell you."

"Really, she went that far back? Abuela told me to come and get you for lunch. We are eating in the back garden. Why don't you tell all of us then?"

"Sure, sounds good. I guess now that I stopped reading, I realized that I am actually starving."

Amelia saw a glint of excitement in Bella's manner. It was refreshing to see Bella engaged in Nayeli's story, and she hoped Bella would succeed in her mission for the sake of many loved ones in the community.

Bella and Amelia stepped out of the woods into the bright sunlight and tropical heat. Amelia realized that the woods tend to be cool, even during summer. Bella saw some of her family sitting at the table, already eating. She noticed Lulu laughing. She thought that Amelia and Torry might have trouble taking Lulu back to North Carolina because, in the past few days, Lulu had gotten used to living in Puerto Rico and playing with her cousins.

"Hey, everyone. Sorry, abuela, I was caught up in reading the journal."

"It's ok. Anything that you want to share with everyone?"

As Bella sat down, she looked at the delicious food Isabella had cooked. In the center of the table was a fresh seafood salad. Isabella also prepared some root vegetables, fresh tamarind and passion fruit juices, and a fruit salad from her trees. It was a feast.

"Yeah, I haven't gotten very far, but I can share what I have learned."

Antonio interrupts, "Wait, what is going on? What journal?"

Bella explained, "Well, that's a crazy story, but I don't think that I can share it right now." Bella gestured towards Lulu. Everyone understood the hint. There are some things they felt Lulu was too young to hear, especially the tyranny of the colonists and the pain of the enslaved. However, Bella would be able to discuss Nayeli's childhood. "But I can share what I have read regarding Nayeli's writings on her early years."

Carlos was intrigued. "That sounds great, Bella. I can't wait to hear."

Bella began her story by explaining how old Nayeli was when she started writing her life down for future generations.

"So, I hadn't realized that Nayeli was forty-two when she started writing her stories. Nayeli begins recounting her childhood and what life was like before the Spanish colonization. She describes a utopian kind of society. Their religion was dedicated to 'the Mother' through caring for the land and following nature's guidance. Look here, I will read this page.

My childhood was pretty typical in our village. I was the eighth daughter of the village chief, so I had fewer responsibilities than my brothers and sisters. I knew that my only duty was to carry on our bloodline with another tribe. However, my father was very lenient, and maybe he spoiled me. He gave me a lot of freedom to play like children should. I had chores to help the village, and when the time came,

I could choose to marry if I wanted to. My older siblings did not have that choice. My favorite things to do were playing with the boys, climbing trees to pick fruit, and going fishing to catch food for the village. My mother often talked to my father about me doing things usually reserved for boys in the village. My father would say that I was meant for something else. To avoid showing favoritism, my father declared that boys and girls could do the same things if they wished. At first, his council questioned this. But my father reminded everyone that he was the chief and that the gods had given him a vision he had to follow. Years later, I asked him why he allowed me to do both boys' and girls' activities. He told me what he once said to the council. While he slept, the goddess showed him a vision of me fighting to save others' lives. The goddess didn't share all the details of the vision because it wasn't meant for him to know. His role was to prepare me by strengthening my body and mind. So, if others in the village judged or complained that he let me do things I wasn't supposed to, he made it easier by proclaiming that all children could choose their activities.

My childhood was exciting and tough, and I felt as if I belonged to something bigger than myself. My father waited to tell me of his vision the night before I was to marry. I knew I had a purpose, even if I didn't know what it was at the time. I was grateful to my mother and father for teaching me what I needed to know and for giving me the opportunity to grow up as a normal child. That helped me connect better with the rest of the village, and the love for my people grew from what they taught me. I thank the Mother for providing."

Bella stopped reading at that point. She noticed that everyone had stopped eating, and their eyes were intent on her. The sound of a parrot broke the silence.

"Wow, Bella." Torry exclaimed, "Knowing how things turned out for her, I feel so sad that she had grown up in a safe and united community that was literally taken away from them. Damn."

Antonio found it challenging to speak. "Yeah, that kind of utopian society is something that we in modern times are searching for. To think that societies in the past lived that way and then it was taken away just pisses me off. It makes me feel so bad for those people."

Lulu was confused at what she was hearing, "Why are you sad? Didn't you hear Aunt Bella? Nayeli had fun as a kid. I think the things she did, like climbing trees and picking fruit, sounded like fun to me." Lulu looked at her grandmother excitedly, "Grandma, can I climb your fruit trees?"

Everyone laughed.

"Sure, mija. But only if your parents allow it, and an adult is helping you. You are not used to climbing trees, and it takes practice. Promise that you will not climb trees without getting someone to help you?"

"Yes, Grandma, I promise. Mommy, can I climb trees to pick fruits?"

Amelia responded, a little worried that her five-year-old wanted to climb trees. She wasn't sure what to say, "Well, that depends on you following the rules. Torry, what do you think?"

Torry was smiling ear to ear. "Of course, I will teach her. I used to climb trees on my grandparents' farm. I used to sit on their branches and pass the time away. From the pecan tree's branch, I was able to see for miles. When do you want to start?"

"Right now!"

Everyone laughed again and continued enjoying their lunch.

"Well, today you have to take a nap, and then we are going to Grandma Cecilia's house."

Bella had forgotten they were in Puerto Rico for her father's funeral. She realized they were supposed to have dinner at Grandma Cecilia's house tonight. She had invited everyone. She wanted to discuss the funeral arrangements. Not that Bella cared, but Carmen insisted she attend.

The rest of the lunch went smoothly. There was still plenty to catch up on. The food was fantastic. Juan Carlos, his son Angel, Olga and her two kids, and Aunt Maria joined them. Grandma always cooked a lot because she expected family to come over, especially since we were visiting.

Chapter 22

None of Carmen's kids wanted to visit their paternal grandmother. Their family had always treated them like strangers. Carmen remembered how often she sent holiday cards to reach out, only to have them ignored. Carmen knew that Cecilia looked down on them because their lineage was a mix of other ethnicities, but Cecilia called her directly and invited them to dinner. Carmen thought that Cecilia was just doing minimal due diligence in this somber situation. Carmen tried to feel bad for Cecilia because Cecilia had lost three sons and one daughter to COVID-19, cancer, and Luis's heart attack. And deep down inside, Carmen never stopped loving Luis, and she yearned for closure.

Amelia, always intuitive, noticed how distraught her mother was. This must be a difficult time for Carmen, laying to rest the one man she ever loved. Amelia, on the other hand, wished that in death, her father's soul would never find peace. But she knew she had to support her mother. So, she went around gathering her brothers and sisters to encourage them to get ready for dinner. She found Torry with Lulu in her bedroom, dressing Lulu like a porcelain doll.

"Wow, baby, where did you get that dress? You look so cute!"

Lulu twirled her dress as she showed off her white lace dress and her leather patent shoes. "Don't I look beautiful, mommy?"

Amelia picked up her daughter and swung her around. "Yes, you look beautiful."

Torry gathered the hairbrush and scrunchies. "Your mother gave this to her. She said that it was yours when you lived in Puerto Rico. Grandma had it stored away. It looks new, doesn't it?"

Amelia was shocked to hear that the dress that Lulu was wearing was originally hers. "This was my dress?"

Torry nodded, "Yeah, and I bet you looked adorable wearing it when you were little. Just like our lovely Lulu." Torry leaned towards Amelia and kissed her. It had been a while since they shared an intimate moment.

The moment was interrupted by Lulu, "Eeww, kissing. Come on, mommy, help me with my hair."

Amelia and Torry laughed. "Well, hurry up, you two. We are leaving in ten minutes."

"Ok, Mel, we will be downstairs soon."

As they approached their grandmother's circular driveway, they were surprised to hear music. Amelia thought that Grandmother Cecilia would be mourning. Bella noticed other cars along the driveway.

"How many people did she invite?" Bella asked as they found a place to park behind the last car.

"I had no idea this was going to be a party," responded Antonio.

"Yeah, I am confused too," exclaimed Carmen. "Well, let's go find out what this is all about?"

Bella had forgotten how big her grandmother's house was. It always made her feel like, at one point in their lives, they had servants. Bella never considered her paternal family or their wealth. As far as she knew, her grandmother lived alone with two dogs. But tonight, a butler opened the door and led them to the family room. Bella had forgotten how opulent everything in this house was. The ceilings had gold leaf and hand-painted murals. You first walk into a beautiful room with an antique crystal chandelier. Each room had its own chandelier, depending on its size. The butler opened French doors that led to an open courtyard. In the center of the garden stood a statue of Ponce de Leon. Rose bushes, a bench, and a water fountain surrounded the statue. Bella had to admit that it was breathtaking.

The butler led them down a hallway parallel to the courtyard. There were more French doors leading into other rooms. Curious, Bella peeked into one of the rooms and saw wall-to-wall bookshelves filled with books. She loved books and imagined herself in a library like this one, surrounded by antique books to read. It actually made her angry that her father's family lived in luxury while their mother struggled to put food on the table.

The butler stopped in front of the final French doors on that side of the hallway. He opened the door and introduced my mother and grandmother. Cecilia was the perfect hostess. She approached them and held their hands. She looked at us and commented on how grown-up we were. Bella sensed the hypocrisy in her grandmother's gestures. But she followed Antonio's lead and greeted her grandmother. Cecilia welcomed them into her house and motioned for them to enter the family room, where other family members were already gathered.

Bella looked around and saw her family members, including aunts, uncles, and cousins, as well as relatives from her father's side. She was able to tell who belonged to which family by their dress and mannerisms. Her immediate family came over and hugged them. Olga whispered to Bella, "I am so glad you are here. I don't know how much I could take from those snobs."

Bella chuckled. The French doors in that room were wide open, giving her a clear view of a large outdoor patio. A band was playing music, and servants moved about with trays of drinks and hors d'oeuvres. She saw Angel talking to Juan Carlos outside. Bella greeted her uncle and Angel.

"I am confused, Uncle. I thought that this was a simple dinner, not a party?"

"Yeah, so did we. But, I guess Cecilia had to show everyone off. Although I would have thought that she would be in mourning after her son's death."

Antonio approached them, "Yeah, me too. This is ridiculous." A server approached them with a tray of pina coladas. "But it doesn't mean that I can't enjoy her hospitality," he stated as he grabbed a cup. Everyone laughed and grabbed their own pina coladas.

Bella noticed her mom sitting in the room, dumbfounded.

"Hey, Mom, are you ok?"

Carmen looked up to find Bella worried about her, "Oh, don't worry about me, Bella. I am fine. I guess I am just confused about this lavish banquet. I thought that her son's death would sadden Cecilia. I don't get it. "

Bella sat down by her mother, "Yeah, I don't get it either. This looks more like a celebration than a somber get-together."

Cecilia approached them and said, "When my son left his family, I thought he would come home, remarry, and take over our family's business. Instead, he moved into our old house and lived as a hermit. The few times we talked, he said that if anything happened to him, he didn't want any recognition. I refused to follow his wishes. I felt I needed to celebrate his life so everyone could remember him."

Bella was growing angry. After all, all these decades they had struggled because their father abandoned them, and now his mother wanted to celebrate HIS life! That was too much to take.

Carmen asked, "You know, when I met Luis, he never told me about his family or their business. I found out long after we married that he came from a wealthy background. Could you tell me what the family business is?"

"Of course. The truth is, I was angry that he married you because we had other plans for him. I guess you wouldn't understand that people like us often marry within our own kind to produce the next generation that can continue and increase our wealth. And when he married you, he broke our family tradition. Our family has been involved in land acquisitions since our ancestors arrived in the Caribbean. For the last forty years, we have expanded to the US and parts of Europe."

Bella was disgusted and intrigued. "How have you expanded to other places? What did you do? Open up business offices in other places?"

Cecilia chuckled, "It's not that simple, dear. I like to think that we are saving neighborhoods that are becoming ghost towns."

"Really, how?"

Cecilia wondered if Bella could understand the good their business is doing for people. "Well, look at Puerto Rico, for instance. There are entire towns where people have moved to the States or other U.S. islands, leaving their neighborhoods as ghost towns. These houses and businesses sit there decaying over time. We step in and broker deals for developers to come in and rebuild in these ghost towns, making them beautiful, modern, and inhabited again." Cecilia proudly finished her explanation. She felt she had every reason to take pride in the work her family had always done to improve many communities on the islands, in the States, and now in Europe.

Bella was confused that her grandmother saw their work as a good thing for people. How clueless was this woman! Her father abandoned them! Her father was the reason Bella had a troubled youth and got involved in criminal activity as a teenager. He was also the reason she needed depression and anxiety medication. And now she is trying to convince her that her family does good for others. As far as Bella could tell, Cecilia and her family are parasites who do not care who they hurt, including families like hers.

"Well, I know that you simplified your description of what the family business is, but I read business documents for company mergers all day. I can understand the business aspect of your company."

Cecilia was impressed. "Oh, would you be interested in joining the family business?"

It took all of Bella's self-control to keep herself from screaming at this woman and storming out of this shindig her so-called grandmother threw for her father. But something inside her told her to calm down and play nice in this situation.

"Oh, grandmother, I didn't mean for you to think that I was asking you for a job."

"No, I don't think that at all. But it's a wonderful idea. Look, your father was supposed to join the company and carry on our legacy, but he didn't. So, maybe in his place, you can join the family business. As a licensed lawyer, we could really use your help, your education, and the fact that you speak several languages would make you especially valuable."

Bella felt sick to her stomach. How could this woman be planning business deals during her son's 'celebration of life'? Bella saw an opportunity opening up, even if she didn't fully understand what that opportunity was.

"Really, Grandma Cecilia?"

Cecilia reacted to being called Grandma, "Grandmother, please, dear."

Bella was glad that she said something offensive to Cecilia. "Of course, grandmother."

"Look, maybe before you go back to North Carolina, you come by to take a look at the work we have done to improve neighborhoods. You can look at our mission statement and business model."

"That would be great, thank you, grandmother. Maybe I will consider it."

"Good, call me when you want to come over. I am sure that your mother has my phone number. For now, I need to tend to my other guests."

Carmen fought the urge to punch that woman. She was confused that Bella would be interested in joining Cecilia's company.

"Mija, what's up with that? Do you want to join their business?"

"Nah, I want to burn the family business if I can. Listen, Mom, when she spoke to us as if we were too dumb to understand anything she was saying, it made me feel like I wanted to punch that woman. But something inside told me to listen to her and keep the opportunity open. I don't know what it all means, but I intend to dig into their company. Perhaps I can uncover some incriminating evidence in their documents that will help me bring them down. And maybe they will understand what it is to go hungry.

Chapter 23

Bella spent most of the evening talking with her family. Many had never been invited to the Castillo home before, and they were amazed at the elegance and clear display of their wealth. Angel described the gold leaf trimmings, the large front doors, and the spaciousness of the house. Bella understood that in Puerto Rico, many communities are so overcrowded that families build on top of each other's homes. Some people in impoverished towns who lack the financial means to move or rent a new place end up building their houses in tight spaces, with neighbors stacked on top of one another.

Angel told Bella that he was feeling uncomfortable being in the Castillo house with the Castillo family.

"You know, Bella, I never realized we were poor before today. I mean, you remember, right? We had what we needed, and our part of town is full of family and friends. I just never saw us as poor." Angel looked at the outdoor garden with statues and water ponds. "I mean, look at this place—filled with antiques from generations of Castillos, luxurious furniture, and from what I heard, our grandmother is the only one living here. Well, being next to the Castillo family, I feel inferior to them. I don't like feeling like this."

Bella understood exactly how he felt. She and her siblings believed they didn't belong in the Castillo home, and they felt unwelcome. Bella reminded Angel that they had come as a courtesy and that they would be leaving soon. She sat alone in the garden because she had lost the ability to socialize with her hypocritical family. She could only fake a smile for so long, and she struggled internally with her emotions. She felt anger and disgust toward these people. She tried to engage with her aunts and uncles, but they talked about their travels to North Carolina, New York, Texas, and various European countries. Bella knew they were showing off and trying to demonstrate that they were better than the Morales family. When Bella realized that her Aunt Luisa had mentioned traveling to Texas, she prodded for more information.

"Ooh, Aunt Luisa, your travels sound exciting." Bella faked the smile.

"Oh, yes, Bella. In Europe, we went to Spain to trace our family history. We also went to Paris and Rome. It was wonderful. We spared no expense."

Bella felt nauseous and angry, but she heard what she thought was Nayeli's voice softly instructing her to calm down. Bella knew that this was a crucial moment, and she had to see it through. Bella played the game, "That sounds great. I plan to travel to Europe myself. I've been planning a trip to Spain for a long time, but I've been so busy at work that I haven't been able to take a vacation."

Cecilia smiled because she saw an opportunity to affect Carmen by taking Bella under her wing, adding her to the family business. After all, why not? Bella looked more European than the rest of her maternal family, and Cecilia was considering having a lawyer within the family company who would have a familial connection to protecting the business.

"Well, Bella, I think that you will be able to travel anywhere you want to go if you join our company. You will be an asset." Cecilia grabbed both of her hands and leaned in towards Bella, and in a warm, touching voice, she said, "I know that your father will be proud."

Bella fought the vomit coming up her throat. Cecilia noticed immediately that Bella seemed unwell.

"Bella, are you alright?"

Bella took several calming breaths and focused on three things in front of her. She managed to steady herself and continue with the charade, "Oh, yes, grandmother. I suddenly realized how my life would improve if I joined your company."

Cecilia smiled, "Of course, sweetheart. I am sure that we can pay you much more than that tiny law firm you work for in North Carolina." Cecilia wrapped her arm around Bella and led her to her oldest son, Manuel. "Manny, good news, Bella is considering joining our company. Isn't it perfect to add a family member to our team of lawyers?"

"Well, I am just considering it. After all, I don't know anything about the family business. Would I be allowed to look at some of the business records, if that is ok, I mean?"

Manny looked at his mother. She had a unique way of conveying messages without speaking. This time, he understood that Cecilia wanted him to agree, even though he didn't know why. His mother had ignored Luis's family ever since she found out he had married Carmen. As a child, she told him and his siblings not to talk about their cousins or reach out to that family. Now, he was confused, but he knew just to follow her lead.

"Of course, mother. You know, we have a new mergers and acquisitions office in Texas that could use a lawyer to lead that team. You would be perfect, Bella."

There it was again, Bella thought, *Texas.*

What was it about Texas that made the hairs on her arms stand up? Deep inside, Bella fought the urge to vomit. She had no desire to get involved with her father's family. After all, they weren't there when she was growing up. If they had been, maybe her mother wouldn't have had to work two jobs to put food on the table.

But at this moment, Bella could hear Nayeli telling her to calm down. However, Bella's anxiety and anger were growing. She took a cup of red wine from one of the servants and took a gulp. The warmth from the wine warmed her stomach. For a moment, Bella fully tasted the wine. The aroma was rich, fruity, and had a hint of spice. The wine tasted unbelievably good.

"This wine is amazing, grandmother. What is it called so I can pick up a few bottles before I leave?"

Cecilia found her question amusing. She giggled as she mockingly told Bella that the wine was too expensive for her to buy. "Oh, Bella, that's nice that you like the wine so much," Cecilia called one of the attendants over. She asked the attendant to go down to the cellar and get a bottle for her granddaughter.

Bella immediately felt humiliated by the charity her grandmother was showing her.

Calm down, Bella looked up and saw a transparent form standing by the doors to the patio. Nayeli smiled at her, as if to tell her that she was not alone. She felt a sense of strength in Nayeli's presence and was able to fake a smile.

Cecilia continued her plan to lure Bella away from Carmen. "Well, I mean that if you keep working at that law firm, you won't be able to afford the finer things in life, like this wine. This wine we bought in Italy twenty years ago. But working for us will allow you to afford these wonderful things." The attendant arrived with the bottle of wine. Cecilia handed it to Bella and suggested she open it at a special time because it was a special wine.

Bella feigned excitement, "Thank you so much, grandmother! This is a wonderful and generous gift. I will treasure it!" Well, grandmother and Uncle Manny, you two make quite a team. I haven't been happy with my salary at the company where I work. But maybe I can come in a couple of days to have someone show me some of your records, tell me more about the new offices in Texas, and discuss the possible salary. I'm having trouble deciding tonight because I'm overwhelmed with everything that's happened. I will call you in a few days." Bella excused herself, saying she had seen her cousin Olga and wanted to greet her.

Unaware to Bella, Carmen had been watching Bella's interactions with Cecilia. She knew Cecilia was a greedy and sly woman. She was aware of what Bella had told her, but she worried about her daughter's emotional health as she engaged with Luis's family.

The rest of the evening unfolded as a smoothly run event. Cecilia was a gracious hostess, engaging with everyone from the Castillo family and their friends, including the funeral director who was there. To Bella's family, she offered quick greetings and excused herself to avoid starting conversations. Bella watched her, noting her as graceful and beautiful for her age. She concealed her age well.

At the end of the event, Cecilia instructed the butler to inform the family out on the patio to come inside for a toast.

With a rehearsed smile, she addressed the crowd, "Please, everyone, grab a glass of champagne for a toast."

Bella noticed that her family seemed confused about the 'toast.' She overheard Angel ask Antonio quietly what they were toasting to. Antonio thought that if someone walked into the house right then, they would assume everyone was celebrating a happy occasion, not the death of his father. Those thoughts made him furious. He felt that, even though he didn't believe he could ever forgive his father, he expected Cecilia to be heartbroken over losing her son. Instead, she was celebrating and showing off her wealth. He thought to himself that these people were cold-hearted, manipulative, driven by greed, and didn't care about each other.

Cecilia's voice was warm and empathetic. She made eye contact with everyone around her. She stood at the front of the room where the lighting would have the most significant effect.

"Dear friends and family, we gather here tonight to honor the memory of my son, Luis." She paused to take a deep breath, seemingly to show her pain of losing her son, but Bella now realized it was just another act by a cunning businesswoman who cares little for her family. "My son lived a difficult life. I had high hopes for him as my oldest son. He had a great talent for business, and during those times, we needed him. But, as you all know, he chose a different path." Cecilia turned to glance at Carmen and offered her a warm smile. Carmen felt repulsed. "Luis did things his way, and when he saw his errors, he quickly withdrew." Cecilia looked at Carmen as if to imply that he had realized it was a mistake to marry her. Carmen felt tears of anger and pain well up in her eyes.

Amelia moved alongside Carmen because she knew that this witch was shooting arrows at her mom. In a gentle voice, Amelia told her mom, "Don't let her upset you, Mom. You know the real reason why Luis left—because he was greedy like them and a coward for not standing up to the family. He paid for that through years of isolation and loneliness." Carmen hugged Amelia's arm and smiled.

"So tonight, we celebrate you, Luis, and all that you could have been. We welcome Carmen and her family in the hope that his passing can unite us more than ever." Cecilia once again looked at Carmen and, with a fake smile, she continued, "I would like to get to know my grandchildren and my great-grandchildren. Carmen, you and I will put the past aside, and you can be the daughter I always wanted you to be."

Carmen squeezed Amelia's arm.

"I look forward to getting to bond with you and the rest of Luis's family. Thank you, Cecilia, for your generosity," Carmen said.

Cecilia walked up to Carmen and took hold of her hand. "Well, of course." Cecilia turned to look at each of Carmen's children. "You are my family too, and I care about you immensely."

Carlos became angry. His uncle approached him and quietly said, "Calm yourself, Carlos. This speech isn't for anyone in this room except your mother. Cecilia has never forgiven Luis for turning his back on the family legacy and choosing Carmen, and for a while, he prioritized his kids over his mother's wishes. This is her way of hurting Carmen."

"I swear I just want to let everyone here know that she is lying about her affections and that once my dad left, she forgot about us."

Juan Carlos turned to face Carlos and said, "Look, everyone knows that she is lying and obviously planning a scheme of some kind. I think it has to do with Bella because I saw them talking for a long time tonight. I am not worried because I trust Bella, and your mother has not responded negatively to seeing Bella and Cecilia warm up to each other. But spending your energy trying to make everyone here see that she is fake is only going to make you feel better and embarrass your mother in front of Luis's family. They would love that."

"You're right, uncle. Cecilia would love that. I won't give her the satisfaction."

"Exactly, so for now, just grin and bear it. There will come a day when she and her brood of nasty kids and grandkids will get their comeuppance."

Cecilia was still performing when she said, "The funeral director, Mr. Mendez, informed me that Luis will be available for visiting starting tomorrow at 9:00 am. He welcomes the family to the Mendez Heavenly Funeral Palace. Interment is scheduled for Sunday at 1:00

p.m., after a family Mass. Guests may join us at the funeral home at 12:30 to pay their respects before he is laid to rest. So, let's raise our cups to my son Luis. May he rest in peace."

She watched to make sure that everyone toasted to her son. This was another minute in the spotlight. She loved it.

Chapter 24

On the drive back to Isabella's house, everyone discussed how crazy and bizarre Cecilia's party was. No one could understand why Cecilia was so determined to hurt Carmen's feelings. They talked about the aunts and uncles and how disconnected they all seemed from the Morales family.

As they approached the driveway, they saw Isabella standing by the entrance door. She turned on all the front lights. After spending an evening with cold-hearted so-called family members, they were filled with warmth from seeing their grandmother waiting for them. They all thought about how good it felt to be back home as a loving family.

Carmen approached her mother and fell into Isabella's warm embrace, exhausted from tonight's affair.

"How are you holding up? I know this must have been very difficult for you."

Carmen couldn't hold her tears anymore. She wept in her mother's arms as she had when she was a little girl. She let out all the concerns she had, the anger that boiled inside her, as she saw how wealthy Luis's family was, while they depended on food stamps, and she worked two jobs.

Antonio approached them. He reached out and rubbed his mother's back, unsure what to say to comfort her. Camen stepped away from her mother, dried her tears, and smiled at her son. "Hola abuela," Antonio said, "you didn't have to wait up for us."

Amelia approached, carrying Lulu, fast asleep in her arms. "Yeah, abuela, it's late."

"It's ok, sweethearts. I didn't think all of you going tonight was a good idea; that woman is a snake, and nothing good can come of associating with that family. How could I go to sleep knowing that this night was going to be difficult for all of you? Come inside. I made coffee and flan. Help yourselves."

"Sounds great. Let me put Lulu to bed. I will join you all in the family room."

Bella wandered up behind the others and hugged her. "Hi, Grandma."

Isabella noticed that her granddaughter appeared tired and upset.

"Bella, what's wrong? You look worried about something, and you look tired." Isabela placed her hands over Bella's shoulder.

"You bet she's tired after spending the entire night talking to Cecilia," Antonio said, still upset.

Isabella was taken by surprise. She knew that Cecilia saw her family as being below her status and would not be talking to Bella if she wasn't planning something. Isabella became worried.

Amelia hugged Isabella when she returned to the group standing outside the entry doors. "Yes, abuela. Cecilia seemed very interested in Bella, and wait until you hear what they were talking about."

Isabella looked at Bella in surprise, worry written all over her face, but then she remembered that she trusted Bella, and she relaxed.

Instead of asking questions, Isabella kissed her granddaughter on the forehead and smiled at her.

"Just be careful with Cecilia," was all she said before waving toward the doorway. "I didn't think that you all going tonight was a good idea, but it sounds like Cecilia's plan to have you attend her soiree tonight didn't go as well as she hoped. You know, Carmen, she never forgave you for stealing Luis from her because she had plans for him to marry Casandra."

Carmen looked up at Isabella in confusion. "What? Who is Casandra?"

Isabella led Carmen through the doorway and said, "Look, sweetheart, let's talk inside. Let's all sit down and talk about what happened tonight."

Isabella had prepared coffee and flan for them. She wanted to hear all about the memorial gathering. Isabella was not surprised to learn that Cecilia turned her son's death into an event about herself. She had never been invited to the Castillo home, so it surprised her to hear about all the opulence in the house. She knew that Cecilia was using this moment to hurt Carmen.

Bella told her grandmother about her experience at Cecilia's house, "So, I was overwhelmed by their house. Abuela, there were antique artifacts throughout the home, including silk curtains and gold leaf on the ceiling, as well as marble floors. I don't remember the house being so big and opulent. And this memorial was more like a ball than a time for remembrance. At first, I snuck away to gather myself because I felt angry, overwhelmed, and frankly disgusted with Cecilia and her family. I found their library. Man, I can't tell you how many original books were in there. The shelves were made of solid mahogany and extended from floor to ceiling. She had two types of ladders to reach the books on top. She had a gorgeous ladder made of brass and mahogany wood, along with a circular iron stairwell that led to a landing at the top, where the restricted books were stored. Up there, she had leather high-back chairs for people to sit down.

I noticed a glass bookshelf with a lock on it. When I looked through the glass, I saw weathered, old, large books. Some had spines with dates, and others had spines that had withered away over the centuries. The ones with dates read 1504, 1507, and others up to the twentieth century. Then, the door to the library opened, and I saw Cecilia standing there, staring at me. I pretended that the drink I had made me dizzy and that I needed a quiet place to rest. She bought that. Then she proudly told me about her library and mentioned some of the original books in her collection, including an original Gutenberg Bible."

Everyone reacted to that in surprise.

"That she kept in a separate glass case with a key. She saw that I was standing by the locked bookcase and went on to explain that the books inside were ledgers dating back to the 1500s. She bragged about having a museum representative visit her home every year to inspect the condition of the books."

"Cecilia asked me questions about my mom, then about everyone else. I dodged the questions by asking her more about the authenticity of some of the other books I saw. She then asked me what I did for a living. When I told her I was a lawyer, her attitude toward me shifted to one of fascination. She asked me about the type of lawyer I was. When I told her I was a corporate lawyer, she immediately started talking about her family business and its potential growth. As she spoke, she led me out of the room and back to the party, where she scanned the room to see how her party was going and if any other influential people had arrived while she was with me at the library. She eventually introduced me to her son Manny, and they both began talking about their business and making plans to meet with me to go over some reports."

Carmen looked at Bella. "Bella, why don't you tell Abuela what Cecilia offered you?"

Bella knew that she had to tell her family so that they would understand what she was doing. She didn't want them to think that she let Cecilia corrupt her.

"Well, Cecilia offered me a job with her company."

The reaction was quick from everyone. They all began to talk at once. They asked why Cecilia would do that. There was confusion and anger.

"Wait, everyone, listen. I saw and heard Nayeli tonight."

Amelia was the first to respond, "Did you just say that you saw her tonight?"

Bella nodded her head and said, "Yeah, I did. She was more transparent than she had been before, but it was still her. I also heard her voice in my head, talking to me. I believed that she wanted me to see where it was all heading. I think that's part of my mission. So, I need to follow wherever it leads. Who knows, maybe it will lead to something important. I asked Cecilia if she would allow me to look at some of the company's business mergers, business model, and finances, and she agreed."

Everyone in the room reacted immediately.

"Bella, are you telling me that she wants you so bad that she is willing to let you look at company documents that none of us have ever seen?" Anthony was skeptical about Cecilia's sudden change of heart.

Torry, not a very trusting person, you had to earn her support and loyalty, said, "Yeah, Bella, why would she do that? I mean, I wouldn't trust Cecilia if she turned into a nun. That woman has a plan, and I bet it's going to hurt you just to get back at Carmen."

"Torry is right, Bella. Are you sure that you want to get involved with these people?" Carlos said, worried about Bella.

Bella knew that her family cared about her and was wary of Cecilia. It made her smile. "Uncle Juan Carlos warned me of the same thing. He said that he noticed that Cecilia was spending way too much time talking to me. He said that whatever she was planning would hurt Carmen because she never forgave Carmen for stealing her son away, and he married below his social class."

"Like I said outside, I didn't think going was a good idea, but Carmen, sweetheart, you never showed anger, shock, or sadness as Cecilia talked to Bella, even though you knew that woman was planning something by simply doing that you defeated whatever vile plans she had for you tonight, but now she has a new target, our Bella. Because Cecilia will never forgive you for destroying her plan for Luis and Cassandra."

Carmen looked up at Isabella. "Mami. Who is Casandra?"

"Think back, Carmen. Do you remember our governor's daughter back then? She was like a celebrity. She was always on TV and in the newspapers. She was beautiful, and still is, and the governor and his family were friends with Cecilia y Roberto, while he lived."

Carmen's memories raced as she tried to remember the governor's daughter, Cassandra.

Chapter 25

Isabella sat on the high-back chair that had been in the family for a hundred years. The chair's position allowed her to address everyone directly.

"I have something to tell all of you." Isabella turned her head to face Carmen. "Especially you, Carmen. I know why it is that Cecilia has been holding a grudge against you."

The room reacted immediately. They all began to speak at once. Isabella lowered her hand to indicate that they should listen to what she had to say.

"Carmen, I asked you while we were just outside if you remember Casandra Ramirez?"

Carmen thought hard, but she couldn't remember that name. "No, Mom, who is she?"

"Well, I am not surprised that you don't remember her name."

As Isabella began to tell her story, Bella's hair on her arms and neck stood up. She felt as if the room was closing in on her and struggled to breathe. She thought to herself that this wasn't how Nayeli felt. This presence was different. It was ominous and dark. The air around her smelled of death. She heard thousands of voices screaming. Unknown to Bella, her family was calling her. Antonio tried to shake her, but she didn't respond. Bella felt as if her spirit was leaving her body, and it frightened her. Somehow, Bella was able to hear her brother and mother calling out to her. At first, it seemed as if the voices were coming from a great distance. But as she continued to concentrate on her family's voices, their words sounded louder, and she was able to hear what they were saying.

'Bella, come back to us! Bella, wake up! Bella breathe!'

Bella did not understand what was going on, but she was scared. She focused on her family's voices, and the screaming stopped. She focused on her mother's voice, and the smell of death vanished. Within moments, Bella noticed the air was clear and the room was lit with a warm glow from the lamps. Bella had not been aware that during this time, she had stopped breathing. Bella noticed that she was lying on the sofa, surrounded by her family. They had tears running down their faces. Bella noticed that her mother's face was pale and covered in tears smeared by her eye makeup. Bella took a few deep breaths and coughed. Slowly, she sat up.

Anthony was beside himself, "What the hell happened?"

"Bella, you stopped breathing!" cried Carmen as she grabbed Bella's hands. "I don't think that I had ever been this scared before." Carmen helplessly cried as she hugged her daughter.

Isabella was the one person who tied this family together. At this moment, she wanted answers, but she knew that everyone, including herself, had just experienced a very frightening moment. So, standing where she was, she walked in front of Bella and sat down.

"Everyone, let's calm down and give Bella a moment to gather her thoughts so that she can tell us what happened." Everyone followed her instructions. Anthony went to the mini-bar and poured himself a drink. Torry saw him and asked him to bring the bottle and some glasses. Isabella looked at Bella and spoke to her in a gentle voice, "Bella, sweetheart, I will tell you what we saw happen to you, and then you can tell us what you were experiencing."

Carlos handed Bella a rum and Coke, and she drank it slowly. She felt the warmth of the rum warm her from the inside out. She hadn't realized how cold her body had become. Carmen draped a throw around her to help her warm up. Bella smiled a loving smile at her mother because she knew her mother had always been the one who gave her the most strength when bad things happened.

"Bella, I began to ask your mother if she could remember Casandra Ramirez. I am not surprised that she didn't remember her because your mom had been living in Florida before meeting your father. Carmen, your relationship with Luis was a surprise to all of us. You two fell in love at first sight at a party you attended."

"Yeah, that's right." Carmen said, "My cousin Linda and I went to a party that night. When we got there, it was filled with people, food, and music. I had a great time. But the scene became too much for me, so I stepped outside to get some fresh air. I was admiring the flowers when I noticed your father sitting on a bench outside by the plants. Almost as if he were hiding. Well, he gave me a scare because I hadn't seen anyone there before. He apologized, and we both laughed. We spent the rest of the night walking around the garden, telling jokes, and talking nonsense. I immediately felt an attraction to your father, and he to me. We hadn't even realized what time it was until my cousin came looking for me. I introduced her to Luis, and the three of us spent a few moments talking and discussing my return to Florida. Linda realized that our curfew had come and gone, so she asked for forgiveness and suggested that we go before my mom got mad. Luis quickly asked for my phone number and asked if we could meet up the next day. Oh, I was so excited! I wanted him to ask me for my phone number. I wanted to spend more time with him before I went back home. We spent the last three days of my trip catching up with each other. He took me and my cousin to the beach, El Yunque National Forest, and we went driving the 'pork highway.' We were devastated when we realized that I would be returning to Florida the next morning. That's when he asked me to marry him. He said that he knew that I was the one he wanted to spend his life with. I never knew he came from wealth; we never discussed our families. But I could tell from the way he spoke and the brands of his clothing that he was at least middle class."

Amelia was curious, "So, what did you say?"

Carmen smiled as she looked back at that sweet and romantic time in her life, "At first, I said no because I knew that he had just graduated from the University of Puerto Rico, and I didn't want to hold him back from a career, and I came from a modest family. I also knew that your grandmother would say no. She knew that I wanted to attend college to become a nurse, and marriage would hinder all my plans. He wouldn't hear about it. He gave me this gorgeous engagement ring. He told me that it belonged to his grandmother, and it was his to give to the woman he fell in love with, and that was me."

She looked around at her children and saw that they all had smiles and tears on their faces. "Well, your father was a persuasive man. The next thing we knew, we were standing at the magistrate's office with Linda as our witness. We were married. Luis told me that he told his family and that one day he would introduce me to his mother. That didn't happen until years later. I told your grandmother, and she almost killed me."

Isabella smiled as she thought back to that day. "So, because your mother lived in Florida at the time, she had no idea who our new governor was. Governor Miguel Ramirez was as corrupt as they came. He was pocketing funds that Congress sent to us by signing contracts with developers and trading companies, which made him very rich. He had two kids, a son and a daughter. Casandra Ramirez was his youngest child. She had turned 22 years old when she returned to Puerto Rico after graduating from Harvard University. While here she was shown in news reports attending galas, fundraising banquets, and cutting the ribbons of new businesses her father helped build. On one of those events, the newspapers printed a photo of Casandra at a ball dancing with a handsome young man, Luis Castillo."

Everyone responded at the same time, "What? Our dad hung out with the governor's daughter?"

Carmen was shocked, "Mom, are you telling me that Luis was dating Casandra when we met?"

"Yes, they were the talk in high society. I had noticed that in one of the photos, he looked as if he were detached from what was happening. He looked as if he had been forced to be there. I found out years later, Carmen, that he had been forced to have a relationship with Casandra by Cecilia."

Carmen was confused, "But why?"

"Cecilia was not content with just being wealthy and part of high society. She craved more power. All her children were married with children except Luis. She saw this as a sign that both Luis and Casandra had graduated from college and returned home. So, she set out to bring them together, to have Luis fall in love with her, and to ask her for her hand in marriage. She didn't care about Casandra or her son; her main goal was to connect with the governor's family, where she could influence decisions affecting her business interests. Cecilia planned this union to increase her wealth. She made it clear to Luis that it was his duty to marry Casandra and to help elevate his family's legacy. And then he met you." Isabella looked at Carmen with a warm smile. "You shattered Cecilia's dreams of joining the Ramirez family and establishing herself in a government position." Isabella turned to her grandchildren, "You see, Luis didn't tell his family about Carmen, and Carmen didn't tell us about Luis. The night before we were to return to Florida, she introduced me to Luis as her husband. Oh, I was furious! My daughter married without me being there to walk her down the aisle. She married a stranger and might have just made the biggest mistake of her life. At that moment, I told Carmen that we would talk later, and in the meantime, I welcomed my new son into the family. You see, I trusted Carmen, and if this is the man she chose, it was because she was deeply in love with him and trusted him. Later that afternoon, the rest of the family came by the house to congratulate the newlyweds. Aunts and uncles brought food, a cake, music, and gifts. We turned that night into a wedding celebration and had a wonderful time. Luis came to me to apologize for what happened. He explained that when he thought about separating from Carmen, when she went back to Florida, it scared him. Luis said he felt deep inside that he couldn't let Carmen go, and he promised to love her for the rest of his life. He also told me that he and Carmen planned a church wedding here in Puerto Rico next year for their first anniversary. Luis stayed true to his words. A year later, they had a beautiful church wedding, with the family gathered around her. I noticed that his family did not attend the wedding at all, so I asked the family to sit in the pews so Carmen wouldn't see that his family had rejected her."

Well, I found out that Cecilia had been discussing wedding plans with Cassandra at the same time Luis was dating Carmen. Once Cecilia found out that Luis was secretly married to what she considered a commoner, she disowned him. The word got out to Cassandra and the governor about the marriage. The governor was furious because he, too, had plans to join the Castillo family. In retaliation, the governor signed a bill to limit companies from expanding into other systems of trade with the United States without meeting specific requirements. So, for Cecilia, that was a massive blow to her business practice, and she blamed Carmen. At first, Cecilia's business took a hit when its profit line dropped. That is when she rebranded her company's name and transformed it into an enterprise, allowing her to invest in other business opportunities. You see, Carmen, Cecilia's hatred isn't because you stole her son; it was because Luis's marrying you closed the doors to her joining the governor's family and creating more profits for her company through corruption and manipulation of the Puerto Rican government.

And now I am not surprised that she is luring Bella away from you. She plans to steal your daughter away as you stole her son and her ambitions."

Isabella faced Bella and saw that Bella wasn't pale any longer and seemed relaxed. "Bella, if you feel better, can you tell us what happened?"

Chapter 26

Bella was feeling better. She listened to Isabella's story and thought about how vicious Cecilia was, and she hated being related to a woman who helped herself to riches while ignoring the needs of the poor. Isabella's story also answered so many questions Bella had while growing up.

"Yes, abuela, I feel a lot better. I am glad that you told us that story because frankly, Cecilia's treatment of us while growing up caused me to feel as if it was my fault that my grandmother didn't like me."

Amelia, Antonio, and Carlos reacted in unison, saying the same thing.

"I am sorry. I had only recently discovered this information from a former maid of Cecilia. Go on, dear, please tell us what just happened to you. We are all concerned."

"Well, I heard you ask my mom if she remembered who Casandra was when the room began to get dark. I felt as if the air in the room was being sucked out, and I struggled to take a breath. I heard the terrible sound of people screaming. It was overwhelming. I smelled rotting flesh, and it made me sick to my stomach, and I lost contact with everything. In the darkness, I didn't see any of you, and the sound of the people screaming was so loud that I couldn't focus on what was happening. I felt the hair on my arms and neck stand up, and felt as if something evil was coming to get me. I felt as if I was not tethered to the earth and didn't have a body. I heard deep laughter and felt as if the room was becoming darker and darker. Something was coming for me." As Bella told her family what happened to her, she realized that she was frightened like never before. She looked around the room and out the windows, and although she did not see anything or anyone, she could still remember the evil presence that was coming for her.

"I felt as if something evil was approaching me, ready to get me. I felt desperate because I was in total darkness with no way to reach you all. That's when I heard, amid all the sounds of people screaming, your voices calling me. At first, it felt as if you were all so far away. It was a miracle I even heard you. I tried to focus on where in the darkness the sound was coming from, and then I heard you call my name again, this time a little louder. That's when I saw a small pinpoint of warm, orange light. The sound was coming from that tiny light. In the darkness, I felt someone take my hand and lead me to the light. Although I couldn't see who was guiding me, I could sense it was someone I knew. The light grew brighter, and your voices became louder. As your voices got louder, the screams faded until I couldn't hear them anymore. I felt a strong hand push me into the light, and I was soon back on the sofa in the warmth of my family. Then I woke up and saw all of you with worried looks on your faces."

Carmen spoke first, "Sweetheart, I have never been so scared before as when I looked at your face. You were pale, and your eyes were rolled over, so the whites of your eyes were visible. We all immediately went to you and called out to you. You weren't responding to us."

With a trembling voice, Amelia stated, "Sis, your body was turning cold, and you weren't breathing. Antonio planned to get the car and take you to the hospital, but you know the hospital here is a half hour away. Since you weren't breathing, we thought about laying you down on the floor and doing CPR when your head went back, and you opened your mouth as if you were screaming. We were petrified that you were having a stroke or heart attack when abuela said that what was happening wasn't medical. She and Mom began to pray. Abuela went for her anointed oil and made a cross on your forehead, telling you to come home. She asked us to call out to you and not stop. After a few seconds, you took a breath, then your eyes returned to normal, you blinked a couple of times, and you were back." Amelia couldn't hold back her tears. "What the hell, sis, what happened?"

"I don't know. It came on quickly. But I will tell you that I knew that something was coming for me, something evil."

Antonio broke into the conversation. He had other questions to ask: "Did you see who led you by the hand and who or what pushed you?"

"No, I didn't see anything but the orange glow ahead in the distance."

"Did you feel anything about this force that was leading you?"

Bella was hesitant to answer this question because she felt that it was her father who had taken her by the hand and pushed her into the light. She didn't know how they would react. And she didn't want to believe that, after all these years of him ignoring her, he would show up to help her now. But she couldn't shake the feeling.

"Well, I know this sounds crazy, but I felt Dad's hand take mine." The reaction was immediate. Her siblings said she must be confused and that she was in a state of crisis, so her mind was playing tricks on her. Bella noticed that the moment she mentioned her father, her mother and grandmother reacted by clasping their hands together and praying.

Bella heard Carmen quietly say, 'Thank you, Luis, for giving me back our daughter.'

"Listen, everyone. I don't expect you to believe me because I hardly believe it myself."

Bella saw her grandmother walk out of the room and pick up her phone. It was 11:00 pm—who would she be calling at this hour? "I think that if we all look back into our childhood, we all have memories of Dad holding us by the hand, hugging us, and, for me and Amelia, dancing with us. I am telling you that I felt his hand take mine."

Antonio, still angry with his father, replied immediately, "Well, I for one don't believe that even in death, Father would come to help you. After all, there was a scary time for you, Bella, during your teen years when you needed your father. Luis never came to help you or even make a phone call to talk to you. So, no, I don't believe it."

Amelia turned to Carmen. Isabella was returning to her seat. "What do you both think about what Bella just told us? Could it have been that Luis came to save her?" Amelia couldn't hold her tears at the thought of losing Bella if it hadn't been for this force pushing her into the light.

Carmen looked at her mom for verification before she spoke, "Yes, Amelia, I do believe that your father would have helped her."

"Mom, you still love that bastard, so you would want it to be Luis's spirit helping Bella. But think of all the times we were in need, and he never even called to ask how we were doing."

"Antonio, you didn't know how much Luis loved being a father. Now that I understand the curse better and his family's role in it, it makes some sense why he left us. Not only was he afraid of Nayeli's curse, but he was afraid of what Cecilia would have done if she found out that Bella and Amelia inherited the gift after it seemed to disappear a century ago. Consider Cecilia's personality and her ambition to earn more money and elevate her family to a higher, more affluent status. Ask yourselves what she would have done back then?"

Antonio walked towards the window so as not to show anyone his tear-filled eyes.

"Look, everyone, I get it. I am just as angry with Luis as you all are because if he had just spoken to me and explained about the curse on his family, I am certain that we could have thought of something. But his decision to prioritize his wealth over his children is something that I still struggle to understand. But I don't believe that in a moment where we almost lost Bella, he would not have come to help her."

The front gatebell rang inside the house, making everyone jump.

Carlos was the first to ask, "Who would be coming at this time of the night? Abuela, were you expecting someone?"

Isabela stood up, "Yes, I am. Wait one moment, everyone." A few moments later, Isabela walked in with a priest by her side. "Everyone, this is his Reverend Pablo. He is my priest at the Blessed Madonna Catholic Church."

Everyone greeted him, asked him to take a seat, and offered him coffee and what was left of the flan.

The priest looked at all the faces of the Castillo children and smiled, "You probably don't remember me, but I used to be your priest. I baptized you all."

Being the oldest, Antonio approached the priest first and extended his hand, "Of course, I remember you, Father. It is good to see you again."

Carlos was next to welcome the priest, followed by Amelia. Bella tried to get up when the world spun just slightly. Reverend Pablo gestured to Bella that she didn't need to get up.

Antonio, always the curious one, asked, "Father, it is good to see you, but isn't it late for a house call?"

Reverend Pablo smiled, "Yes, of course, but your grandmother called me because we feared this attack on Bella would occur."

It was Antonio who became alarmed, "What? Abuela, you knew something like this would happen and didn't warn us about it?"

Reverend Pablo used a calming voice, and with a gesture of his hand, he indicated for Antonio to sit down. "Listen, children, there is more to the story to tell. The minute your mother told Isabela of the girls' abilities, I started researching your family's lineage and if there was any written history of the chosen ones."

Bella had a million questions, "Wait, Father, do you mean you researched through church records? Wouldn't that be strange?"

Reverend Pablo explained, "Yes, Bella, through church records. I want you to think back to your childhood. From what you know of your family, they have always been in tune with nature and this place. In the past, your ancestors and community members would have seen a gifted one as someone blessed by God or cursed by the Devil. For either case, they would go to the church for answers and intervention. The church's priests kept detailed records of daily events at the church. We have records that date back to the colonization period of Puerto Rico. It took me several years, but I discovered that the chosen ones were not only provided with a gift of foreknowledge, allowing them to view into the past, speak with and see our long-passed ancestors, but they also possessed the power to influence change. Rio Piedra was a prosperous place, thanks to the help of our chosen ones, for many years. But, without a chosen one this past one hundred years, Rio Piedra had lost its protector."

Isabella handed Father Pablo a coffee.

"Thank you. In the records, I found that some of the chosen ones chose not to get involved and moved out of Rio Piedra. Other chosen ones were not strong enough to be open to Nayeli and push away the evil presence that tried to take Bella away tonight."

Torry asked, "Father, do you know what or who this presence is, and where it comes from?"

Father Pablo put his coffee down on the coffee table. He looked at everyone with stern eyes. They all focused on what the Reverend was about to say, "The presence is pure evil. It manipulates and controls humans to bring about pain, destruction, and fear. This presence sickens men to desire gold, land, and conquest as it did to your ancestor, Ponce de Leon. Men become blind to the pain they cause. A single human would struggle to fight this evil presence alone. The records showed that some chosen ones fell under the power of this dark force and turned away from the light. I found several records of exorcisms that were performed to try to cleanse the evil from those chosen. In 1699, Father Juan Batista spent three days exorcising one of your ancestors, Juana Rodriguez. In the end, he was successful, but the ordeal left him completely drained of energy. You have to understand that Father Batista was only in his 30s, full of life. He documented the daily activities he performed for the people of this town. His writing was optimistic even in troubling times. After the exorcism, he changed."

Isabella noticed how quiet it had become. Everyone was focused entirely on what Father Pablo was telling them. She knew some of this history was dark and scary, almost like the things you see in movies. But she knew that it was all real.

"When he stepped outside the church doors after the exorcism, the crowd waiting outside with candles gasped and prayed. His black hair had turned entirely white, and his face was lined with wrinkles. He looked like he had aged during those three days as he took on the evil force that had attached itself to Juana. He became a recluse afterward, and the Church replaced him with another priest. Sixty years later, another person in the community started showing signs of the same evil. His wife and mother approached the priest to request an exorcist. At that time, things in the Church were changing, aiming to distance itself from medieval and ancient practices. It took the priest several months to get permission from the Church to perform the exorcism, and he had to provide proof that a possession had occurred. The exorcism went well, and the young man fully recovered. Unfortunately, he was mistrusted by the community afterward, and his wife and children were avoided. People feared him because of his transformation and the things he said and did while possessed."

"The church's libraries are filled with daily records of every birth, death, marriage, and tragic events like hurricanes, floods, diseases, and exorcisms. When your grandmother spoke to me about your gifts, I looked into your family history and learned about Nayeli's curse. Years later, I discovered that Luis had left you all and returned to Puerto Rico. Everyone suspected he did it to join the family business and enjoy his wealth. I found it strange because I had spoken to Luis the nights I met with him for the wedding and at each of your baptisms. He often showed me photos of how big his kids were getting. I knew in my heart that your father loved all of you, so moving back in with his family felt wrong. After your father left you and you all came back home to be surrounded by friends and family while dealing with his abandonment, I convinced your grandmother to tell Carmen about Nayeli and her curse."

"Was it you, Father, who gave Abuela Nayeli's diary?" Bella asked.

"No, Bella," Isabella said, "after Father Pablo spoke to me about the chosen ones and the exorcisms in the past, I dug around our attic. As you know, the attic spans the entire length of the house and is filled with boxes and boxes of old paperwork and antique furniture. It took me a few years to find Nayeli's diary and our family's beginnings here in Puerto Rico. I learned about our Taino and African heritage from the diaries and journals others kept. I know that some of our ancestors followed Ponce's push for gold and conquest. This house is several hundred years old and was built in the Spanish style when a family member sought to emphasize their Spanish lineage more than their Taino and African heritage. But, as time went by, our lineage to Africans and Tainos became more important to our ancestors, the love for the land that Nayeli and her people left us became vital to their sense of identity. They were Boricuans. Nayeli's people reclaimed this land and proudly lived as descendants of a great people that were persecuted and murdered for gold and silver."

Father Pablo continued his story, "Together, we spoke to Carmen when you all came back home. As you can imagine, Carmen was beside herself. She yelled at your grandmother that if she had known this, she would have said something to her when her daughters showed signs of having the gift. We had to explain to Carmen that you girls were too young for us to know if Nayeli's gift was with one of you. You see, women with the gift had been present in your family for centuries, but women with Nayeli's gift were rare. Your grandmother immediately contacted me when Nayeli began to show herself to Amelia and Bella."

Amelia reacted, "Wait, wait, Father Pablo, I don't remember ever seeing Nayeli. At least I don't think so."

"When you were very young, you told your mother that there was a lady in your room. And that she was nice to you. You also described this lady. Now, I had never seen Nayeli, of course, but I had read testimonies from others who had seen her, and they described her as an Indian woman with long, black hair and a warm smile on her face. Carmen told me that you began to see her around the time you were three years old. Carmen then told me that Bella had been seeing a woman who matched that description since she was almost two, and she continued to see her for many years. But we now know that Nayeli was contacting Bella in her dreams throughout the years. After that, Bella began to have nightmares that showed Nayeli and other people from different eras. Carmen was worried for Bella, but at that time, Carmen did not know about Nayeli and the family history."

Chapter 27

"And now that you all know your family's history and how Nayeli plays a pivotal role in the protection of her people, you also understand that Amelia and Bella's ability to step into the veil between here and our merciful God's kingdom can expose them to negative forces that still influence our world."

Carmen's children were frozen as they heard Father Pablo speak about natural and supernatural forces. As the oldest, Antonio had felt that he had to protect his family ever since his father abandoned them. His siblings and wife would accuse him of being too controlling in some of his actions. She now sat next to him, wondering how he was feeling, knowing that this was something that he couldn't control. She thought about how scared he must be feeling, knowing that he would no longer be able to protect Bella as he had always done. She leaned into his arms and grabbed his hand. Antonio looked at his wife and knew that she had a sense of what he was thinking. He gave her a weak smile and wrapped his arms around her.

Upstairs, a door slammed, making everyone jump. Isabella was quick to let them know that it must have been the wind that came in at the landing on top of the stairs and the one at the end of the hallway.

Amelia reacted immediately, "Father, will you excuse me? I need to go see if that sound woke up Lulu."

Father Pablo nodded.

"I will go with you." Torry was already standing next to Amelia. After hearing a priest talk about dark forces and the supernatural, she was not going to let Amelia out of her sight.

"You don't need to come with me. I can check on her and be right back."

Torry would not let herself be persuaded; even as Amelia gave her one of her beautiful smiles, which usually convinced Torry to do what she said.

"Are you kidding? Something dark just attacked Bella. They failed, and maybe that was because we were all around her." Torry looked at Bella and the rest of the group before continuing. "I do not want to even think about what would have happened if Bella had been alone and not able to hear us calling her. Do you think I'm going to take a chance that something might happen to you? Nah, Mel, I am going with you."

Bella hadn't thought about that, and her sense of security was diminishing with the more she learned about what was happening to her. A sense of dread came over her as Torry's words rang in her head. Bella could still feel the desperation that she felt when she was surrounded by complete darkness until she saw the tiny ball of warm orange light. What if her family had not been around to call out to her? She remembered that they said that she had stopped breathing during the incident. Bella realized that her life had been in danger. Anxiety was quickly growing inside her. She felt her mother's hand grab hers. She looked beside her and found Carmen had moved to sit by her. Her mother smiled at Bella and, without using a word, gave Bella a sense of reassurance and security. Bella hugged her mom like she hadn't in years. The warmth of her mother's hug reminded her of her childhood and running to her mom's bed after having nightmares. Those feelings reassured Bella and helped lower her anxiety.

Amelia and Torry walked back in to find Father Pablo pulling things out of his bag. Everyone but Isabella and Carmen watched him curiously. Father Pablo placed a couple of sticks of palo santo on the table, followed by a glass jar filled with some black sand, several candles, garlands of rosemary and roses wrapped in ceiba branches, and a necklace with a small bottle of water inside it.

Father Pablo knelt to pray over the items on the table before sitting on the sofa again to address the family.

"Isabella called me immediately after Bella returned to us."

Carlos beat Antonio to the question, "What do you mean she was returned to us?"

"Just exactly that." He turned to Bella. "Bella, have you ever felt like you went somewhere else? Like a place you didn't know, or saw others experiencing things that you wouldn't have known about?"

Bella nodded.

"That's because you can spirit-walk. We know it today as astral projection. Throughout history, people believed that shamans could transcend to the spirit world and communicate with their ancestors. Taino and African peoples practiced shamanism. They lacked a sense of God and the Devil. They believed in nature and our connection to it. They were also able to practice divination that was granted to them through their connection to the earth and the spirit world. Many cultures, including Tanios today, still practice shamanism for healing and divination.

With the introduction of Christianity during the colonial period, the colonists introduced the concept of good versus evil, as well as the ideas of heaven and hell, to the native people of the islands and the

Americas. Christianity and other later-established religions challenged those who practiced shamanism, particularly women. This gift was passed down from mother to daughter, and Christian leaders did not like women to hold that kind of power and influence over the community. The Church relied on making people dependent on their leaders. So, they used the term witchcraft to influence the masses and control women. Luckily, priests and monks kept good records of the things that occurred back then. The church's record showed the atrocities done to women and some men who continued to practice shamanism once Christendom was established throughout the island.

Father Pablo lit the incense burner and swung it back and forth in all four corners of the room as he continued with his story.

"We have to take steps to keep you safe. There are dark forces that seek to harm you to maintain the status quo in Puerto Rico. If people aren't paying attention to what is going on within their communities and government, malicious entities can continue to take what they want and cause pain and hardship. For your safety, Bella, I am going to cleanse the house, and we will set up protective barriers. I will also bless you and Amelia. While you are dealing with Nayeli's mission, I want you to follow my instructions on keeping your space safe from malevolent forces."

Father Pablo had everyone kneel and pray, saying a prayer for protection. He handed everyone a small pouch with what looked like black sand, a book of matches, and a candle.

Bella asked about the black sand. Father Pablo explained that it was black salt mixed with palm ash.

"I blessed this," he said, "it will form a protective barrier around the house." Father Pablo turnsed to face everyone, "take the black salt and sprinkle it on every window and doorway in the house, light the candle, and with a strong, confident voice, pray out loud repeating these lines, 'Only light can enter this house. God's will be done, ' and then blow out the candle."

"Tomorrow, each one of you will take what is left and sprinkle black salt on the exterior property line. I know that Isabella's house is surrounded by thick forest, but you cannot miss any part of the property line. If you don't remember where the property starts and ends, I suggest that Isabella provide you with a map."

Bella noticed that he wasn't addressing her or instructing her with this task. "Father, I don't have enough salt inside my bag. I am going to need more."

Father Pablo stared at Bella in a kind of way that frightened her. "Bella, you are not to leave the house until they are done with their task. You would be alone out there in the woods, and that could be the opportunity it needs to try to take you away." He leaned in to stress the severity of the situation, "No one would know that you needed help, so this time there may not be a light to direct you back home to your family. Please promise me that you will stay safe in the house while they do this."

Bella found herself scared like she had never been before. With wide, frightened eyes, she agreed to do what he said.

Father Pablo continued his instructions. "It is vital that you do not show fear in your voice when you speak the prayer and then blow out the candle." Father Pablo handed out a cord necklace with a small lanyard containing dried flowers. He then handed Amelia and Bella each a garland of dried rosemary and roses. Take these garlands and hang them over your headboard. Amelia, here is an extra one for Lulu. I understand that she can see Nayeli as well, so let's start taking steps to protect her."

The idea of something happening to her little girl made Amelia angry. "Yes, Father, I will. I have to admit that I hadn't thought about something happening to Lulu. Thank you, Father."

Everyone took the supplies the priest handed them and dispersed throughout the house. Carmen, Isabela, and Antonio's wife, Maria, worked on cleansing the first floor while everyone else went upstairs. Antonio went to the attic. One by one, they laid the salt down, placed the candles, said their prayer, and blew out the candles.

Bella was able to hear Father Pablo walking around the first floor, reciting God's prayer. By the time she was done with the windows she had been responsible for, she saw Father Pablo finish his blessing, then begin to make the sign of the cross with anointed oil over every archway. As the priest moved upstairs, Bella felt that the air around her seemed lighter. There was the scent of flowers in the air. One by one, they all gathered back in the family room and waited for their priest to return.

Bella knew that her mom was religious and still followed the Catholic faith, but she couldn't remember a time when she saw her mom have a priest bless their house or discuss curses and place relics around the house to ward off evil spirits. She and her siblings turned away from faithfully practicing any religion after their father walked away from them. Throughout the years, Bella would ask, "What kind of God lets a man walk out on his family?" And now she felt immense gratitude for Father Pablo's presence. Bella accepted her supernatural abilities. She had always believed there was good in the world, and now, after her spirit was pulled into the darkness, she truly believed in evil.

Isabella took a deep breath and slowly released it.

"Do you all feel that?"

Antonio and Torry took deep breaths and looked around the room. There was something different about the room and the rest of the house.

"Yeah, something is different, but I can't put my finger on it," Antonio said as he began to pace the room. He looked in every corner of the room and out the windows. He noticed that Father Pablo was outside praying and placing potted plants around the yard.

"Hey, what is Father Pablo doing?"

Everyone rushed to the windows. Isabella knew what he was doing and was grateful that Father Pablo was so thorough.

"He is placing strong herbs, mainly sage, throughout the yard to keep negative spirits from invading our property. He is using the same plants that he burned tonight." Isabella faced Bella, "But don't worry, he is only warding off evil spirits. Our ancestors' spirits will always be on this property."

Bella was glad to hear that from her grandmother. She recognized that throughout her life, she had been dreaming and seeing the spirits of her ancestors. And now that she knew who they were and why they were here, she wasn't sure if she wanted all of that to stop.

Bella craved a normal life without faces in the dark staring at her or people being slaughtered in her dreams. But now that she understood the severity of the situation and saw the evils that her paternal family had committed throughout the years, she wanted to help her ancestors, protect the land they had saved for them, and pay back Cecilia and her family for the pain they had continued to cause to people. Bella suspected that somehow, Cecilia and her company were part of the problem that she must figure out.

Father Pablo walked into the room. He gestured to everyone to gather around him, hold hands, and together recite The Lord's Prayer to close the blessing.

In a quiet tone, they discussed the things they would need to do regularly to keep themselves safe.

"So, is everyone here aware of what happened tonight?"

"Frankly, Father, I am still confused," Antonio said as he passed his hand through his hair repeatedly. "What was all of this?" He looked at his mother, "Mom, I didn't know that you believed in this kind of stuff."

Carmen smiled, "I think that moving to Florida and acclimating to the American culture, you learn to rely less and less on the old-world beliefs, and after your father left us, I had to work a lot and make time for all of your needs. I didn't have time to teach you all our family's old beliefs."

Father Pablo asked again, "Do any of you doubt what happened tonight?"

Everyone shook their head and said no.

He continued, "Good because there cannot be any doubt that Bella was taken from us, and if it hadn't been for the spirit's intervention, Bella would have been lost. A powerful spirit was able to reach into our realm and pull her spirit out of her body. It was fortunate that your grandmother called me immediately. As Bella is becoming more and more aware of her abilities, the evil that has been around your family for centuries will try to stop her from completing her task." Father Pablo faced Bella, "Bella, you must be very close to figuring out why your ancestors' land is in danger. Keep searching, follow your instincts, and find Nayeli, as it's vital for everyone's security. I want to thank everyone for following my instructions without questioning my actions or being resistant to the blessing of the home. From now on, everyone must follow these instructions. First, the plants I strategically placed around the property must be planted and properly cared for. The plants form a barrier that only good spirits can pass through. Nothing evil can pass or even exist where these plants grow. Be aware that you cannot neglect the herbs. Evil spirits will continue to push themselves into this world. If you notice leaves turning brown, even after watering and fertilizing them, it means that your barrier is weakening. If that happens, replace the herbs because the malevolent forces have weakened their protective barriers. Also, plant them throughout this hill. I have placed more of these herbs throughout the hill, but they require constant monitoring, and I admit that I haven't always been able to do that."

Bella realized that she had seen those plants before, "Wait, Mom, you had these bushes in your garden in our old house. In fact, you put potted plants outside my apartment window, even though I had told you that my landlord would not allow it. Oddly, he never said anything about the plants."

Carmen smiled, "As soon as I realized that you and Amelia were born with our family's gift, I knew that I had to take steps to protect you. I contacted your grandmother and Father Pablo. He recommended that I monitor your abilities and protect you girls by creating a barrier. That is why you saw Nayeli and other ancestors and not these evil spirits that are trying to stop you now."

Antonio and Amelia realized that Bella was right. Their mother had gifted them sage plants whenever they moved into a new home. Amelia now understood why her mom insisted on planting herbs under every window and hanging herbs by the front and back doors. She was setting the barrier of protection for Lulu and herself.

Father Pablo continued, "Secondly, once a month, we will have to bless this house and each other. Amelia, Torry, and Bella, please follow the same instructions when you return to North Carolina and wherever you move to. And finally, Amelia and Bella, you must practice mindfulness practices such as Tai Chi and meditation. By setting time out of your busy day to do this, you will be more in tune with your surroundings, it will help relieve anxiety, and heighten your abilities. Bella, you must be completely in control of your abilities while meditating, or you could be overwhelmed by any wandering spirit. You two are like bright lights in that darkness, but you, Bella, you are like a lighthouse that they will head towards. Learn to set boundaries before and after your daily meditation. You both need to start this while you are here in Puerto Rico. Amelia, you must teach Lulu how to be mindful because I suspect that she was born with the same abilities. From everything I read in the church's archives, Nayeli only appears to her descendants sporadically. Still, when Isabella and Carmen mentioned to me that Lulu shows signs of abilities, it means that she may have her own destiny to fulfill."

Amelia immediately said, "Oh God Father, do you think that Lulu will have to deal with the same things Bella has been dealing with?"

"Well, I can't tell you what will happen in the future, but your family's ability is common with the women of your family, but the strength of the ability is determined by what is happening or will happen. From what I understand, Lulu can see Nayeli. My best suggestion is not to hide her ability, but to help her strengthen it and set boundaries for herself. That way, she will be prepared and won't run away because she fears what she may not understand," stated Father Pablo.

Bella felt a pang of emotional pain because she remembered her teen years. "You mean like I did. I ran away from my family, I made friends with the wrong type of people, and my fears and anxieties led me to experiment with drugs. I didn't understand why I was different from other teens. I even thought that I was crazy, and I didn't make any friends because I was afraid that they would think that I was crazy and abandon me."

Antonio, Carlos, Amelia, and Torry together hugged their little sister. Each of them filled her with words of affirmation and how grateful they were that she wasn't completely lost to them during those years.

Amelia faced Father Pablo, "I promise Father that Torry and I will prepare her and teach her what she needs to do to protect herself."

Father Pablo stood up. It was 1:30 am, and he was tired. From the looks of it, everyone looked exhausted. Bella was still a little pale, but it was no wonder, since she had experienced what many living people cannot: the transitional void between the living and the eternal.

"I suggest that everyone get some rest. Be assured that nothing will harm you tonight. I will check on you in a couple of days. Please plant the bushes, and you girls start researching meditation techniques."

Amelia and Bella responded immediately, "We will, Father. Thank you for your help and guidance today."

Bella added, "Thanks to you, I know that I will be safe tonight."

Father Pablo smiled and said his goodbyes.

Chapter 28

Bella woke to the sound of birds outside her window and the smell of coffee in the kitchen. For once, she felt energized after waking. Although she had been in danger the night before, she now had a renewed sense of strength and focus. She headed downstairs to find her family sitting at the dining room table, enjoying breakfast. They immediately greeted her, and Carmen set a plate for her at the table.

"How did you sleep, Bella? Any nightmares?" Carmen asked as she prepared Bella's tea. Carmen could see that Bella was still pale, and that worried her. She knew that her experience may have drained her more than they all thought.

"Mami, what kind of coffee is this?" Bella asked as she held her nose over the cup.

"It's not coffee, Bella, it's a special tea to help your defenses. Father Pablo sent it to us this morning. He said that you will be 'drained' for a couple of days. It tea is a combination of herbs high in nutrients, particularly iron and vitamin B."

Bella took a sip, and the flavor of dirt, mown grass, pepper, and spearmint flooded her mouth. She spit it back into the cup. "Mom, this tastes terrible! Is everyone drinking this thing?" Everyone around the table shook their heads.

Amelia smiled, "No, sis. You are the only one who has to drink that. I am sure that it tastes as bad as it smells, but you have to drink it to get your strength back."

Isabella walked over and placed a dish of sliced lemon next to Bella, "Squeeze some of this in it, Bella, the vitamin C will help your body absorb the other vitamins." She lightly smacked Bella on the shoulder. "And drink it all, it's good for you." In her mind, she was six again with a cup of onion tea in front of her, her mother's miracle cure for a cold. Then, like now, her siblings sat around the table staring at her. All of them eager to watch her choke down the remedy.

Bella squeezed the entire plate of lemons into the cup, then added sugar. She drank it as fast as possible, and she slammed the cup down on the table. Head held high, she stared at her siblings and stuck out her tongue.

"Geez, what are you five?" Antonio asked.

Isabella set a plate of food in front of Bella.

"See, Bella, it wasn't that bad," her grandmother said.

While Bella ate, they discussed how different things were now that they understood how they could help Bella. Soon, the conversation shifted to the wake. Carlos explained that, regardless of what Luis did to them, going to the wake was a good way to have closure with the part of their childhood that had the most traumatic impact on their lives. They all agreed to support each other and attend the wake. In the meantime, they decided to take Lulu sightseeing by taking her to the beach and Old San Juan to pick up souvenirs.

The phone rang, and Isabella went to answer it. "Oh, Manuelito, how are you? Good to hear it. Yes, she is here. Hold on a minute, and I will get her." Isabella turned to face Bella. "Bella, mija, it's Manuel on the phone." All talking ceased. Everyone was curious as to why their uncle would be calling.

Bella thanked her grandmother and answered the phone. "Hi, Uncle Manuel, what can I do for you? Are you sure? Well, that makes sense. Not today, we are taking Lulu to the beach. Can I come tomorrow before the wake? That's great. I will see you then."

Antonio couldn't wait any longer to find out what their uncle wanted from Bella. "Well, what did he say? Why did he call you?"

Bella noticed that everyone was staring at her. "Oh, he finally invited me to go to their home office to go over the company's ledgers and business plan."

"I can't believe you would want to be around those people. Are you going to go?" Carlos said.

"Yeah, I am because something is telling me that they are the source behind Nayeli's awakening. He wanted me to go today, but I told him that I could go early tomorrow before the wake, and we could review the books in the morning. He agreed to that. Boy, what a loving, devoted brother that he wants to do business on the day of his brother's wake."

"Yeah, there is no love lost there. Manuel only cares about Manuel. The whole family is like that." Isabella said.

"Well, I told him tomorrow so that we can enjoy Puerto Rico today, and I wanted to go visit Magaly today. I haven't seen her since we arrived in Puerto Rico. Olga explained to me that Magaly had been ill and was still recovering. So, I thought that I could go visit her."

Isabella was glad that her grandchildren were making time to see their other family members. "Oh, that's wonderful, Bella. Let me give you the bone soup I made for her yesterday so that you can take it to her. I intended to ask one of you to take it, although I can still walk up this hill, I get tired faster. I am getting old, you know."

Everyone laughed because their grandmother still looked very young for her age and was a force to be reckoned with. Isabella packed the soup in a travel container and handed it to Bella.

As Bella walked up the hill to Magaly's house, she was greeted by family members and friends, including Olga. She stopped at Olga's fence to talk to her. "Olga, how is your mother?"

"She is about the same, Bella. It's not only her failing physical health, I think it's also depression."

"What makes you say that?"

"Think about it, Bella. Rio Piedra has changed a lot. There are more homeless people on the streets. Hurricane Maria forced some of our friends and family to leave for America because they lost their homes and jobs. You have no idea how grateful we all are that your family helped us during those difficult times. Isabella distributed the food, clothes, and money that you all sent to her to give to us. This place looks very different than how it looked when my mother was growing up and raising us. Many of her friends left or died after the hurricane, and the government forgot about us. That resulted in abandoned houses, and the crime rate went up. I keep suggesting to her that she see a counselor, but she refuses to go." Olga noticed that Bella was carrying something. "Hey, what's in the container? Are you going somewhere?"

"Yeah, you told me that Magaly was sick, so my grandmother made her bone soup. I wanted to go see her since she is too sick to come see us."

"It will make her happy to see you. Magaly was such a strong woman, so very joyful. She got sick with COVID, and she has struggled to regain her strength ever since. We all take turns caring for her because her son is still in the Army and is stationed in Germany.

But he calls her almost every day, and he sends her money so she can get her medicine and pay the power bill. I'll talk to you later."

"OK, I will go see her now. Oh, hey, we're taking Lulu to the beach. Do you want to come with us?"

Olga became excited to have been invited. "Ay Prima, I wish I could, I don't get out to do fun things anymore. Today, my mom's health nurse is out, I need to take care of her, but when I can, I will see if I can get up hill to see if Magaly needs anything."

Bella sighed as she headed back up the hill. Walking down from her grandmother's house to Olga's had been easy compared to the steep hill now in front of her. By the time she reached the top of the mountain, she was out of breath, and she realized how out of shape she was. She remembered Magaly's house as a brightly colored house with flowers in her front yard. Bella was shocked that the garden was overgrown and dried up. The walls were no longer painted in bright colors, and there was mold on the exterior wall, likely also inside the home. A blue tarp still covered most of the roof. Heading to the door, Bella had to be careful where she stepped. Fallen trees lay all over the yard. Some of them were already decaying; they must have been from Hurricane Maria. "Magaly, are you home? It's Bella."

Bella heard a low voice from beyond the small house's iron security door.

"Bella, you came. Yes, I am home. Push the door open."

Bella noticed that had dishes on almost every surface, and trash bins overflowing with garbage. All the windows were closed, and unpleasant smells floated in the air. Bella heard the sound of a television coming from a back room. As she walked further inside, she found her cousin on a bed surrounded by clothes and sheets.

"Magaly, I heard that you are not feeling well, so I came to see you."

Magaly sat up in bed and smiled so earnestly that it made Bella sad.

"Thank you, Bella, for visiting me. You have no idea how happy it makes me feel! I was told that you and your family were in Rio Piedra for your father's funeral, and I planned to make my way down the hill."

"Don't you worry about visiting us. We can definitely visit you. Oh, and Abuelita made a bone soup for you, and she also sent a piece of bread and an avocado. Are you hungry? Let me heat it up for you. I will be right back."

Magaly heard Bella washing dishes and smelled the delicious soup heating up. She went to clean herself up and then cleared some space in the living room. It wasn't often anymore that she had a visit from a distant family. Having Bella there filled her with energy and excitement. She felt a bit embarrassed about having her house in such a messy state.

"Bella, I am sorry that the house is such a mess. I meant to clean, but I don't have the energy to do it. I will start cleaning one of the rooms and feel drained because of the effort."

Bella set Magaly's bowl of soup on the coffee table and cut the bread and avocado.

"OK, Magaly. Enjoy. You know that Abuelita is going to ask if you liked it."

Magaly chuckled, "You're right. From the smell of it, I know that it's going to be great!"

Bella asked her what had been happening since the last time they saw each other. Magaly talked about the hurricane, her husband's death from pneumonia, and how, without jobs in Rio Piedra, her son Alberto joined the Army. She expressed pride in her son for turning a military life into a career. Magaly mentioned Alberto's girlfriend and her excitement for her son. She also spoke about contracting COVID and how the virus took many Puerto Ricans. Bella noticed Magaly's energy fade as she discussed the virus and the family and friends she lost. Magaly shared her realization that she was just a shell of her former self and couldn't seem to become her old self again.

"Of course, you lost yourself. You have gone through a lot! In a way, you lost your husband and your son because the military keeps him away from you. You may be experiencing depression and the chronic effects of COVID. Have you seen a doctor?"

Magaly shook her head. "I only saw the doctor at the community clinic, and she prescribed some medicine. But I need a specialist, and unfortunately, I can't afford one. Our state insurance isn't very good, you know."

Bella could relate to that. "I don't think any insurance is good. They are happy to take your money, but they don't like to pay for your medical care. It's all a joke. What about a psychotherapist to treat your depression? Are you seeing a therapist?"

Magaly looked offended. "Not you too, Bella. Everyone wants me to see a therapist, even my son, but I am not crazy."

Bella held her hands, and in a calm and compassionate tone, she pushed further. "Are you calling me crazy, Magaly?"

The question stunned Magaly. "Absolutely not! You are not crazy. You are smart and kind. You are not the one people consider to be crazy."

Oh no, did you forget about my behavior problems as a teen? I want you to know that I started seeing a therapist a few years ago after I had an anxiety attack in court. Yeah, I froze in the courtroom, struggled to breathe, and fainted. After ruling out all kinds of illnesses and disorders, my doctor suggested that I see a psychotherapist. I thought the same as you — that he was telling me I was crazy. But I went to see her and discovered that she was good at listening, and I started talking about my childhood. A few sessions later, we discussed what happened in court that day. She and I worked on my coping skills and sleep issues. I still see her once a month. She has helped me immensely.

"I didn't call you crazy, Magaly. I just suggested it because my depression and anxiety prevented me from truly living. I had no friends, and honestly, I didn't even want to socialize with my family. It was a struggle for me to groom myself or keep my home clean. But after a couple of months working with my therapist, I noticed I was talking with coworkers more often, and I was actually happy to see Amelia and Torry when they visited me. Magaly, therapy has really improved my life."

"Really, Bella? You feel better?"

Bella nodded.

"OK, I will see if my insurance covers a therapist."

Bella was happy for Magaly when she looked at the pile of mail at the end of the coffee table. Bella recognized the envelope.

"Magaly, is this the same letter Olga received in the mail about the property being sold?"

Magaly looked at the envelope and instantly became mad.

"Yup! Those bastards sold our properties and land to some corporation, and now we have to present ownership of our homes or leave. Can you imagine? Me leaving my mother's house? And, go where? I don't have money, and I don't want to live anywhere else. I was born in Rio Piedra, and I will die here."

Bella remembered what Olga told her about her mother's house. "Magaly, do you have the deed to your house?"

Magaly stood up to show Bella all the documents piled on the table. "No, Bella. This was my mother's house and my grandmother's house.

This house has been in our family for over seventy years. Things were different then. People paid for a house in cash, and it was understood that it was their house. I didn't think that they had the right to kick people out of their homes."

Bella noticed that Magaly's joy was suddenly gone. "Can I borrow that letter? Olga lent me her letter, too. You know that I am a lawyer, and I want to check on the legality of these letters."

"Yes, you can have it. I forgot that you are an attorney. If you find anything that can help me keep my house, please let me know."

"I promise."

They spent some time reminiscing about the Rio Piedras in which they had grown up and discussing the families and friends that had left the island. It seemed to Bella like every family had someone who left the island. Many were forced to leave for work simply so they could send money back to those they left behind. As the conversation became melancholy, Bella shifted the topic.

As Bella spoke about her siblings and their children, she saw Magaly's face soften with quiet joy, as if she missed a house full of children she once had.

"I'm sure Amelia will be happy to bring Lulu by so you can see how much she has grown," she said as she stood, "but that reminds me, I have to get back, we promised her a trip to the beach."

Magaly stood and walked Bella to the door. Her steps were firm and confident, unlike those she made when Bella first arrived.

"Bella, please revisit me. And tell your brothers and sisters to visit me. I heard that Amelia has an adorable little girl. I promise that I will clean the house to make it safe for your niece to come visit me."

"Absolutely, Magaly! I promise."

Bella leafed through the papers Magaly had loaned her as she walked back to her grandmother's house. She couldn't shake the nagging suspicion that someone was involved in something corrupt, but she couldn't quite figure out why. Why were they forcing people out of their homes? Money seemed like too simple an explanation; there had to be more to it than just corrupt politicians and greedy corporations. Her thoughts drifted to what might happen to her friends and family if they couldn't find the deeds to their property. Bella made a mental note to talk to Laura and see if there was anything the firm could discover. Before stepping into her grandmother's house, she looked at the letter again. She paid close attention to the logo at the top of the page and the P.O. Box address. Bella knew that one reason private companies use P.O. Boxes is to stay anonymous. One thing was sure: the P.O. Box was in Texas. She remembered Cecilia and Manuel bragging about their new office in Texas. Could all of this be Cecilia's doing? Bella hated to think that Cecilia could be so desperate for money and power that she would betray her fellow Puerto Ricans. Considering what Isabella had told her about her plans for Luis and Cassandra, she realized it might also be another way for Cecilia to get back at Carmen.

As she entered Isabela's house, Lulu ran up and wrapped her arms around Bella's legs in a hug, almost knocking them both to the floor. Lulu stepped back after a moment and held her hands out to her sides.

"Look, Titi, my mommy bought me this bathing suit, hat, and a bucket with a shovel. I am so excited." Lulu looked over Bella and didn't see a bathing suit. "Are you ready? Where is your bathing suit?"

"You are so clever." Bella lifted her shirt. "But see, I am already wearing my bathing suit, and I have a cooler with snacks. Are your mommies ready to go?"

Bella heard her sister coming down the stairs.

"Yup, we are ready to go. Abuela isn't coming. She said that she has to go check on some friends to see if they found any documentation that they could take to the Department of Housing." Amelia held a beach bag over one shoulder. "Torry is getting the car, and Mom is talking to Angel and Olga to see if they are ready as well."

"Ooh, that's great!"

Isabella walked out of the kitchen and handed everyone a silver chain with a small vial pendant filled with some of the same herbs and the black salt Father Pablo used to cleanse the house.

"Wait, everyone, Father Pablo sent these chains for everyone to wear. He said these will keep you safe when you are not home." Isabella handed one to everyone and showed the group that she was already wearing hers.

Bella thanked her grandmother. "Thank you, Abuela. By the way, Amelia told me that you are going to visit with some friends and family."

Isabella nodded.

"Good, can you please go visit Magaly. I visited her today, and she became super excited and energized. She needs help with home repairs and cleaning her house. Maybe you can ask some of the family to help her. And Mel, she really got excited when I told her how big Lulu has gotten. Could you find some time to take her by for a visit? I think she misses her son. I'm sure it will do her good to get a visit from all of us."

"Yeah, Bel, no problem. Torry and I will take Lulu to meet Magaly tonight."

Isabella felt proud of her grandchildren. Despite the hardships they had faced after Luis abandoned them, they grew up to be considerate and passionate adults. She felt a pang of sadness at the thought of everyone leaving next week. In the meantime, she would enjoy every day she had left with them.

Chapter 29

Lulu bounced in her seat with excitement as she stared out of the car window. She constantly asked for the names of statues and parks, and repeatedly asked if they were almost to the beach. Torry handed Lulu a pair of child-size sunglasses.

"Lulu, Puerto Rico is very sunny. I want you to wear sunglasses and a hat to protect your eyes."

Lulu followed Torry's instructions and asked Bella how she looked.

"Lulu, you look grown up." Bella gave her a high-five.

Lulu beamed with confidence. She started wiggling in her seat. Bella smiled as she realized Lulu was dancing to the music coming through the car windows. It seemed like every street they drove through had a new song playing along it.

"Why's everyone playing music?" Lulu asked. "Is it a holiday?"

"No," Bella told her, "the music is coming from everywhere because people enjoy listening to music, dancing, and spending time with friends. Music is part of us." She took a deep breath. "Do you smell food? That smell is coming from the many food trucks, restaurants, and vendors selling traditional Puerto Rican food. Smells good, right?"

Lulu nodded her head. "Yeah, it's making me hungry. It smells yummy."

Bella was captivated by the sound of music and the chatter of people walking up and down the streets, talking to friends. As they drove into San Juan, Bella saw the clear, emerald water of the beaches on the horizon. She knew Puerto Rican beaches were among the most beautiful in the world.

"Look, Lulu, the beach." Bella pointed to show Lulu the emerald waters.

Lulu began bouncing up and down in her chair again. She stopped suddenly, a look of wonder on her face.

"Titi, why is the color of the water green and blue? It's so pretty."

"Well, during late Spring to early Fall, the beaches are very shallow. The water appears to be emerald green glass, and it is quite warm. You know, when we went to the beaches of North Carolina, the water was dark green-gray, almost blue, and it was not very warm. The beaches in Puerto Rico are gorgeous and clear. They are great for swimming and snorkeling. Your mommy brought your snorkeling mask, and you will be able to see small, pretty fish swimming along the coast."

"Are we there yet?"

"Yeah, kind of. Before we go pick out a spot on the sand to set up our picnic, we are going to Old San Juan to have lunch, take photos, and buy some souvenirs."

Amelia parked her car in the parking deck in Old San Juan. Bella grabbed Lulu's hand to help her walk on the cobble streets and to keep Lulu safe.

"So, some of the streets are narrow and they wind up and down small hills and slopes. So, while we are here, you must take one of our hands. Is that ok, Lulu?"

Lulu stopped and pointed to the structure in front of her. "Is that a castle? Are we in a castle?"

Bella wasn't sure how to explain the Old Spanish Wall to a five-year-old without giving her nightmares. She knew that the history of colonization was complicated, and she tried to simplify it in her mind, to remove the bloody massacres, the mistreatment, and the near extinction of the native people. She stood frozen as she tried to sanitize it for a young mind, but just couldn't see how to. After a moment, Torry rescued her. She knelt next to Lulu and explained.

"Those are the garitas, little houses where soldiers used to stand watch to look out for ships. Do you remember when we talked about the Spanish Conquistadores?"

"The guys with the funny helmets?" Lulu asked.

"That's right, when they came to the Island, they built forts to protect the colonists who lived here. They connected them with a big wall so they could see ships coming. There are more than fifty garitas all around the city."

Bella mouthed a heartfelt thank you to Torry for the assist as they changed direction and walked toward the garita.

"Been sneaking off to tour the island on us?" Amelia asked her wife.

Torry grinned, "What I'm not allowed to take an interest in the Island the love of my life was born on?"

"Not at all. What you're not allowed to do is run off on tours without me."

Torry laughed.

"It wasn't from a tour, well, I guess in a way it was. The first time you brought me here, we went to El Morro. I bought a book about the castle's history in the gift shop, and Torry shrugged, "I guess I finally got around to reading it."

Amelia took photos of Lulu standing in front of the turret, trying to climb a palm tree, and chasing one of the island's orange iguanas with Torry. Amelia found it quietly rewarding to see Lulu adapt to the island's raw, untamed nature.

Bella took in the beauty of Old San Juan. Its Spanish colonial architecture and the roots of the island's indigenous peoples seemed to seep into her spirit as she walked its streets. Even though some buildings could have used a fresh coat of paint, Old San Juan was full of positive energy. As they walked, she felt a cool breeze from the sea wash over her, and she found herself relaxing like a weight she hadn't known she carried had been lifted from her. A soft smile began to play around her lips.

Amelia put her arm around Bella. It had been so long since she had seen Bella so relaxed and even happy. "Hey sis, we made reservations at Raices. It's a couple of blocks up the hill. Are you ready for lunch?"

"Absolutely, I'm starving. We've done so much walking since we got here. I never walk like this in North Carolina. I'm glad that I brought my sneakers."

"You know, Puerto Rico looks good on you," Amelia told her, "I haven't seen you smile like this in a long time, you're practically shining."

"Yeah? I guess it's because I feel the sense of community here. I feel like everyone around me is happy to be here, and they all accept me as part of their world. I don't just mean the family; even strangers I've bumped into treat me like I'm someone they know, or someone they want to know. It's so different than up North."

Amelia nodded. She understood how Bella felt. She thought about the conversation they had with the family about how living in the States felt like a trap. Maybe no one around them in the North was happy because they all found themselves trapped in the same endless cycle.

Torry ran past them, chasing Lulu. When she caught her, she spun her around several times, laughing, before she placed her on her shoulders so that she could see over the promontory and out to sea. Coconuts hung heavy from the palm trees around them, and the hibiscus bushes were full of brightly colored flowers. Torry thought that the scene was breathtaking; she admired the skill that went into building many of these structures, some of which had endured for centuries. She was inspired to sketch the landscape. Setting Lulu down, she took out her phone and took photos of the turrets, the cannons, and Lulu trying to pick up a cannonball. As she went to send that one to Amelia's phone, she saw the time.

"Amelia, it's 1:00 pm, and I think the restaurant is a few blocks up. Let's save souvenir shopping for after lunch." Torry showed Amelia the tourist map to indicate where *Raíces* was located.

"Yes, Mama, I am hungry, and I want to go play at the beach."

"Alright, alright, let's go. I am getting hungry too."

The group arrived at the restaurant just on time for their reservation.

"Wow! Mama, it smells so good in here." Lulu ran to touch the palms that decorated the inside of the restaurant. "Mama, look at these palms and flowers. They are so pretty."

The hostess sat them at a window seat. Bella looked around and couldn't help smiling because of the décor. The restaurant was decorated in *Jíbaro* style with paintings of banana harvests and the streets of Old San Juan. Straw hats and farm tools hung on every wall, with clay and wooden jugs sitting on every spare flat surface. It looked as if the restaurant was celebrating the working class while still embracing all the people who make up Puerto Rican history.

Torry and Amelia toasted with piña coladas. Lulu joined them, tapping everyone's glass with her pineapple juice. They took turns telling riddles to each other, and their laughter soon rang across the restaurant. When Lulu's plate was clear, she turned to Torry.

"Thank you for lunch, Mama. Can we go to the beach now?"

Everyone laughed.

"Yes, Lulu. Let's go."

The sight of the emerald green beaches took her breath away. It felt familiar to Bella. The smell of salt hung in the air. Although it was a hot day, the breeze felt wonderful on Bella's face. Living in North Carolina, Bella forgot how blue the Puerto Rican sky was and how clear the beaches were.

Puerto Rico is indeed the Island of Enchantment, she thought.

They spent the afternoon swimming, snorkeling, and buying food and souvenirs from the vendors who walked up and down the beach. Bella, Amelia, and Torry noticed the many new condos that had been built recently. It had been a few years since their last visit to San Juan, and it had grown. But the island still had some beautiful and quiet beaches available for those who dislike crowded beaches.

Vendors walked up and down the beach, yelling about the goods they had for sale: cold cut coconuts, Puerto Rican icees, snorkeling equipment, boogie boards, and delicious-smelling traditional food that enticed the appetite. Bella sat on the shore, and the waves tickled her feet. She thought to herself how relaxing it was just to sit there, watch her family swim and play with Lulu, and not think about any problems. Today was a day for relaxing and having fun. Bella wished that Carmen had come with them, but Carmen was going to assist Cecilia with Luis's funeral arrangements.

At first, Cecilia rejected Carmen's offer of assistance, but then changed her mind and asked Carmen to come to the house to make plans. Bella felt a sense of mistrust that Cecilia had changed her mind, but at this moment, she was glad to be at the beach rather than at Cecilia's house.

Bella watched families snorkeling, teaching children to swim, and splashing around. She couldn't help but smile when she saw Amelia and Torry doing those same things with Lulu. The air was salty and cool under the palm trees. Music, salsa, and merengue rang all around the beach as people celebrated, danced, and enjoyed food from their grills.

Torry called out to Bella, taking her out of her reverie of peace and joy, and signaled for her attention.

"Hey, what's up, Torry?"

Torry smiled. She hadn't seen Bella this relaxed and happy in a very long time. "Bella, your smile looks good on you. I can see that being back home has done you a lot of good."

Bella nodded and looked around. "Yeah, I do feel like I am at home here. Look all around you, Torry, life! People are enjoying the beauty of this island with family and friends. There is music in the air, the waves are calm, the beach is a light emerald green, and I can feel my connection to the land." She lifted a handful of sand and let it sprinkle through her fingers. "Of course, I am happy."

Torry looked at the families playing with their children, young couples walking on the beach, and teens splashing each other in the water. Bella was right, the scene was like something from a movie. "Yeah, you are right. It's almost as if the troubles of the world are gone from this place and people can be people, enjoying what life has to offer." Torry looked at Bella, "So, hey, we are going to have a snack and then put Lulu down for a nap. Can you help by getting us some food and drinks? I will set up our beach towels and a place for Lulu to sleep."

Bella agreed and went to find vendors offering food. The variety was so great that Bella wanted to buy a little bit of everything. The many vendors along the beach provided a foodie's paradise of traditional and savory Puerto Rican food. While walking along the coast, people greeted her and wished her a good day. Bella thought about how different it all was compared to living in the States, where people are more individualistic and are often wary of strangers. Bella was happily returning salutations when she spotted two vendors; One sold sodas, fresh fruit juices, and cold coconut water, the other sold *alcapurrias* and roast pork shoulder in onions on a Puerto Rican bread. Bella bought tamarind and mango juice, three *alcapurrias*, and one pork sandwich because they were big sandwiches. On the way back to her family, Bella spotted another vendor selling grilled *salchicon* with yucca fries.

Bella returned with her bounty and saw Amelia washing the salt water off Lulu. Lulu saw Bella and ran to her.

"What did you buy for me, Titi?"

"For you? Oh, I didn't realize that I was buying food for you."

"Nah, I know that you bought me food cause mommy told me."

Bella laughed, "You are too smart for my jokes. Yes, yes, I found some tasty food for us to share."

"Did you invite the whole beach?" Torry asked, looking at all the food Bella had brought. "I said a snack, not second lunch."

Bella shrugged. "She's a growing child. Besides, I wanted to try everything."

The group enjoyed their snack. Lulu ate and fell asleep as Amelia, Torry, and Belle had to discuss their plans for the rest of the trip.

Amelia reached out and grabbed her sister's hand, and with compassion in her face, she asked, "So, Belle, how are you feeling? Are you still overwhelmed and sad?"

Torry put her drink down and spoke quietly to Bella, "Yeah, Bel. You have been saying for years that you don't feel like you belong anywhere, and that worried Amelia and me. How are you feeling now?"

Their words touched Bella. She realized that she hadn't actually thought about it since arriving in Puerto Rico. And now, with their questions, Bella realized that she had not been sad, anxious, or overwhelmed. This has all been a new experience for her, but deep down, she had already sensed that she had a "gift."

"Honestly, I hadn't thought about it much. Since coming home, I've felt a strong connection to our family and the island. But now that I think about it, I can honestly say that I'm thrilled to be here. It's been wonderful reconnecting with our cousins and other relatives. It feels like we never left. I do worry about Grandma, though. Even though she's independent, I hate that she's alone in that big house. So far, I don't feel overwhelmed, sad, or like I don't belong here. In fact, it's quite the opposite." Bella looked for the right words to say so she wouldn't worry her sisters. She knew they had been concerned about her mental health, and she wanted to reassure them. And it's been nice not being at work, right?"

Amelia and Torry nodded their heads in agreement.

Torry lifted her chin and answered, "Hell yes!" She looked at Amelia, Bella, and Lulu sleeping and felt a deep sense of peace. "Mel, I think we should have visited the family long ago."

Amelia smiled with a gentle smile, and her eyes shone in a way Torry hadn't seen in a long time.

"Bella was right, living on the United States continent sometimes felt like a trap. Always on a tight schedule, rushing to get things done, flooded with commercials tricking you into buying things that you don't need. We use our credit cards as if money will never stop, but the day we don't get a paycheck, we're screwed."

Torry saw the differences between their life in the States and Amelia's family in Puerto Rico. Torry looked at Amelia and grabbed her hand.

"Maybe we can visit your family more often."

Amelia smiled, "I would love that!"

"Yeah, and we need to reconsider our lifestyle in the States and reduce our debt so that we are free to take more vacations." Torry looked at Bella, "Do you know, Bella, that I was so busy at work last year that I didn't take a vacation?"

Bella was surprised because she knew Torry was employed at a good company with great benefits.

"No, I didn't. So what, can you take two weeks off this year?"

Torry laughed, "hell no! We lose our vacation time every December 31st. So, the other thing that I propose is that we take the daycare tuition and pay all our credit cards and cut up the cards, then take that little bit extra and put it away for our next trip here."

"Are you serious?" Amelia asked. "I've felt run down and trapped for months, too, but being here has rejuvenated me."

"Well, with Lulu starting Kindergarten soon, we can save that tuition and pay off our credit cards. I am ok with cutting them up because we have too many, and for too long, we've been using credit to rob Peter and pay Paul. I mean, it's awful when we have to use a credit card to buy groceries. OK, so do we have a plan?"

Amelia reached over and kissed Torry.

"I love you," she whispered.

"I'll take that as a yes, then."

Amelia looked at Bella. It was the kind of look that Bella knew. The one she couldn't say no to, whatever it was Amelia was about to ask, it was either something Bella would not like, or it was important to Amelia.

"Oh no, I know that look. What is it?"

Amelia's smile widened.

"Could you please watch Lulu while Torry and I go for a walk on the beach?"

"Of course, pick me up a snowball or a cold coconut to drink."

"You can't be hungry after all this," Torry said, waving to the remains of the 'snack' Bella had brought.

"I'm thirsty," Bella said with a pout.

"A snowcone is a food, not a drink."

Amelia pulled at Torry's arm, "Let's walk, sweetheart, that's not an argument you can win. Especially against my lawyer sister."

Amelia pulled Torry away, and they began walking down the beach.

Bella was delighted to see Amelia and Torry taking time for themselves, and the spark that brought them together was there again.

Lulu was still sleeping and would probably sleep for another thirty minutes or so. Bella pulled her knees close to her chest, crossed her arms over her knees, and lay her head on her arms. She closed her eyes and took a few deep breaths. She inhaled the salty ocean breeze, listened to the gentle waves crashing against the shore, and blocked out the chatter of people and the children playing in the water. She listened only to the gentle snore of her niece on the towel beside her. The amulet Father Pablo had given her was around her neck, along with the silver cross necklace from her grandmother. So, Bella knew that she had nothing to fear as she eased into her meditative state. She felt the warmth of the sun on her skin and heard the palm trees swaying in the breeze. She was in her secret place, and everything around her was calm. She did not feel the heavy sense of oppression that was always in the background. Instead, she felt as if someone had opened the blinds and windows, letting nature in. She was in a peaceful place, full of joy.

In her mind's eye, Bella saw people approaching her. She was not afraid. These people felt familiar, and she knew she had nothing to fear. As they drew closer, Bella could see Nayeli, and behind her, her ancestors. She noticed that their skin tones included many shades. They shifted from snow white to dark molasses, and their clothes were just as varied as if they came from different eras. In the crowd, Bella recognized her great-grandmother Aurelis, who stood smiling proudly at her. Aurelis had passed away when Bella was nine. She also saw other family members from her childhood. Bella felt safe. She expected to see her father in the crowd, but he was not there, and she was surprised to feel disappointed that he hadn't joined them. Nayeli spoke.

"We are gathered here to remind you that you are not alone. And, now that you can control your meditative state, you can call upon us for guidance and protection. You have been given a great task. With your return to our Mother Island, your connection to her is growing. For centuries, your family has been born on this island, fought revolutions for freedom, and the gifted ones have taken on similar tasks like the one you face today. Allow that connection to the Mother to grow because you, like all your ancestors, are of this island and connected to it."

Bella found that she could think words that the others could hear.

"Nayeli, why isn't my father here? Did he not want to see me?"

"Bella, do you recall the night you entered that void?" Neyeli said with a warm smile.

Bella nodded. She would never forget that night.

"Your father was in there, and it was he who brought you back to the light." Nayeli walked closer to Bella. "He will remain there, in purgatory, until you complete this task. He has done many wrongs in his life, and he feels responsible for the way you have been dealing with your emotions because of what he did. But know that he chose to stay there to ward off the evil that had been trying to stop you. He is protecting you."

Bella was surprised that this revelation made her smile. Nayeli and her family slowly began to fade. Bella didn't want the warmth to end or her family to go away.

"Wait, please don't go. I am happy here. I want to talk to my cousin and my grandmother. Nayeli, I still need your help. Please don't go."

"Bella, we have to go. You are using your life's energy to be here with us. You cannot stay here because you are part of the living."

Bella heard low voices saying goodbye to her. They told her that they loved her, that they were proud of her, and that they would always be with her. Bella felt tears running down her face.

"Bella, you have to find me. That will be the key to completing this task. Talk to your family and neighbors. They are facing hardship and uncertainty. You will know what to do. Pay attention to everything. And remember that your life's journey was always meant to end up here protecting Borikén."

Bella saw Nayeli fade away. Bella realized that while in her meditative state, she never stopped hearing the waves, Lulu's soft breath, or feeling the sun on her face, and the tropical breeze. Bella blinked at the bright sunlight when she opened her eyes. The people around her were still laughing and playing. It was strange that Lulu was still sleeping because Bella had been in her secret place for a long time. She looked at her phone. To her surprise, it had only been a few minutes. She was confused because it felt like she had been there much longer.

Lulu woke up a short time later. She looked around for Amelia and Torry.

"Where are my mommies?"

"They went on a walk."

Lulu sat up in panic, "Without me!"

"Yes, you were asleep, and I didn't want to be lonely, so I asked them not to wake you so you could keep me company, and they agreed. Here, Lulu, I saved you some juice. I will put more sunblock on you and your arm floaties so we can go swimming. How does that sound?"

Lulu quickly forgot about the walk. She learned that she really loved the warm tropical ocean better than the beaches that Amelia and Torry went to back home. That water was always cold and, most of the time, dark green. But here the water was so clear that you could see the bottom, and the water was warm.

Torry and Amelia returned from their walk. Torry went up to them as Amelia headed toward their towels.

"Hey, you two, we brought guava pastries and mango smoothies. Come and eat."

Bella and Lulu got out of the water.

"Guava pastries and smoothies," Bella asked Torry as they reached the towels. "You can't be hungry after all that," Bella said with a grin as she waved at the pile of wrappers and cups from their earlier snack.

Torry shrugged, "Walking makes me hungry."

For the rest of the afternoon, they played on the shore and searched the sand for pretty shells. While Torry and Bella snorkeled, Amelia took photos and videos to show her mom and grandmother how much they were enjoying themselves and what a good time Lulu was having.

Chapter 30

Bella woke up to the smell of bacon. For a moment, she considered staying wrapped in her blankets to enjoy the warmth of the sunlight filling her room. She felt safe in her bedroom and wanted to hold onto that feeling. After a tough childhood of always feeling like she didn't belong anywhere, Bella now felt welcome, at peace with herself, and was certain that she was where she belonged. She sat up, stepped onto her balcony, and admired the beautiful view of Isabella's Garden and the small forest surrounding Isabella's house. An ocean breeze rustled her hair. She asked herself why she would ever want to leave this place.

Bella knew her answer. She had thought about this for years, but her depression kept her from seeing things clearly. She was part of Borikén. She was connected to the island and its people. Since returning, she felt grounded in this land. Interacting with her family felt familiar and meaningful. She knew they would fly back to North Carolina in just a couple of days, and that made her anxious. She took a few deep breaths. She knew she wouldn't get on that plane. She had found where she belonged, where she was needed. She could also help Isabella around the house and with her appointments. There was no way she was going back to her hectic life.

Bella heard Isabella call her to breakfast. Before returning to her bedroom, she thought of her siblings and how much she would miss them. It tore her apart, and her eyes filled with tears as she replayed in her mind what she was going to tell them. Bella heard her name in the wind and went back to her balcony. She thought she would see Nayeli at the edge of the woods. Bella believed that Nayeli and her past family would be happy to know she was staying in Puerto Rico.

Instead, the instant she stepped onto the balcony, the hair on her arms stood up. Her heart felt heavy. It became difficult to breathe. She wondered what was going on. She had been on the balcony and felt great. But now she felt heavy; a sense of oppression came over her.

Bella heard Nayeli say in her head, "Get your amulet."

She took the amulet and necklace off to rinse the salt water off and forgot to put them back on. She knew that if she didn't go back into her bedroom and put on the amulet and the necklace, she would feel frozen where she was standing. Panic filled her at the thought of being pulled back to that cold darkness without any of her family being around her to help bring her back. Tears streamed down her face. She heard a low, deep laugh all around her. The laughing became louder, and a terrifying growl accompanied it. Bella felt herself falling and couldn't stop it. She knew she was being drawn into that place of nothingness, where evil forces awaited her. Bella called out to Isabella and Lulu for help, but no words came. She was unable to scream for help.

Lulu was sitting on the floor of her room playing with a wooden top she had found under the bed. It was painted in different colors; one side was red and the other was blue. When she spun the top slowly, the two colors flashed at her one after another, and it fell over on its side after just a few turns. When she spun it fast, the colors blurred into a beautiful purple, and it seemed to spin for a long time.

As she went to spin it again, her tummy flipped, and she felt like she was going to be sick. Her fingers slipped as she tried to spin the top. It bounced off the floor and ricocheted out the doors onto her balcony. She crawled over to get. Her head felt heavy, as if she wanted to fall asleep, but she had just woken up. She stopped at the threshold. The top was just out of reach. She remembered that Mama had told her not to go out on the balcony.

Does one step really count as going out? she thought.

Lulu heard someone call her name. "Mama, is that you?"

She knew that it wasn't Torry or Amelia. In Lulu's head, they felt different.

No, it's not them.

Lulu felt the urge to get up and find who had called her. She felt like this on the night that Aunt Bella got really sick. Forgetting about the top, Lulu walked out into the hallway.

Nayeli was standing in front of Bella's room, staring at Lulu.

"You have to hurry and go get help for Bella. Sweet Lulu, you have to get your grandmother and mommie. It's important. Do you understand?"

"Yes, I understand. Bad things are hurting Aunt Bella. I will go find my mom and my grandmother."

Lulu ran down the stairs as fast as she could. She did not find anyone in the living room. Lulu heard dishes being moved about. She ran into the dining room and the kitchen. She saw the entire family either sitting down at the table or in the kitchen. Lulu took a deep breath and cried out, "Hurry, Aunt Bella is in trouble. Nayeli told me to get my grandmother and my mom to help her."

The group immediately responded. Those at the table got up and began to run to Bella's bedroom. Carmen was the first up the stairs.

She could think of nothing but Bella. The fear that Bella would be taken away from them again gripped her heart. As Carmen, Amelia, and Lulu approached Bella's room, they felt an oppressive force crushing down on them. It was a struggle just to move forward, as if ghostly hands were holding them back.

Carmen panicked, "Boys, run in there and take Bella out of her room. Mom, get the blessed olive oil that Father Pablo left with us. Amelia, can you move faster?"

Amelia also found it difficult to move. Amelia and Lulu cried out simultaneously. They heard loud laughter and growling. Lulu raised her hands to cover her ears. "Mama, I don't like the laughing."

Torry responded first, "Mel, what's wrong. Lulu, sweetheart, can you tell me what's wrong?" Torry patted Lulu to see if something was hurting her. But she couldn't find anything on Amelia or Lulu, so she began to panic.

Carlos and Tony came out of the bedroom with Bella in their arms. Her face was pale. Her eyes were wide open, and she was not blinking. Her breathing was fast and shallow, and her face had streaks of tears running down it. They quickly moved her down the stairs and laid her on the sofa.

Once Bella was out of her room, Amelia, Carmen, and Lulu were able to walk freely again. They all shifted into protective mode. Carmen put a pillow under Bella's head and began to pray. Isabella returned with the olive oil and began chanting the Lord's Prayer as she drew the sign of the cross on Bella's forehead with the oil.

Amelia pulled a throw blanket off a nearby chair and wrapped it around her sister. When she looked at Lulu, she realized how scared she was.

"Lulu, don't worry. Titi Bella will be fine."

"Nayeli says that we have to get around Titi Bella, Mama, Mima, the three of us need to hold hands, and think about her and how much we love her," Lulu said. Everyone turned to look at her. Nobody moved.

"Nayeli says that we need to hold hands now," Lulu said more firmly.

Tony, Carlos, Isabella, and Torry stepped out of the way to give them room. Carmen went behind the couch and reached out for Lulu and Amelia's hands. Carmen's tears ran down her face at the thought that she might lose her daughter today. With joined hands, the three of them closed their eyes and thought of Bella, like Lulu said Nayeli wanted them to do.

"Mima Carmen, Nayeli says that it's almost too late. She said to call out Bella's name again and again."

Torry's heart sank at the thought of her little girl also being a chosen one. What terrors would await Lulu when it's her time to answer the calling? Torry thought how surreal it all was that Lulu was talking as if Nayeli were in the room, talking to her. Torry couldn't help but look around the room. She didn't see anything.

In a low voice, Tony addressed Carlos and Torry, "We may not be sensitive, but I say let's all call out to Bella in our thoughts. I feel like it worked last time, so let's give it a try."

Both Carlos and Torry nodded their heads, and the three of them held hands. They took deep breaths to calm themselves, and when they were calm, they began to call Bella. Isabella had run to phone Father Pablo. When she returned, she grabbed Tony's hand and joined them. Isabella noticed that Bella was not wearing her protective amulet and cross. She felt a sense that Bella would need those to come back to them. She ran up the stairs and into Bella's room. On the dresser, she saw the amulet and the silver cross. She grabbed them and ran into the family room. She ducked under her daughter and granddaughter's linked arms and placed the amulet and cross over Bella's head.

Amelia and Lulu sensed cold and darkness all around them; it was pushing them away, keeping them from Bella. The moment Isabella dropped the necklaces over Bella's head, both Amelia and Lulu felt hands pushing them forward. They all felt it as the air around them warmed.

When Tony opened his eyes, he saw Bella's face change; the pale complexion colored to a healthy, rich glow. She began to blink and started breathing deeply. She sat up suddenly when she realized what had happened. She looked at her family and then sank into her mother's arms, crying.

"I am so sorry! I am so stupid for forgetting to put on my necklaces. I don't know what I was thinking. It had been such a perfect day, and I had to ruin it." Bella hugged her mom after seeing her face covered in tears. "Mami, I am sorry."

Carmen was overjoyed to have her daughter back, and tears of joy streamed from her eyes. "Bella, you don't have anything to be sorry for. We are grateful that you are back with us." Carmen kissed her daughter as if it were the last time she was to see Bella.

One by one, the rest of the family came up to Bella to hug her. Bella saw the scared looks on their faces and the dried tears on their cheeks.

"I am so sorry to cause you worry!"

Everyone told Bella not to worry about that because they were just glad that she was back with them. The doorbell rang, and Isabella went to get to the door while drying her face with one of her late husband's handkerchiefs.

"Oh, Father, I am sorry to call you."

"It is God's works that bring me to your house."

When Father Pablo saw Isabella, he was filled with worry. He knew that she was 78, but she hid her age well. She had never looked old to him; in fact, she could pass for a woman half her age. Not tonight, though. Tonight, Isabella looked like she had aged well beyond her 78 years.

"What has happened, Isabella? I can see it in your face, and it worries me."

"I don't understand it myself. Maybe Bella can tell us what happened. But Father, I am so scared. I thought that we were going to lose her." Isabella wiped more tears from her face.

Isabella led Father Pablo to the living room.

"Good morning, everyone." Father Pablo made the sign of the cross as he walked into the living room. The group looked up, and they felt a sense of security. Father Pablo knew what was going on. Carmen was the closest to the door and stood up to greet the father.

"Good morning, Father Pablo. I'm glad you could come. I am afraid that it is very serious, and we almost lost Bella again."

Father Pablo approached Bella. He looked at her and noticed the pale face covered in tears. He also noticed that Bella was trembling. "What is it, Bella, that has you scared? What happened?" He knew he had to alleviate her fear and help her calm down. "Bella, go ahead and lie back down and close your eyes." Father Pablo took a small bottle of anointed oil from his pocket and made a cross on Bella's forehead. "I want you to take three slow, deep breaths. As you exhale, I want you to feel your arms and legs becoming lighter, and I want you to concentrate on the sound of the birds chirping outside the window. Can you hear them?"

Bella nodded and began the breathing exercises.

The priest realized that it was going to take a little more time for her to stop shaking.

"OK, Bella, I remembered that you were going to the beach yesterday with your family. Tell me about that."

Bella smiled at the memory. She recounted the things they did and ate. Father Pablo looked around the room and realized the others had started to relax as well. To Isabella, the room felt less oppressive, and she took a big, deep sigh of relief.

Once she was completely recovered, Father Pablo helped Bella sit up.

"How do you feel?"

"Better Father. Thank you."

"You don't have to thank me. It is my pleasure to see you looking better. So, tell me what happened."

"Well, I am not exactly sure. One moment, I was on my balcony and started feeling something. I don't think I can describe it accurately, but I immediately felt fear. The worst part was the laughing and growling; they were in my head, but at the same time outside. I knew that whatever this was, it was coming to hurt me. I managed to look around the backyard and the entrance to our house, and I thought I saw a fuzzy shadow in the shape of a man standing at our entryway. And I knew that the laughter was coming from him."

Isabella handed Bella a cup of tea.

By the time I knew it, I couldn't move. I was cold and frozen where I stood. I saw that my necklaces were on my dresser, and I realized that I had let something take control of me. I felt tears on my face, but I couldn't move or speak to scream for help. I felt myself beginning to float out of my body, and I saw a darkness all around me, starting to sap the light. I knew that they were trying to take me, and

I felt helpless to stop it. That's when I thought to call out for my mom, Amelia, and Lulu."

Carmen excitedly told the priest about her experience. "That's right, Father. I was in the kitchen helping my mom cook breakfast when I felt the hair on my arms and neck stand up. I felt a humming in my ears, and I knew that something was wrong. That's when Lulu ran into the kitchen and told us that Nayeli had sent her to get Amelia and me to get to Bella's room right away. She said that Nayeli told her that Bella was in danger. My mom and I ran upstairs, but we couldn't get to the room. I called out to the boys." Carmen paused, overcome by emotion, and tears began rolling down her cheeks as she remembered the feeling of helplessness. She took several deep breaths to calm herself, then continued.

"I sent my mom to go get the oil you left us. When Lulu, Amelia, and I reached the top of the stairs, we felt something pushing us backward. Tony and Carlos ran up the stairs and saw what was happening to us. They tried to help us, but I sent them into Bella's room. They carried her out and took her to the family room. Father, I will never forget the look on Bella's face!" Carmen wiped more tears from her face. "She was as white as a ghost. Her eyes were wide open, and she wasn't blinking. Her pupils were dilated and staring at nothing. I saw tears on her face. We called out to her, but she didn't respond. We remembered what you told us to do, and we began to pray. That's when my mom noticed that Bella wasn't wearing her charm and her silver cross, so she went upstairs, brought them, and put them around Bella's neck. And that's when she woke up." Carmen took a deep breath and smiled around the room at her family."

"So Lulu came down to get you," the priest asked as he knelt next to the five-year-old. "Did you see Bella in trouble?" he asked.

Lulu shook her head. "No, Nayeli told me to get mama and mima."

"Really."

Lulu nodded, her chin bouncing off her chest. Father Pablo listened to every detail.

"I was playing with a little toy I found in my room. It rolled onto the balcony. I remembered Mama telling me to go out there, so I didn't get it. " She looked around the room at her aunts and uncles as if she had done something amazing. "Then I started to feel bad, and I heard someone call my name. When I went into the hall, Nayeli was there. She said Titi Bella was in trouble and to get help. Then I heard Aunt Bella cry out in my head, so I ran downstairs. When they brought her down, Nayeli told me to make a circle around Titi and think about how much we love her. I did that, but Abuela just kept praying." A soft chuckle echoed around the room, and Lulu looked up to see who was laughing at her. Nayeli said that Bella was really hurt and only my mom, my grandma, and I could help. So I did what she told me to do because I love my Aunt Bella." Everyone sighed because Lulu sounded so grown-up.

This five-year-old must have stronger abilities than I first believed, the priest thought.

"So, Lulu," he said as he reached out and drew a cross on the little girl's forehead, "it sounds like you were the hero today."

Lulu giggled and beamed with pride..

Father Pablo wanted to know more. "So, you first felt bad and then you saw and spoke to Nayeli?"

Lulu nodded her head. "A huh, when I was thinking about getting my toy. I felt like I was too heavy and couldn't keep my head up. Then I heard Bella call me."

Father Pablo smiled.

"You did a very good thing today. But you must promise me that if you ever see anything that scares you or if other people come to talk to you like Nayeli does, you will tell Amelia or Torry right away. If they aren't around, you tell Abuela or Tia Bella. Okay?"

Lulu nodded her head again and held out a pinky. "Promise."

Father Pablo smiled and shook her pinky.

Torry walked over to the priest and helped him stand. "Thank you for that padre," she patted his shoulder, "you can't believe what that little promise means to me."

Father Pablo reached over and hugged her. "I am happy to help in every way I can. Please, when you return home, stay in touch. I would like to keep your little family in more than just my prayers." Torry smiled.

Bella stood from the couch. "Thank you so much, Father, for all you have done for us."

"Oh, look at the time. I have to be at Cecilia's to look over those company records, and we have the wake to go to."

"Bella," Carmen said, "what if I came with you? I can sit with Cecilia to discuss the funeral arrangements and keep an eye on you. I don't want you to see that terrible family, but I know you must. I \ know that you are now wearing your protective necklaces, but I still want to be there."

Bella knew that her mom was probably not going to let her out of her sight for a while, so she agreed. This new encounter with malicious forces left her scared. This time, it was her own absentmindedness that had left her vulnerable to whatever was trying to stop her from helping Nayeli.

Bella couldn't help noticing that everyone in the room was either pretending not to be worried about her or asking her again and again if she was ok.

"Listen, everyone, I know that you are worried about me. I realize that it was my fault and that I let this happen, but I will learn how to build stronger barriers for the future if something like this happens again."

"Father Pablo, do you know where I can go to train how to protect myself?"

Father Pablo thought about it for a few seconds and sipped his coffee. He looked at Bella. She thought he looked worried about how his following words might affect her. Finally, he spoke.

"Is it ok if I ask you some personal questions?"

Bella nodded.

"Do you go to church? Do you have people of faith back home in North Carolina?"

"No, Father, I do not. I never felt as if the Christians there and their religion ever cared for me or what my family and I needed. I tried several churches when I first moved there, but after a few months in each, I realized that I didn't truly belong with any of them. I thought that if I tried to get involved with the children's nursery, women's auxiliary group, or the choir, they would make me feel like I belonged. Instead, I felt treated like an outsider, always looking for that sense of community. I waited for that feeling, and never got it. I would hear after the fact of some cookout they hosted and never told me. I heard of volunteer work for fundraising events that I wasn't included in. And when I was sick, no one even called to check on me."

Bella looked at Carmen.

"I am sorry, Mom. I know that you have a church community that you depend on, but I got tired of trying so hard to fit in just to be rejected."

Bella faced Father Pablo and continued to explain, "So yeah, Father, I did not find that being in any of those denominations helped me get close to God. I began to do acts of charity on my own, reading with local children's programs. I raised funds for schools to purchase supplies. I found peace in simply doing what my heart told me to do. And you know what? Even through my pain and depression, I felt connected to the universe and the land without the need for a church. I learned to meditate, and I talk to the flowers and trees outside my window, as well as at the staff garden at my job. I know that I have a lot to work on myself, but when I stopped stressing about going to church, I felt better. Sorry, Father." Bella looked at his family and saw that they were smiling at her, indicating that they approved. Bella felt validated.

Father Pablo listened carefully and smiled, "Bella, what you are describing are the beliefs and actions our ancestors, the Taino and Africans, who were brought to this island, believed. These people had a strong connection to the land, and they practiced acts of charity. Although they worshipped many deities, they still believed that one creator, in Puerto Rico's case, the Mother, created life, and the other gods served as her minions to guide them. So, you are, as some would say today, spiritual, just not religious, and that is ok. It's this strong connection that opened your mind's eye to see what others cannot. So, I recommend that when you get back home, you look for a medium to help teach you how to protect yourself and how to control your gift."

Bella was relieved that she did not offend Father Pablo, and in fact, Father Pablo was very progressive. Isabella looked at her watch and let out a yelp, "Bella and Carmen, you need to go, or you will be late to meet with Manuelito and Cecilia. Everyone else will meet you at Cecilia's house for the wake later."

Chapter 31

Bella rushed to her bedroom to change her clothes. She thought about what she was going to wear. She needed something that showed the remorse of saying goodbye to her father, but would also show the authority she wanted to project during her meeting with Manuel. Apprehension crept in as she approached her room. She stood in her doorway, scanning the room and trying to sense a malevolent force. But instead, Bella smelled the scent of flowers in the air, roses, her favorite flower. A sense of tranquility and safety washed over her, and she no longer feared her room. She moved to the balcony doorway and softly spoke to Nayeli, "Thank you, Nayeli, for protecting me."

She opened her closet and chose a dark, tailored suit, simple, grave, and unflinching. It would do.

Bella walked into the family room to look for her mom. Through the glass patio doors, she saw Torry and Amelia outside playing with Lulu. Bella thought about how traumatizing this whole thing must have been for her niece.

Isabella walked in and kissed her on her forehead.

"Remember, Bella, never take this off," she lifted the necklace, "and if you feel unsafe at Cecilia's house, look for Carmen. I am sure that she will be close by."

"Thank you, Abuela. I will."

Bella stepped outside.

Bella hugged Torry, tears in her eyes, "I am so sorry, sis."

"What for, Mel? None of this is your fault."

"Because of my stupidity, Lulu was part of something that at her age she probably doesn't even understand, and it must have scared you. I am so sorry, Torry."

Torry pointed at Lulu.

"Look, does it look like she is traumatized? She told me that she felt like a hero because she saved you." Amelia walked up to them, hugged her sister, and whispered in her ear, "It was terrifying for me and Torry."

Torry took Bella by the hand, "Look, I am not going to pretend that it didn't freak me out. I thought about the kind of life Lulu would have growing up with this ability and what type of challenges she would face. But I was worried for you and Amelia, too. Now we know how to prepare Lulu for her possible future, and maybe she won't have to face the challenges that you faced. The nightmares, voices, and haunting images, we know why now, and when the time comes, if it comes, Mel and I will be ready."

All three of them walked up to Lulu, and she looked up. Lulu smiled and jumped up when she saw Bella. She ran up and hugged Bella.

"Hey, little one, how are you feeling? That must have been very scary for you to go through."

"Are you feeling better?"

Bella was touched that Lulu was more worried about her than herself.

"Yes, Lulu. I feel great thanks to you. You are my hero."

Lulu giggled.

Bella squatted in front of Lulu to make eye contact with her. "Tell me, Lulu, weren't you scared because of what was happening? I know that when I was your age, I was so scared that at night I slept under my blankets."

Lulu found that funny and silly. "Oh, Titi, I wasn't scared because Nayeli is my friend and she told me that I was the only one who could save you."

All of the sisters looked at each other.

Bella couldn't help being curious, "What do you mean she is your friend. How long have you two been friends?"

"Since we came to Puerto Rico. I saw her in the woods, and she told me to follow her. You remember Mom. You saw me that day, moving rocks by the waterfall. Nayeli told me to look under the rocks, but then you showed up and I had to stop. I really enjoyed turning the rocks over because lizards and tiny frogs were hiding underneath them. Now, Nayeli plays with me in my room, and she shows me pictures in my mind of people from long, long ago. Nayeli showed me kids running, playing, and swimming in the pond." Lulu looks at her mom, "Mommy, where did those kids go? I want to play with them."

Amelia chose her words carefully because she did not want to lie to her child, "Well, Lulu, I think that those kids lived around here a long time ago, and Nayeli was showing you how happy they were."

"Will I get to play with them another day?"

"Lulu, I think that she showed you those kids so that you can learn more about them and the things that they did."

"Oh. Maybe they made that flowerpot that I found underneath one of the rocks."

"What flowerpot?"

"The one by the waterfall. It was broken, so I left it there."

A jolt of urgency surged through Bella. She felt a sudden rush, like some instinct whispering that this, somehow, was part of what Nayeli needed her to do.

"Lulu, can you show us where you found the flowerpot?"

Lulu smiled and happily grabbed Bella's hand and led the way into the forest. They walked through a less-worn path covered in bushes. Bella thought that she knew every inch of the forest, but this area looked unfamiliar. It had more trees, and the path upward was steeper. They cleared the trees and shrubs, and Bella realized that they were at the top of the waterfall.

Amelia was frightened when she thought of her little girl up so high above the pond below. "Lulu, how did you get up here?"

"Nayeli told me where to go."

"Weren't you scared?"

Lulu giggled, "No, she said that she would protect me. She told me that it was important that I move the rocks around."

The sense of urgency Bella felt had grown with every step she took up the trail. What was it that Nayeli wanted Lulu to find? The waterfall had two landings where water streamed down; one on the top where they were standing and another halfway down the slope.

"Amelia, where did you find Lulu?"

Amelia pointed to the landing halfway down the hill, "There, and I couldn't guess how she even got to that spot. It's covered in shrubs and large rocks."

Bella looked at Lulu, "Lulu, just point where you found the flowerpot. I want you to stay here while I go look."

As Bella started down the slope, she realized how treacherous it was. The large boulders were covered in moss, and the overspray from the waterfall kept them slick and slimy. She stopped after a few steps and looked around for something that she could use to stabilize her trek. She found a thin, sturdy branch and used it as a walking stick.

"Nayeli, keep me safe."

Step by step, Bella grabbed onto small trees, balanced herself by grabbing boulders, and tapped the ground and rocks with the stick to check for stability before stepping on them. All the while, Amelia and Torry stood above, terrified, but they knew not to distract Bella. They held each other's hands and silently prayed for Bella.

The trek was arduous. She struggled to grab onto some of the overhanging branches because they were flimsy and offered no secure hold. After what seemed like hours, she reached the landing and looked around. The rocks here looked like they were placed intentionally, almost stacked. If she squinted and tilted her head to one side, she thought it might look like a spiral. She couldn't be sure, over the centuries, the elements had worn down the stones and disfigured the shape. To her left, in her peripheral vision, Bella noticed a small green boa staring at her. Down below around the pond, Bella saw transparent figures of Tainos looking up at her. She knew that she must be at an important location.

Sticking out from one side of the piled rocks was a large earthen pot, half covered in rocks and soil. Bella began to work. Slowly and gently, she moved small stones out of her way to get a better look at the pot. She knew enough physics to realize that if she moved too many too fast, the whole cliffside of the falls might crumble down with her caught up in the slide. After moving a few rocks, Bella noticed that the dirt underneath was black and moist. It looked pristine, and she wondered if the reason for that was that no one ever thought of scaling a dangerous cliffside to dig under these rocks.

Only dummies like me do this type of craziness, she thought.

Bella used a wide piece of bark as a shovel and dug out the rock when she saw what looked like the base of the pot. Her heart raced and pounded. She wondered how long this pot had been here; how many centuries. The wonder that filled her was edged with bitterness as she realized that this was made by her people, the ancestors who lived on, thrived in, and cared for this land. But how did this pot get up here?

Bella cried out to the group, "I think I found it! Give me a minute to get it out. It looks ancient, and I don't want to damage it."

Meticulously, she moved every rock and pebble out of the way. She stopped using the bark and instead used her hands to avoid damaging the pot. Soon, she was able to see markings on the pot and detailed carvings. Now that it was halfway exposed, Bella noticed a 2" crack from the brim to the neck of the pot. She took particular care when clearing off this area in case it was fragile. She removed the dirt and was able to see that the pot had a cover on it. A piece of tanned leather had been tied around the top of the pot, and other than the crack, it was in excellent condition.

"Amelia, do you two have something that I can use to wrap the pot in?"

Immediately, Torry removed the vest she was wearing and tossed it to Bella. Bella carefully wrapped the pot in the vest. She started back up the cliff carefully. Bella found that going back up was easier than when she came down, since the boulders all slanted toward the pond. The four of them walked very slowly and carefully back to the house with their precious cargo. As they approached the patio doors, they called out for Carmen, Isabella, and their brothers.

Carmen was the first to meet them in the entrance and was shocked to see Bella dirty.

"Bella, are you covered in dirt? Did you fall? What's going on?"

"Mom, you are never going to believe what we found!!"

Gently, they unfurled the pot and put it on the table. Everyone looked at the pot and recognized it for what it was: a piece of their people's history. They were mesmerized by it as they slowly walked around the table to look at its details.

Isabella broke the silence, "Mija, where did you find this?"

"On the cliffside of the waterfall."

Isabella, Carmen, Tony, and Carlos looked up at her in horror.

Carmen was the first to react, "What!! Are you crazy? Why?"

"Because Lulu told us that Nayeli showed her that location and told her to dig there. Lulu told us that she found a flowerpot, but Amelia found her, and she wasn't able to keep digging."

The group realized how horrifying it was to think of Lulu climbing down that cliffside. They looked at Lulu in wonder. This little girl had discovered something that had been lost for centuries.

Tony grabbed a rag to clean the layers of dirt off the pot when Carlos stopped him.

"Wait, Tony. Hold on. If this is from our ancestors, we should contact someone who knows about antiquities."

"Ok, what do you suggest?"

"Bella, you and Mom go to Cecilia's and do what you have to do. We will meet you there for the wake. I will take some photos of the flowerpot as it is and send the information to the Indigenous Studies department at the University of Puerto Rico. I want to speak to an archaeologist or anthropologist who knows more about the people who lived here over the last few centuries. I will let everyone know if someone contacts me back."

Chapter 32

Cecilia greeted Carmen and Bella in her entryway. The tension in the air was so thick it could be cut with a knife. Carmen understood that Cecilia blamed her for Luis turning away from her planned marriage and a future in politics. Regardless of her true feelings, Cecilia smiled and was a gracious hostess to her son's family.

"Welcome, Carmen and Bella. You came right on time. Carmen, I would like to discuss with you some of the funeral arrangements, and Bella, Manuel is in the study." Cecilia turned to face her butler. "Go ahead and show Bella to the study, please." Cecilia led Carmen away to discuss funeral plans.

Bella recognized the study and found Manuel in front of a filing cabinet, sorting through files. He turned when he heard the butler introduce Bella.

"Ah, Bella, good, I am glad that you are on time. I've pulled out our financial statements for the last five years if you're interested in reviewing them. Here, come look."

Bella immediately noticed that some information was redacted, making it impossible for her to read. Manuel highlighted the information that he and Cecilia wanted her to see. Most of it was financial records in large sums. However, Bella wasn't able to account for the transactions for those invoices. Bella decided to play to his ego.

"Manuel, this is really impressive. I had never realized that this business was so prolific, and from the looks of the deposits, it's growing."

Manuel was more than eager to talk about their successes. He described details about the Jones Act shipping to and from the island and the profits the company and its American investors were making. Manuel gave her a breakdown of how their business sought opportunities when their ancestors first arrived on the island. Although Bella knew about their so-called opportunities, she decided to continue to play to his ego and act as if she wasn't aware of history.

Manuel showed her ledgers and journals from the locked glass case, which painted a disturbing picture to Bella of what they considered opportunities. It seemed that the enslavement of the Taino people, genocide, African slave trading, and the annexation of indigenous land were their twisted version of opportunities.

Manuel opened an old leatherbound book. There was a map inside, showing whole parcels of land and the names of the indigenous tribes that lived in those areas. Bella also saw lines across the map throughout what was now called the Arecibo and Ponce areas. Bella knew that some of her ancestors had lived in the hills of Ponce, and they had taken refuge in the mountains, where the Spanish wouldn't find them.

"Hey Manuel, what are these lines?"

Manuel was only too happy to tell her.

"Those are gold and silver mines. And see how they run from the hills and mountains." Manuel pulled out a journal and opened it to narratives written by Ponce De Leon. "De Leon and Columbus knew the riches this island had. Colonists focused their attention on these

Caribbean islands for the riches they held for the taking. Gold, silver, coffee, slaves, and other products generated a substantial amount of wealth for Spain."

It took everything for Bella not to scream at him or walk out. She could see that he was very proud of their heritage and the riches it brought the family, regardless of the pain their greed cost people and their land.

Manuel put the books back inside the locked glass cabinet.

"Geeze, Tio, you should have those books in a museum or something." Bella giggled.

Manuel stood up, looked up to stare at an oil painting of Ponce de Leon, smiled, and turned to Bella.

"Well, over the centuries and decades, we've lent the books to museums throughout major cities in Europe. But they are delicate, and we decided to stop exhibiting them and keep them with us. There is a curator who comes once a year to inspect them and look for fungus, mites, or anything else that can damage them."

Bella smiled, "That makes sense. Do you have more recent financial records that I can review? After all, I want to make sure that I am not risking my job in North Carolina, joining the family business, and then the company files for bankruptcy in a year."

Manuel let out a booming laugh. His face turned red from laughing.

"Dear Bella. No worry about that. With our latest ventures and expansion to Texas and Europe, our great-grandchildren will not be able to spend all our money."

"Oh, that's right, you mentioned Texas to me before. You and Cecilia said something about me running the Texas branch, or something like that."

"That's right, Bella. We want family in charge of our offices in Texas, and with your corporate law experience, you would be perfect."

Bella pretended to be impressed. "Thank you, Manuel. Thank you for the opportunity. However, I looked up the company name in Texas and couldn't find Ponce Industries anywhere in the State. So, is this a new branch you are opening?"

Manuel looked at his watch. He collected the ledgers and began filing the documents and books away. "People will begin arriving for the wake in a few minutes."

Bella repeated her question.

"No, no," he answered, "we've had a branch in Texas coming on five years now. The reason you couldn't find it is that this branch focuses solely on land acquisitions for the development of real estate properties. We decided to call it the Morning Glory Corporation."

Bella stopped. That name sounded so familiar to her. Something bothered her about it, but she couldn't put her finger on it. She knew that this was important, but she just couldn't make the connection. She caught up to Manuel as he walked out of the study toward the indoor garden.

"Ok, I get it now. Why did you feel that you had to change the name of the company? After all, Ponce Industries is a legacy that your family has built an empire on?"

Beaming Manuel responded, "Well, because Puerto Rican companies are heavily taxed in America, but American companies that do business in Puerto Rico actually receive tax breaks and incentives. We are maximizing our profits by paying less in taxes. As a lawyer, I am sure that you see the advantages of making Morning Gloria an American company based in Texas."

Bella was seething inside. For years, she had known how Puerto Rico was dying due to unfair trade policies, unemployment, an aging population, and the purchase of protected lands so that millionaires could own paradise. All the while, Puerto Ricans, born American citizens, lived in one of the poorest parts of the United States. Bella had to put that aside and keep pretending. She knew she had learned a great deal of important information today.

"Absolutely. I get it. The American tax system is created to maximize profits for corporations and the wealthy. You know, that is very smart. And you want me to run this branch because I am a lawyer, family, and I grew up in the American culture."

"Bella, you catch on quick. And by joining us, you will be helping your family because of the money you will be earning as President of the Morning Glory Corporation."

Cecilia walked up to them and embraced Bella. Bella knew that Cecilia was going to ask about the position, so she had to continue pretending to be interested.

"Well, Bella, what do you think? Our company is doing well, and there is money to be made. You are the perfect candidate to run our Texas branch."

Bella showed gratitude. "Thank you, Abuela Cecilia. Your family has built an amazing legacy."

"Ah, it is your family too, Hija," Cecilia said a little too quickly. Bella wished she hadn't known she was part of this family. These terrible people's blood was in her as well, and although she could not hide that fact, she could learn from it and do better for the next generation.

"I stand corrected, our family. So, Grandma," Cecilia's smile faded slightly at the word, and Bella remembered how the woman had practically demanded she call her Grandmother at the dinner party. "Is it okay if I let you know tomorrow, then I could go back to North

Carolina to pack and say goodbye to my brothers and sisters? I'd like to speak with them first, if that will be ok."

"Of course, Bella." Cecilia clasped her hands over Bella's. We will talk tomorrow." She looked past Bella to make eye contact with the priest who walked in. "Father Ignicio, welcome. Here, let me show you where my son is laid."

Guests began to arrive, including her family. Carmen spotted Bella and came to her side.

"Bella, are you ok? How did it go? Did you learn something?"

Bella looked directly at Carmen and whispered, "I sure did, Mom. Let's talk about it when we go back to Grandma's. Let's just get this day over with and head back."

Chapter 33

Bella saw Isabela standing outside her house, waiting for everyone. She stood under the entryway with a smile on her face, welcoming her family back home. Bella thought of the years that she had stayed away from Puerto Rico and her grandmother. Isabela is the traditional grandmother who overfed you, overworried about you, and was a warm person to everyone. Bella knew that by staying in Rio Piedra with Isabela, she would make her grandmother happy, but it would also make her mom and siblings sad. It was not going to be easy to tell her family she intended to stay.

"Welcome home, everyone. I have ceviche in the refrigerator, tamarind juice, and crackers. I figured that you needed a little bit of comfort food after the wake at Cecilia's house."

Isabela spread out a serving tray with the ceviche, condiments, and freshly sliced mango. Bella hugged her grandmother and served herself food. Lulu ran down the stairs and jumped into Amelia's arms. Torry set Lulu at the table and served her food. With everyone sitting at the dining room table, enjoying Isabela's cooking, the conversation about the Wake began.

Tony started it.

"So, I am not sure who half the people that showed up today were. I mean, I knew that some of the guests were Cecilia's family and friends, but I did not know the suits that showed up." Tony looks around the table. "Does anyone know?"

All of a sudden, Carlos became excited.

"Listen, everyone, I just received an email from Professor Montoya from the University's Indigenous Project."

That got everyone's attention. Carlos kept looking at his phone, reading the email.

"Tell us what they said, Carlos. Don't keep us waiting," Carmen said.

Carlos began to read the email.

'Good afternoon, Carlos,

Thank you for reaching out to me. I must say that we at UPR are excited by the photos you sent us. Although we would need to examine the earthenware vessel, I feel sure that it originated from the Guaynia people in the late 1500s. Our records show that they fled to the hills and mountains after Ponce De Leon's diaspora of the indigenous people from the coastlines, where he established his harbors, throughout the Puerto Rican hills. Would it be possible for me to visit with you later today to examine the vessel closely?'

Please do not clean the earthenware. Today's chemicals will damage the artifact, and I will be taking a soil sample.

Professor Juan Montoya, PhD

Department of Archeology, University of Puerto Rico

"Mijo, that is so exciting." Isabela hugged and kissed Carlos. "To think an archaeologist is coming here."

"And to think Amelia said, "the pot Lulu and Bella found can tell us a little bit more about the people who lived in this area hundreds of years ago. I can't wait."

Carmen served everyone coffee.

"So, Bella, what did you learn about Cecilia's company?"

The conversation around the table became centered on Bella's investigation into Cecilia's company. She described the financial records and the several multi-million-dollar bank accounts in Puerto Rico and the US. She also told them about the various projects they are involved in.

"Ok, so Manuel showed me Ponce De Leon's ledgers and journals."

"Wait, what?" Carlos explained, "Did you say Ponce De Leon's actual ledgers and journals?"

"Yup. You should have seen how pompous he was, stressing how privileged they were because they are related to that monster De Leon, and they had some of his stuff."

Bella finished her coffee. "And listen to this, that new Texas branch they were bragging about isn't called Ponce Corporation. They're taking advantage of Puerto Rico's tax laws—using incentives meant to attract outside investment. These let corporations pay far less in taxes than everyday Puerto Ricans. If your business is based in Puerto Rico and sells to the mainland, you're hit with higher shipping and tax costs. Here's the twist: if you open a company in the U.S., say in Texas, and then do business in Puerto Rico, you avoid those penalties. The Castillos are maximizing profits by playing both ends—buying local resources, but routing sales through their stateside branch."

Isabela was curious because the Castillos had never shown an interest in her family before,

"Mija, what is the position they want you to take?"

"And now they want me to be president of their Texas subsidiary."

"Wouldn't they have had to register as a Puerto Rican company first, though?"

"They did—but when they expanded, they created a U.S.-based subsidiary. That's how they're skirting the extra costs."

"Wait, Bella," Torry said. "Their business was started here a few centuries ago, and the family has been building an empire from the land they stole and the Tainos and Africans they enslaved. Are you telling me that the Castillos' business has been growing by doing the same things that the colonists did?"

Bella nodded.

"They've named it the Morning Glory Corporation."

"Bastards!" several of her siblings said together.

Isabella let out a sigh and seemed to collapse into a chair. Everyone reacted; they jumped up to make sure she was okay. She waved them off and assured them that she was fine, but everyone could see how pale she had become.

Bella ran to her grandmother with a glass of water.

"Grandma, what's wrong. Here, drink water."

"Bella, everyone, I am ok, but I know that name. Bella, go to the study and bring me the box of records."

Bella didn't ask why; she had never seen her grandmother like this. Isabela has always been a tower of strength and control. Seeing her so pale was unusual, and it frightened her. She laid the box at Isabela's feet and opened it.

"Ok, Mima, what am I looking for?"

Isabella picked up a yellow folder full of letters and handed Bella a letter to read. But Bella didn't have to read it. She had seen this letter before, and she finally recognized the name on the letterhead, Morning Glory Corporation. Feelings of anger, bewilderment, and an immense sense of sadness filled her at the sight. Her family and her people were once again being exploited for land.

After a moment, she realized they were all staring at her.

"What is it, Bella? What is going on?"

Bella looked up at her mom and then at everyone else, tears welling up in her eyes. She faced Isabela with an unspoken recognition of what was being done to them.

"Mom, back with Manuel, I thought that I recognized the Morning Glory Corporation name, but I wasn't able to remember where I had seen it. Do you remember that Mima told us about how so many of our family and friends are losing their homes due to some corrupt deal with a real estate corporation and our local government?"

"Yeah, but what does that have to do with the Castillos?"

"I visited Olga and Magaly, both received the same letter, and Olga's mother was very depressed because she was being forced to leave the home that had been in their family for generations, because she did not have a deed to the house. They don't have anywhere else to go. The letterhead said Morning Glory Corporation. So, our friends and family's homes are being stolen by our family, the Castillos."

Tony was the first to react, "So what do we do about it?"

Bella stood up and, with resolution on her face. "I finally figured out why I am here. I am going to need everyone's help. Abuela, can you find out how many Rio Piedrans received this letter?"

"Of course, I have a file here with everyone's copies. Let me see." Isabela counted the letters in her hand. "Eighteen that I know of. I am sure others received this letter, but they didn't come to me, so I can only guess."

"Wait, are you saying that there is a good chance that our grandmother is evicting everyone up and down this hill?" Carlos asked.

Bella saw the rage and pain in his eyes. As the oldest, he spent more time here than the rest of his siblings. He had friends he grew up with in the neighborhood, and he was outraged to think they would all be forced to leave their homes because of Cecilia, just so her family could make money.

"Carlos, look, I told Manuel and Cecilia that I would consider their job offer. Let's review the information I was able to gather. I know that there is something we can do about this. We need to put our heads together and do some more research to stop this. I am going to call my supervisor to see if there is an injunction that we can place on the city's transfer of property to Morning Glory. In the meantime, some of you can help our family and friends register their homes, which will protect the ownership of their homes."

Their conversation was cut short by the sound of the doorbell.

"Oh yeah, that might be the professor." Carlos said, "Remember? His email said that he would be coming by to look at the clay pot."

The group went into the family room to meet Professor Montoya. Carlos walked into the family room with a man in her late forties who had a satchel over his shoulder. He had sun-weathered skin and short hair streaked with gray.

Isabela, always the perfect hostess, approached the professor to introduce herself.

"Good afternoon, professor. My name is Isabela. Welcome to my house. May I get you a cup of coffee?"

Professor Montoya agreed to a cup of coffee. He scanned the house. He took in the antique paintings, furniture, books, and the painted tiles that went up the stairs. He seemed fascinated by them.

His attention was pulled away from the tiles when Isabella returned with coffee.

"I want to thank you for letting me come to your home on short notice," he told her. "I have a conference on Monday and I will be away for a few days."

"It's no problem, professor. We are glad that you responded so quickly." Carlos said, then turned to Bella. "Bella, why don't you tell Professor Montoya where you found the pot?"

Bella explained that they had seen her niece up on a cliff on the hillside, where a small waterfall ran into a pond. She did not mention Nayeli or the family history. She was afraid that if she did, he would think that all of this was a joke or that they were crazy, so she chose her words carefully.

"Now, has anyone ever found anything like that before in the woods or after digging a garden?"

Carmen responded, "No, professor. I grew up in this house, and I can tell you that nothing like this has ever been found anywhere near this property."

Carlos walked in with a large covered wicker basket.

"I thought it might be easier for you to move around in this."

"Did you try to clean it?" Montoya sprang to his feet, eager to see their find.

"No, no, we followed your instructions." Carlos handed the basket to the professor and opened the curtains, allowing more light to enter the room.

Everyone remained seated to give the professor room to examine the pot. He opened his satchel and slipped on a pair of white cotton gloves before lifting the pot out and setting it on the center table. He pulled out a pen and a notepad and began taking notes and sketching some of the images on the pot.

Bella received a call from Laura, and she stepped out into the hallway to take the call.

"Good afternoon, Laura."

"Good afternoon, Bella. I looked into Morning Star Corporation and found that it is a legitimate company founded by your family in Austin, Texas. They seem to be purchasing land in poor neighborhoods and then developing luxury apartments. According to what I found, they invest heavily in the communities that they are about to buy they donating supplies to schools and neighborhood clinics, and of course, by making rather large contributions to elected officials ."

"Yeah, well, I know what you mean when you say invest in the communities. You mean that they bought the politicians to get permits so they could gentrify poor neighborhoods and evict the current residents."

"This must be their standard business practice because Laura, that is exactly what they are doing here. My family and friends are being thrown out of their homes, and the local politicians sold their land out from under them to the Castillos to make it happen."

"Yeah, I know, but unless you can prove they bribed someone, what can you do about it?"

"Well, can you help me find a lawyer here in Puerto Rico who isn't influenced by Morning Star Corporation or Casillo's money or one of their pet politicians. We need to put in a petition with the courts to place a temporary injunction on the evictions. I need a little more time to come up with resources to help this community."

"Sure, let me make some phone calls. I will call you back as soon as I have a lead."

Chapter 34

The family sat in silence, watching as the professor took out a toolbox containing small jars and various tools. He took samples of the dirt surrounding the pot. He scraped the inside of the pot to dust off the clay. Professor Montoya took photos of the outside, inside, and at the base of the pot. Lastly, the professor sketched the pot and the carving designs on its surface. He then turned to the group.

"I have to tell you that this is exciting. I cannot tell you much about it now, in case it's a replica. It will take me a couple of days to run these samples through the spectrometer and carbon-date the clay. Give me until next weekend, and I will call you with the results."

The professor packed up the toolbox with the samples. "Again, I want to thank you for letting me barge into your weekend to look at the vessel. I will process the samples today, and my TA will inform me of the results later in the week."

The professor said his goodbyes. Isabella was the first to speak up, "Well, that was exciting, huh? A professor is coming to our home to research the pot that Lulu found." Everyone nodded.

Torry leaned over and whispered in Amelia's ear. "At this rate, if we stay much longer, our child is going to think she is Supergirl." Amelia giggled and kissed Torry's cheek, "Our child is Supergirl."

"I hope he gets those results right away," Isabella said. "Even if the results say that it is a replica of something, it's still exciting to imagine that it may be a real artifact from our ancestors who lived in these hills."

Bella was feeling a little overwhelmed. Her near-death episode, her father's wake, and the discovery that her father's family was stealing people's homes and making millions of dollars off their neighbors' suffering. Now, a professor came to the house to research the clay pot they found. It was all too much to bear in one day. She had to get out of the house for a little bit.

"Hey," she said to the group, "how about if we go do some sightseeing today. I have a lot on my mind, and I need a break. You know we are close to the National Forest. Let's take Lulu there, we can spend the rest of the day exploring."

Lulu sprang out of her mother's arms and headed upstairs, hollering, "I'll get my shoes."

Everyone laughed, and the thin thread of despair that had hung in the air since Isabella heard the name Morning Glory broke. Everyone stood and agreed.

Isabella took out her picnic basket, and she and Carmen filled it with fruit juices, sandwiches, and snacks. Amelia gathered throws to lie on the grass. Torry packed a tote with frisbees, badminton rackets, and a soccer ball. Torry knew that they all could use a day of fun. Tomorrow was Luis's funeral, and on Tuesday, they would fly back home. Torry felt a bit sad thinking about returning home. She felt like this house on this hill was her home as much as it was Amelia's. She was conflicted, but she knew that she couldn't be in two places at once. After all, Amelia had her career, and Torry knew how much she loved nursing. She promised herself that they would make trips to Puerto Rico more often so Lulu could spend more time with her great-grandmother and her extended family.

Isabela reached out to her nearby family and invited them to the park. Together, they set up a picnic under the shade of some trees near a creek. Bella felt a sense of peace and nostalgia upon seeing her family together, just as they used to be. This is her family. This is her community. There was no reason for her to return to an empty apartment in North Carolina and feel detached and isolated again. She knew she was making the right decision. And she knew that she had to find the time to tell her family.

Chapter 35

Luis's funeral went as expected. Bella thought how sad it was that her father was being interred today, and his family did not mourn for him. His mother and nephew showed no sadness at his passing; his death was simply an inconvenience they endured. Bella wondered at the lack of remorse and couldn't help but wonder if Cecilia would ever forgive her son for ruining her plans. Cecilia, always the showman, paid for an elaborate casket, satin sheets, and expensive flowers not native to Puerto Rico. She played the perfect hostess while Manuel played politics as company staff and customers paid their respect to a man they had never known.

Bella saw Tony and Carlos walking up to the casket together. They quietly restrained their tears. After all, as children, they spent the most time with Luis, and they remembered him as a good husband and father. And yet here they were, after so many years apart, saying goodbye.

Tony quietly whispered to Luis, "Dad, I don't know if I can ever truly forgive you for hurting us and robbing us of a future with our father, but I want to thank you for helping Bella when she was lost to us in that darkness. Thank you, Dad."

Carlos followed, "Yes, Dad, thank you for bringing Bella back to us. I disagree with the way you handled the situation back then, and you chose money over us, but keep protecting Bella, and maybe someday you'll be forgiven." Carlos and Tony turned away from their father's casket with a sense of relief and closure.

Amelia sat in the front row, staring at her father's body. Torry and Lulu sat beside her.

"Hey Mel, how are you? Can I do anything to help you?"

Amelia looked at her wife and child and thought how fortunate she was, having the kind of family she had always wanted to have as a child.

"I am fine. You know, I was so worried about seeing him again after so many years. But I realize that there wasn't anything for me to be anxious about. When it comes down to it, I am still angry with him, but when I look at him, I see the dad who danced with me, protected me, and played with me. Well, up to a certain age, that is. I would have preferred him to leave with another woman than choose to abandon us for his family's money."

She stood and moved toward the casket. Torry started to stand.

"It's okay, I got this, stay with Lulu," Amelia said.

Amelia set a hand on the edge of the casket, her head bowed as if in prayer.

"Goodbye, Dad," she said, "I will always miss what we could have had if you hadn't left us."

When she returned to her seat, Torry leaned into her and whispered, "Is that San Juan's Mayor over there?"

Amelia turned her head to look. "Yup, that's him. And I see Richard Williams with First National Bank. I am not surprised that

Cecilia invited her investors and a politician to do business at her son's funeral. Disgusting!"

Tony approached his sister and handed Amelia the funeral program. "Have you seen this?"

Amelia looked at it, and her eyes widened. Torry noticed Amelia's response. "What is it?"

Amelia handed her the funeral program, took a deep breath, and gathered herself. "Well, why am I surprised?? She arranged for the reading of the will to be held after the guests leave. I guess she is ready to say goodbye to her son, now and forever."

"But why?" Torry asked, "It's not as if they won't inherit his money. What's the hurry?"

Tony thought about it for a minute. "Did Cecilia tell any of us that there was going to be a will reading after the funeral?"

Both women shook their heads.

"Me either. Let me ask Mom since she helped plan out the funeral. I'll be right back."

Carmen was sitting quietly outside on the patio, lost in her own thoughts. She was quietly talking to Luis, hoping that wherever he was, he would hear her.

'Luis, you were my first and last love. I really don't know if I can forgive you for abandoning our children. You didn't just leave my side; you walked out of their lives. I will never understand why you didn't reach out to them over the years. You caused a lot of damage. But I do want to thank you for the few wonderful years we had together. Living with you was exciting. And now I know that you walked away from the governor's daughter to elope with me. I would say to you that maybe you shouldn't have turned away from your mother's plans to conquer the world. But I know that our children wouldn't have been born. My kids are the most important thing in my life. And I want to thank you for helping Bella. Please protect her and your granddaughter, Lulu. I am sure that you know that although Amelia and Torry didn't want to know whose egg conceived Lulu, there's no denying that she has our blood in her because she can see and talk to Nayeli. Please protect her as well.'

Tony sat beside his mom. He noticed her eyes filled with tears. "Mom, you don't have to hide your tears from me. I know that you two loved each other, and you have more memories of being with him than we do. It's ok."

Carmen hugged her son. "Thank you, Tony. I came out here because I didn't want Cecilia to see me cry."

"I get it. Did you notice the politicians and the bank executives here?"

"I recognized the mayor, but no, I wouldn't have noticed any executives."

"Yup. Manuel and Cecilia have been holding little meetings in the study with different people. It's disgusting! Listen, Mom, did Cecilia show you the program? Did you know about the reading of the will right after the funeral?"

Carmen's eyes widened. "What? No, I didn't know. She wrote the program and didn't show it to me. Why would she do that so soon after burying him?"

"That's what I was thinking. The fact is that she did not want us at the reading of the will, or she would have invited us to it. I guess she knows that we were cut out of the family inheritance a long time ago."

Carmen and Tony walked back into the solarium when they saw everyone walking in. They assumed the priest was ready to say the final rites. Carmen saw Cecilia out in the hallway, arguing with someone.

Carmen made her way to the doors to see if she could hear what they were arguing about.

"Look, Ms. Castillo, I am bound by the courts, and I have to follow the law. Your son left a will, and his wish was that his wife and children be present. That's the way it has to be."

"Look, Mr. Perez, maybe we can come up with an arrangement of some kind. I can be very generous, you know."

Mr. Perez appeared to be offended. "Ms. Castillo, I do not know what you mean. After the priest completes his service, we will all gather in your study." Mr. Perez walked into the solarium and took a seat, leaving Cecilia flabbergasted. She had always been able to buy her way through problems and red tape; who was this lawyer to disregard her wishes? She walked to her seat in the front row, dabbing at her dry eyes with a tissue, once again performing the role of a distraught mom.

Carmen walked back to sit next to Tony and whispered, "Tell everyone not to leave after this. We are crashing the reading."

Tony smiled. He hadn't seen his mom this worked up in a long time. He knew that look on her face. It was the look that said not to argue with her, or she would destroy you. It was the look she had on the day her husband left her —a look of resolve.

After the priest blessed Luis, he turned around and gave a rose to Cecilia and his condolences. Bella noticed that he didn't approach her mom. She thought to herself that these people are hypocrites, and they deserve each other. With the solarium empty, Carmen whispered to her kids. "We aren't leaving. I overheard the lawyer tell Cecilia that it was your father's wish that we be present for the reading. Cecilia was mad, and she tried to bribe him. It didn't work, and she was visibly upset. That is, until she walked into the room. So, we aren't leaving. I have a feeling that she is going to walk into the study where the lawyer is set up and claim that we didn't want anything to do with Luis and leave. So, we are just going to walk in. Come on."

Carmen's children beamed with pride at seeing their mother taking control away from Cecilia.

Carmen opened the door to find Cecilia telling the lawyer that they had already left. "Thank you, Cecilia, but we haven't left." Carmen looked at the lawyer to address him. "I am sorry that we are late. But, here we are."

Mr. Perez smiled at Carmen's bravery. He knew the Castillo family. Everyone knew the Castillo family. One thing that everyone knew was that you don't say no to Cecilia Castillo or grandstand her.

"Well, good. Now we can begin." Mr. Perez broke the seal of the envelope he was holding and pulled out one document.

"Mr. Perez, there must be a mistake. My son's will is eight pages long. I helped him write it. Did you leave a file at your office?"

Mr. Perez was savoring the moment. His family had made their wealth by helping Cecilia and her husband bend the law in their favor. His father would do anything that the Castillos wanted him to do. He grew up watching his father simper and grovel to the Castillos his whole life. He hated that and vowed to find a way to undo their retainer legally. He let the pause linger, and then he answered.

"Oh yes, I remember that will. That was when he turned eighteen. My father documented that will."

Cecilia was glad that Mr. Perez remembered the original will, and she relaxed in her seat. She thought to herself that Mr. Perez had never been as detail-oriented and loyal to the Castillo family as his father was. *This imbecile is the reason I'm looking for another law firm to represent us,* she thought.

Mr. Perez made direct eye contact with Cecilia. He wanted to savor this moment as she saw all her plans fall through. "Oh yes, I remember that will."

Cecilia smiled, "Yes, that will. Where is it?"

Now to savor the moment, "That will was made null and void back in 2010 and replaced with this one." He held the one sheet up. "This is the current living will of Luis Castillo."

Carmen couldn't help smiling. This was unprecedented. Cecilia planned for every detail in people's lives. Her primary goal in life was to accumulate wealth and elevate her family to the 1%, the elite who controlled the world.

Cecilia jumped up from her chair. "What are you saying? What new will? Let me see that?"

"I am sorry, Ms. Castillo, but only I am permitted to see this will at this moment. Your son contacted me shortly after he returned to Puerto Rico. He handed me a doctor's report of his most recent physical and mental health assessment. Your son was of sound mind and body when he drafted this will, and it is my obligation to read it now in front of his family. Would you please sit down?"

Cecilia had never been caught off guard, let alone talked to in the way Mr. Perez spoke to her. She looked at Carmen's family and saw small smiles on their faces. This burned her to her core.

Mr. Perez broke into her thoughts. "Ms. Castillo, please sit down so that I can continue. I still want to enjoy the rest of my weekend. You know I usually don't work on the weekends, but you insisted that we hold this meeting after the funeral. Well, let's continue."

On the outside, Cecilia was still playing the part of the perfect hostess, distraught mother, and a person with power. She sat down.

"Well, like I was saying, Mr. Luis Castillo wanted all of you here for the reading. He wrote a short narrative addressing you all:

Mother,

I had always known that you were a cunning and ruthless woman when it came to growing your enterprise. I know that you were proud of your family lineage and felt that you were superior to most because of your pedigree. You planned our futures for us and made our lives a living hell. The word Mother or Parent has specific meanings that mainly account for a person who loved, provided, protected, and forgave her children. I realized, much too late, that you don't love us. You do not love anyone but yourself, your money, and your power.

I will always regret abandoning my family. You tempted me with the prospect of losing my inheritance, so I left them. But, mother, you are in for a surprise. You never asked me why I left Carmen and the kids. You just immediately made plans for me to join the business and follow in your footsteps. That is why I left your house and lived the rest of my life as a recluse. Honestly, I couldn't stand being around all of you.

My siblings, aunts, uncles, nieces, and nephews,

I feel sorry for you. You weren't living your own lives. For money, you joined the devil. Ask yourselves, are you happy with your life? Did you do the things you always wanted to do? My life is over now, but yours is still going, and you still have time to follow your passion.

Carmen,

You were the only woman I loved. I wanted you to know that I didn't leave you for another woman. I went to protect my kids. I think you know what I'm referring to by now. I come from a very powerful family, and their greed for wealth and power is insatiable. I did not want them to be crushed under my family's evil.

My beautiful children,

You do not know how often I woke up sobbing in bed because not only did I walk out on Carmen and all of you, but I missed seeing you grow up. Please know that I kept tabs on all of you. A few times I went to North Carolina and laid my eyes on you from a distance. All I can say is I'm sorry I was not there for you when you needed me. Carlos and Antonio, I am so proud of the men you have become. Amelia, you've found a loving partner and have a beautiful family. I am sorry that I wasn't there to share those moments with you. Bella, by now, you know why I left. I want you to know that you were always my baby. I have seen you grow up. I blamed myself when you were struggling during your teen years, but I knew if I went back to living with you, all your lives would have been in danger from the evil that plagues my family.

I want you all to know that I have always been proud of the men and women that you have become.

Please forgive me,

Your father'

Mr. Perez continued, "With a sound mind and body, I make these statements before my lawyer, Mr. Angelo Perez Jr., and his public notary. I am bequeathing to Carmen, Tony, Carlos, Amelia, Torry, Bella, and my granddaughter my entire estate."

Cecilia jumped out of her chair. Manuel cried out in disbelief. "Mr. Perez, you have the wrong document. The document we wrote listed numerous items of inventory, property, and money that Luis inherited. I know that he didn't use it, so it should still be there. Let me see that document because I know that this isn't the correct will."

Mr. Perez did not give her the document because he was afraid that she would tear it up. Instead, I placed it inside the folder and sealed it before standing up.

"Ms. Castillo, I already told you that the original will was destroyed many years ago. This is the most recent will your son made. I am sorry, but if you keep interrupting, I will make an appointment with Ms. Carmen Castillo on another day."

Cecilia was still confused. She felt numb. Her son had a sizeable inheritance that she was counting on for the new development she planned for Rio Piedra. Cecilia sat down.

"Alright, let me list the estate. To my wife Carmen, I leave $250,000. I know that this doesn't make up for the hurt I caused. But I want you to know that I had always planned to provide for you. To my son Antonio, I leave $500,000, my 1982 Harley-Davidson, and my small boat. I know that you love fishing. To Carlos, I will leave $500,000 and the cabin I bought in Maine the year you were born. I don't know if you remember us going to the cabin, but I will always cherish the memories I have of hiking and riding the trails with you. My strong and beautiful Amelia. I love you. I will leave $500,000, some of my grandmother's jewelry that is in a safe deposit box, the key to which I have left in the care of Mr. Perez. Additionally, when you were little, you told me that you wanted a car like the 1978 Ford Mustang we had in Miami. I have restored it and have kept it in storage for all these years. It is now yours and Torry's to enjoy. Mr. Perez has the key to the storage facility in Miami. Bella, my baby. I am leaving you $500,000, my house in Ponce, all the furniture at that house, and the furniture that I have in a storage facility. I am also leaving you three antique oil paintings. And finally, Lulu. I will always regret that the only time I could see you was from a distance. You are smart and kind. To you, I want to give the means to make your own choices when you grow up by leaving you $250,000 and two crates of old family toys. I have collected them over the years, and I am now passing them on to you. Take good care of them.

Children, please accept what I leave you. I know that you can't forgive me, but let me do this one last gesture to provide for you."

Mr. Perez handed the file to Carmen. Clasping her hand, Mr. Perez presented her with the documentation. "Mrs. Castillo, allow me to offer you my condolences. I knew Luis. More when he came back to the island. He spoke about all of you and how proud he was of each and every one of you. He wanted to help you meet your life goals with this inheritance." He looked at Carmen and her kids. Their faces were masks of disbelief. He noticed that they all had tears in their eyes. He felt sorry for this family because he knew Luis to be a caring parent, all the while they thought the worst of him. Who wouldn't if their father left with no real explanation, leaving them with feelings of resentment, anger, hatred, and bewilderment? And today, they heard from their father when it was too late for them to tell him what they wanted to say.

On the other side of the room sat the other Castillo family. Manuel was talking to his mother. Cecilia sat in disbelief, shaking her head. There weren't any tears in their eyes. The adults were visibly upset. Their kids seemed not to care. Why would they? After all, their money is still there. The Castillos will endure through time, continuing to use their money to pay for backroom deals to increase their wealth. He thought to himself how despicable they were.

Cecilia walked up to Mr. Perez. "Mr. Perez, I will sue you for this trickery. My son's inheritance was supposed to be bequeathed to his siblings and me." She looked at Carmen. "Is this your doing? Did you and Mr. Perez plan this? I knew that you only married my son for his money. This will not be the end of this."

Mr. Perez turned to face Cecilia. "Listen to me, Ms. Castillo. The first will was destroyed, and your son wrote this new will. Luis came to my office several times to provide me with details that were to be put in the will. This document cannot be altered or destroyed by anyone except Mr. Luis Castillo, and I don't foresee that happening, do you? Of course not. This legal document has been registered with the county clerk. You can waste money and lawyers' time to contest this will, but it is sealed and closed. Don't waste your money." Mr. Perez smiled at Cecilia. "After all, you are probably the richest people on the island. A measly 2 million dollars that your son left his family is nothing to you. In fact, it's petty cash for you." He turned back to Carmen, indicating that the conversation with Cecilia was over.

"Mrs. Castillo, your late husband put the information about safety deposit boxes, and the keys to the motorcycle, the boat, and the cabin in here." He removed another folder from his case and handed it to Carmen." Ms. Bella, here are the keys to the storage facilities and his property. The addresses are also in the folder I have given your mother."

He turned back to Carmen.

"On Monday, I will transfer his accounts to you and your children. I will need you to sign a confirmation of acceptance of the terms of this will. I also need each of you for a minute to get your banking information so your inheritances can be deposited into each of your accounts Monday morning."

One by one, they signed the documents and provided Mr. Perez with their banking information. They walked out of the study, confused as to what had just happened. They had inherited money and property from a father they thought had abandoned them.

"Everyone, let's get out of here before Cecilia comes out to accuse me of stealing from her. Let's meet up at Abuela's house," Carmen said.

From the hallway, they heard Cecilia yelling at Mr. Perez, but he was smiling as he walked out. He closed the door and left Cecilia and her family in the study. He knew that on Monday, he would refund Cecilia the rest of the retainer she had paid his firm because he didn't want to do any business with them. He took a deep breath and sighed.

As he caught up to Bella and her family, he called out, "Ms. Castillo, do not let them bully you out of that inheritance. It is yours. This was his last will. He wanted to provide you all with something that could help you. He talked to me about his childhood and how much he hated his mother. He knew that this was going to make her angry, and it was his final way of telling his mother that she had never been able to control him, not even in death."

They walked out together, and Mr. Perez wished them well.

Chapter 36

Isabela heard the cars drive up the hill, and she knew that her family was returning from the funeral. Isabela didn't want to show it, but she was sad because she knew her daughter and her grandchildren were leaving in two days. Although she has friends and had plenty to do, it was wonderful being together with family. Isabela's loneliness had gone away for a week. Her house felt nostalgic when she remembered the children running and playing around the house. Isabela wiped her tears and headed to the doorway to greet her family.

Carmen practically ran to her mother. "Mami, mami, come inside. I have something to tell you." Everyone else quickly followed into the family room.

"What happened? Why are you all so excited? Wait, what did Cecilia do to you?

Carmen took a deep breath before answering, "No, Mom, Cecilia didn't do anything to her. In fact, it appears that Luis was rebellious one last time against his mother. Mom, Luis left his kids and me his inheritance!"

"Well, he should. I mean, he owed you. But the man lived in a decrepit house in Ponce. How much money could he have left you?"

The group yelled it out at the same time, "two million dollars and property!"

Isabela's eyes widened, "Qué?"

Carmen told Isabela what happened during the reading of the will. Isabela sat there, amazed, wishing she had been there to see Cecilia deflate and put in her place.

"So, you're telling me that Luis was still rich after walking away from his fortune?"

"Yes," Tony said, "Mr. Perez said he inherited money and property when his grandparents passed, and Cecilia never touched the original will because in that will, she would have inherited everything. She didn't know that Luis changed it, so why would she do anything different? Luis was living a hermit's life and was not involved with the business. So, when he died, she would gain his wealth. Well, the joke's on her." Tony looked up, as if gazing at the sky. "Dad, I don't know if you can hear this, but good one."

"Well, Abuela, I think this is a moment for celebrating our financial troubles gone, and we were present when Cecilia lost." Carlos gave his grandmother a hug and a smile wide enough to make Isabela smile.

Isabela was happy that her family was laughing and joking around after all that had happened.

"OK, sounds like a good plan to me. Let's gather our friends and family for a cookout, and let's forget about our problems for today."

The family sat around the dinner table enjoying breakfast. Carlos and Amelia drafted plans for the day's activities. They knew that their flight departed the next day, and they had to make arrangements for their inheritance. They agreed to leave the items stored away on the island and deal with them another time. All of them received messages from their banks confirming the deposits that were made into their accounts. There was a process for inheriting more than $10,000 and depositing it in a bank. With that out of the way, they discussed their plans for managing their money, including investing, using CDs, donating to charitable organizations, and traveling.

Bella felt guilty for not having told her family that she was staying behind. This was the time to do it. But before Bella could speak to her family, her cell phone rang.

"It's Laura. Give me a minute." Bella answered the phone. "Hi, Laura. How are you? What did you find out?"

Everyone around the table stopped moving.

"Yes, Laura. It is a parcel of land that my mom's family developed."

"Listen, Bella, I made some calls. The land deal is iron-clad. There's no way to stop it. Your grandmother's lawyers used an antiquated law that established land rights to someone who could develop it for the betterment of the island." Bella knew betterment meant people with money had the first rights to buy land. Laura referenced a case from 1899, where an investor purchased 600 acres of land from the city, with plans to build houses for sale to the wealthy who were discovering the Caribbean. Her petition claimed that most of the properties in Rio Piedra do not have titles and are there for reclaiming by someone who can improve the situation and bring in commerce."

"What? Are you serious?"

"Yes. Your grandmother is a cunning businesswoman, and she has lawyers doing her bidding. I am sorry, Bella, there is nothing you can do but help your friends and family move."

"Thank you, Laura. It's tough to hear. Thanks for all the work that you did."

Bella hung up the phone and looked at her family.

From the look on her face, Tony knew that it wasn't good. "Ok, so tell us. There is nothing that can be done about the evictions, right?"

"No, Laura found out that Cecilia used an 1899 law to purchase this land. Although the sale hasn't been finalized, there is nothing that would stop that from happening. Morning Star Corporation is set to buy this land next week."

Bella walked away from the table, went out the back doors, and walked into her forest. This was her place to think, to cry, to relax, and to get away. She walked along some of the paths that led to the pond. She thought to herself how beautiful everything was. Bella knew that her grandmother had a title to her house, but so many of the surrounding neighbors didn't, and all of this land would be destroyed. She stopped to look at a sapling of a mango tree. Bella knew that this tree would not get any taller. She was certain that Cecilia would not stop until she acquired this land. Her plans depended on it. In front of her was the waterfall and the pond. The rays of the sun came through the canopy, bathing the water in a magical shimmer, as if this area were enchanted. Bella sat on the boulder to think about everything that had happened. *Our lives here on the island could be the plot to a movie or something,* she thought.

Bella felt the answer was near. But she blamed herself for not discovering the solution. Bella cried in a way she hadn't in a long time. She found her community and chose to stay behind, only to have it taken away by Cecilia. And she felt she had let Nayeli down. She failed her.

"Nayeli, why did you choose me? I am a failure. Always have been. You chose wrong."

Bella rested her head on her hands. She looked up when she realized she wasn't alone anymore. Nayeli stood on top of the waterfall. This time, she looked solid.

"Nayeli? Wait, is that you? Are you real?"

Bella saw a smile on her face and heard in her head, "You still have to find me. Don't lose hope. You are closer than you think. Don't give up."

Bella wiped tears from her face.

"Where are you? In a book? A portrait? Where?"

"I am where your heart resides." Nayeli disappeared.

"Wait, wait, I need your help. What does that mean?"

Bella heard her name being called and looked up to see Tony running down the path towards her. Panting, he stopped in front of the boulder.

"Listen, sis, you aren't going to believe this. Professor Montoya called. He wanted to let us know that the clay pot is authentic pottery from the 1600s. And he wants to come over with some of his students to search the area. Plus, he wants to talk to you about where you found it. He is on his way."

Bella was excited to learn that she held in her hands a piece of her ancestors' history. She wondered if it was from Nayeli's people.

An hour later, the family was gathered in the family room.

Isabella welcomed the professor and his two assistants.

"Professor," Carlos said as he shook the Professor's hand, "I thought you would be at the conference today."

"I have canceled my plans." She said, a wild smile forming on his face. "It's much more exciting to look for new artifacts from our early indigenous era. What you have found here is far too important. " He turned to Isabella, "Señora, I am sorry to barge into your home with such short notice."

Isabella waved away his concern, "Señor, you are welcome here always."

Professor Montoya grinned, a slight blush rising to his cheeks. He looked around the room and addressed everyone.

"The results came in and confirm that the earthenware vessel you found is from a Taino tribe that migrated to these hills seeking safety from the colonists. The relief on the pot is commonly found in Guania archaeological sites. I wasn't able to find any research on artifacts from that tribe in this region. All known sites are in and around Lares. This may be the first artifact from the Guania to be found here."

He turned to face Isabela. "As the owner of the property, may we have permission to dig around the area where this pot was found?"

"Of course you can. All I ask is that you put the land back the way it was."

"Thank you, Sra. Isabela. We will." He turned towards Bella, Amelia, and Torry. "Can you show me where you found the pot?" He turned to look at his students. "Please get the equipment out of the van and meet me in the backyard."

Chapter 37

Isabel was motivated to prepare lunch for everyone. The past few days had been both exciting and frightening, but having a professor researching on her land was truly exhilarating.

Tony and Carlos helped the students carry their gear and supplies to the backyard. They knew that the cliff where they found the pot was narrow and treacherous.

"Professor," Carlos said, "the trail and cliff are pretty narrow, so my brother and I will stay here. Too many people may be too crowded, and we would just get in the way. We'll stay behind to help our grandmother."

Torry knelt beside Lulu. "Honey, maybe when you tell the professor about how you found the pot, you shouldn't mention Nayeli. She might not want everyone to know about her. Okay."

"Yes, Mama." *The last thing they needed was an investigation into their daughter's state of mental health,* Torry thought as she led her child down the hill to play with her cousin Angel at her house.

Bella led the professor and two students through the trail that led to the upper cliff of the waterfall. She heard the students talking about how beautiful the woods were.

"Isn't this place amazing?" Iris whispered to her classmate.

"Yeah, I know. It is so peaceful. I mean, look at this place. It looks like something from a fantasyland like they show in movies." Claudio scanned the forest around her in awe.

"You wouldn't know that the city is less than a mile from us."

"And I know this sounds crazy, but I swear that I feel like we are being watched." Iris looked all around her.

The professor broke their silence with a joke, "Well, maybe we are being watched by fairies."

The students stopped walking, "Wait, fairies professor, really?"

The professor laughed and apologized for the silly joke. Bella thought about how close he was to the reality of this place. Fairies are not the ones watching. But how could she tell them that her ancestors' spirits were the sentinels of this place? She knew she couldn't say anything about Nayeli and what had happened over the past week. If she talked about it, they might turn around and leave. She knew somehow that their research played a vital role in completing her task and helping her friends and family.

The group began their hike up the hill just as the rays of sunlight bathed the pond. Bella heard a gasp from Iris as the sun's rays shimmered on the water, making the scene magical. The group stopped to take in the view, mesmerized by the beauty of nature.

"This is beautiful, Bella. Did you grow up here?" Iris's voice was full of curiosity, filled with eagerness to learn more about the place written all over her face.

Bella noticed that all three of them were staring at the pond with wonder. With a smile on her face and a sense of pride, she replied to Iris.

"Yes, I was born in Puerto Rico and grew up here. Even when we moved to the continent, we visited regularly. My favorite place in all of Puerto Rico has always been this small forest. I spent my childhood playing with my brothers and sister here, swimming in the pond, picking fruit, and drawing on that boulder down there. I would feel an intense sense of loss for this place every time we returned to the US. I'm glad you're enjoying it. I always feel re-energized after spending time in here." Bella addressed the professor, "We can go down to the pond later if you want to check it out after you examine the site where I found the pot."

The professor loved that idea. "Can I get some soil and fauna samples as well?"

"Of course. Please know, Professor, regardless of what your research suggests, we are not interested in selling or commercializing this land. We feel that we belong to this land, and it belongs to us. Our family history tells us that our ancestors lived in these hills. We do not want to destroy our past."

Unknown to Bella, the professor, as a historian and archaeologist, had always advocated for the protection of Puerto Rican land. He had even lost some funding because of a protest that he led four years ago, when a developing company and a Washington, D.C. senator drew up a bill that would allow U.S. investors to buy protected land and beaches to set up million-dollar houses and condos in Puerto Rico. The outcome was a disaster for his career and his research. It seemed that Puerto Rico's governor would financially benefit from this deal. The university president informed the professor that he was not allowed to protest political issues again, or he would risk losing complete funding for his research and possibly his position at the university. Since then, he had to get creative and partner with Professor Eliana Rodriguez from the University of Santo Dominguez. Her research into the impact of the Spanish colonization on the native people in the Dominican Republic was breaking new ground. He didn't mind if she took the lead on this study as long as he found a way to continue to research the native and slave population in Puerto Rico affected by conquest, capitalism, and its impact on the island, then and today.

"Bella, thank you. I can see that you cherish this land."

The professor appreciated that Bella and her family felt a strong connection to this land in a time when Puerto Ricans were being enticed to move to the United States for better work and living opportunities. The aging population they left behind would most likely not be politically active or willing to protest the lengths corporations would go to seize their land. Professor Montoya thought to himself that he would like to interview the family in depth at another time.

"Yes, I do, and I will do anything to protect it." Bella looked up at the top of the cliff. "So, professor, if you look at the top of the cliff and then look further to the right and down, you will see a large flat boulder in between some bushes."

The professor nodded. "Yes, I see the rock."

"That rock is kind of flat, and it allows a person to stand on it. I wouldn't risk two people, though." Bella continued to guide the group up the hill. "Alongside that rock is a patch of dirt covered by moss that has been untouched for a long time. When I found the pot, I asked my grandmother if she could remember if anyone had ever been up to that spot before. She told me that even when she was a child playing in the woods, she had never spotted that rock because no one was allowed to go near the pond. She spoke about a legend around the pond that kept the children away."

That piqued everyone's curiosity.

Iris was the first to ask, "What legend?"

"Well, she said that the children were told that there was a malevolent presence surrounding the pond, you know, a 'cucu.'"

The professor was fascinated, "A boogey monster, here in this special and magical place."

Bella smiled, "Yeah, right. My mom would find me here whenever I disappeared from her side and would reprimand me for being on the boulder in the pond. She swore that 'el cucu' was going to get me because this was his home, and he didn't like it when people trespassed. My grandmother told me that in her time, children were punished if caught near the pond. She explained that they were only allowed to come into the woods to pick fruit with a grown-up. She told me about how an eight-year-old child was found floating on the pond back in the 1930s. She died the next day at the hospital. She told everyone that El Cucu wanted her to find something at the bottom of the falls. I'm not sure if this is true. I never thought about it. But I never believed that this beautiful place was the home of any monsters. This place felt peaceful and wonderful, so I snuck out and came here whenever possible. So, I may have been the only child to hang out at this pond."

The thought of a piece of land untouched by modern humans was too good to be true, thought the Professor. Bella had disturbed it when she dug up the pot, but from her description of the delicate way it was worked, he did not believe she had done irreparable damage. He was ready to look for her excavation of the site, but other than that, it sounded like the cucu legend kept children away for a long time.

Once at the top of the waterfall, the professor set up his rock-climbing equipment and secured it to the base of a large tree. He would rappel down to the rock and assess the area for risk factors. The students set up a small 4'x4' tent and tables with bins and mesh filters on them. They unpacked vials, labels to record the samples, and digital equipment. Iris placed an outdoor camera on top of the tree that held the rappelling rope, in front of the tables where samples would be processed, and one at the edge of the cliff to record the professor. Then she set up another rope, connected it to a basket, and sent it down to the professor.

Bella was curious. "Why the cameras?"

Iris explained, "To verify site authenticity. We don't want anyone to dispute any of our findings. So, we will record the entire time we are here, documenting how we process any samples the professor sends to us. We want the third camera to record everything the professor is doing, so no one can accuse him of falsely tainting the samples or putting replicas in the ground and declaring them authentic."

Bella was shocked. She knew that the legal world was frighteningly competitive and cunning, but she was not aware that academia was just as ruthless.

"Wow, does that happen often?"

"Every time. Everyone is out for the next big discovery. When you make a significant find, people working on the same research will pick your work apart to protect their studies. You see, not only can the research team become famous, but they will publish their findings in peer-reviewed journals, sometimes get the spotlight on national television, and, most importantly, they will secure contracts with the corporation or university they work for. New contracts come with increased funding. So, we want to do everything by the book, so our professionalism can't be questioned."

As he set up bins around the table, Claudio laughed, "Yeah, we don't want to be bogged down by court battles while someone else takes over our research, or worse, if our research is affecting corporations and politicians' wallets, research can be stopped and forgotten."

"I had no idea."

From the boulder site, everyone heard the professor. "Is everyone ready. I am recording. This is Dr. Juan Montoya with the Archeology Department of the University of Puerto Rico. We have been asked to visit an undisclosed site to investigate a recent artifact discovered by a resident in this location. With me are graduate students Iris Rodriguez and Claudio Morales. I am standing on a 2'x2' piece of land hanging off a cliffside. I am secure and ready to analyze the site. I will be taking soil, rock, and fauna samples from this site to establish any human interaction. We are also looking to establish who inhabited this region. Is everyone ready up there?"

"Yes, Professor."

"Alrighty, here we go."

Amelia showed up with cold bottles of water and a fresh fruit salad. Claudio set up a small camping table by the trailhead. "I'm sorry to put you way out here," he told her. "But there is a chance that food could contaminate our artifact processing. And at this early stage, we wouldn't want to risk site integrity." Amelia walked up to Bella with a raised eyebrow, "Site integrity?"

Bella smiled. "Apparently, archeology is more cutthroat than nursing."

"No way."

"Apparently, they attempt to discredit any research that doesn't put them at the top of the charts."

Amelia looked at Bella, "Okay, so just like nursing then."

The woman laughed together for a moment, then Bella pointed toward the camp.

"Pretty cool, huh?"

"Way cool," Amelia agreed.

The researchers took a break to enjoy Isabela's lunch and hydrate with water and tamarind juice. They sat on the ground, away from the research camp, to maintain site integrity, as Claudio told them.

Iris looked around. "This place is so relaxing, I can see why the family wants to protect it. Almost like the outside world is far away, and while I am here, I am stress-free."

"Yet if we walk a mile in any direction, we'll be back in civilization."

Professor Montoya nodded in agreement.

"Yes, I know what you mean. By the way, Amelia, please let your grandmother know that the food is delicious and we appreciate it. Bella, tell me what it is about this forest that you want to protect?"

Bella took a moment to think of how to explain her attachment to this land without revealing family secrets. "Well, I was born here. During my childhood, I was allowed to run around and walk to my extended family's homes, where I had a sense of community, but this place always drew me to it." She laughed, "My mom and grandmother would get mad at me when they found me sitting on that boulder by the pond because of the legend that surrounded it. We were only allowed to go a few yards into this forest to pick fruit, but we weren't allowed to get close to the pond. But I felt as if I belonged in this forest. I felt I was a part of something wonderful and meaningful. It had a difficult time when our dad moved us to Florida. We moved into a new development in Miami. To me, it was a concrete prison. My connection to the earth was gone. I feel like I can say that my depression began when I realized that we were alone in Miami without any of our family, our community. The times we visited home were the happiest moments because I could feel that connection again."

Iris interjected, "I am so sorry, Bella. I understand what you're saying because I moved to UNC Wilmington to study pre-colonization coastal indigenous peoples. During the school year, I struggled to fit in. I felt lost being so far from my community. I couldn't understand why people led isolated lives. And where were the trees? I learned that Wilmington was a tourist hub, and land was destroyed to build more homes and businesses. It was so hard for me to come home during the holidays and then return to my isolation at Wilmington."

Bella was glad to find someone who understood her. "Are you back in Puerto Rico for good?"

"For now. I am working on my master's degree under Professor Montoya, and I plan to continue researching the impact of colonization on the Taino and Carib peoples."

"There were Caribs in Puerto Rico," Bella said.

"No, the Taino belong to the Arawak language group that inhabited the Greater Antilles, the Carib belong to the Cariban language group, and were in the Lesser Antilles." Iris replied, "I am originally from St. Thomas, though my father is Puerto Rican. Studying the Carib people will give me the opportunity to return home and do for the Carib people what Professor Montoya is doing here for the Taino."

The rest of the afternoon, Bella watched as dirt was brought up. The students were bottling and carefully labeling the jars and vials of soil with the time and place they were taken from. It looked to Bella like the professor had laid a grid over the area and given each one a number. Every time he sent a basket up, he would call the grid coordinates to them.

Bella heard a bell ring.

The two students smiled and high-fived each other, then raced to get the basket Professor Montoya sent up.

"What is it?" Bella asked.

"The bell means he found something."

Iris retrieved the basket. She gently placed it on the table, brushed off the dirt caked on the artifact, and placed the dirt in a sample jar. Using a magnifying glass, she looked at the artifact and gasped. She quickly put it in an airtight container.

"Bella, come here and look."

Bella was able to see some kind of cloth. "What is it?"

With a smile, Iris said, "If the analysis comes back positive, it is a piece of hemp-made fabric used by one of your ancestors."

Bella widened her eyes with a confused look on her face. "What, I can't tell that is a piece of fabric."

"Yeah, we can tell it's fabric. You can actually see the weave in the cleaner parts. Hemp was commonly used for fabric. But when we get it to the lab under a microscope, we'll be able to see the actual fibers. Hemp fibers are long, kind of like thick plant threads with little bumps along them. You have to know what you are looking for, but that's why you called us." She smiled at Bella, her face beaming. "We will clean the sample in our lab and determine its origin. This likely belonged to someone who lived in this region, if not directly in this forest."

A few hours later, Bella heard the bell again. The professor once again sent the basket up for the students to process. This time, Claudio retrieved the basket, placed it on the table, and followed Iris's previous steps to gather soil samples. As Claudio brushed the dirt off the artifact, he put the object into another airtight container.

"Look, Bella, if it's authentic, this is a shell bead necklace that may have belonged to one of your ancestors."

Bella's head was spinning. Her ancestors lived here, and in her hands were real objects that may have belonged to them. She thought about how this made their history so real, and she felt an immense sense of pride in belonging to this land and its people.

"I can't believe this. It's amazing. Why do you think no one ever found these things before?"

Claudio thought about the question, "Well, maybe because, from what your grandmother told you, people were not allowed to explore so close to the pond. I mean, look where the Professor is standing. It's a hidden cliff edge."

Bella knew that Claudio was right. Carmen would have grounded her if she ever found Bella up on this ledge.

Once again, they heard the artifact bell. Iris retrieved the basket and took it to the table. Professor Montoya informed the students through his walkie-talkie that he needed to stop digging and return to the campsite.

Iris did the same thing she had done with the other artifacts. This was a small pot with a lid. Bella asked if she could remove the lid to see what was inside.

"No, we will remove the lid under controlled lab conditions; even a microscopic particle of pollen could ruin the sample and skew our research."

The professor removed his rappelling equipment as he joined the group.

"OK, everyone, listen up. It is my professional opinion that we have found a burial site."

Bella's eyes widened. "What?"

"Yes, a burial site. I believe it is a woman. So far, I have found a piece of fabric and a beaded necklace; pots such as the one your niece found were often placed inside burial sites. Typically, the pot contains cleansing herbs to purify the departed's soul, allowing it to then enter the spirit world. Though we haven't had it translated yet, the script carved into the pot is most likely a prayer. When we clean it up at the lab, we will be able to see more and confirm my hypothesis."

The professor told his students to close down the campsite and secure all documentation.

"Bella, this is exciting," the Professor said with a smile. "Well worth canceling my conference. We do not have records of burial sites in this region. We will need to bring in an entire team, including Dr. Fernandez Sanchez and her students. We will have to get a permit from the local government to excavate this area. There are formalities that we must carefully follow to ensure the authenticity of the research. Do you think your grandmother will mind if we stay for what could be three months to a year of research? It will depend on whether we find the burial itself."

Bella's excitement disappeared. "I am sorry, Professor, you won't be able to research this area after the 30th of this month."

Professor Montoya was confused.

"The county sold this land to Morning Glory Corporation without consent from the people who live up and down these hills. They are being evicted from their homes."

Montoya was well aware that American corporations were purchasing land at low prices and profiting from its development by constructing inexpensive buildings, even on protected land, to create apartments, million-dollar homes, and commercial properties. A protest against such a move was what had gotten him in trouble with the University. But he had not been aware that they were evicting people.

"How can they do that? These homes aren't abandoned. People are living here."

"Because many of the resident do not have a title to their homes, the county took the property back and sold it. So, you see, people here are scared because they have no other place to live. It's not fair."

Montoya reacted, "Wait, Bella. This may be a Taino burial site, and by law, we are required to excavate the site before anyone or any company can access the land. Some research excavations can last for years. Our university had lawyers who represented the University's research projects. Your friends and neighbors need a lawyer."

"What will that do?"

"This dig will be protected by law, and we will be digging throughout this hillside. The residents need to permit us to dig on their properties to participate in the research project, and they can not be evicted during the research period. They need a lawyer to finalize their part of the agreement. Do you know of one?"

"I think that I do. What do you need from us?"

"To allow us to dig on your property? We will be setting up dig sites throughout the area that belongs to your grandmother. Therefore, your lawyer will draft the terms for us to sign. For now, allow me to return with my colleague and a couple of her students so she can review the site and co-sign my findings. We can then have our legal department begin the legal process. I need to talk to your grandmother about us returning."

"Bella, we are going to cover both areas with a plastic tarp to protect the site from wind and rain. I am asking that no one come up here, because if the quarantine seal is broken, it will render the research null and void. No one can come here until we return in a few days. I will bring a few more people and validate my findings. Please have contact information for your lawyer for us to give to the legal department."

"I will. Thank you so much. This research may lead to a deeper understanding of Taino knowledge, as well as benefit the people who live in this town. So, most of my family is flying out tomorrow, but I am staying."

Claudio and Iris smiled.

"Do you need anything from them before they go?" The professor shook his head. "Ok, one more thing, I haven't told my family that I am staying here with my grandmother, so please don't say anything."

"I understand, Bella. We won't say a thing."

Chapter 38

Professor Montoya debriefed the family. Isabela clasped her hands together and said a silent prayer. Carmen hugged Bella and called out to Nayeli, "Nayeli, pronto vamos a salvar este pueblo."

Bella wanted them to think through this logically. After all, as a lawyer, she was well-informed about how projects can get stalled in the courts because the one being blocked often has the power to make people give up their claims due to financial hardship. Like Luara used to say, it's not always the one with the best lawyer who wins; usually, it's the one who can pay their lawyers the longest.

"Ok, look. There is still a chance that the artifacts they found today are not from the pre-colonization era, but rather more modern. So, as a lawyer, I think that we should be prepared for a long battle in court."

Carlos replied, "Yeah, Bella is right. I mean, Cecilia wants this land, and there are millions of dollars already invested in her plans to take ownership of it." He faces Bella. "Ok, so what do we need to do?"

"The first thing that we have to do is retain the services of a lawyer. I already have one in mind. I think that Mr. Perez showed bravery in challenging Cecilia the way he did. He may want to take this on. We will need everyone to sign. I can call him today and ask him if he wants the case and to send us digital retainers for us to sign, along with the initial funds he will need to start."

"How much are you thinking?" Tony asked.

"Be ready to pay somewhere between $35K to $100K." Everyone seemed taken by surprise. "Look, I know that Cecilia is going to fight this. She will have a team of lawyers and archaeologists to contest Professor Montoya's initial findings. She has the money to wait for it out in court until we give up. I am not giving up. I can't ask any of you to share some of your inheritance money in this case, but I want you to consider it. If we have a combined $100K, we can ride out Cecilia's plans and push back."

Carmen stood up and hugged her daughter. "You are so generous because you know that none of our friends and family can pay lawyer's fees. You can count on me. Just tell me what you need, and I will give it to you."

Tony stood up and, with a proud look on his face, offered $50,000. Amelia and Torry also pledged $ 50,000, and Carlos promised $50,000.

"Bella, you are the lawyer, so we are putting this in your hands. I am sorry that we can't do more to help. Just let me know how much you need. It would be amazing if we could reclaim everyone's land for them and push back on poor Grandma Cecilia." Carlos burst out laughing. Soon, they all began laughing.

Bella knew that she couldn't keep her secret any longer. She had to tell them.

"There is something else. Grandma, can you join us again?"

"Absolutely, Bella. I was calling your Aunt Maria to tell her our exciting news."

"Ok, I don't know if you can understand what I am about to say. You all know how I have struggled with depression and stress for all these years. I have never felt welcomed in the U.S, no matter how hard I tried to fit in." Bella took a deep breath. "I feel like it's time that I acted on my feelings and stayed here with our grandmother." Bella turned to face Isabela, seeking approval. "If she will have me."

"Of course, Bella. That makes me incredibly happy."

"Well, I also thought that being the lawyer, I can stay on top of the court battle that is about to come our way. I can also help my grandmother around the house, reconnect with our family, and thanks to my inheritance, I won't need to go looking for work for a while. I can dedicate my time to this case."

With tears in her eyes, Amelia walked up to Bella and clasped her hands. "Bella, we all were already suspecting that you were going to stay." Bella seemed surprised. "There has been a transformation in you since we returned here. You are comfortable and even happy. I don't want you to think that because we are getting on that plane tomorrow night, that we are abandoning you and this operation. I can tell you that we enjoyed Lulu's acclimation to this town and our family. It will be different for her back in North Carolina. Torry and I are going to take a deep look at our finances and obligations to see if we can move back to the island."

Torry smiled at Bella. "We can pledge money, but what you are about to do takes more support. You call me, and I will fly here to be at your side."

Tony, Carlos, and Torry nodded. Bella looked at Carmen.

"Bella, sweetheart, I can see that you have reconnected with your friends and family. I was able to see you find your sense of purpose. If you need me, I will be here in a flash. The flight from Miami is the same as the flight to Charlotte after all." Carmen hugged Bella. "I am so proud of you."

Isabela joined the hug. With tears in her eyes, Isabela looked at her grandchildren and told them how proud she was of all of them. "Do you all know how proud I am of all of you?" The group smiled. "I am going to be sad to see you all go, but I have a feeling that you will be back soon. Not just because of the burial site, but because you are all taking a piece of this community, this Puerto Rican culture, and your reconnection to your family. Having you here made me so happy, and I don't want you to go without promising that you will come back."

Isabela's grandchildren gave her hugs, wiped their tears, and promised to come back soon. They set the burial site aside because they wanted to make some last visits with family and buy souvenirs for friends and coworkers. Bella sat quietly in front of the large windows in the family room, which looked out onto the forest, and made a phone call to Laura. It was difficult to let Laura know that she was resigning and staying with her grandmother. She explained to Laura that her grandmother is older and she wanted to stay to help her and spend time with her.

Bella made a phone call and updated Laura on what had happened and the burial site.

"Are you kidding me, Bella? A burial site of the Taino people on your grandmother's land? That's incredible."

"Yeah, I know. Can you believe it? I want to hire your firm to do some background work."

"Wait, Bella. You want to hire me? You know that we are not licensed to practice law in Puerto Rico??"

"I know. But I don't want you to represent us in our case. I was hoping you could research relevant Federal statutes that would help us petition for an injunction regarding the land deal. It must be iron-clad to be accepted in court. That's why I want to hire you. Look up US laws on corporate annexation of protected lands and federal statutes for the protection of indigenous people and indigenous landmarks. And since Cecilia decided to open up a whole new company, Morning Star Corporation, out of Texas, I will need legal representation in the US to begin an investigation into Morning Star's finances and previous land deals."

Laura became excited. She had known Bella for years, and she knew that when Bella set her mind to do something, she became focused and detail-oriented. Laura almost felt sorry for Cecilia. She does not know her granddaughter well, and she is about to find out not to piss Bella off.

"Ok, Bella. We will be thorough and help build the background you need to present your case. But Bella, this will not be cheap, I will need two of our paralegals, Mike, who specializes in land acquisitions, and me. I don't think the board would let me run it pro bono."

Bella became excited to hear that Mike would be assigned to this case. She had known Mike for several years, and he is a bloodhound when it comes to finding case precedents and statutes.

"Don't worry about money, Laura. I haven't told you the most exciting news yet."

"More exciting than possibly finding a Taino burial site on your property??"

"Yes, my dad saved his wealth for us. Without Cecilia knowing, he went to the lawyer and wrote up a new Will."

"Why would he have done that?"

"To spit in his mother's face one more time. Look, Cecilia and her kids are super wealthy. They do not need any more money or property. It's just greed. Something tells me that they were counting on the $2 million that they would have inherited if my dad hadn't changed his Will. Now it was divided among all of us, including my mom. I also inherited a small house. I haven't seen it, but I was told that it needs repair. My brothers and sisters pledged to transfer some of their inheritance to me to pay for the legal fees. We figure that if they authenticate the burial site in a few days, Cecilia is going to do whatever it takes to stop us. So, I am placing security around the site to keep Cecilia from destroying the camp."

"Damn, Bella. I have to remember not to get you mad." Laura laughed. "I will draw up the retainer and send it to all of you for signing. Please send me your family's email addresses. Also, if this goes to a hearing, let me know in advance. I want to be there to help in any way that I can. Plus, I want to see this Cecilia bitch for myself."

They laughed and then talked about Bella's trip, the beach, and her family.

Chapter 39

It was a somber day. The family was due to fly home at 8:00 pm. Isabela and Carmen made breakfast, and Tony helped to serve it. Tony could see tears in their eyes even though they were smiling. Isabela took in the sight of her grandchildren talking, laughing, and planning their day. Of course, they bought more souvenirs than they planned to take home. Isabela gave them one empty suitcase that they could use to store their souvenirs.

"Hey everyone, your aunts and uncles are calling to wish you a safe trip. How about if we get together for lunch with our extended family to do one more celebration?"

Everyone liked the idea, and they made plans to buy groceries, set up the outdoor chairs and tables, and Carlos asked Isabela if he could bake a dessert. The house was busy with activities. Isabela wouldn't have it any other way. Friends and family slowly came to the celebration. They wanted to be there to say goodbye to the family. Carmen hugged her mother with a deep embrace. The two women cried.

Carmen whispered to Isabela, "I will be back, Mom. I have things to attend to in Florida. But I will be back as soon as I can. I am so happy that Bella is staying with you."

The two of them looked at Bella with pride and concern.

"Mom, you call me if something happens to Bella. Ensure that she wears her talisman, and Father Pablo performs the routine cleansing. More importantly, you and I know Cecilia well. Bella is stepping into a land mine, and we need to help her. Her success affects everyone in this town. Bella has dealt with loss, depression, and years of nightmares."

"I know. Don't worry. She will not be alone. Bella is a smart person, and she knows the law. I think that all of this, including her becoming a lawyer, was all for this moment. For the battle to come."

It was time for Amelia, Torry, and Lulu to say goodbye to Bella, Carmen, and Isabela.

"Bella, we are so proud of you. I know that you are doing what's best for you. Please keep us in the loop, and I promise we will see you soon. You, too. We will miss you so much!"

Lulu began to cry. "Mommie, do we have to go back home? I can stay with Aunt Bella and Grandma."

Torry picked up Lulu. "I am sorry, peanut, but we can't stay right now. But, how about we go home and plan when we can come back?"

Lulu hugged Torry. "Ok. You promise that we will come back."

Amelia hugged her little girl, "Yes, Lulu. We will be back." Amelia hugged her mother and grandmother one more time and climbed in the car.

Tony and Carlos said their goodbyes to their mother and grandmother.

"Listen, grandmother; please call me if you need me. In fact, call me if you need anything." Tony said.

"You both don't need to worry. You all made me so happy that you came. It was really special to hear the sound of laughter in the house again. I hadn't realized how much I missed that. Please come back when you can."

Bella watched as her mother and siblings drove away and felt a small pain in her heart. She was going to miss them. But she also had a purpose, and she was going to win against Cecilia and her empire.

Bella hugged her grandmother. "Ok, Abuela, it's time to work on our plan. When we first arrived, you told us that you had been going through old documents to find anything that could be used to claim our family's property. Can I help you look through that?"

"Absolutely, I can use your help."

"Great, let me hire a lawyer to begin to work on Puerto Rico land grants, protected land sanctions, and real estate law."

Bella begins to dial.

"Do you know a lawyer here in Puerto Rico?"

"Sure, do." Someone answered the phone. Isabela heard a man's voice on the line.

"Good afternoon, Mr. Perez. I have something to discuss with you. May I come by your office?"

Isabela wasn't able to hear his responses, but she heard Bella agree to meet with him that afternoon.

Bella spent the time until her appointment helping her sift through the family documents. They separated personal documents, love letters, and journals from official records, car titles, tax forms, and such. Then she started looking through the personal documents, looking for any mention of buying or selling property. She hoped that having at least a statement from one person mentioning the transfer of land would help build a case showing ownership for someone.

An hour later, Bella returned. She smelled her grandmother cooking as soon as she got out of the car. Bella heard music playing. She knew that her grandmother was happy not to be alone again.

Isabela greeted Bella with a cup of coffee. "How did it go?"

Bella smiled her Cheshire cat smile. "Oh yes, he is in. He didn't provide any details as to why he didn't like Cecilia. I noticed at the will reading that he enjoyed dropping the bomb on Cecilia. I thought that I even saw a small smile. So, I wanted to find out if he was willing to take on Cecilia the giant. I gave him our US lawyer so that they can coordinate their work. Laura sent the retainer, and everyone signed it. Mr. Perez said that he will draw up his retainer tomorrow."

"That is wonderful news. What's next?"

"Well, I plan to go visit our friends and family to see if those who have titles in their names are planning to sell their properties, or if they are unwillingly being kicked out because they don't have a deed. I need to gather testimonials and any available family history. Once the retainer is signed, Mr. Perez will form a team to handle this case, and they will conduct their own investigation. We are also waiting for the professor to contact us again."

"You really have thought all this through. So, let's have dinner and then we'll start by visiting my sister, Maria. She may know other things that I don't know or remember. I know that she has boxes in her storage room, and she said that we can go through them. Let's go look at them."

"Sounds like a plan."

Just as they were heading out to see Maria, Professor Montoya called Bella.

"Hey, professor. What's up?"

Isabella couldn't hear what was being said, but she heard Bella agree to meet with the professor and his colleague the next day at 10 am.

Chapter 40

The professor and his group were on time. Isabela welcomed the professor and his colleague into her home.

"Oh, I thought that there would be more people coming today."

"Yes, we brought a few of our grad students with more equipment. They're taking things out of the van."

Bella walked down the stairs.

The professor was happy to see Bella. "Bella, this is my research partner, Dr. Fanderez-Sanchez. She and I will be evaluating the site today. Do you have any questions for us?"

Bella shook Dr. Fernandez-Sanchez's hand. "I am pleased to meet you, Dr…"

"Oh, please call me Lucienda."

"Thank you, Lucienda. No, I do not have any questions."

"Excellent, in that case, Bella, can you show us the way?"

Bella led the group along the path up to the cliffside. Bella noticed that the group had stopped walking. They were staring at the pond, where the rays of the sun peeped through the opening in the canopy.

Butterflies were flying from bush to bush on the shore around the pond. Bella smiled as these scientists appreciated the beauty in nature.

She whispered, "Beautiful, isn't it. Feels magical."

The grad students and Lucienda nodded in agreement.

Lucienda looked around, "It feels like we are trespassing in a sacred space."

"You are not trespassing, Professor. You were meant to be here. From this point, you should be able to see part of the camp and the alcove on that rock ledge where we found the pot."

Everyone craned their necks to see. They continued with their trek. Professor Montoya noticed that the seal he had placed all around the camp was still sealed. Once at the campsite, the professor downloaded the security videos to make sure no one else found a way in and tampered with the site. Bella noticed how precise their movements were. They set up the new equipment and attached it to a small generator for power. Bella felt that the area was too small for everyone, and she would only get in their way, so she excused herself and returned to the house. She had other things to do.

Isabela wanted Bella to let the researchers know that lunch was ready. As soon as Bella stepped outside, she saw the two professors walking back to the house.

"Abuela, they are coming."

Isabela joined them in the patio.

The professor had a smile on his face. "Sra. Isabela, we can say without a doubt that you have a burial site on your property. There are artifacts that would only be found in a burial chamber, and we found a metatarsal, a bone." The professor shows Isabela and Bella a small, sealed glass jar with a small bone inside it.

"Wait, are you saying that someone IS buried at that site where we found the pot? And this is what? What did you call it?

"A metatarsal. Our hands and feet have tiny bones. This is one of those bones. We will take what we found to the lab to analyze everything and meet with our department head to request permission for the dig. In the meantime, now that we confirmed that a human was buried there, you are to contact the lawyers, talk to your neighbors to explain to them what is going on, and how it will affect them. We need them to permit us to excavate around their property if possible."

Lucienda clasped Bella's hand. "If it gets approved, we will be back in 2-3 weeks. Our legal department will address the injunction to stop the takeover of this land. Be ready for your grandmother to come at you. She will most likely have a lawyer draw up her counter-response and hire her own "experts" to disqualify our findings. We are ready for that. It's not the first company to dispute our injunction when we find artifacts and human remains. Your defense has to be strong, and that includes your documentation."

"I have signed retainers with two law firms."

Lucienda was impressed.

Professor Montoya thanked Isabela for allowing them to come. "I can't thank you enough. A finding like this one doesn't come very often. Especially now that corporations are bribing politicians, buying land cheap, and pouring cement over the dirt so the earth keeps its secrets. We will be back in two to three weeks, ready to go. Here is the contact information for our legal department. Please give this to your lawyers. As of today, this area is claimed for further research. Please remember that the site is currently closed. No one can go up there."

The professors and their team waved goodbye and left. Bella and Isabela hugged and cried. Bella knew that this was simply a small window of opportunity, and they had a lot to do to prepare for the fight against Cecilia.

Grandma, you can't tell anyone about what we found. We don't want Cecilia to find out. We have a surprise on our side, and it's going to catch her off guard. And remember, this discovery, along with its historical documents, will tarnish her precious reputation. She will fight to defend it. They are so proud of what Ponce de León did, and they have used their name and influence to sell their own people. No one must know. For now, we are privy to secrets best kept hidden.

Epilogue

Cecilia hired the services of another law firm. She would make that idiot Perez pay for betraying her. She was still seething at the loss of Luis's inheritance to that bitch and her kids. She had plans to open a Morning Star office in Spain, and now those plans had to be put on hold. She was counting on that money, and now she had to make new plans without it.

Cecilia stood up to pour herself another drink. She thought about how she would get revenge on Carmen and her brood. 'Fucking bitch! She stole my money.' Cecilia stared at Ponce De Leon's portrait as if asking for help to get revenge.

'Tell me what I have to do to get back at her. She stole my son away from me. She destroyed all the plans I had for Luis and our company. Now that bitch took my money.'

Cecilia poured herself another drink and walked outside. Without realizing it, she walked through her garden to the family mausoleum. Inside were marble coffins of her family. Everything looked pristine. This was the resting place for the elite. The De Leons and the Castillos were Puerto Rican royalty. The coffins all looked the same, made of top-quality marble with a gold plate bearing the deceased's name.

Cecilia walked up to the most recent coffin, her son's. She stared at it until her hatred came through. "I can't believe that I gave birth to you! Where did I go wrong? You should have died in labor because you never brought me any joy. And then you go off and marry that gold-digger and ruin all my plans for you!" Cecilia filled another cup of brandy.

"You cost me $2 million."

Cecilia spat at her son's coffin.

"I hope that you rot in hell!"

As Cecilia turned around to walk out, she heard a menacing laugh behind her. She looked around the mausoleum, but did not see anyone else. The voice was in her head. *I must be drunk,* she thought.

"You are not drunk. Do you want my help?"

Although Cecilia didn't think that this was real, she nodded nevertheless.

"Yes!" *I mean, for all I know, I passed out in my study, but just in case that isn't the case, I will respond,* she thought. "Yes, I want help to take down Carmen and her kids. They are of no value to me, and they will not live happily ever after. What do you want me to do?"

"I want you to get rid of your granddaughter, Bella. She is the real threat."

Cecilia threw her head back and snickered, "That brat is no family of mine. I will do as you wish. I just want to make sure that they die broken, especially Bella. We gave her the opportunity for a better life, and she turned it down. The hell with her."

Cecilia turns the knob to leave the mausoleum. "What are you going to do for me?"

"I will give you everything. I will get your money back to you, and I will help you make even more. You think that you are rich and powerful now, you wait, daughter, you will know true power."

Cecilia walked out of the mausoleum with a smile on her face, hearing the laughter behind her.

Did I just make a deal with the devil? Oh well, wealth and power. It's too good to walk away from such a deal.

Cecilia walked back inside, called her son Manuel, and invited him to her house. "I want to talk to you about something. When can you come by? We have work to do?"

FIN